KU-540-624

Suzanne Wright lives in England with her husband and two children. When she's not spending time with her family, she's writing, reading or doing her version of housework – sweeping the house with a look.

She's worked in a pharmaceutical company, at a Disney Store, at a primary school as a voluntary teaching assistant, at the RSCPA and has a First Class Honours degree in Psychology and Identity Studies.

As to her interests, she enjoys reading, writing, reading, writing (sort of eat, sleep, write, repeat), spending time with her family, movie nights with her sisters and playing with her two Bengal kittens.

To connect with Suzanne online:

Website: www.suzannewright.co.uk
Facebook:
www.facebook.com/suzannewrightfanpage
Twitter: @suz_wright
Blog: www.suzannewrightsblog.blogspot.co.uk

By Suzanne Wright

The Dark in You
Burn
Blaze

SUZANNE WRIGHT

BURN

piatkus

PIATKUS

First published in Great Britain in 2015 by Suzanne Wright
Published as an ebook in 2015 by Piatkus
This paperback edition published in Great Britain in 2016 by Piatkus

3 5 7 9 10 8 6 4 2

A CIP catalogue record for this book is available from the British Library.

ISBN: 978-0-349-41316-7

Typeset in Goudy by M Rules
Printed and bound in Great Britain by
Clays Ltd, St Ives plc

Papers used by Piatkus are from well-managed forests and other responsible sources.

MIX
Paper from
responsible sources
FSC® C104740

Piatkus
An imprint of
Little, Brown Book Group
Carmelite House
50 Victoria Embankment
London EC4Y 0DZ

An Hachette UK Company
www.hachette.co.uk

www.piatkus.co.uk

For my own little demons

Acknowledgments

I have to thank my husband and kids for being so amazing and supportive. I don't know how they put up with me disappearing into my head all the time, but they do. I adore them for it.

I want to say a huge thanks to my Beta reader, Andrea Ashby – she's a star, and she always takes time to help me. I'm so grateful for that.

Last but not least, thank you to all my readers. I really appreciate you taking a chance on this series, having no idea if it will be something you can enjoy. I hope you did!

If for any reason you would like to contact me, whether it's about the book or you have any other questions, please feel free to e-mail me at suzanne_e_wright@live.co.uk.

Take care,
Suzanne Wright, Author

CHAPTER ONE

From her seat in the large dome, Harper Wallis winced along with the other spectators as one of the contenders in the combat circle collided with the ceiling. His opponent looked on with a blank expression, seemingly unmoved.

"That guy doesn't show an ounce of mercy," commented her cousin, Ciaran. "It's awesome." He was referring to the reaper that, like many demons, often dueled for money in the Underground.

The subterranean location was like the Las Vegas strip on steroids. There were restaurants, bars, nightclubs, casinos, hotels, and amusement rides, among many things. Considering their kind was impulsive, plagued by restlessness, had instant gratification problems, and were prone to pursue cheap thrills to chase off their oppressive boredom, the Underground was every demon's version of heaven.

Moreover, it was a place where they could blow off steam and didn't have to pretend to be anything other than what they were.

Harper winced at the snapping of a bone. Fighters were always guaranteed to leave a duel with injuries, broken bones, or even internal bleeding. Some had died during or after duels, despite demons having an accelerated healing rate. That was why she wasn't joyful at the idea that her other cousin, Khloë, was due to enter the combat circle any minute now. Even if Khloë won the duel, she was still liable to be badly hurt by the end of it.

Harper watched in morbid fascination as the losing contender dealt the reaper, Levi, a series of blows that barely managed to register on the reaper's radar. He just lifted his contender by the throat and flung him across the dome. Levi's eyes bled to black, which was a tell-tale sign that his inner demon was in control.

Much like shifters, all demons – no matter the breed – had a dualism to the soul. Whereas shifters shared their soul with an animal, demons shared theirs with a conscienceless dark predator that lacked empathy, was unable to emotionally connect, and had a strong sense of entitlement. An inner demon could surface, enabling it to then talk and take control. The only outward indication of such a thing would be that the person's eyes would turn totally black.

"Levi will easily end this," stated Ciaran. "I don't know what Franklin was thinking when he agreed to this fight. *Fuck him up, Levi!*" he hollered along with the rest of the crowd. She winced as the reaper proceeded to do just that by telekinetically sending Franklin crashing into the ceiling once again.

Some demons were relatively harmless in that their only abilities were to cause nightmares and read thoughts. At their strongest, however, demons could do things such as possess others and steal souls. Although Harper was powerful, she wasn't particularly impressed by it. She liked to earn the things she had, and her demonic abilities were something she'd been born with – not the same thing at all.

She scowled at Ciaran. "You're supposed to be supporting Franklin!" Her scowl deepened at the shifty expression on her cousin's face. "You bet on Levi, didn't you?"

He gave her a sheepish look. "Hey, I like Franklin, he's my friend . . . but I also happen to be fond of money. That meant backing Levi."

"Where's the loyalty toward your friend?"

He pointed at himself. "Duh. Imp. You know . . . selfish, sneaky, fickle, not to be trusted under any circumstances."

He did have a point about imps. Her family, like all imp families, had a reputation for being what her grandmother Jolene liked to call 'multi-talented.' Humans would term them criminals. They tricked, they stole, they lied, they cheated, and they could get in and out of any place without being noticed . . . and they were completely casual about it.

Jolene had ensured that Harper was just as 'multi-talented' as every other Wallis, despite that Harper wasn't an imp. There were no hybrids in the demon world. If two different breeds procreated, the child would be one or the other. Harper was the same breed as her absent mother.

Ciaran elbowed her lightly, practically radiating excitement. "Look, Levi's ready to finish him off."

The reaper was currently looming over Franklin with his hand hovering over his chest, palm down. Franklin was crying out, his back arched like a bow. A few seconds more of what was clearly excruciating pain and Franklin raised his arm – a signal of surrender. The crowd went wild, cheering and chanting Levi's name. He stood clenching his fists and breathing deeply, clearly battling his inner demon for complete control. Finally, his eyes returned to normal and his muscles unlocked as the entity retreated.

Levi didn't strut cockily around the circle like many others did. He was too busy glaring at Franklin, and she got the feeling that he was annoyed with his opponent for surrendering so soon.

"No wonder he's Knox's sentinel," continued Ciaran.

And who was Knox? Well, Knox Thorne was not only the creator of the Underground, but a demon whose lair spanned most of Nevada and even much of California. The Prime was a ruthless billionaire who owned a chain of hotels, restaurants, security firms, bars, and casinos. That was what demons did: they hid in plain sight, mingled in with unsuspecting humans; often in positions that provided them with power, control, respect, and challenges. Many were entrepreneurs, politicians, stock brokers, CEOs, bankers, lawyers, police officers, journalists, chefs, surgeons, and people in the media. Harper herself co-owned a tattoo studio that had many oblivious human customers.

Knox blended in with humans so easily that she doubted even other preternatural species would suspect him of being anything other than human. However, there wasn't a demon in the world who hadn't heard of Knox Thorne, since he was rumored to be the most powerful demon in existence – something apparently he'd never denied or confirmed.

There were many other rumors about Knox: that he was dangerous, calculated, notoriously sexual, and someone who lived by his own rules on his own schedule. It was also believed that he had the ability to call on and control the flames of hell, which was extremely rare. It was also scary, because nothing was impervious to the flames of hell.

Hearing her cell phone ring, Harper fished it out of her pocket and frowned at the name on the screen. It was Khloë. "Shouldn't you be immersing yourself in 'your zone'?" teased Harper on answering.

"I need you to come back here." Pain dripped from her words, making Harper stiffen.

"Khloë, what's going on?"

"Quickly." With that, she ended the call.

"Khloë needs me for something." Harper gave Ciaran her half-eaten hotdog for safekeeping, though they both knew he'd eat it. "I'll be back in two minutes."

Harper rushed to the end of the row, vaulted down the steps, and headed to the manned door that led backstage. The doorman, who knew her family well, said, "Khloë's in room twelve. You're not going to like what you find."

Shit. Harper dashed down the corridor before reaching the door she was searching for. Stepping into the room, she came to an abrupt halt. Anger whizzed through her system. "Khloë, what the fuck?"

The small, olive-skinned girl's attempt at a smile earned her a wince; she put a hand up to her split, swollen lip. Her clothes were torn and she was covered in bruises and scratches. Peeking up at Harper through one eye, she said, "It wasn't my fault."

Well that would be a first. Khloë had a tendency to get in deep shit. "Who did this to you?"

"Mona's little group attacked me in the restroom a few minutes ago."

"*What?*"

Mona was not only Khloë's opponent but a bitch who had a hard-on for Khloë simply because she'd once slept with a guy Mona liked. Demons tended to hold a grudge.

"I wondered if maybe Mona put them up to it," said Khloë. "But would she really think she'd get away with this?"

Yes, Mona would. The harbinger thought herself untouchable because her anchor was a demon within Knox's Force. Demons were predominantly psychic creatures. They didn't have soul mates, but they came in pairs. That meant they each had a predestined psychic mate, or 'anchor,' who made them stronger and gave them the stability that prevented them from turning rogue.

By fusing their psyches, a powerful, unbreakable link formed between the demons. It wasn't sexual or emotional, it existed on a psychic level. Demons were very protective of their anchors, but Harper didn't give a shit who Mona's anchor was – no one messed with her family.

"Where are Mona's little bitches now?" demanded Harper, pacing.

Khloë's expression was grim. "The doorman went searching for them, but they're nowhere to be found – conveniently. They got what they wanted; I can't go out there. I can't fight like this."

It was true. Not even their accelerated healing rate would have Khloë back to normal within the small timeframe she had.

"No, you can't," agreed Harper. "But I can."

Hearing a knock on the office door, Knox turned away from the reflective glass that provided him with a perfect view of the combat circle. "Come in." Three of his sentinels – Tanner, Keenan, and Larkin – entered. Glimpsing the hard set to Tanner's jaw, Knox knew he wasn't going to like the information he had sent them to attain.

Setting his glass of gin and tonic on the desk, Knox said, "Tell me."

Tanner halted directly in front of him, and the others flanked him. "More strays have gone missing than we thought. We checked to see if there have been disappearances in other areas, but it seems to only be happening in Las Vegas right now."

The matter had only come to their attention a few days ago, since Knox didn't monitor the population of strays – demons that chose to live outside of a lair. But it seemed that someone was simply plucking them from the streets. Strays weren't under his protection, but that didn't mean Knox liked anyone using Las Vegas as their own personal hunting ground. Unlike shifters, demons didn't claim territories, but they were protective of the places where the demons of their lair resided.

Keenan pulled a flask out of his jacket that Knox knew was filled with vodka. The incubus was a heavy drinker, but since it didn't affect his efficiency as a sentinel, Knox never called him on it. "Las Vegas is highly populated with demons," the incubus pointed out. Demons liked bright lights, gambling, thrills, and adrenalin rushes. It made Last Vegas a popular place for their kind. "A perfect place to hunt strays."

"The ones we spoke with are scared." Larkin moved to the sofa beside the window. "Usually when there are crimes like this, you hear of at least one witness or one person who managed to avoid a kidnapping attempt. There's been nothing like that. The strays that were taken weren't weak in power, but they were easily taken."

Knox leaned against his desk. "I have to wonder if Isla has something to do with it."

Keenan frowned as he took a swig of his vodka. "Isla?"

"She's been calling for changes that have been ignored up until recently. Those changes would offer strays protection. If they're scared . . ."

"They're more likely to listen to her," finished Keenan.

"Exactly." Demons didn't have a global leader, they simply existed in lairs which were ruled by a Prime. The lairs weren't organized into any kind of hierarchical structure. Demons only answered to their Primes. Isla, however, had suggested electing one of the Primes – more specifically, her – to rule above all the lairs of the U.S. For a long time, no one had listened to her. But now some demons were supporting her idea, and she'd found a true voice.

"Considering it's rumored that she rents out her own demons to dark practitioners to use in their spells, I doubt she'll have any qualms with plucking strays off the street," said Larkin, toying with her long, brown braid.

"Why would Isla bother appealing for this?" Keenan shook his head. "We had a structure like that once, and it resulted in fucking chaos. Why ask to bring that back?"

"Power," Larkin answered simply.

She was right. And there was always someone looking for power, control, and money. After so many years of being surrounded by such greed and calculation, everything had started to feel predictable, boring, and cold for Knox. Now a numbness was beginning to settle in for both him and his demon. "I had a call from Raul," Knox told his sentinels. "He's holding a conference on Saturday in Manhattan for every Prime of the U.S. to discuss the matter." Raul's lair spanned most of New York. "Personally, I think it's best to have a formal discussion about it."

"Do you think Isla has a chance of implementing any changes?" Keenan's tone said that he didn't believe so.

"I think she's very cunning and calculated, and we shouldn't underestimate her," Knox told the incubus. "She-demons can be pretty ruthless."

A grin played around the edges of Tanner's mouth. "Speaking of ruthless she-demons, you might want to know that Kendra has got herself a boyfriend. She's flaunting him like crazy, obviously hoping it will get a jealous reaction out of you." And the hellhound seemed to find far too much enjoyment in that.

Inwardly, Knox groaned. "Last time we spoke, she promised me I'd regret letting her leave me and I would beg her to come back."

Tanner laughed. "She sensed your demon lose interest?"

"Yes." Story of Knox's life. His demon could be very obsessive when fixated on a female, but it got bored so easily that the infatuation was always short-lived, leaving Knox to deal with a pissed-off female nursing a bruised ego.

Their inner demons couldn't 'care' for others, but they could form attachments to people. When that happened, those attachments were incredibly intense, because every ounce of a demon's natural intensity and focus was channeled into them. The only people his demon was attached to were his four sentinels. It obsessed over women it wanted, but it didn't wish to 'keep' them, despite that it experienced the same loneliness that all inner demons were plagued by.

Knox snapped out of his thoughts as another knock was followed by the entrance of Levi; he'd clearly washed and changed. "You fought dirty, as always."

Levi grinned. "There's no other way to fight."

"I think Mona's up next," said Larkin, looking out of the window. "Here comes the umpire."

Speaking into a microphone, which was wired to the speakerphones in Knox's office, the gray-haired male announced, "There has been a change in the program. Due to Miss Wallis' poor physical state at this time, she has been substituted—"

"Hold on, that's not allowed!" insisted Mona as she suddenly stomped into the combat circle. "If a contender decides to pull out, it means their opponent automatically wins."

"In many cases, yes, but Miss Wallis hasn't *decided* to pull out. She's been rendered unfit to duel. Miss Wallis is within her rights to select someone to replace her."

The rage that flashed across Mona's face told Knox that there was something very personal about this. But that wasn't what had him stepping closer to the window. No, it was the sight of the dark-haired female now making her way into the circle. She was a petite thing. Five-foot-four inches tall at most. But there wasn't anything delicate about her. Even through her neon orange t-shirt and jeans, he could tell that her body was sinuous and toned. She had a sinful flare to her hips – perfect for a guy to hold onto while he thrust in and out of her. "Who is that?"

"I've seen her around," said Tanner. "But I've never seen her fight before. She's a Wallis."

"And a teensy little thing. I think Mona's got this." Larkin sounded disappointed, which was most likely because the harpy wasn't a fan of Mona. Larkin wasn't a fan of many people.

While it was true that Mona seemed to have the advantage in the duel, being that she was taller and quite powerful . . . "I wouldn't be too sure of that," said Knox. There was just something about the other she-demon; about the way she cocked her head as she ran her gaze over Mona. She was a predator searching for a weakness. No easy target. And he suddenly found himself . . . interested. Not much truly interested Knox anymore. It was a refreshing feeling.

"You think the little one has a chance of winning this?" asked Levi.

Yes, he did. The bell suddenly rang. "We're about to find out."

Seeming to revel in the noise of the crowd, Mona tossed Harper a dismissive glance. "Joining me in this circle was a big mistake, Harper." She said her name with utter distaste. Yeah, a lot of people felt that way. Why? Because Harper was known amongst her social circle for being the sphinx without wings. An oddity. An abnormality. Some people made the mistake of believing that made her easy prey. Mona was clearly one of them.

Harper simply taunted, "Prove it."

With a smirk, Mona conjured an orb of hellfire – a standard ability that most demons had – and hurled it at Harper. Sharply stepping to the side, Harper dodged the orb. But in spite of the anger threatening to steal her self-control, she didn't retaliate, which clearly puzzled Mona. What the harbinger didn't realize was that Harper didn't want to duel with her, she didn't deem the bitch worthy of one. All Harper wanted was to get a grip on the dumb heifer.

Of course, she had abilities which would allow her to hurt Mona from a distance. But if she wanted to cause the harbinger *real* pain, she'd need to get her hands on her. Unfortunately, Mona seemingly intended to attack from afar. Harper needed to lure her close. That meant pissing her off – something which Harper was totally okay with. By nature, Harper was a reasonably collected person. But she had a temper that ran quick and hot. "You know, I can't work out why you thought you'd get away with having your little friends attack Khloë," sneered Harper. "Do you feel empty inside? I mean, like, in your skull?"

"Bitch," hissed Mona. She launched one orb of hellfire after another; aiming for Harper's head, chest, legs, and abdomen.

Harper evaded most of them, purposely allowing one to clip her shoulder and another to graze her leg. She didn't want Mona to know how fast she was. She wanted Mona to be confident enough to come closer. "All this because Gael chose Khloë over you three years ago? Really? How pathetic."

"He didn't choose her. She lured him away."

Khloë could control most minds, but she had too much self-respect to ever use the ability to get a guy who didn't want her. "We both know that isn't true. But even if it was, two wrongs don't make a right. Your parents have proved that."

Snarling, Mona conjured two orbs of hellfire and threw them simultaneously. Harper ducked, evading both. Lightning fast, she whipped a stiletto blade out of her boot, curving her hand around the ruby-red marble handle.

Mona laughed. "You think a little knife will save you?"

Ordinarily, probably not.

"It's almost cute."

Harper sidestepped the orb of hellfire that flew her way. Conjuring orbs was something Harper had personally never been able to master. She could *create* hellfire, but she couldn't shape it into anything. She could, however, do something else.

Generating hellfire in her left hand, Harper then infused it into the knife. Like that, the blade was aflame and totally lethal. Stilling, Mona gaped. For a brief moment, the crowd fell silent. They had all obviously assumed that the reason Harper wasn't retaliating was that she didn't have any offensive gifts to boast of – wrong.

Wearing a patronizing smile, Harper twirled her blade on her finger. "Personally, I think this beats orbs." Because she could infuse hellfire into any object, making them instantly deadly. A blade. A pen. A hairclip. Anything. "If I didn't know any better, I'd think that was fear on your chimp-like face."

Mona caught a dagger that one of her friends threw her and then launched herself at Harper – giving her exactly what she wanted. Harper evaded the sword, slashed Mona's thigh, and then slammed her palm into Mona's abdomen. Mona dropped to her knees, shuddering, with her mouth open in a silent scream of excruciating agony. It wasn't because of the hellfire eating away at her flesh. No, it was because of something far worse.

The crowd once more turned quiet, no doubt confused as to why a mere slice and a single hit had taken Mona down.

Harper squatted in front of her. "*No one* fucks with my family. Go near any of them again, and this pain will seem like a fucking slap on the wrist. You got me?"

Mona fell onto her side and curled into a fetal position, sobbing, just as the umpire dashed over. "What's happening?" he asked.

Harper returned her blade to her boot. "She's getting what she deserved." With that, she strode out of the combat circle. It took a few minutes to squeeze through the cheering, congratulatory crowd before she reached her cousins near the exit of the dome.

Keeping in step with her, Khloë fanned her face. "I'm so happy, I could cry."

Ciaran looked pissed. "I can't believe the bitch sent her friends to—" They halted as two demons suddenly planted themselves in front of them. The male was broad-shouldered and dark-haired with golden eyes that made her think of a wolf. The female was tall, slender, and had a stunningly sleek braid hanging over her shoulder. Harper had seen them patrolling the Underground many times, knew exactly what they were – sentinels.

The male told Harper, "Mr. Thorne would like to talk to you."

Fuck. "Oh yeah? I'm not really the chatty type."

The female smiled, genuinely amused. "I'm sure you won't mind sparing Mr. Thorne a few minutes."

Well, actually, Harper did mind. Given everything she knew about Knox Thorne, the prospect of meeting him didn't exactly fill her with joy – especially since there was a little something else about him that bugged their kind: no one seemed to know what breed of demon he was. Harper didn't like blind spots. But it was vital to never show weakness to a predator, and backing away from the challenge in his sentinels' eyes would definitely make her look weak. "Fine."

"Just you," the male said.

Harper inclined her head. "Wait at the Xpress bar," she told her cousins. "I'll be back soon."

Without giving them a chance to object, she followed the two sentinels behind the dome and up a flight of stairs. When they finally stopped outside a door marked 'Office,' the male rapped his knuckles on it. She could feel Knox's power from there. It reached out, and encased the door almost protectively. When a shockingly sensual voice summoned them to enter, the male sentinel opened the door and signaled for her to enter. Then the two sentinels backed away and left her.

Inhaling deeply, Harper slipped inside . . . and found herself fighting the urge to stare in awe at the tall, imposing figure standing behind a glass desk. Deep-set dark eyes that matched the color of his hair locked on Harper, and the intensity there rocked her. Her body instantly responded. Molten lust licked at her, making her breasts ache, her nipples harden, and every inch of her skin suddenly feel hypersensitive. *Well, shit.*

All demons had natural sex appeal, and she'd heard that Knox's effect was more potent than most, but Harper still hadn't been prepared for the sheer impact of him. He radiated alpha energy, projected a raw sexual magnetism that would make any girl sensually starving. As she took in his bold stare, powerful stance, and air of self-possession, lots of words came to mind: Powerful. Forceful. Confident. Controlled. Dauntless. Determined.

Damn if it didn't make him intimidating.

Refusing to buckle under the force of it all, Harper shut the door and waited. He said nothing. Didn't greet her. Didn't invite her to sit. Just stared at her with that dark, penetrating gaze that was sizing her up, and the atmosphere seemed to thicken with tension. But there was no chance that she would avert her eyes. This was a test of her strength, and she wasn't prepared to fail it.

Finally, looking like he'd just stepped out of a GQ magazine, Knox slowly rounded the desk and walked towards her. No, walked wasn't the right word. He breezed, glided – moved with an animal grace that demanded attention and could easily keep it.

Her inner demon froze, feeling threatened by this male that

exuded danger. And he *was* dangerous – it was apparent in the way he moved, in his posture, in the tension coiled in his muscles that rippled beneath his black suit. She would bet that suit cost more than her entire wardrobe.

"I'm Knox Thorne." He tilted his head, those dark eyes still locked on her. He was even more imposing up close. "And you are . . . ?"

"Harper Wallis." It worried her that he unnerved her demon, who was rarely rattled by anything. To Harper's utter frustration, she couldn't get a read on him, couldn't identify what breed of demon he was. But every instinct she had told her to tread carefully; that she was in the presence of a very powerful predator.

"Harper Wallis." He didn't say her name, he tasted it. Tasted it with a voice that was like smoke, whiskey, and velvet. And Harper knew she'd be entertaining some seriously dirty fantasies about him later. She sure hoped he couldn't read her thoughts – now, that would be embarrassing.

She wasn't offended when he didn't hold out his hand to shake hers. Demons were tactile, psychic, sexual creatures, but they were also very selective in who they gave permission to touch them. "Nice to meet you, I guess." She didn't sound at all genuine. And for some odd reason, that made his mouth curve into a crooked smile which caused her libido to do the fandango. Great.

Well now, this she-demon had surprised him yet again.

When she'd walked into the room, her eyes – glassy, reflective, much like that of a cat – had been the color of warm honey. But as Knox had moved to stand in front of her, the honey had begun to swirl like liquid, fading into an entrancing misty gray. He had the feeling it wouldn't be long before the color changed again, and he was intrigued as to just what color that would be.

Intrigued.

A simple feeling, but not one he'd experienced for a while until he'd caught a glimpse of this she-demon in the combat circle. Her facial features were soft and feminine. Except for that mouth. Plush, glossy, and a tempting cherry shade, it was straight out of his fantasies. He could imagine sliding his cock between those lips while knotting his hands in that sleek, dark hair that was tipped with gold.

His inner demon had perked up the moment she entered the office, going from bored to alert in an instant. It liked pretty, shiny, unique things, and that was exactly what Harper was. "How are your injuries?"

Harper rotated her shoulder. "All right." The wounds had mostly healed, but they still stung like a motherfucker. Demons were invulnerable to normal fire. Hellfire, however, could cause serious harm. The flames of hell, on the other hand, could turn someone into ashes on the spot. And it was just possible that the guy in the room with her could call on them. Fate was mostly likely laughing its ass off.

"If you're a Wallis, you must be from the North Las Vegas lair." At her nod, Knox added, "How closely related are you to Jolene?"

As he took a small yet prowling step closer, Harper's demon tensed even further. "She's my grandmother." In addition to being the Prime of her lair, Jolene Wallis was a hard-assed bitch. She was also thirty levels of batshit crazy and had been known to reduce entire buildings to rubble when in a foul mood . . . though Jolene preferred the term 'demolition expert.'

"I have a loose alliance with Jolene." Knox had always liked imps. Why? Because you knew where you stood with an imp. You knew that they would rob you blind if you were dumb enough to not pay attention. You knew you would only get the right answers if you asked the right questions. And you knew that expecting obedience from them would be an exercise in frustration. But having Harper so close, filling every one of his senses, he realized . . . "You're not an imp." He wasn't sure what she was. The Wallis family was pretty notorious, and he'd assumed they were all imps.

"No, I'm not," Harper confirmed, impressed that he'd sensed it.

Knox felt an unexpected tingle of amusement at her typical imp response – vague and evasive. Apparently she was, for all intents and purposes, an imp. "Sit," he invited, gesturing to the chair opposite his. Before taking it, her unusual eyes did a quick sweep of the room. And he knew that, in that small moment, she had assessed what was of value, the most likely places for a safe to be positioned, and every possible exit. It would be instinctive for a Wallis.

He noticed that she didn't make a sound as she moved – another imp trait she had mastered, despite not being one of them. "What are you?"

Watching as he melted into his chair, she parried, "What are *you?*"

Oh, that little bit of fire made his demon chuckle. Like Knox, it didn't have much time or respect for weak, frightened little lambs. This female clearly wasn't easily intimidated. He could have pushed the matter, but he found that he liked the idea of watching her, studying her, and solving the mystery for himself.

Harper was surprised to see his mouth twitch in amusement, since she'd expected anger. Knox Thorne made her think of a jungle cat that was choosing to behave *for now* but whose mood could change at any given moment. Regardless of that, she was stupidly wondering if his short, ebony hair was as silky as it looked. Yeah, well, she'd never been all that smart.

Seeing that the huge window offered a perfect view of the

combat circle, Harper guessed he'd watched her duel with his she-demon. "Look, if this is about Mona, she got what she deserved."

"And what is it exactly that she 'got'?" No answer. "Your touch can cause soul-deep pain," Knox guessed. A rare ability.

"Very good." It had always been effortless for Harper to do it. Whenever she felt angry, threatened, or frightened, a dark protective power instinctively built inside her and rushed to her fingertips, making them prickle. As a child, it hadn't been easy to control. Now that she was an adult, she was able to push the power back down if necessary.

He drummed his fingers on the desk. "If you believe she deserved soul-deep pain, I'm assuming Mona did something I need to know about. Tell me."

Be a tattletale who whined to people's Primes? "No."

"No?" Knox echoed with disbelief.

Evidently, he wasn't denied things often. Well, Harper did like to introduce people to new experiences. It was more of a calling, really. The air chilled as his eyes very briefly bled to black, communicating his inner demon's displeasure at being refused; hell reigned in those dark pools. A frisson of apprehension tingled down her spine.

"If one of my demons has done something they shouldn't have, I need to deal with it."

She shrugged. "It's been dealt with."

"That fight was personal. Tell me why."

The guy was seriously tenacious. "Ask Mona."

"I'm asking you."

"Shame for you that I won't answer, huh."

His demon was impressed by her. It liked that she pushed back, and believed she would be delicious prey to hunt. Not a weak, defenseless prey – no, she would be entertaining. "So very stubborn."

"Yes." It was indeed one of her best qualities.

It was right then that his instincts told Knox . . . "You're a sphinx." He knew it as sure as he knew that this greedy ache to possess her wasn't going anywhere.

Oh, points to the Prime. "I am."

No wonder she was so obstinate, Knox mused. Like a bird, sphinxes were winged, swift, graceful, and could be challenging to pin down. Like a lion, they were strong, fierce, brave, and would single-mindedly trail, stalk, and run down their prey. In short, there wasn't a more elusive, daring, persistent demon than a sphinx.

Rising to his feet, Knox rounded the table and came to stand in front of her. She quickly stood, meeting his stare boldly. At that moment, her eyes changed again as the misty gray swirled and became a silvery violet. It was fascinating to watch the transformation. "If you're not going to answer my questions about Mona, you can answer another. Are you involved with the male demon that's with you?" Knox didn't share, and he intended to have Harper Wallis.

She frowned. The guy sure liked to throw out random questions. "Why do you want to know?" Both she and her inner demon stilled as his eyes again bled to black. The demon living inside Knox was staring back at her, and it was fucking chilling. Those eyes . . . they were so cold, menacing, and *old*. The temperature of the room seemed to drop five degrees.

The demon covered the remaining distance between them and spoke in a flat, disembodied voice as it lightly tapped her cheek with one finger. "Answer the question, little sphinx." So much silken menace in those words. "No more evasiveness."

The entity was admittedly a scary fucker, but Harper would be damned if she'd let it intimidate her. Nobody, *nobody*, got to play with her like she was prey. "My private life is exactly that – private. But I'll share with you if you share with me. What are you?"

After a long, tense moment, that erotic mouth curved on one side. The obsidian eyes weren't so cold now. They glinted with challenge and amusement. Then suddenly the demon retreated, and she was once again looking at Knox.

"Your demon's not prepared to answer that one then, huh," said Harper. "Now who's evasive?"

Her fire made his demon smile. "You're free to take a guess at what I am," said Knox.

"If I got it right, would you admit it?" Her stomach clenched at the crooked smile that curved his amazing mouth. He was so achingly hot it simply wasn't fair.

"No."

"Something tells me I'm best not knowing what you are." Because whatever lived inside him was too dangerous for words.

This she-demon seemed to have a talent for surprising him. "You're absolutely right." At the sound of his cell phone ringing, Knox dug it out of his pocket.

Some of Harper's tension left her as he moved away to take the call, leaving her personal space. Oddly enough, her demon had started to relax around him. It was intrigued by his supreme confidence, his dark sensuality, the power that cloaked him, and the air of the forbidden that surrounded him. Stupid, stupid, stupid.

The tension returned to Harper's muscles as he stalked toward her, his eyes on hers as he spoke into the phone, promising the caller he'd be there quickly. Good. Because she wanted to get out of there quickly.

"I have to go," Knox told her as he opened the office door. "It was interesting meeting you, Harper Wallis." His demon snarled at the idea of leaving her. It wanted the pretty sphinx; wanted that hot little body beneath it – or above it, or against it as it backed her into the wall and fucked her senseless. The demon wasn't fussed.

"Likewise." To her shock, he held out his hand. It was an invitation to touch him, permission to break the skin-to-skin barrier. But if she touched him even once, she would be returning that invitation. He'd have the same permission to touch her as and when he wished – and not just physically, but psychically. It was no little thing. But Harper had never been a coward.

Meeting his dark eyes, Harper shook his hand, unprepared for the flare of heat that assaulted her when his touch met her skin. Her heart jumped when he brushed his thumb over her inner wrist, and he no doubt felt her pulse briefly spike. But she wasn't going to give herself a hard time about that moment of weakness. As he released her hand, his mind stroked hers, a farewell that could have come from Knox, his demon, or both of them.

And then something totally fucking weird happened.

A pressure built in her head as some kind of magnetic energy pulled at her mind . . . like something was tugging at her psyche, trying to fuse with hers. She was sure she stumbled, and not just from her sudden disorientation, but from the realization of just what this meant. Meeting Knox's gaze, she saw the same recognition in his.

Ah, hell.

"Anchor," said Knox, knowing he looked as shocked as she did. The word came out more like an accusation, a dare for her to deny it.

"Anchor," Harper quietly conceded. Maybe a lot of demons would be jumping for joy right now. After all, having a psi-mate was good, right? Not necessarily. There were plenty of hiccups that came with having an anchor. Her inner demon, however, wasn't concerned with those issues. It saw this male as belonging to it, and it wanted nothing more than to connect their minds.

It was strange to watch Knox's composure crack slightly as he seemed torn between staying to discuss their little predicament and leaving to attend to whatever problem had been discussed during his phone call.

After a long moment of silence, he sighed. "I have to leave. We'll talk tomorrow. I'll find you."

He was gone before she could respond to what was a half-promise, half-threat. And Harper knew that everything in her life was about to change.

Shit.

CHAPTER TWO

Locking the door of her apartment behind her, Harper puffed out a long breath as she leaned against it. Anchor, she'd found her anchor. She still wasn't having warm, fuzzy feelings about that discovery. Oh, she knew that was odd. Just as a shifter needed their fated mate to complete their soul, a demon needed their predestined psychic mate, or 'anchor,' to complete their psyche. An anchor did exactly what it said on the tin – it anchored a demon and made them stronger, so that they no longer struggled to maintain dominance over their inner demon, meaning they could never turn rogue.

It was easy for a demon to lose their way, since it wasn't possible to fully control the entity that lived within them. The entity could take over if a demon didn't have the mental strength to be the dominant figure. It was a constant fight. Demons that didn't find their anchor often turned rogue, went insane, or even committed suicide due to their struggle.

Once a person was anchored, however, they no longer had

to fight as they had the stability, power, and strength to maintain the dominant position. It didn't mean their inner demon wouldn't still surface from time to time, but it did mean that it couldn't permanently hold the reins unless permitted to do so.

There were other good things about having an anchor. For instance, it meant having someone you could rely on, someone whose loyalty would be absolute. In most cases, anchors became tight friends and confidants. They would protect, support, and defend their anchor if necessary. It was instinctual.

However, there were downsides. Anchors could be possessive and overprotective, which often also caused them to be annoyingly meddlesome. Additionally, demons could find it mentally uncomfortable to be away from their anchors for long periods of time. There was also the fact that if a demon died, it was very psychically painful and draining for their anchor if the bond had been formed. That psychic pain could be bad and long lasting, in some cases.

When Harper had been a little girl, the idea of having an anchor – someone who would protect her and always be there for her, no matter what – had been thrilling. Of course, that could have been a lot to do with the fact that neither of her parents were anyone's definition of 'dependable.' Not once in those girly daydreams had she envisioned an anchor who was *anything* at all like Knox Thorne.

But then, would anyone imagine their anchor being someone who was potentially the most powerful of their kind? Doubtful.

Despite knowing that about him, Harper didn't fear him. She couldn't deny that he unbalanced her. And she had to admit that she found him a little overwhelming. But even before she'd known he was her anchor, there had been none of what would be considered very rational, plausible fear. So either she'd sensed who he was to her on a subconscious level, or this was just part of her not being smart.

Still, she couldn't say she was eager to bond with him. Not just because of all she'd heard about him, but because there was no doubting that Knox Thorne would be hard to have as an anchor. Just fifteen minutes in his company was enough to tell her that he was controlling, authoritative, and wanted what he wanted exactly when he wanted it. He'd interfere in her life and dictate to her. Being that she was stubborn, willful, and contrary – traits she was proud of – she'd drive him insane.

Having spent most of her life traveling with an emotionally immature nomad for a father, she'd taken most of her leaps in life all on her own. She had become so independent that she found it both difficult and uncomfortable to have people do things for her. Being alone was her comfort zone, it was what she knew. That kind of thing didn't go hand-in-hand with having an anchor like Knox Thorne.

There was also a little complication she would bet that Knox wasn't aware of; something that could mean he would decide not to accept her as his anchor anyway. She supposed she'd find out soon enough.

In the meantime, she needed to know more about him. Settling on the sofa, she pulled out her cell phone and dialed a familiar number. "Hey, Grams."

"Hello, sweetheart." Jolene Wallis might be a bossy, meddling, master manipulator that even Lucifer found hard to deal with, but she loved and protected her family ferociously. She had also trained and prepared Harper to take over as Prime one day, but it was a position that held no appeal for Harper.

"How are you doing?"

"Fine," replied Jolene. "You sound tired."

"It's been a long, busy day at work." And an even busier night.

There was a heavy, frustrated sigh. "I teach you to lie, steal, extort, embezzle, commit identify theft, and hack into bank accounts. And what do you do? Get a job."

Harper rolled her eyes. "Anyway . . . I called to tell you that, um . . . I found my anchor."

"Really? Who is the lucky bastard?"

"You've actually met him."

"Well, don't keep me in suspense. You know I don't like that."

"It's Knox Thorne." Total silence greeted that announcement. "Grams, you there?"

Another heavy sigh. "I suppose I should have anticipated that your anchor would be someone strong-minded and powerful. They would be no match for you if they weren't."

"You don't disapprove?"

"Knox Thorne is a powerful demon who will do whatever he has to do for those under his protection – and that now includes you. How can I disapprove of that? Quick warning: he won't accept any of your 'I don't want an anchor' shit if he wants the bond bad enough."

"Yeah, I know. But there's a lot I don't know. I've heard rumors about him, but that's all. I need some facts."

"Well, he has one of the largest lairs and, from all accounts, is a very protective Prime who polices his demons well. He runs a pretty tight ship. I've heard many tales of his versions of 'punishment.' Not so long ago, one of his demons was kidnapped by vampires. Knox hunted the vampire responsible, subjected her to gruesome torture, placed her in a solid brass coffin and then set a fire beneath it."

"I heard a little about that."

"He can be merciless and brutal. And if you ask me, he's even more powerful than we believe. But he's never caused our family any problems. He doesn't war with other lairs. He could have abused his power by trying to rule at least the U.S., if not the world. But he hasn't. Not like this Isla-bitch who's been making plenty of noise lately – she's cold and greedy for everything that represents power. Knox isn't like that, which says a lot about him."

"What do you think he is?"

"I don't know. Some think he's simply an extremely powerful incubus, given his incredible allure."

Harper didn't believe that. He was something . . . more. Something she instinctively knew she'd never encountered before.

"In any case, don't let Knox or his demon bully you. Any weakness you show will be pounced on. I'm not saying provoke him or lose your wariness of him – anything that dangerous should be watched carefully. But don't be afraid to stand your ground."

"It's likely that I'll piss him off."

Jolene cackled. "Of course you will. You're a Wallis. That's what we do." A pause. "It's safe to say that Carla isn't going to like you being Knox's anchor, whether you form the bond or not."

"Don't think I don't know that you're smiling right now."

"Anything that causes that bitch upset is worth smiling about. If she gives you any trouble, you call me."

So that Jolene could turn the woman's house into rubble? It was tempting, but it would only cause problems. "She's not worth it, Grams."

"Oh come on, allow an old woman her fun."

"Your ideas of 'fun' tend to attract the attention of humans."

A huff. "I don't know why you have to be so judgmental."

Harper shook her head. "You're unbelievable."

"Thank you." She sounded genuinely pleased with the comment.

Amused despite herself, Harper chuckled. "I gotta go, I'll see you soon."

"I'll hold you to that, sweetheart. Remember, stand your ground with Knox."

She would. Because Harper never folded. Not even to a guy who could scramble her brain and play her body without even touching her.

"Either you've got your tampon in too far or something's bugging you. Which is it?"

Looking up from where she was cleaning her tattoo station, Harper sighed at her fellow lair-member. "Like I already told you a hundred times, I'm fine."

Devon gave her a reassuring smile. "Of course you're fine." There was no sarcasm there, only total faith in Harper. "But that doesn't mean something isn't playing on your mind. Share it. You've been like this all day, and I can't take the suspense anymore." That was the thing about hellcats, they were unbelievably and annoyingly curious. "I even waited for Khloë to leave in case it was something you didn't want to discuss with your family. I know they're meddlers."

It was true that there were no worse meddlers than Wallis imps.

"Your sour mood isn't because of Royce, is it?" asked Devon, her cat-green eyes wary. "I mean, honestly, you can do a lot better."

"No, it's not Royce. Although it's definitely not fun working across the street from my ex." Particularly since said ex was being an asshole, despite that *he* was the one who did the cheating.

Raini, another member of Harper's lair, appeared. "What are we talking about?" Both she and Harper were not only senior tattooists but owned the business together. Devon was an apprentice and also specialized in piercings while Khloë worked as their receptionist.

The place had a rock/art/Harley-Davidson vibe. The she-demons had treated the white walls that ran throughout the office and work area as one big canvas. The metal wall art on display were actually enlarged copies of tattoos – flames, swirls, animals, and Chinese dragons to name a few. Framed photographs of tattoos also decorated the walls.

The reception area had a large L-shaped sofa and coffee table on either side. There were also some glass display cabinets of various types of jewelry here and there. The chrome reception desk was almost a full circle, leaving plenty of workspace and was kept obsessively tidy by Khloë, who guarded her territory like a bulldog. Khloë was a total contradiction. She was obsessively tidy – everything had a place, and everything had to be kept in that place or she would totally lose her shit. And yet, Harper had never met anyone who dressed *less* neatly than her cousin.

"Harper was just about to tell me what crawled up her ass and died."

"Ooh, spill, spill, spill," encouraged Raini before taking a sip of her coffee. Somehow, she was able to make it look like a sensual experience. Like all succubae, she exuded sex. She was also celibate at the moment.

"Did I tell you I love this new look?" Harper asked Raini, admiring the soft pink highlights she had added to her white-blonde hair. It made Harper think of strawberries and cream.

Raini held up a hand. "I will not be distracted."

With a resigned sigh, Harper told them, "I found my anchor."

Devon's face lit up with excitement, but then she frowned in confusion. "Why is this bad?" Raini seemed just as puzzled.

"Because even if I did want an anchor, this guy is the last person I would choose."

The intrigue that flashed in Devon's eyes was expected. "Ooh, why?"

"It's Knox Thorne."

Raini's mouth dropped open. "Seriously? Huh. I sure didn't see that coming. But I don't understand why you wouldn't want him as your anchor."

"He's a control freak. I'd make him crazy."

Raini snorted. "You'd make any guy crazy. It's a gift you have, and I envy you for it." Probably because it would never matter how hard Raini tried to repel a male, they would be drawn in by her sinful curves, flawless skin, innate sensuality, and piercing amber eyes – all succubae had a body that screamed 'sex,' it was part of the package. A package that Raini always covered with casual, non-revealing clothes, since she didn't like attention much.

"This is a *good* thing," insisted Devon. "Knox is incredibly powerful. Having him as your anchor would be like the ultimate form of protection. Given that the demon world can be brutal, protection is nothing to sniff at. And I seriously doubt anyone would even consider harming you if they know they'd have Knox to deal with."

Raini's brows drew together. "I have to say, it would be a heavy weight to carry the responsibility of keeping a demon who's potentially the most powerful demon alive mentally stable."

"Thanks for pointing that out," said Harper dryly.

The succubus smiled sweetly. "You're welcome."

Harper wanted to strangle both she-demons. "There's one thing that you guys aren't considering. Being his anchor would make most people hesitant to harm me. I stress *most*. He has a lot of enemies. I'll bet some of them would be either stupid enough or angry enough to hurt me just to strike out at him."

Devon tilted her head, conceding that. "Consider this, though: our lair is small and mostly contains imps. Imps live for pissing people off. If your grandmother wasn't so damn crazy that she almost destroyed the Golden Gate Bridge when a lair in San Francisco decided to challenge ours, we would have had *way* more trouble. In other words, we're always in danger. Knox would bring you less problems than more. And just think, you might learn the mystery of what breed he is."

Harper shook her head. "I wouldn't have access to his thoughts unless he wanted me to." Anchoring minds was like joining two spheres where they intersected only slightly, still remaining separate entities while making each other psychically stronger. The anchor bond didn't allow them to hear each other's thoughts, sense each other's feelings, or uncover each other's secrets. It wasn't emotionally intrusive.

"Yes, I know that," confirmed Devon impatiently, flicking one of her long, ultraviolet ringlets over her shoulder. "But most anchors spend a lot of time together, they need it. Being around him might give you some clues as to what he is."

"Personally, I think you should totally bond with him," said Raini. "You'll have serious protection, and you'll be stronger and more powerful. He'll probably be pushy, but you're no pushover. So it's all good."

Was it? Harper wasn't so sure. Everything in her life suddenly felt off kilter. "You can't tell anyone, okay. Especially no one from our lair or my family. This situation is . . . delicate." Raini and Devon both nodded solemnly, but Harper wasn't reassured.

The fact that her ex then waltzed inside the studio didn't at all improve her mood. Royce was good-looking in a rugged, cowboy kind of way. Their brief fling had ended after he cheated on her. She couldn't say she was heartbroken, since their relationship had been rocky at best. Royce believed she was too independent, which was true. She was very headstrong, used to not needing anyone. She could admit that she was also pretty guarded and tightfisted when it came to giving her trust. Yes, she had her flaws and she knew she needed to work on them. But Royce had wanted to insultingly 'fix' her and mold her into someone else, which quite clearly pointed out that they weren't what the other needed. The fact that he'd slept with someone else only supported that theory.

Still, he'd been pissed when she ended the relationship. She couldn't figure why, nor could she figure why he'd be so spiteful as to have his sister ban Harper and the girls from entering the café across the street that his family owned.

Being around him was like remembering how she'd once studied a little quantum physics – she'd recall that she spent time out of her life on him and just have to ask herself . . . why?

Sighing, she turned to face him while the girls flanked her. "What are you doing in here?"

He held up his hands. "I just want to talk."

"About the fact that you had us banned from the café?"

"It wasn't like that."

"It totally was."

He sifted a hand through his brown hair, making it stick up everywhere. "So yell at me."

Harper blinked. "Huh?"

He flapped his arms. "Yell at me. Curse me to hell and back. Demand I fix the situation."

As understanding hit her, she gaped. "You did it for a *reaction*?"

"I wanted to know if you still care for me." He flushed when Raini and Devon snickered.

Unreal. "Why would you even care? You fucked someone else."

"I've apologized for that a million times." He inhaled deeply. "I miss you, all right."

"You should. I'm fucking awesome."

Exasperated, he insisted, "You must still feel *something* for me."

"Sure." She tilted her head. "Irritation. Anger. Disgust. Oh, and pity." She stilled as something odd happened: another mind slid against hers. It 'felt' familiar, felt like—

She peered over Royce's shoulder as the door slowly swung open and a rich, insanely hot fucker strolled into the studio. Knox's eyes swept his surroundings before honing in on Harper like a laser. Her body melted, her inner demon instantly shot to alertness, and the pressure to bond with him once again slammed into her. She breathed through it all, doing her best to remain composed.

Royce turned and then stiffened in apprehension. Even humans recognized the danger in Knox, though they couldn't know that he was a preternatural being. She sensed Raini and Devon not only stiffen with nervousness, but melt with arousal at the sight of him; both reactions would be instinctive.

"Harper," Knox greeted simply, though there was a wealth of intimacy in the one word. "Time to have that talk."

"Who are you?" demanded Royce.

Knox looked at the human male who stood a little too close to Harper than he liked. Close enough to suggest they knew each other intimately. That wasn't something Knox liked either. His inner demon loathed the human on principle. "I'm Knox Thorne."

"Royce Yardley." He pointed one finger at Knox. "I've heard of you, you own most of the—"

"Harper and I need to talk, Mr. Yardley." Knox moved aside

to clear the doorway – an act that told Royce to leave. Looking a little befuddled, the human did.

Raini leaned into Harper as she quietly said, "I'm at risk of swooning from that dominant vibe he's got going on."

Harper rolled her eyes. "We'll use the office," she told Knox. She headed straight for the back of the studio, hearing his confident footsteps following her. Finally inside, Harper thought about standing behind the desk to put some space between them, but that stank too much of fear. So instead, she remained in front of it, arms folded across her chest.

He stalked toward her, but didn't invade her personal space. His unflappable confidence was apparent in the way he just stood there looking like he owned every inch of the space around him. His power and strength radiated from him, impressing her demon and drumming at Harper's skin. "I won't ask how you know where I work." He'd probably done some research on her the moment he realized she was his anchor.

Knox almost smiled at her defensive posture. Apparently his little sphinx wasn't entirely comfortable with the anchor situation. Initially, he'd also been a little uneasy. As a Prime, he was always surrounded by people. He was used to being responsible for others. Used to supporting and protecting them. But it wasn't intimate, there was still personal distance between him and his demons – even between him and his sentinels.

A relationship with an anchor, however, wouldn't allow much distance. They would be intimate on a psychic level, and they would most likely play a large part in each other's life. With the exception of his sentinels, Knox didn't have people in his life. Existing around his life, yes. But not part of it. He knew by the force and depth of the protectiveness and possessiveness that hit him hard on realizing she was his anchor that it would be different with Harper.

Knox hadn't known if he was ready for 'different.' Unlike most demons, he hadn't been eager to find his anchor. He didn't believe he needed one. Didn't see how having one would improve his life. But as their minds had briefly touched and he'd realized what she was to him he'd thought … *Mine*. Simple. Primal. Instinctual. And the feeling didn't seem to be going anywhere.

After taking some time to consider it all and become accustomed to the idea, he was no longer uneasy. It was as simple for him as it was for his demon. This female belonged to him, was meant for him, and it was his role to protect her. Harper, on the other hand, didn't appear so agreeable. "You're hesitant to bond."

"So should you be. For someone like you, I'll be a total pain in the ass."

"Someone like me?"

"And be honest, I'm not at all what you imagined your anchor would be like, am I?" They couldn't be more different, had totally different lifestyles.

She was definitely unexpected, but that wasn't at all relevant to Knox. "I'm probably not what you expected either, but it doesn't change anything." As he studied her manic, brown eyes, his enhanced vision picked up something that immediately agitated him. "You're wearing contact lenses." He wanted to look into her unusual eyes, watch them change color.

"Obviously. I have to hide my eyes from humans. Anyway, back to this anchor thing. You're powerful enough all on your own. You don't need me or anyone else to make you stronger."

"Oh, little sphinx, do you really think I can't sense how powerful you are? In any case, that doesn't matter. I don't want you for power. Or even to stop me from turning rogue."

"Then why?"

"Because you're mine. I don't walk away from what's mine."

Filled with restless energy thanks to the pressure in her head that was swelling and becoming painful, Harper began to pace. "Look, it wouldn't work out."

The comment vexed his demon, but Knox decided to be patient with her – sensing that any bulldozing would make her more determined to keep him at bay. He'd let her list her issues and then he'd address them, because there wasn't a chance he'd leave her alone. "Why do you think that?"

"I don't know you, granted, but I can sense that you like control and having your own way all the time. You'll try that with me."

It was true that Knox liked control. A long time ago, every minute of his waking time had been controlled. He'd been told what to wear, what to eat, where and when to sleep, and even how long he was permitted to sleep. He hadn't been allowed any individual possessions, hadn't been allowed to make any decisions for himself. When he'd finally gotten free, he'd seized control of his life and taken everything he'd been deprived of: power, control, possessions, independence, knowledge, and freedom.

He *needed* to keep those things – particularly control. Especially since without it he might not keep his abilities and demon in check. "I'm controlling," he conceded. "And I won't deny that I'll interfere in your life in an effort to make it better, and you naturally won't like that. You'll push back. It'll be hard, so it means we just have to learn to compromise and find a balance."

Why did he have to sound all calm, mature, and reasonable? It made her complaints and reluctance seem dumb. The reality was, though, that this wasn't dumb, because there was something else. Halting, she said, "There's another thing that would make this hard."

"What's that?"

"You're protective of your demons, you're loyal to them and would choose them over an outsider. Right?"

Knox narrowed his eyes. "Where are you going with this?"

"My mother is part of your lair."

That had definitely been unexpected. The background check he'd done on Harper hadn't found the identity of her mother. "I'm sensing you believe this is a bad thing."

"She and I don't have a relationship. She won't want me anywhere near a single demon in her lair. As her Prime, you have a certain loyalty to her. You're responsible for the emotional and physical well-being of each and every one of your demons."

It took only a moment of recalling the few sphinxes in his lair to guess who she was referring to. "Carla Hayden is your mother?"

Harper simply nodded.

The depth of anger he suddenly harbored for Carla Hayden, someone who had clearly hurt his anchor, was shared by his demon. "I'm not sure what's happened between you and Carla – we'll get to that later. I *am* loyal to my demons and I take my responsibilities to them seriously. Ordinarily, they come before outsiders. But this isn't an ordinary situation, and you're not an outsider. You're my anchor, and I have a certain loyalty to you as well. If, as you believe, she won't like that, it's her issue to deal with. No one makes my decisions for me." Not anymore.

"You're a tenacious fucker, aren't you," she grumbled. Silence fell as he studied her with those bottomless pools of dark silk. She'd never met anyone who had such a bold, unapologetically direct stare. She still couldn't get a read on what he was, nor could she get a read on his state of mind. This was someone whose emotions were very tightly controlled. Someone who could also wrench a viciously sexual response from her body that was pissing her off.

"Know what I think, Harper? I think some of your hesitation comes from the fact that anchors tend to rely on each other and you don't want to – maybe don't even know how to – rely on anybody." Her eyelids flickered. *Bingo.* "I understand that." He really did, because he was just as opposed to depending on others. "But being anchored doesn't mean losing your independence. I don't intend to take over your life." But he'd interfere in it to the point of making her crazy, she was right about that.

Seeing the resolve on his face, she sighed. "Do you always get your way?"

"Yes." He approached her cautiously, like he would a skittish animal. "You need to accept the situation, Harper. You're my anchor. That means you belong to me, I'll always have rights to you, and I'll always be in your life."

Feeling his mind coaxingly stroke hers, she scowled. "Stop it." That sounded petulant even to her. He looked amused rather than irritated.

"Tell me the idea of me backing off doesn't bother you, Harper." He ate up the space left between them in one stride, curling a lock of her hair around his finger. He wasn't above using the attraction that hummed between them to weaken her defenses. "Tell me it doesn't send your demon insane."

Swamped by his forceful presence and raw sexuality, it took everything she had not to back up. Unfortunately, she couldn't deny that the idea of him staying away from her disturbed both her and her demon.

"Even if I was prepared to walk away from you, which I'm not, I wouldn't manage to stay away for long. Our demons wouldn't allow us to ignore this. Mine is already extremely possessive of you. Are you going to tell me that's a one-way street?"

"No," she admitted in a low voice.

Her honesty pleased his demon, who was extremely impatient to bond and was rearing to do it right then. But Knox knew it wouldn't be that simple. Harper still wasn't fully convinced it was a wise idea, and he had the distinct feeling that pressing her any further would make her object just to be contrary. "I have plans for dinner. You're coming with me." When one of her brows imperiously slid up, his cock twitched – it made him want to bend her over that desk and fuck that attitude right out of her.

"I am?"

Knox almost smiled at her soft yet dangerous tone. A lesser demon might have cowered. "I'll rephrase. Come with me."

Knowing that was as close to a request as he was capable of delivering, Harper asked, "Where? Why?"

"We need to get to know each other better." He'd use the opportunity to make her more comfortable around him. The sooner that happened, the sooner she'd be comfortable with their situation and agree to bond.

Curling a hand around her wrist, he led Harper out of the office and through the studio – passing her colleagues, who were shooting her enthusiastic, supportive looks as they said their goodbyes. Once she'd slipped on her jacket, he put a hand on the small of her back and urged her outside.

At the sight of the gorgeous, sleek, black Bentley that was totally out of place in this area, Harper halted abruptly. "Holy fuck."

Knox gestured to the two males guarding the vehicle. "Harper, this is Tanner and Levi, two of my sentinels. Tanner, Levi – this is Harper Wallis, my anchor."

Harper exchanged nods with the two seriously hot demons, one of whom she recognized as the male sentinel that had escorted her to Knox's office in the Underground. Both sentinels regarded her with a respect that took her by surprise, considering that lairs weren't quick to accept strangers. Apparently their respect for their Prime automatically extended to her now.

As Tanner opened the rear passenger door, Harper and Knox slid inside. She pretty much sank into the buttery-smooth leather, inwardly groaning in pleasure. It was good to be off her feet.

Once Tanner hopped into the front passenger seat, Levi threw the car into gear and pulled out of the parking space.

She looked at Knox, who was currently focused on his cell phone. "You didn't tell me where we're going."

"Patience, little sphinx."

"It's not a trait I possess."

Still consulting his phone, he said, "Patient isn't something I can claim to be either. Relax, you're safe with me. It's just dinner, Harper."

She snorted. "No, it's not. This is you making sure I'm seen with you. You want it known that I'm under your protection."

"You're partly right," he admitted, liking how astute she was. "After all, if anyone harmed you, I'd have to kill them. They should know that in advance. Call it a preemptive measure. But I also want to know you."

He wanted to unravel the mystery of her. His anchor was a complex creature. She had a tough, almost aggressive exterior, but he had the feeling that there lay a lot of softness under that hard shell. He wanted to know what had formed that hard shell; wanted to know her better than anybody else did. It was an unexpected urge, but he didn't care to overthink it.

"I have to warn you that once you know a little about me, you'll change your mind about bonding."

"You sound very sure of that."

"Look, I might biologically be a sphinx, but I'm an imp in

every other way that counts. That means I'm unmanageable, stubborn, secretive, I don't like rules, and I make people tired and irritated – and I take pride in it."

Knox caught Levi's amused smile in the rearview mirror. "I consider myself warned."

Stubborn-assed motherfucker.

CHAPTER THREE

When Levi opened the car door and Harper slid out, her jaw almost dropped at the sight of the huge, luxurious hotel that she realized was on the Vegas strip. She found herself once again saying quietly, "Holy fuck." She suddenly felt out of place in her jeans and t-shirt, particularly since she was standing next to Knox, who was looking rather edible in his dark tailored suit.

Seemingly unaware of her attack of self-consciousness, Knox took her by her wrist and led her inside the hotel. The interior was even more impressive; so grand and lavish it was intimidating. Several staff members, most of whom were demons, came to Knox to chat with him; he didn't even break his stride or release her as he replied to their queries.

Realization dawned on her. "You own it, don't you?"

"Yes. And stop panicking."

"I don't panic."

His mouth twitched. "Of course you don't. My mistake."

Moments later, she and Knox were walking into a restaurant

located within the hotel. It too was extravagant and classy – and crowded enough to make her even more nervous. "I'm not really dressed for this kind of place," she told him. It wasn't as if she could remain inconspicuous while she was being dragged around by Knox Thorne.

When Knox pulled her into a private dining room, she seemed to sag in relief. *The conversation that's about to follow wasn't something I wanted to have in public.*

Harper blinked at the unexpected telepathic contact. It was an ability most demons had, including her. *We could have just had it in my office.*

But then we couldn't have eaten.

As they sat and the server offered a choice of different fancy-named wines she'd never heard of, Harper just shrugged. "If it's red, I'll like it." Hearing that the starter was oysters, she almost died. *No way* was she eating an aphrodisiac around the demon opposite her. He *was* an aphrodisiac. "I'll just skip straight to the main meal, if that's okay."

Knox shrugged. "Order whatever you want." The last thing he'd expected a little thing like her to order was a 12-ounce grilled steak. She kept on surprising him. He found that he liked it. Having ordered his Italian beef stew and watched as the server left, Knox spoke. "What made you become a tattooist?" From what he'd heard, her business was quite successful and she was very popular among humans.

"It was my family's idea. I've always loved art." It was the one thing she was good at. The talent had been honed by years of creating counterfeit paintings for fun . . . but that was off topic and not something that he needed to know.

"Speaking of your family, I'd assumed Richie was your father."

"Nope." But Knox wouldn't be the first to assume that was the case.

From what Knox had learned, Jolene only had three children. Richie, who'd bred over a dozen kids. Martina, who hadn't birthed any despite that she had plenty of practice in the making of them. And . . . "It was definitely a shock to find that you're Lucian's daughter. I knew he had one." Lucian's daughter was apparently the only living being that the demon had any true attachment to. "I'd assumed she was an imp. But then, you're very good at seeming like one."

He'd said it like she was deceptive. "I grew up with imps, so I was hardly going to be any other way."

"What about your mother?"

She was a selfish bitch who Harper hadn't seen since—

She cut off the thought, determined not to waste time on the woman. "Look, I'm not really a fan of personal questions."

Her guard had slammed up so fast and hard, Knox was surprised it hadn't shook the room. "Personal questions in general or personal questions about your mother?"

"Both."

Her glare almost made Knox smile. "Why do you look so offended by me asking you questions?"

Harper's brow furrowed. "Why are you even asking me questions? I know you did your research on me."

"I did," he admitted unrepentantly. "I learned a lot about you. For instance, I learned that you're responsible for the breakdown of an ex-boyfriend's bank account—"

"Allegedly."

"—that you hacked a human police database and messed up their filing system when your friend was unjustly arrested—"

"Hearsay."

"—that you beat up a male demon who hurt your cousin—"

"I have an alibi for that."

"—and that you infected an old teacher's computer with a

virus that caused clips of gay porn to pop up on his screen every thirty seconds."

"Closet gays do the strangest things when the pressure gets too much." As his mouth curved into a shadow of a smile, the lust pooling in her stomach seemed to thicken. His dark, direct stare probably should have unnerved her but – for some inexplicable reason – having his entire focus on her was a turn-on. She got the feeling that when Knox Thorne was interested in something or someone, it or they had his total and unbridled attention.

Just then, the server returned with their wine. Tasting it, Harper raised her eyebrows. "This is actually pretty good."

Once he was alone with Harper again, Knox said, "Personally, I think your methods of revenge are very creative." Demons always got even, one way or another. "I learned something else about you." He was wondering how best to phrase his question, not wanting to seem insensitive, when she spoke.

"It's true that I don't have wings."

He'd heard whispers of a sphinx without wings, but it hadn't occurred to him that it was Harper. "You've never had them?"

Veiling her hurt, she replied, "No."

"Do you have the marks?"

"Yes." They looked like tattoos of wings on her back. They should become real wings at her command. But they'd never come. "Before you ask, it's also true that I can't throw orbs of hellfire. I can, however, do this." She infused her fork with hellfire.

"I noticed you do it during your duel with Mona. In many ways, it makes you stronger than demons who can throw hellfire orbs. You can make anything into a weapon." She was a walking, talking surprise to him. "Now, back to my question about your mother . . ."

"It's not important."

"Carla Hayden's a member of my lair, and you're my anchor, which means this is very important to me."

"Why aren't you even a little hesitant about this anchor business?"

"Why would I be hesitant? The vast majority of demons look forward to finding their anchor." It was typical that his anchor would be one of the exceptions. But if she was someone he could steamroll, Knox had to admit he wouldn't have found her half so intriguing.

"Yeah, mostly to stop them turning rogue and to become stronger. We both agreed you don't need me for any of that."

"Doesn't matter. I've told you before; I don't walk away from what's mine."

"Oh," she drawled. "You like possessions."

Actually, yes, Knox did like possessions. Having been deprived of those things as a child, he refused to do so as an adult. But she didn't need to hear that story. Nobody did. So instead, he gave her a different truth.

Leaning forward, Knox said, "Since my mind brushed against yours, every instinct I have has told me that you're mine and I should protect you and bond with you." Of course, he also wanted to fuck her until neither of them could walk. But that had nothing to do with her being his anchor. "You *are* mine. Deserting someone I'm supposed to protect isn't something I'm prepared to do. Now, tell me about your mother."

After a long inhale, Harper replied, "Carla wanted my father to accept her as his mate. He didn't want to. She wasn't happy about it."

"*He* didn't want to or his demon didn't?" In order for their kind to have a deep relationship, to take someone as their mate, both halves of the soul needed to choose the partner.

"Neither wanted her as a mate," replied Harper. "So Carla left me on Jolene's doorstep when I was two months old."

Knox felt a low rumble begin to build in his chest as anger whipped through him. "Why Jolene's doorstep?"

"Lucian Wallis doesn't have a doorstep. He's a nomad."

"And he then took care of you."

"Not exactly. Lucian convinced Jolene to take care of me, because he didn't know what to do with a baby. She agreed because she knew he was out of his depth, and she wanted to be sure I was okay. But she made him promise to visit me regularly."

"Did he?"

"He turned up every six months or so, which to him was the equivalent of full-time parenting. When I was four, Jolene forced him to take me."

"She passed you to him like a parcel?" The idea made Knox's blood boil.

"No. She wanted her son to learn some responsibility, and she thought it was wrong that I didn't have either of my parents playing a big part in my life. She also thought it might make him settle somewhere."

"But it didn't."

"No. We moved constantly." She'd attended thirteen different schools before graduating. Being 'the new kid' over and over had been irritating in itself, just like repeatedly experiencing the cycle of curiosity, acceptance, and desertion got old fast.

"How did you end up here in Nevada?"

"After I graduated, I told Lucian I was moving here to be around the rest of my family."

"You were sick of flitting from place to place," Knox assumed, but she shook her head.

"My upbringing wasn't horrible or something I'd change if

given the chance. I liked traveling, it was an adventure, but I wanted to put down some roots."

She'd wanted a real home, not a motel or a rental house or someone's sofa. Wanted a place she could decorate and settle in. She'd gotten sick of repeatedly leaving her friends, her school, and her favorite places; sick of missing her family and all their special occasions.

"Do you see Lucian much?"

"He's never out of contact for more than five months at a time. I know that doesn't sound like much, but it's a lot for him. He never really embraced the dad role. He had no behavioral expectations of me, and he allowed me to make my own decisions. He believed I should learn through experience rather than through rules. I'm grateful. It's made me fiercely self-reliant."

Knox didn't understand how she couldn't feel even a slight element of anger or bitterness. When she spoke of Lucian, there was even affection in her voice – the kind a parent would have for a clueless child. "But you weren't raised. *You* were the adult."

"You sound angry."

"I am. He put his needs before yours." At that moment, the server entered with their meals. Once he'd left, Knox asked, "Has Carla ever made any attempt to contact you?"

The piece of steak melted in her mouth, and she groaned. "Nope."

As an almost orgasmic look flashed across her face, Knox's body clenched. "You don't seem in the least bit upset by it. Why?"

"I figure if that's the kind of person she is, it's better for me that she wasn't in my life. Be angry at Lucian if you want, but at least he accepted and cared for me in his way. That's more than she was ever willing to do."

Thinking it was best that she knew, Knox said, "She has a

mate and two sons now. The oldest is twenty-three. The other is sixteen."

"Yeah, I know, I saw her with them a few times." Harper sipped at her wine. "Enough about my life."

Inwardly, he tensed, expecting her to start asking about his life. But she didn't, she turned her total attention to her meal. And he realized it was because she didn't see the point in getting to know him as she had no intention of forming the anchor bond. Knox had to wonder if – maybe even on a subconscious level – it was because she didn't trust him not to leave her. She'd been abandoned by both parents, never had many fixed people in her life thanks to her years of traveling, and quite possibly lacked the ability to trust that anyone would want her bad enough to stick around.

It was then that he recalled what she'd said in the car; that he'd change his mind about bonding once he knew her. So it could be that he was right and she expected him to leave her – maybe not now, but eventually since, to her, people came and went all the time.

If that was the case, he would need to gain Harper's trust before he had any hope of getting her to form the anchor bond. She would need to be certain she had his complete loyalty, confident that he would be a constant presence in her life. And he *would* be a constant presence. "You'll come to know me. You'll come to trust me. And you'll see that I can be relied on. Then we'll bond."

"Yeah, in your imaginary world."

Her unimpressed, flippant, elusive air was like a challenge to his demon, who was currently fixated on Harper – and not because she was its anchor. It liked her quiet confidence, her refusal to be intimidated, and the strength that allowed her to withstand Knox's forceful personality. Knox could admit the demon had good taste, and he made his decision there and then – he'd have her. But one thing he could sense about the guarded creature in front of him was that she wouldn't be easy to seduce.

He'd been around many women, had thought he knew her gender pretty well. He'd found that the majority had some sort of agenda. Some wanted him because they found a thrill in being so close to danger. Some wanted him because of his wealth and status. He'd also found that seduction itself was one big game. A lot of females played coy and hard to get, while others were very forward.

Harper, however, was like no female he'd met before. She didn't have an agenda and she wasn't playing a game. Not once had she flirted with him. He knew she was attracted to him – he could detect the lust building in her, could clearly see the glint of need in her eyes. A need he knew was in his own. But it was as though she'd dismissed their attraction as unimportant, meaningless. Something was holding her back from him. Neither he nor his demon liked it.

Pausing in his meal, he said, "You strike me as someone who prefers it when people are upfront."

It was true that Harper had no time or patience for mind games. "So?"

Knox leaned forward, wanting her to see the resolve in his expression. "I want you."

And Harper nearly choked on her steak. When she'd finally swallowed it down with the help of her wine, she shrugged. "Thanks for sharing."

"You want me." She cast him a glare but didn't deny it, which soothed his demon slightly. "But you're going to fight it, aren't you?"

Every step of the way. It wasn't that she had any hang-ups

about casual sex – and that was all it would be if she got involved with Knox Thorne. Demons were very sexual creatures, so casual sex among their kind was pretty much the norm. But that was the thing. "I don't get involved with our kind – not even for a single night."

That was the last thing he'd expected her to say. His demon was just as shocked. "You don't date demons? You've never been with one of our kind?"

She took another sip of her wine. "No."

"Why?" He wasn't all that surprised when she didn't answer him. Shamelessly using his most compelling voice, Knox said, "Tell me." But, of course, she shook off the compulsion.

"No." Didn't he understand yet that she was a very private person? Harper was also a person who preferred to avoid complications. Like parking tickets, speed restrictions, and red lights – which was why she no longer had a driver's license. When it came to relationships, male demons liked to make things complicated. They were extremely possessive, annoyingly demanding, and incredibly intense. Human relationships, by contrast, could be simpler. Most human males wouldn't demand everything from a girl, whereas demons would accept nothing less.

Of course, she could have simply settled for a series of one-night stands with her own species rather than stick to humans. But that kind of lifestyle held no appeal for Harper. Her father flitted from person to person, and he was never happy. Not to mention that human males were more accepting because, unaware of what she was, they didn't see her demonic flaws. The lack of wings, the strange ever-changing eyes, and the inability to conjure a simple fucking orb of hellfire therefore meant nothing to them. She thought Knox would push her for an explanation, but although his mouth tightened, he shrugged.

Picking up his wine glass, Knox sank into his chair. "Okay, we'll play it your way."

"I'm not playing."

"No, you're not." And that just made him want her even more. His cock was hard, heavy, and aching with the need to be in her. The dark predator inside him now wanted her more than ever; it wanted to be the first demon to possess her. "You'll come to me."

Harper narrowed her eyes. "Is that so?"

There was a taunt in her voice that made him arch a brow. "It will happen."

"Do you think that sex will make me more inclined to bond with you, is that it?"

"This has nothing to do with us being anchors. This is about me wanting you, and you wanting me."

"You're very sure of yourself. And you mistakenly seem to think you can be very sure of me." She pouted. "How sad for you."

He gave her a pointed look. "I will have you in my bed, Harper. I always take what I want. Right now, that's you."

"But you also want the anchor bond. Adding sex into the mix would just complicate things."

"Sex never has to be complicated."

But of course he'd think that. He was a guy who approached sexual intimacy on a purely physical level. For him, it could never impact an emotional situation. "You like control in all things. You'll never control me," she reminded him.

No, he wouldn't. And that should have dulled her appeal. But if anything, it made him want her more. Knox didn't understand it. "You could never desire a man you could control."

"Is that a fact?"

"It is. You're a very strong personality, Harper. You would

only be attracted to someone who's either stronger or equally strong."

It pissed her off that he'd read her so easily. "And you think you're stronger, don't you?"

"What I think is that when I'm deep inside you, neither of us will care."

Harper shook her head. "It won't happen."

His eyes bled to black as his demon pushed for supremacy. "It will, little sphinx." The voice was toneless, flat. "I promise you that."

To Harper's total frustration, their conversation had sent so much lust curdling inside her that she lost her appetite. Her food sat like lead in her stomach. Knox's knowing look told her that he knew exactly why she suddenly didn't feel so hungry – at least not for food anyway.

When they were done with their meal, he led her out of the room with a hand on her lower back; his touch seemed to burn her flesh right through her clothes. As they were nearing the restaurant's exit, Knox ever so slightly tensed. Harper would have asked what was wrong, but then she noticed that the beautiful blonde heading toward them, arm in arm with a guy half her age, was glaring hard at Knox.

She stopped in front of him. "Knox."

He sighed. "Kendra."

If Harper was guessing correctly, this was an ex-bed buddy of Knox's who wasn't very happy about the 'ex' part. The she-demon spared Harper a brief, dismissive glance.

Feeling unusually protective as Kendra turned her glower on Harper, Knox slid his hand around Harper's back to cup her hip. Kendra noticed the move and didn't appear to like it.

She leaned into the male demon at her side, stroking his arm as she smirked at Knox. "Have you met Brandt?"

"I haven't. Have you met Harper?" Seeing that Brandt was raking an appreciative gaze over her, Knox possessively flexed his grip on her hip.

Kendra's smirk was quickly replaced by a sneer of distaste as she studied Harper's appearance. "No, I haven't had that pleasure. I expect that's because she clearly doesn't travel in our social circle."

"This is Harper Wallis, my anchor."

Kendra froze for a moment. Then jealousy briefly flashed across her face, and Harper understood why. A demon would often be jealous of their partner's closeness to their anchor. Kendra clearly didn't want anyone having any kind of claim on Knox.

"I see," drawled Kendra. "Did you say she's a Wallis?" Kendra chuckled, but the sound was forced. She was still too jealous to be truly amused. "You drew the short straw, Knox. Poor you."

Used to the prejudice, Harper just smiled. "It's good to see you're not bitter."

"Enjoy your evening," Knox told Kendra and Brandt. Shackling Harper's wrist, he then guided her through the exit, out of the hotel, and into a waiting car. "We're taking Harper home," he told Levi, who immediately pulled away from the curb. "I take it Tanner's still dealing with some issues in the hotel." Levi merely nodded in confirmation.

"What did you do to that woman to piss her off so much?" Harper asked Knox.

"My demon loses interest in its sexual partners very quickly." It was probably better that his little sphinx knew that upfront. "Females tend to be offended by that."

"Is this a warning?"

Knox shrugged. "It's simply better that you know."

"Since I've no intention of hopping into your bed, it's not something I need to know."

He pinned her gaze with his as he spoke only loud enough for her to hear. "I will have you, Harper. I don't give up until I catch my prey."

"I'm nobody's prey."

"We'll see."

No sooner had Harper stepped into her apartment than her cell phone rang. It was Khloë. "Hey," answered Harper, locking the door.

"*Why am I only hearing* now *that Knox Thorne is your anchor?*"

Harper frowned. "Who told you about that?"

"I heard Jolene and Beck talking about it." Beck was Jolene's anchor.

"Eavesdropping again?"

"Why didn't you tell me? You knew that night in the Underground, but you didn't say anything." Khloë sounded genuinely hurt.

"I was kind of in shock. It's a big thing, and I didn't really know how I felt about it. We both know what your reaction would have been."

"If you're insinuating that I would have interfered in any way, shape, or form—"

"You would have hounded me until I gave in and bonded with him, and if that failed you would have concocted some sort of plan with the rest of our family to make it happen – and we both know it. This has to be my decision, and mine alone."

"But you told Raini and Devon," she whined.

"Because although they're full of opinions, they don't believe it's their right to mess with my life. That's a Wallis thing."

Khloë huffed. "Fine. You can at least tell me if you've bonded with him yet."

"I haven't."

"You didn't say 'yet,' which means you're considering refusing to do it. Look, I know you find it hard to trust and let people in. But you have the comfort of knowing that Knox can't possibly be any less reliable than either of your primary blood relations." Primary blood relations being Carla and Lucian. Khloë simply refused to refer to them as 'parents.'

"That's true," Harper allowed with a sigh.

"You sound really glum. How about we go back to the Underground this weekend? Sunday night's the best. It's too hectic on Fridays and Saturdays." As demons could go for days and days without sleep, they didn't need to worry about staying up late on work nights.

"Sure. But no more duels."

"We'll see."

It occurred to Harper as she ended the call that those were the last words Knox had said to her. If it turned out that Knox was just as mentally resilient as Khloë, then Harper would definitely have a problem getting him to do anything she wanted him to do – including walking away from her. Not great.

CHAPTER FOUR

Come to me, Harper.

With a gasp, Harper bolted upright in bed. And cursed. That rumbly, velvet voice called to her day and night; tempting her and teasing her with a promise of sexual satisfaction. Worse, the words snaked over her skin like demanding hands, making raw need inflate inside her – an overwhelming pressure that had nowhere to go. Her whole body felt hypersensitive, edgy, and tingly.

Cursing him to hell and back, she clambered out of bed and headed for the kitchen area, where she switched on the coffee machine. She had seen him twice during the past week; on both occasions he had collected her from the studio and taken her to dinner. It had been a different restaurant each time. He was clearly trying to ensure as many demons as possible saw them together.

As she'd watched people rush to aid, serve, or talk to him wherever they went, it had quickly become clear that he wielded a shit load of social power. That fear of him was always present, though. Even humans sensed that there was something dangerous about him.

Each time they were together, he surprisingly made a distinct effort to get to know her, asking questions about her family and the places she'd seen during her travels. He shared some of his own memories with her, though nothing too personal. He'd also hinted at her accompanying him to the conference in New York, wherein the Primes would discuss the matter of electing a U.S. Monarch, since many demons took their anchors to important events. Harper was nosy enough to be considering it, but she wasn't yet totally sure she—

Come to me.

Again, his voice snaked over her skin. Squeezing her eyes shut, Harper shook her head. For the first time, she responded to his call. *Why are you doing this to me?* She'd seen the way females responded to him, doubted he'd ever be short of women eager to hop in his bed. She'd also noticed that those women were just like Kendra – tall, elegant, and well-groomed. Harper was none of those things and she was totally okay with it. That didn't change the fact that she wasn't his usual type.

I want you.

Like it was truly that simple for him. She scratched at her arm, feeling itchy with the restlessness that was taunting her entire body. His mind brushed against hers, almost as if he was trying to comfort her. She was glad her mental shields were tough enough to withstand him or he'd no doubt pour into her mind until she could feel him everywhere. Telepathy wasn't an invasion of the mind. It was like one mind picking up the frequency of another and using that channel of communication to speak.

Maybe you only want me because I'm not tripping all over myself to get to you. Demons loved challenges.

A vibe of male amusement touched her mind. *We both know it's more than that, but I'll admit that your stubbornness is refreshing.* His mind stroked hers once more . . . and then it was gone. And for some stupid, irrational reason, she felt more alone than she ever had before.

It wasn't only her stubbornness he seemed to find entertaining. Knox also seemed to be enjoying how difficult she found it to adjust to having someone who looked out for her. He'd installed a high-tech security system at her apartment and the studio. He'd also assigned Tanner to be both her driver and bodyguard – something she'd expected Tanner to resent, given that it had to be a boring job. But her new bodyguard made it clear to her that since she was important to Knox, her safety was equally important to Tanner and the other sentinels.

Part of her balked at having a driver, felt it impeded on her independence. But traveling in a Bentley beat using public transport any day. As such, when she left her apartment later that morning to head for work, Tanner was waiting outside. They talked a little during the short journey, at the end of which he parked in a spot outside the studio and, as usual, remained in his car while she went inside.

"Morning," sang Khloë, who was sitting at the reception desk. "I brought bagels."

"You mean you *stole* bagels."

Khloë just shrugged.

Peeking at Tanner through the window, Devon asked, "Is he ever going to come inside?"

"I doubt it," replied Harper. "He takes his sentry position very seriously."

No sooner had Harper began setting up her station than Raini appeared, took her by the arm, and started pulling her toward the back of the studio. "What? What is it?"

"I have something to show you," said the succubus. Inside the office, Raini dug into a black store bag and pulled out a pair of tailored black pants and an elegant blouse. "What do you think?"

Harper gave the suit an approving nod. "It'll look good on you."

Raini rolled her eyes. "It's not for me, it's for you."

"What?" squeaked Harper. "I don't do 'elegant.' I can't."

"If you go to the conference in New York, you'll have to. And if you just lose that expression that dares the world to come at you, you'll easily pull off elegant. Oh, and I got you shoes to match."

"I'm not good at—"

"Think of this suit as armor. You're going to be in a place swarming with high-profile demons, and they'll undoubtedly be dressed all prim and proper. You'll feel better if you're dressed just the same."

"Armor," echoed Harper. "I can work with that."

Raini gave her a beaming smile that lit up the room. "Excellent! One more thing before we get to work: have you tested the bed springs with Knox yet? Why are you scowling? I was just asking."

Carla Hayden, Knox noted, didn't look much like her daughter. Although they were both petite, she lacked Harper's delicious curves. Her facial features were exotic where Harper's were soft. In addition, Carla's skin was a golden shade while Harper's was ivory perfection. There were only three physical traits they seemed to share: height, hair color, and the slightly pointed chin.

When Harper looked at someone, it was with a bold, daring 'fucking try me' expression that amused both Knox and his demon. Carla, however, was all smiles and grace and pleasantness. They both had a certain sensuality to their movements. But whereas it was innate and unconscious with Harper, it was superficial and practiced with Carla.

Standing in the office of one of his casinos, Carla nodded. "Mr. Thorne."

"Sit," he invited, forcing himself to be civil. He'd suspected the woman would come at some point, wanting to know if the rumors circulating about the identity of his anchor were true. It had been three days since he'd last seen Harper. Three days of his demon hounding him to seek her out, to take her as they both wanted. There was no denying that it was utterly fixated on her.

Knox could admit to being just as impatient to have her. One of the things he liked most about her, despite how contrary it made her, was her independent streak. He also liked that she was upfront, tenacious, and unpredictable. It was a package that fascinated him.

Nervously, Carla cleared her throat. "I hope I find you well and . . ." She trailed off when Knox held up his hand.

"We both know you didn't come here to enquire about my welfare, so I'd prefer it if you didn't make unnecessarily small talk."

"Very well." She paused briefly. "I heard that you found your anchor."

"You heard correctly."

"I heard her name is Harper Wallis."

Something about the way she stumbled over the name made Knox realize . . . "You didn't name her, did you?"

She averted her gaze. "I had some difficulty deciding on one."

"You also had difficulty being a mother to her, as I understand it." So much difficulty she hadn't even bothered to give Harper a name before dumping her.

"So she told you." Carla exhaled heavily. "I ask you not to take everything you heard as gospel. The Wallis family have a very one-sided account of what occurred back then."

"You *didn't* leave your child with Jolene Wallis?"

"It's not as simple as that. I have no idea if Jolene and Lucian told Harper lies about me or if she, like them, enjoys exaggerating the tale. But there is much more to the story than whatever she told you."

Knox sank into his seat, regarding her thoughtfully. "Why come to me with this?"

"You're my Prime, and your opinion of me is important to me. I just ask you not to judge me on the information you've been given by Harper. It's clear that – as I feared – you're angry with me because of what you've heard, but please be fair. You have known me for some time. Harper's your anchor, but the reality is that you don't *know* her."

"I'd say it's you who doesn't know her." Carla seemed abashed, but he wasn't buying it. "Are you implying that she lied to me? That's a very serious allegation to make." And it offended both him and his demon that anyone would accuse Harper of such a thing.

"I know," agreed Carla, sounding distressed to even consider it. "But it's *that* or she's simply repeating lies the Wallis family have told her."

"As I see it, if you truly had any regard for her, you wouldn't have abandoned her."

"It wasn't as simple as that. I thought that if I left her with Lucian for a little while, he would bond with her and then we could be a family. It was a foolish plan, and I saw that soon enough. I went back for her, I did. But Jolene refused to let me take her. I tried again and again, but then Lucian took her away. I never had a chance of finding her after that, he was always moving."

If Carla was lying, she was very, very good at it. According to

Harper, Jolene had sent her to live with Lucian when she was four. Was it possible that Jolene had done that to keep her out of Carla's reach?

"Soon after that, I met Bray and we eventually had our sons. My focus had to be on them."

"In short, you're saying that if Jolene and Lucian hadn't tried to come between you and Harper, you would have been a mother to her?"

"Yes, of course."

"Hmm. She's been in Vegas without Lucian since she was eighteen. Yet, you've made no effort at all to see her. That strikes me as odd for someone who claims to be so unhappy about not having their daughter in their life."

"I thought about going to see her, but I knew Jolene and Lucian had filled her head with a pack of lies. I worried that she'd slam the door in my face. I don't think I could take that." Carla swallowed hard, the image of an emotional mess. "Do you think she would ever want to speak with me? Has she given you any indication that she might be prepared to do so?"

"Anything Harper tells me will remain between her and me. I'd never break her confidence."

"Naturally. I'm sorry, I shouldn't have asked that." There was a pause before Carla timidly enquired, "How is she?"

"That's a question for Harper to answer. I'm her anchor. But I don't speak *for* her. Now if you're finished, I'm a busy man." But he got the feeling that she wasn't finished, that there was something else.

Carla immediately shot to her feet. "I understand. Thank you for your time, Mr. Thorne." When she reached the door, she glanced at him over her shoulder. "Before I go . . ."

And here it is. "Yes?"

"Please give Harper a message for me. Please tell her that,

whatever she may think, I have always loved her. I never stopped thinking about her, wondering where she was and how she was doing. Not even for a single day." Then Carla was gone, and Levi slipped inside.

"You heard that?" Knox asked him.

The sentinel nodded. "Do you believe her?"

"I'll concede that there are always two sides to every story, but that's not to say that I believe Carla's account. You?"

"She sounded truthful. But . . ."

"Yes. But."

"If you asked her sons whether she's a good mother, I think you'd get conflicting answers. Roan is a self-righteous prick who hops, skips, and jumps at her say-so. Her youngest, Kellen, seems to despise her." Levi tilted his head. "Are you going to give Harper the message from Carla?"

"I haven't decided yet. You think I should."

"I think you want her to trust you. She won't if you keep things from her – even if your reason is to protect her or her feelings." Levi grinned. "It bugs you that you can't control this."

Of course it did. Knox took control of whatever situation he found himself in. "And that amuses you far too much."

An unrepentant shrug. "I always figured you'd be indifferent to your anchor, since you don't need one."

"It's not that simple, which you'll learn for yourself when you find yours. Then *I'll* be the one who's laughing."

Knox?

He instantly tensed at the wariness in Harper's voice. *What's wrong?*

Who the hell is Silas Monroe? Because he just walked into my office.

Shit. *I'm on my way.*

* * *

Harper eyed her visitor with a mixture of distrust, irritation, and confusion. She'd been going through the accountancy books when there had been a rhythmic knock at the door followed by the *immediate* entrance of a dark, gangly guy who apparently didn't have the manners to wait until he'd been summoned to enter someone's office.

She could sense he was a demon, so he should know better than to invade the personal space of another demon uninvited. That had annoyed her, and because she was in a shitty mood after arguing with Royce again, she'd simply asked, "Who the fuck are you?"

He'd presented her with a huge grin, ignoring the disapproval radiating from her colleagues in the doorway. The grin was pleasant enough, yet . . . there was something sly in the curve of it. A cunningness that seemed to match the callous glint in his eyes. "Silas," he'd replied in a British accent. "Silas Monroe."

"What do you want?" She highly doubted it was a tattoo, since he could have discussed that with Raini or Devon – it was Khloë's afternoon off. No, this wasn't about a tattoo. Something was very weird here. She'd instantly called out to Knox, wondering if he knew the guy. She hadn't expected Knox to declare he was coming, but maybe she should have.

You don't have to come. No answer. So she focused solely on Silas, who was glancing around the office, as if admiring the décor.

"He said he wanted to speak to you," Raini told Harper, though she was glaring at his back. "I explained that you were busy right now, but he said he could smell you and then just barged right past me."

Did he now? Harper slowly got to her feet as she repeated, "What do you want?"

He shrugged. "To have a little chat."

"I don't chat."

"Really? That's sad."

"No, it's not."

Harper, don't let Silas touch you, said Knox, his voice hard. *I don't think he'll be stupid enough to try to harm you, but he's obviously stupid enough to bother you.*

If the fucker tried to touch her, he'd find her pen – which she'd infused with hellfire – lodged up his rectum. He cast the object a wary look as he said, "Come on, luv, there's no call for rudeness. Let's start again. Hello Miss Wallis, I'm Silas."

"Yeah? Well, I'm bored. You can go now."

He didn't look in the slightest bit offended. "Now that wasn't nice."

"If you want 'nice,' you came to the wrong fucking person. I'm a fully qualified bitch who'll happily rip you another asshole if you don't get the fuck out of my office." She arched a brow when he didn't move. "Why are you still here?"

"More to the question," began Tanner as he strolled past the girls and into the office, his gaze hard and intent as it locked on Silas, "why are you here at all?" No doubt Knox had sent him inside to protect her if necessary.

"Tanner," Silas greeted pleasantly. "It's a surprise to see you." Yeah? He didn't actually look all that surprised.

"I asked you a question. I never ask twice. So tell me, why are you here?" Tanner sounded more dangerous than she'd ever heard him.

Silas shrugged casually, though he no longer looked so relaxed. "I'm simply having a friendly chat with the little she-demon here."

Tanner glanced at her briefly. "She doesn't look like she considers you a friend."

"I think I offended her by walking into the room without waiting for a 'come in.' I suppose it was kind of stupid."

At that moment, another demon breezed inside. "Stupid is coming here in the first place." Just like that, the atmosphere snapped taut with tension. How Knox got there so fast, she didn't know. Some kind of teleportation, maybe ... She didn't care to figure it out right then.

As his dark eyes locked on hers, her body immediately responded – heating, burning, longing. Her inner demon perked right up, excited to see him, despite the circumstances. He scrutinized her from head to toe, as if checking that she was fine. Then his eyes slammed on Silas, instantly hardening.

"Knox," mumbled Silas nervously.

When Knox arched a questioning brow at Tanner, the hellhound said, "Silas here claims to be having a friendly chat with Harper."

Knox narrowed his eyes at Silas. "Just why would you concern yourself with my anchor?" He was so composed, it was chilling. Harper actually felt the room temperature lower.

"Anchor?" echoed Silas.

Tanner tilted his head. "You haven't heard the rumors about Knox and Harper? Strange."

Strange? More like doubtful, in Harper's opinion. Knox had made it public, and news traveled fast in the demon world. But why would Silas play this weird game if he knew Knox was her anchor?

"I'm going to ask you a question," Knox rumbled as he advanced on Silas. His inner demon wanted nothing more than to rip him apart, and Knox found the idea particularly tempting. But he needed something from the little shit, and he'd get it. "It would be good for you to answer me honestly. I don't like it when people lie to me. It's very disappointing." Silas swallowed hard as

Knox halted in front of him. He didn't cower, to his credit. But his fear was easy to see, and it satisfied Knox's demon. "Did someone put you up to this, Silas? Or was this little test your idea?"

"Test?" repeated Harper.

Knox didn't move his gaze from Silas as he explained to Harper. "A test to see just how important you are to me. Just how protective I am and just how quick I'll act on any issue you might have. The answer to that, Silas, is that she is very important to me. And it would be the height of stupidity to harm her by word or deed, because I *will* eviscerate anyone who dares to do so."

Picking up movement near the doorway, Harper noticed that Raini was fanning her face; it was typical that she would find the dominant, protective routine arousing.

"This is the part where you assure me that you are no threat to Harper," Knox told Silas.

"I'm no threat to her," Silas swore.

"Good. Before you leave, I want the answer to my question."

"This was my idea. It was wrong, and I apologize."

Knox narrowed his eyes as he invaded the demon's personal space. "I told you that I don't like it when people lie to me. Why would you want to disappoint me so badly, Silas?"

Harper eyed Knox curiously. He looked merely mildly irritated, but his rage pulsed around the room, unnerving even her inner demon despite that it believed he wouldn't harm it.

Silas, on the other hand, was sweating with fear. "I can't tell you," he mumbled, licking his lips nervously. "I would if I could, but I can't. I'm under a compulsion."

There was a long pause, so Harper asked, "Is he telling the truth?" That was when Silas fell to his knees, crying out in sheer agony. He rocked back and forth as he cradled his head, and she instantly knew what was happening. "You've thrust your mind into his," she accused Knox. And that scared the shit out of her.

"The compulsion is strong," commented Knox, withdrawing from Silas' mind. "I sensed it. You *are* unable to give us a name. But I also learned something else, Silas. Do you know what that was? I learned that you were eager to do this. So eager that you volunteered."

"He didn't expect you to come," Tanner theorized. "Did you?"

Silas got to his feet. "You don't have loyalty to anyone outside your lair," he said to Knox. "You don't exactly keep people around you. I didn't think you'd care."

It was true that although Knox protected his lair fiercely, he only kept his sentinels around him. And now Harper.

"I didn't think she'd be important to you," continued Silas. "You're too powerful to need an anchor."

"Do you think flattery will get you out of this?" chuckled Tanner.

Drawing on every bit of strength he had, Knox resisted killing the bastard. His inner demon wanted it badly, reminded Knox how effortless and satisfying it would be. But Knox had to be smart about this. "There's only one reason I'm allowing you to live ... for now ... and that's that I need you to go back to whoever sent you and tell them just how suicidal it would be to harm my anchor. You should also let them know that if they, or anyone else, ever considers using her against me, they'll pay in ways they don't want to imagine."

A paling Silas nodded and, after one last look at Harper, quickly scampered.

Devon stepped into the room with Raini. "That was really all a test?" Her face suddenly scrunched up and she hissed at Tanner, looking ready to pounce.

Pure male amusement took over the sentinel's face. "What's wrong, kitty?" Yeah, hellhounds and hellcats had an instinctive aversion to the other.

"Tanner, follow him," ordered Knox. "I want to know who sent him." The sentinel swiftly left and, taking a deep breath, Knox held out his hand to Harper. "Come." He needed to get out of there, and he needed her with him to keep him calm. Levi should have arrived in the Bentley by now, considering the expertise of his driving skills.

"I'm at work," she pointed out.

"But she can totally leave early." Raini was such a bitch. "I'm Raini, by the way. That's Devon."

Knox gave them a simple nod of greeting before gripping Harper by the wrist. "Let's go."

Harper was impressed by how easily Knox shrugged off Raini's succubae allure. Tanner, too, seemed to have withstood it very well. As Knox hauled her outside where Levi waited and practically shoved her into the Bentley, she cursed. "You might find this surprising, but I don't like being dragged around." He didn't respond. "Where are we going?"

"My home."

His 'home' turned out to be a goddamn mansion. *Holy fuck.*

They had barely reached the door when it opened wide, revealing a tall, elegant demon who nodded respectfully at Knox. "Evening, Mr. Thorne."

"Dan, this is Harper Wallis, my anchor."

Dan presented her with a polite smile. "I'm happy to meet you, Miss Wallis."

Unaccustomed to gentility, Harper merely responded, "Um, you too." No sooner had Dan taken her jacket in the marble foyer than Knox urged her into a high-ceiling living area that was like something out of a magazine. With its mahogany walls and light pine flooring, it might have looked plain if it wasn't for the blue-tinted windows, the incredible paintings, the ocean blue Persian rug, and the spotlights in the ceiling and on the walls.

At Knox's gesture, Harper gingerly sat on one of the two beige half-moon sofas that circled a pine coffee table, feeling completely out of place and unable to relax.

A few moments later, a small Hispanic woman appeared. "Mr. Thorne, dinner won't be ready for another hour. Can I get you and your guest anything?"

"Meg, this is Harper Wallis, my anchor. Harper, this is Meg – the best cook you'll ever have the pleasure of knowing."

Flushing, Meg smiled at Harper. "It's a pleasure to meet you. Is there anything I can get for you?"

"I'm good, thanks."

"We're both fine for now, Meg." With a respectful nod, the woman scurried away. When Knox saw Harper open her mouth – most likely to castigate him for not asking in advance what she'd like to eat – he said the one thing guaranteed to distract her. "I had a visit from Carla today."

She blinked. "Really?"

"She wanted to know if there was any truth in the rumors that you're my anchor. I confirmed that you are."

"Did she cry?"

Her expression was so hopeful, he had to smile. "No."

"Damn," she muttered. Knox moved to a little bar behind them that she hadn't even noticed until then.

"Drink?" She shook her head, so Knox simply prepared himself a small glass of gin and tonic. "What did your family tell you about her over the years?"

"Not much, actually. Just that I should never think there was anything wrong with me simply because my mother dumped me; that some people are just too selfish to care about anyone but themselves."

"She claims she tried to see you over the years, that Jolene and Lucian kept her away."

Harper snorted. "They probably *would* have kept her away if she'd tried. But I'm pretty sure she didn't." Knox's expression was inscrutable, but she suspected, "You believe her."

Knox lounged on the sofa, directly opposite her. "What I believe is that it's important for you to have the facts about your life."

"The fact is that the woman doesn't, and never has, wanted me."

"She asked me to tell you that she's always loved you, thought of you often."

"I'll bet she did." Carla was, according to Jolene, as cunning as they came. "She's taking preemptive steps, worried I'll switch to your lair and request for her to be cast out."

Knox *did* want Harper to join his lair, but they'd get to that at a later point. He had to do things one step at a time with Harper or she'd withdraw from him rather than accept his place in her life. "You've very sure she doesn't care for you?"

"Since moving to Vegas, I saw her a couple of times. She dismissed me with a haughty look. So, yes, I'm very sure."

That had anger bubbling inside of him. "Knowing that makes me want to cast her out."

"Nah, it'll be more fun to have her stick around. She likes to pretend I don't exist. But you can't pretend someone doesn't exist if they're being paraded in front of your entire lair, can you?"

Her impish grin made him smile. "You have a lot of Jolene in you."

"I'll take that as a compliment."

"You should. Your grandmother is strong and a good Prime." He took a swig of his gin and tonic.

"So . . . you can crash right through people's mental shields and invade their minds."

He could see that it concerned her. "Even if your shields

weren't impenetrable, it's not something I would ever have done to you. You never have to fear that I'll harm you."

"Because you're one big, cuddly bear, right?"

"Cuddly? Definitely not. But you're my anchor, you're safe with me." He took another drink of his gin and tonic. "Have you thought any more about attending the conference with me in New York?"

"So you can introduce me to all the other Primes as your anchor?"

"The sooner your importance to me is well-known, the sooner you'll be considered untouchable." And the sooner people like Silas and his friends would think twice about bothering her to 'test' him.

"I don't see the point in you introducing me to everyone."

"I've already told you, whether we bond or not won't change anything. I'll still be in your life. I have rights to you that no one else will ever have."

At the sound of approaching footsteps, Knox turned his head to see three of his sentinels striding into the room. He knew them well enough to sense something was wrong. Rising, he asked, "What is it?" When Keenan slanted a glance at Harper, Knox assured him, "You can talk freely in front of her." One way to get Harper to trust him would be to show her that he was willing to give her that same trust. "Harper, you already know Levi. This is Keenan and Larkin, two of my sentinels. Keenan, Larkin – this is my anchor, as I'm sure you've already guessed."

The moment Keenan's hooded, blue eyes met hers, waves of need assailed Harper, bringing her senses to life. *Incubus*, she knew. Like succubae, they oozed sex and stirred a person's lust with a mere look. Still, it was nothing compared to the effect that Knox had on her body.

Keenan was what someone might call cutely hot with his

boyish face, adorable smile, and tall, defined body. Larkin was, in a word, stunning. She had a warrior-type figure, and her wide eyes were an unusual blend of gray and green. She was also the female who, with Tanner, had escorted Harper to Knox's office in the Underground. Harper wasn't sure what breed she was.

"A whole building of strays has gone missing," revealed Keenan. "You know how they sometimes group together for protection, right? Well, every single stray in that building has gone."

"Where did this happen?" asked Knox.

"In a neighborhood close to where Harper lives."

Knox stiffened. "No witnesses? No sign of foul play?"

"None," said Larkin, lounging on one of the sofas. "They just disappeared."

Harper spoke. "Strays have been going missing?" Knox merely nodded, his gaze suddenly burning with intensity as it focused on her. "What? Why are you looking at me like that?"

"Your current address isn't a safe place. It's in a high crime area."

"I'm aware of this. But you say it like this makes me a special case. Lots of people live in that area and similar areas."

"Their lives aren't important to me. Yours is."

As understanding hit her, she shook her head. "Hell no, you are *not* setting me up in another apartment."

"You heard what's happening. Strays near *you* were taken. I know you're not a stray, but you can't deny that it would be better for you to be in a more secure building in a safer area."

"You installed a security system at my building, remember?"

Keenan suddenly spoke to Harper, wonder in his voice. "You're not an imp, are you? I figured you were the same breed as the rest of your family." He studied her closely as he and the other male sentinels took a seat. "What are you?"

Harper didn't answer, too intent on making Knox see reason.

"A better apartment doesn't equal safety. People from all walks of life are targeted by criminals."

"Moving away from there would dramatically reduce your chances of being targeted. If you're worried about rent, don't. I own the building I have in mind for you."

"Of course you do," she muttered. "I'm not accepting any grand shit from you."

"Is this about pride? Pride won't keep you safe, Harper."

"Come on, tell me, what are you?" Keenan begged her as he pulled a flask out of his jacket.

Again, she ignored him. "I can protect myself just fine. I've been doing it for a long time."

The reminder that she'd pretty much raised herself didn't lessen Knox's frustration. Just as agitated, his demon pushed to the surface – making Knox's eyes bleed to black for a second. Knox pushed it back down. "I don't doubt that you're capable of protecting yourself. But those strays were probably capable of it too. Yet, they were all taken."

Keenan interrupted, "*Seriously*, what are you?"

She sighed at him. "I'm a sphinx." Seeing that Knox was about to speak again, she held up her hand. "I appreciate the gesture, but no. I don't want expensive things from you, and I don't want to move away from my lair. It's not going to happen."

"So damn stubborn."

"I believe I did warn you about that."

"She did," Levi verified, smiling.

It took supreme effort to make Knox stop grinding his teeth. The she-demon drove him insane. It was a wise person who acknowledged their strengths and their weaknesses, and Knox was smart about many things. He was good at reading people and what they wanted, at predicting how people would react to situations, and at figuring how to get what he wanted from them – and then at getting it. Harper, however . . . she left him stumped. "Then we find a compromise."

"What kind of compromise?"

"Something that enables me to ensure your protection without requiring you to change address. You can come with me to the conference."

Taking a swig from his flask, Keenan's brow furrowed. "It might not be a good idea for Harper to be there."

"Why?" asked Larkin.

"Isla might be offended by Harper's presence," Keenan pointed out. "Might even try to harm her."

"Isla Ross?" Harper turned to Knox. "Is she some kind of jealous ex? Did you two shake the sheets in the past?"

Knox frowned. "No."

"Then why would she have an issue with me?" When Knox didn't respond, she sighed. "Fine, you don't have to tell me." Harper refused to believe that it was disappointment that hit her on the realization that he didn't trust her.

If he hadn't spent the past week studying Harper so intently, he might have missed the hurt in her tone. "It's not that I don't trust you with this information. But much like you, I don't like sharing details about my personal life." Especially anything related to his past. Seeing that she looked mollified, he relaxed. "But . . . I won't have you walk into a situation blind, and as I fully intend to take you to the conference, I will trust you with the facts."

"I won't repeat them," she promised.

"I know you won't. When I was twelve and my parents died, I was placed in a sanctuary for stray demon children. That's where I met my sentinels. Isla was also there. We all watched out for each other."

"So, you're all kind of close?"

"Yes."

"Then why would she wish to harm your anchor?" At his shifty expression, she narrowed her eyes. "What?"

"Isla convinced herself I was her anchor. I knew she was wrong, but she refused to listen to me. She was angry with me because she believed I was rejecting her. So she left us and joined the lair that she was made Prime of only a decade later." Knox shrugged. "It could be that she's realized she was wrong. We've come across each other over the years and she never mentioned it. Hoping that it could be forgotten, I never raised the subject. Maybe it has been forgotten. After all, it's been a long time."

That made Harper wonder how old he was. Once demons reached their late twenties, the aging process slowed to a crawl. She couldn't guess his age based on how he dressed or how he spoke. Demons adapted and changed with the world around them – it was how they blended.

"But if she does still believe I'm her anchor, she'll have some serious anger toward the person she thinks has taken her place."

"Then announcing I'm your anchor isn't the wisest thing to do."

Knox pinned her gaze with his. "I'm not going to keep you a secret just to placate one person who may or may not still be deluded about something. You're in more danger if people *don't* know who you are to me."

"He's right," Levi told her.

Harper sniffed at the sentinel. "I don't believe I asked for a glass of your unimportant opinion."

The guy just smiled. "Knox, can I bite her?"

"No." If anyone would take a bite of that ivory skin, it would be Knox. His demon was in full agreement with that. "Although I don't like the idea of you being in the same room as Isla when there's a possibility that she could resent you, I think it would be better for you both to be introduced in a safe environment while I'm at your side."

"Otherwise Isla, if she is still convinced you're her anchor, would track down Harper and you might not be there to intervene," said Levi, correctly guessing where Knox's thoughts had taken him.

"It's best to get it over with and find out for sure," agreed Larkin.

Keenan looked at Harper, seemingly concerned. "Unless you'd rather not go. We'd understand if you were reluctant to be in a dangerous situation like that, if you're scared."

Knowing full well that the incubus was using reverse psychology, Harper scowled. "Are you always such an annoying motherfucker?"

Keenan laughed. "It makes life more interesting."

Hearing his cell phone ringing, Knox retrieved it from his pocket. *Tanner.* "Tell me."

"Did you know Silas can travel using shadows?" It was a form of teleportation.

"I'm guessing this means you lost him."

"He went down an alley, I followed him and watched him blend into the shadows. Then he just disappeared."

Knox sighed heavily.

"I don't think whoever sent him will risk pissing you off again. They were just testing the waters. They have their answer now, so there's no need to do anything else."

"Maybe so. We'll just have to be extra vigilant about her protection." Hanging up, Knox updated the others.

"He *tested* you? Some people are just fucking clueless." Larkin flipped her braid over her shoulder. "You should have at least dismembered him."

Keenan chuckled. "Tanner's probably right; they won't try it again. That would be a death sentence, and they have to know that."

After they talked a little more about it, Knox gestured for the sentinels to leave the room. Turning to Harper, he said, "I won't coerce you into attending the conference. You can say no." He wanted her to understand that although he'd be interfering and controlling, he wouldn't try to make her into a puppet. He liked that she was strong minded and stood up to him.

Feeling at a disadvantage while she was sitting and he was towering over her, she rose to her feet. "I want to go with you." She was curious about Isla, and this would be one way to stop him from repeatedly moaning about her living situation.

"Fair enough."

"I still think it would be better for you to walk away from me."

He threaded his hand through her hair, marveling at how soft it was. "That won't happen." It was so very tempting to take advantage of the need pulsing between them and seduce her into his bed. But he wanted her to come to him, willing in body, mind, and soul. He decided not to question why that was so important to him.

"I told you, I don't get involved with our kind."

"This was always going to happen, Harper." From the moment he'd first seen her in the combat circle, when she'd pierced the numbness settling over him, it had been inevitable. "It's too late to fight it."

Considering how much her body craved his and how badly her demon wanted him, Harper feared that he might just be right.

"Now come on, let's eat."

CHAPTER FIVE

"Of course you have a private jet," Harper said dryly. Didn't everybody?

As Knox guided her inside, she saw that the interior of the sleek black jet was just as impressive as the outside. She should have guessed the rich bastard would have his own plane. Sinking into a gray leather reclining seat that seemed to mold itself to her body, she happily accepted some refreshments from the animated stewardess.

Opening a can of Coke, she said, "Okay, I'll admit, this is seriously cool."

Sitting opposite her with only a walnut table between them, Knox briefly peered up from his phone. "Glad you think so."

Tanner and Levi had taken seats in a separate cabin at the other end of the jet, giving Knox and Harper plenty of privacy. Watching as Knox's fingers moved furiously over the screen while his face was set into a mask of concentration, she said, "A bit of a workaholic, aren't you?"

"There are worse things to be obsessive about." He'd no sooner put his phone away than the aircraft began to move. "Why didn't Jolene want to travel with us?"

"She thinks you and I should have plenty of 'alone time' to get to know each other the way anchors should."

"She's right." Knox twisted his mouth. "So ... if you don't date demons, does this mean you're celibate or that you stick to humans?"

He had a way of totally throwing her by shooting random questions. She had a feeling that was exactly why he did it. "What does it matter?"

"I want to know." As her mouth set into an involuntary pout, he smiled. "You really do hate personal questions, don't you?"

"It's something we have in common."

He inclined his head. "All right. How about an exchange? You answer my questions honestly, and I'll do the same for you. Nothing too invasive." The latter words were both an assurance and a warning.

If he was anyone else, the offer wouldn't have at all appealed to her. But the guy was such an enigma that he had her curiosity well and truly roused. It was frustrating that he had the very same effect on her libido. While she believed it was better not to know what he was, she couldn't help but *want* to know. "Fine. To answer your earlier question, no I'm not celibate. I only date humans." He narrowed his gaze at that. "Now it's your turn to answer a question."

Her eyes were daring him to back down. Knox didn't. "Ask."

"Does anyone know what you are?" He was silent for so long she didn't think he was going to respond.

"Only my sentinels," he finally replied. "Do humans totally satisfy you and your demon?" He didn't expect her to answer that, but she surprised him – as always.

"No," she reluctantly admitted. "Are you really as brutal and unforgiving as everybody says?"

"Yes." If that answer scared her, she didn't show it. "Are you at all afraid of me?"

"Sometimes." She was afraid of her body's response to him, and she would be dumb if she wasn't at least a little unnerved by something so dangerous. "Why are you secretive about what you are?" Because that could give her a clue as to just what he was.

"Our kind fears me enough as it is. They don't need an additional reason." He drummed his fingers on the armrest. "What do you think I am?"

"When I was coming up with a worst-case scenario, it crossed my mind that you could be one of Lucifer's offspring."

He laughed. "Lucifer keeps his offspring close; you should know that." He tilted his head. "That's the best theory you have?" If so, he was disappointed.

"That's another question. I haven't had a chance to ask mine yet. Are you a hybrid?"

He frowned. "There are no hybrids in the demon world." Even cambions – demons that were half-human – were still classed as a demonic breed in their own right.

"I know, but stranger things have happened." Like the fact that she was even answering personal questions.

He deliberately nudged her knee with his beneath the table. "No other theories?"

"None. Some think you're some kind of super incubus. Don't act like you don't know the effect you have on people."

"I'm not a . . . super incubus." He smiled at her irritated look. She clearly didn't like being in the dark about anything. "Why don't you get involved with our kind?"

She arched a reproachful brow. "That's a little invasive."

"Asking me what breed of demon I am isn't invasive?"

"Ah, but I didn't ask you what breed you are. I asked questions that might hint at the answer. That's different."

"Okay, I'll rephrase. Do you avoid getting involved with demons because one once hurt you?"

"No. How old are you?" She could tell he wanted to pursue his own line of questioning, but he didn't push.

"Much, much older than you."

She narrowed her eyes at his evasive response. "Can you really call on the flames of hell?"

"Maybe. Do you expect me to leave you, abandon you?"

That question demonstrated a perceptiveness she didn't like. "Maybe."

"I won't."

He didn't say anything else, and she knew that was as much as both of them were prepared to reveal for now.

The flight to Manhattan felt a lot longer than it probably was. A short drive later they arrived at a high-rise, black glass building. Tanner and Levi flanked Harper and Knox as they strolled through the foyer. Recognition flickered across the faces of the staff as they spotted Knox, quickly followed by a dose of fear.

A demon nervously directed Knox, Harper, and the two sentinels to a room at the rear of the building. As they entered, Harper's brows flew up at the size of the long, square boardroom table that looked like it would fit better at a wedding reception. Many demons were seated while others were standing in small groups as they chatted quietly. Every single one of them had the same reaction to Knox – their eyes flashed with respect, awe, and blind fear.

It was easy for Harper to forget just how much of a threat to their kind he truly presented, because she felt safe with him; had that instinctual knowledge that he would never hurt her, his anchor. Oh, she still found him unnerving and she never forgot she was in the presence of a powerful predator, but she also never felt threatened by him like these demons here did.

Her inner demon didn't like being in the company of all these Primes, didn't like their curious, assessing looks as they noticed Harper. Knox must not have liked it either, because his hand slipped around her nape as he guided her to the table, broadcasting that she was under his protection. Tanner stood on guard behind her chair while Levi took position behind Knox's seat.

"Jolene's not here yet," she noted with disappointment. She whispered, "Which one is Isla?"

Knox glanced around the room. "She hasn't arrived yet."

Hearing the empty chair beside her scrape along the floor, Harper turned her head to – *oh joy* – see a familiar male. Malden Lester had an alliance, though it was tenuous at best, with Jolene. He flashed Harper a wide charming smile, like they were good friends. Sure, she'd met him a few times, but they were barely even acquaintances.

"Hello, Harper," he drawled. Why he seemed to think he was suave and charismatic, she had yet to figure out. In reality, he was sly, smarmy, and bursting with a sense of self-importance. He had to sit pretty high on the power spectrum, but she suspected he wasn't quite as powerful as he liked to believe.

Harper forced a smile. "Hi, Malcolm."

"Malden," he corrected; a muscle in his cheek ticked – just as it always did when she called him that, knowing he hated it.

"Sorry, I'm not good with names."

Draping an arm over the back of her chair, Knox looked at Malden. "I see you've met my anchor." Knox also saw that Malden was trying to charm her, and he didn't like it.

Malden's gaze danced from him to Harper. "Yes, I have. I know Jolene quite well. Here she is now."

Harper couldn't help but smile at the sight of her grandmother, aunt, and Beck. Harper rose to her feet, immediately gaining their attention, and they headed straight for her. Jolene had a very confident walk – shoulders back, spine straight, chin up, and her stride purposeful. No one walked better in high heels than Jolene Wallis. A smile spread across her face as she reached Harper and gave her a one-armed hug. "Harper, I've missed you."

Stepping back, Harper said, "Grams, you look smart." Jolene had a very natural veneer of elegance, her clothes always sleek skirts and blouses.

"As do you. I'm guessing you're uncomfortable like that, though."

"So true." Harper nodded at the burly guy who was Jolene's anchor. "Hey, Beck."

He winked at her. The guy was like an annoying yet amusing uncle.

As her aunt pulled her in for a hug, Harper had to force a smile, wondering why the hell Jolene would bring her to something like this. Martina Wallis was fun, high-spirited, and so beautiful she could bewitch any male. She also liked to set shit on fire.

"Aw, it's so good to see you." Martina kissed Harper on the cheek.

No fear in her eyes, Jolene turned to Knox, who was also standing. Not much rattled Jolene. And if something did, she destroyed it – problem solved, in her opinion. "Knox Thorne, it's always a pleasure."

He nodded, a slight smile curving his mouth. "Jolene."

"I expect you to be a good anchor to my granddaughter."

"I expect you wouldn't allow anything else."

Jolene cackled, clearly quite happy with his answer. "I didn't realize you had a sense of humor. You'll need one if you have Harper in your life. Let's sit." She looked down at Malden. "You don't mind shuffling along, do you um . . . ?" She clicked her fingers, as if struggling to recall his name, but she knew damn well what it was.

"Malcolm," Harper helpfully supplied.

"*Malden*," he instantly amended, the tic in his cheek going crazy, though he did shuffle along. Jolene and Martina then sat on Harper's left while Beck stood behind Jolene.

Jolene leaned into Harper. "And *you* criticize *me* for messing with people." She patted Harper's hand. "I taught you well."

"You brought Martina?" Harper whispered.

"She distracts people, it makes them easier to read." It was true that many of the males were drooling over the woman already. "The security here isn't all that good, which concerns me."

"You snuck inside, didn't you?" Not that Harper would expect anything different from an imp, particularly a Wallis.

"Of course." Glancing at the doorway, she said, "That's Isla Ross."

The woman was amazingly beautiful, her features were eerily perfect, and her skin was flawless . . . but there was something almost robotic about her as she slowly crossed the room. It was odd.

When Knox tensed ever so slightly, Harper knew he'd spotted her. "Here goes," she said. His hand squeezed her thigh gently, almost soothingly.

Isla was searching for an empty chair when she finally glimpsed Knox. She came toward him with a half-smile. "Knox, it's been a while."

He stood, not speaking until she'd exchanged greetings with Tanner and Levi. "Isla, you look well."

Her smile brightened a little. "Thank you. We should talk before you leave." Then she walked on past, not even acknowledging Harper.

"That was easy," Tanner said quietly.

"I don't think she realized Harper was with us," said Knox,

retaking his seat. "I usually come to these events with only two sentinels as company."

"Is there a problem I should know about?" Jolene quietly asked Harper.

Harper leaned into her. "In sum, there's a possibility that Isla believes that Knox is her anchor, which means . . ."

"She might not be so happy to meet you," finished Jolene. Then she shrugged. "You can take her."

When a blond, smartly dressed male with an air of authority waltzed inside, all the demons standing then immediately took their seats. He settled in the chair at the head of the table. "Afternoon, everyone. For those of you who haven't met me before, I'm Raul Harlan. As you all know, we're here to discuss . . . well, the fact that Isla's making a lot of noise about things that don't interest me. But her noise is getting louder, and it's time to get the whole thing settled."

Harper liked his no-bullshit manner.

"Isla, maybe you'd like to explain to us why you wanted this meeting."

The she-demon straightened in her seat opposite Malden. "In short, I'm proposing that a pyramid hierarchy be put in place in the U.S. as opposed to our lairs all existing around each other."

"With you as the ruler," said Raul, to which she nodded. "Why? Why fix what isn't broken?"

"But it *is* broken. The small lairs have no protection from larger lairs, strays are easy targets because they have absolutely no one to turn to, and we are so divided that we are vulnerable to dark practitioners. If we worked together against them, they wouldn't have a chance. But because we all cling so tightly to the idea of power and refuse to answer to each other, we're making our kind easy to prey on."

"Odd that you would criticize people for wanting power when

you yourself are asking for power over us all," observed one of the Primes.

Her face hardened. "There's nothing wrong with wanting power. But if the search for it makes our kind suffer, it's not a good thing."

"The U.S. has had a Monarch before," called out a Prime at the far end of the table. "It didn't work. It resulted in lairs constantly attempting to overthrow others."

"Yes," confirmed Isla, "but there wasn't a pyramid hierarchy then."

Raul crossed his arms over his chest, looking bored and tired. "Explain this pyramid hierarchy."

"There would be levels of power and influence," she said. "A layout of authority exists within each lair; there's the leader, the sentinels, the Force that defends the lair, and the other demons that are part of it. Layouts work."

One of the Primes scoffed. "You want some of us to be sentinels for you?"

"Not at all. I am simply making the point that each level within a lair's hierarchy has a certain amount of authority – the same would apply to the pyramid hierarchy I am proposing. Depending on where a Prime sits within the structure depends on how much power they have."

Another Prime spoke up. "And what about Primes that sit on lower levels?"

"Obviously they wouldn't be influential over the others," replied Isla, "but it means they would have the protection of the others. At the moment, small lairs are very vulnerable to larger ones. Plenty of small lairs have in fact been overtaken by others. I'll bet even some of you here are guilty of that."

Harper watched as some of them averted their gaze or shuffled in their seats.

"We have no laws," continued Isla. "Nothing in place to protect the demons of our country. Having a Monarch would prevent that."

"That's a very pretty answer," said Jolene, lounging casually in her chair, "but realistically all lairs existing on the lowest level would be crushed under the power of the others if such a hierarchy was implemented." Murmurs of agreement spread throughout the room.

Isla arched a brow. "Are you not crushed now?"

"No, because there's no law or Monarch that says I can't retaliate against any lair that tries to give me trouble. If we accept your changes, it would mean lairs with a high level of power and authority over me could come along, demand I hand over my lair to them, and there'd be nothing I could do about it. Of course, I'd tell them to shove that order up their ass. I don't think they'd like that. So we'd war. It's possible I could lose. Then what?"

"You could come to me, I would ensure the crime was punished."

"But it's not a crime if their authority exceeds mine. And by then, I'd probably be dead, so I'd be unable to go to you for help. That would make me very unhappy."

Harper's mouth twitched into a smile.

"Okay, here's what I don't understand," began another Prime. "Why would you care about the fate of small lairs, Isla? They don't affect you in any way."

Isla looked affronted. "The suffering of any demon should be the business of all of us." She suddenly appeared saddened. "There's also been an issue with the strays in Nevada – many of them have gone missing." She looked at Knox, daring him to deny it.

Knox narrowed his eyes. "Now just how would you know about that?"

"I know everything that occurs in my country. Never doubt that." She swept her gaze around the room as she continued. "If strays living in the state of who is potentially the most powerful demon alive are not safe, who is?"

That comment had a lot of people casting nervous glances at each other.

Raul sighed heavily. "All right, let's put this to a vote. All those who aren't in favor of a change, raise your hands."

Almost every demon raised their hands, and Harper noticed that Isla seemed startled to see that Knox was one of them. It was as if Isla had assumed he'd automatically support her, no matter what she did . . . much like an anchor would.

Raul turned to one of the Primes who hadn't voted against Isla's proposal. "Dario, you're the last person I'd have thought would be happy to answer to someone else."

Dario shrugged. "I think the idea of a Monarch has merit. I would be interested in such a change. But . . . I would wish to be the Monarch." That had Isla scowling at him while whispers circulated the table.

Malden, who also hadn't voted against Isla, spoke then. "I, too, support a change. But I will not answer to another – not to a ruler, and not to a demon on a 'level' higher than mine in any kind of hierarchy. For that reason, I am proposing that I be Monarch."

Raul looked at Knox curiously. "You're not interested in electing yourself as Monarch?" It probably did seem odd that someone as powerful as Knox wouldn't take this chance to get more power.

"I will never bow to another," said Knox. "But I do not have any desire to rule over every demon within the U.S. I'll never support any changes. The fact is that power structures do not work for our kind. When such a structure *was* in place, too many demons were vulnerable. The strongest were plucked from their lairs and forced to join the more powerful ones, making the large lairs stronger while making the small lairs weaker. Only the demons that were considered 'upper class' had any real say in their own lives, and the small lairs became nothing but packs of servants. It's been proven time and time again that that kind of power corrupts – there would be chaos, not peace among us." Many nodded their agreement.

Raul shrugged at Isla. "Only two other Primes are in favor of your proposal, which means you've been overruled, Isla."

"No, I haven't," she insisted, appearing oddly pleased with herself. "The U.S. as a whole hasn't been given a chance to vote."

Raul pinched the bridge of his nose. "What are you saying?"

"I don't think this matter should be decided by Primes. Demons who hold no power shouldn't be overlooked. The decision should be as much theirs as it is ours. Here we are, speaking for our lairs and families. But is it fair?" She looked around the room as she continued. "There you sit with your family or anchors, but they're given no say. Does it occur to you that they may feel differently? I suppose Knox's demons will feel whatever he feels, since no one will go against him," she chuckled. "But dismissing me now will not silence me. I feel too strongly about this."

"As do I," said Dario. Malden nodded. Apparently the idea of having ultimate power over the other Primes was attractive enough to make them fight the decision.

Raul looked like he wanted to bang his head on the table. "There are twenty-two Primes in this room. We have all humored you by having the vote. We don't *want* another one, we—"

"When the rest of our kind learn that their right to vote on something so serious was dismissed, they will not like it," said

Isla. "Naturally most Primes don't want to lose any of the power they hold. But the rest of our kind have little to no power, and they are the ones that will be affected most by the changes. Is it not fair that they have their say? How do you think your families, friends, sentinels, and Force members will feel when they learn you didn't give them a chance?"

Knox raised a brow. "Are you threatening us?" Because it sure sounded like Isla intended to spread the word of what had happened to incite other demons.

"Of course not. I'm merely pointing out that many demons already heard of the changes I requested, and many know this meeting is being held. If they learn that their votes were discounted when three Primes here spoke up on their behalf, they won't like it."

Irritatingly, Isla was right. Demons, especially sentinels and Force members, would be angry that they weren't considered important enough to have a say – despite that they served their Prime.

"The problem is I don't see how we can involve other demons in this decision," Dario said to Isla. "There's no way we can hold an event for every American demon to attend."

"No, but we can hold an event for any Prime who wishes to come forward with suggestions for changes. It can be recorded live. Demons unable to attend can still learn the facts. Afterwards, we can put it to a vote."

Malden frowned. "That wouldn't be something that could be done in one day."

"Then we hold a weekend event during which each Prime wishing to be elected as ruler can suggest their proposed changes and present their promises for the future," said Isla.

Malden nodded. "The voting could be held a short-time later and—"

"Wait, you're automatically assuming demons will *want* a Monarch," interrupted Knox. "That may not be the case. It certainly isn't the case for me."

"Knox is right," said Raul.

Dario proposed, "Then we'll make it so that when each demon is required to vote, they are asked to state 'yes' or 'no' to a change, and if they *do* vote 'yes' they then have to state their chosen Monarch."

Isla smiled. "Sounds fair to me. And if the rest of you truly feel a hierarchical structure will not appeal to the rest of our kind, what harm is it to hold a voting?"

Seeing that there was a very high chance this voting would take place, Knox offered, "I'll hold the weekend event at one of my hotels in the Underground two weeks from now."

Harper almost rolled her eyes. It was typical of Knox to attempt to take control of the situation.

"This doesn't mean I support a change," Knox added. "I've made it quite clear that I don't, and I will not change my mind on that."

Isla actually smiled. "Don't be so cynical, Knox."

Rising from his seat, Raul shook his head at Isla. "You won't get what you want." Then he crossed the room to one of the Primes, dismissing her.

"I had a feeling this would happen." Jolene stood just as Harper did. "The bitch will have known in advance that the people here won't want to lose any of their power; she always intended to suggest we include all U.S. demons in the voting."

"I doubt anyone in our lair will be in favor of it."

Jolene snickered. "Of course they won't. My demons are smart. *She* doesn't seem to be, though." She gestured over Harper's shoulder, and Harper twirled to see Isla walking toward Knox with her guards close behind her. *Great.*

"I was expecting you to support my proposal, Knox," Isla admonished gently.

He shrugged, though he didn't look casual. "I won't vote for something I don't believe in."

"You would go against me on this?"

"I would."

"Sweetheart, I have to leave," Jolene said louder than necessary, kissing Harper's cheek. "We'll talk again soon. Knox, you take good care of her."

Isla, having overheard the little exchange, peered at Harper. "And who is this, Knox?"

As he slightly tugged on her wrist, Harper stepped forward. Figuring it was best to get it over with, she said, "Hi, I'm Harper, Knox's anchor."

For a few seconds, Isla didn't respond at all. Then her face hardened, her body tensed as if to spring, and her eyes bled to black. The demon glared at Harper with a promise of pain. Knox, Tanner, and Levi gathered closer to Harper protectively even as Harper's dark protective power rushed to her hands, ready to deliver some soul-deep pain. Still, her inner demon literally charged to the surface and took control.

Alarm shot through Knox when a chill surrounded him and Harper's demon rose to the fore. As it glared at the predator that lived within Isla, he saw a fierce temper – saw an entity that would protect Harper against absolutely anyone or anything.

"Don't," it warned Isla's demon. "You won't find me the easy prey you assume me to be."

"You are nothing," scoffed the other demon.

Harper's demon smiled cruelly. "You are not what you pretend to be. I see it. I see what you are."

His anchor had a real talent for surprising him. Knox had never known anybody to sense that there was more to Isla than what their kind believed. "Isla, seize control before this goes any further."

She blinked a few times, and then Isla was once again in control. Her glare shot to Knox. "You refuse to see who I am to you. I have been patient. My patience is fast running out."

"I'm not your anchor, Isla. I never was."

"You can't change the truth, Knox, whether you choose to accept it or not." She cast Harper a scathing glance before striding out of the room.

Knox slipped his hand around Harper's nape, hoping to soothe her demon. "She's gone."

Black eyes honed in on him. "If the bitch attacks me, I will kill her." It was a warning: the demon knew he had a long history with Isla and it was letting him know that it didn't give a flying fuck. Then Harper was back, her eyes a swirling ocean-blue that told him her contact lenses had dissolved when her demon surfaced.

"My demon *really* doesn't like her," stated Harper.

"That's a bit of an understatement," chuckled Martina. As she kissed Harper and started babbling about her new boyfriend, Knox turned to Tanner and—

If you ever hurt my granddaughter, I will hunt you down. I don't care who you are or what you can do.

Knox almost laughed. Nothing in Jolene's expression gave away that she'd just threatened him. *She's the one person I'd never harm.*

Jolene studied him for a long moment, then nodded.

Tell me why she's so reluctant to bond.

That's for Harper to tell you. Amusement was in every word. *I should warn you that Lucian won't like this anchor business. He's not the most attentive father, but she's still his baby girl and he'll see you as too dangerous for her. Carla probably won't like it much either.*

She told me that she tried to see Harper several times in the past.

A snort. *She always was a good story spinner.* Jolene touched Harper's arm. "We need to leave now, sweetheart, before people start to realize that Martina has stolen their wallets or that she set her ex's car on fire." Jolene hugged Harper once more. "You take care now." She shot Knox a warning look before leaving with Beck and Martina in tow.

Tanner smiled at Harper. "You've gotta love Wallis imps." She just snorted.

It wasn't until they were back on the jet, high up in the air, that Harper's demon finally settled down. Isla had really pushed its hot buttons, and that was largely because the bitch had tried to lay claim to Knox – someone the demon believed belonged to it.

"I wondered when that demon of yours would show itself," said Knox. "It's very protective of you. And very feisty."

"My demon seems to think that Isla isn't just a banshee. In fact, it picked up a vampire vibe from her. But I don't see how that can be possible."

"She is a banshee . . . to an extent," said Knox. "A vampire tried to change her. She was strong enough to survive a transition that has killed many other demons, and so she is a blend of the two species. It's not known if it was done against her will or not, but I believe it's something she did in the hope of gaining more power."

No wonder Knox worried so much that Isla would try to hurt her. She was basically a Super She-Demon-Slash-Vamp. Possibly even invincible to most demons . . . except for the person opposite her. "But *you* could kill her."

"I could." He hoped it wouldn't come to that. But if he had to choose between Harper and Isla, he'd choose Harper. "That's why I wanted to be present when you two met. I had hoped she'd realized I wasn't her anchor, but apparently not. And that presents us with a big problem. To her, you're an imposter. A creature she believes she could easily crush, since she believes you're an imp and knows that you belong to a small lair."

Harper narrowed eyes that were currently amethyst. "I'm not going to move to your lair. Why do you look so surprised that I'd guess you would ask it of me? You're set on 'improving' my life. It wasn't such a stretch to conclude that your next step would be getting me to switch lairs."

"You would be safer that way."

She smiled knowingly. "And if you were my Prime, I'd have to answer to you. You'd have a level of authority over me. You'd just love that, wouldn't you?"

Knox cocked his head. "I'm beginning to find that I don't want to control you. You're much more interesting as you are."

Okay, that comment totally threw her. "You do it on purpose, don't you? Try to catch me off guard."

"It's only fair. You surprise me all the time. My own personal little mystery. I asked Jolene why you're hesitant to bond. She wouldn't tell me."

"Ah, maybe this is why you haven't walked away from me yet. You not only see me as a challenge, but you find the mystery refreshing."

"Let's find out. Tell me why you're really so hesitant to accept me as your anchor."

She balked at that . . . but maybe she should tell him. Maybe the sooner he solved the mystery and she was no longer so interesting to him, the sooner he'd walk away. "Although anchor bonds only exist on a psychic level, it doesn't stop some anchor pairs from wanting something more. I've seen firsthand what happens when a demon falls for their anchor and those feelings aren't reciprocated."

Knox stilled as realization dawned on him. "Carla and Lucian are anchors."

She nodded. "He never wanted the bond because anchors need to stay in contact; Lucian doesn't like attachments. But he had no problem sleeping with Carla and setting her aside. The problem was that Carla and her demon also wanted Lucian as a mate, but neither he nor his demon wanted them."

"He rejected her on two levels."

"Yes. And I can understand that must have hurt, despite that she had to have known in advance that Lucian didn't do commitment. And I can understand that her inner demon must have been enraged that the attachment it had formed to Lucian was only one-sided. It's really no surprise that Carla turned bitter and hateful toward him. But those feelings twisted her up so much inside that she abandoned her child simply because it reminded her of him and she wanted to hurt him."

When Knox's expression darkened, she added, "Don't get me wrong, I don't feel sorry for myself. I have a family who loves me and I've had a good life, even if it wasn't a typical upbringing. But it wasn't easy being a single sphinx among a family of imps."

Knox got it then: she'd become so much like an imp because it enabled her to blend.

"Kids can be mean about shit like that. When neither of your parents are around, it's easy to believe that those kids are right and your parents don't think you're good enough for them. Jolene never stood for that shit, though. She made sure I knew that I wasn't at all to blame for the mistakes of either Carla or Lucian."

"Is this part of why you avoid having relationships with demons? You don't want to repeat their mistakes?"

She sighed. "It's more that male demons make relationships too complicated. I don't want that."

He was silent for a minute. "I can understand now why you're hesitant to bond. But we're not Carla and Lucian. You're not delusional and selfish, and I'm not a self-centered playboy. As for you avoiding relationships with demons . . ."

"What?"

"What happens when your demon decides it's ready for a mate? It won't settle for a human, and it will drive you insane because you're not giving it what it wants and needs. You know what happens to people who do that, because you've seen that firsthand too." People like that became like Lucian – lost.

"I'll deal with that when it happens," she said with a nonchalant shrug. In truth, it was a worry, but she didn't let it play on her mind.

Figuring one truth deserved another, Knox said, "The fact that my demon gets bored very quickly with women isn't the only reason I don't do relationships. I know I wouldn't be good at them, and I don't like being involved in things I'm not good at."

She laughed. "So you're a perfectionist as well as a total control freak."

"And yet, your rebellious personality doesn't irritate me the way it should. Except for when you fight accepting me as your anchor, of course."

She gave a little shrug. "I'm just not convinced that accepting this anchor thing is the smart thing to do, I told you why."

"It's not just about Carla and Lucian's experience though, is it?" He was coming to read her quite well.

"No, it's not."

"Is it because I'm controlling or because of what Isla might do?" He doubted it was the second. "Or because you find it too strange and uncomfortable to have someone look out for you?"

Sensing that he was playing with her somehow, she said nothing.

"The first should only bother you if you believe I have the

power to steamroll you." Yes, that was a little reverse psychology but he wasn't above using it.

"You don't."

"The second should only bother you if you don't believe you can truly protect yourself or that I won't protect you if necessary." Yes, more use of reverse psychology.

"I *can* protect myself."

"And the third . . . I'm not going to imply that it shouldn't be strange for you, because I understand. But is it really so bad having someone there for you?"

No, it wasn't. Although she didn't say that aloud, it must have been in her expression because a hint of smugness glistened in his eyes. "Arrogant bastard." His smile widened.

CHAPTER SIX

She shouldn't have gone home with him. She knew better.

He just wanted to feed her and ensure she relaxed, he'd said – after all, it had been a weird and trying afternoon. Still, it was one thing to have the occasional meal with him; it was another to spend pretty much the entire day with him. But . . . Harper hadn't wanted to be alone. And, honestly, she was coming to like his company.

He could be almost fascinating at times. She'd grown up around imps, creatures that were expressive, temperamental, wild, and passionate. She wasn't used to people like Knox, who was so collected, focused, and emotionally disconnected. Also, she'd never before met anyone who had such a huge amount of personal power. People were always eager to please him, always respected him in spite of the fear he inspired.

She ached a little for him, though. Despite being surrounded by people all the time, he seemed to stand apart. He was so solitary, like a tiger. But demons weren't built to be alone. They were social, tactile, sexual creatures. And yet, this was how he lived.

When his staff came to him with issues, every order he gave them was quick, objective, and unemotional. He always knew exactly what he wanted, and he always did exactly what he had to do to get it. And she had to face that fighting their anchor bond was pointless. Not even the things she'd told him on the jet appeared to have made any difference. But, as he'd said, they weren't Carla and Lucian; they were totally different people. Knox would never give up, never cease tormenting her until she gave him what he wanted.

After they'd eaten a seriously delicious meal and she was perched on one of the breakfast stools while he made them both coffee, she sighed. "You're not going to let this go, are you?" It wasn't really a question.

Placing the mug in front of her, Knox then braced his hands on the counter. He didn't pretend to misunderstand her. "No. I've told you before, I don't walk away from what's mine. And you *are* mine."

She blew over the rim of her mug. "Hmm."

"No matter how much or how long you fight the bond, it won't keep me away from you. Nothing will. I'll always be in your life, Harper." He paused as they both sipped at their coffee. "Haven't I proven that I plan to be a constant presence?"

"Oh you've been around a lot, sure . . . but what happens if we bond? You wouldn't need to try to prove anything to me anymore. You'd have what you want. The link would be formed. I'd officially be your anchor. You could only visit me when the time apart gets uncomfortable. I wouldn't blame you." She honestly wouldn't. "I mean, we don't have much in common. We have different lifestyles. I'm not part of your lair and I have no intention of changing that. Anchors are supposed to make each other's life easier and better. You already have everything you want. You don't need me for anything. There's literally nothing that I can offer you." It hurt her pride and, dammit it, just plain hurt.

He tilted his head as he mused, "You're so used to people leaving you that you expect everyone to do it."

"Yeah." Harper was a self-aware person, she owned her faults. "It's cliché and even a little pathetic—"

"It's not pathetic." He rounded the table, and twirled her stool so that she was facing him. "Now, let me address your little issues so we're very clear. I'm not going to pretend we'll see each other as often as we have since we met. I put aside a lot of work so that we could spend time together and get to know each other. But I have a busy schedule and I travel a lot. That doesn't mean I won't remain in contact with you. It doesn't mean we won't still see each other often."

He tucked her hair behind her ear as he continued, "It's true that we don't have a lot in common, though I don't see that as a bad thing and I'm not sure why you do. It's also true that I have everything I want." He shrugged. "Going after the things I want is part of who I am. Do you make my life easier? No. You're willful and contrary and you'd snort at any order I tried to give you."

"This is not making me feel better," she grumbled.

"But . . . you intrigue me, which is a surprise in and of itself. I can never predict what you'll say or do next. You're a quirky, complex, fierce blaze of fire in my otherwise numb, predictable world. See, despite that I have everything I want, it hasn't made me satisfied. If anything, it has made me bored and restless. There have been no challenges, no obstacles, and nothing I couldn't manage or control one way or another . . . until you." It drove him crazy, but it also energized him. "I *like* having you in my life. I intend to keep you in it."

As his cell phone started ringing, he crossed the room to

grab it from the counter and answer the call. Harper used that moment to gather her composure. He'd meant every word, she realized with a start. He actually liked having her around. If he was any other guy, she'd have been startled by all that honesty. But Knox Thorne wouldn't care to hold back, because he wasn't interested in anyone's opinion of him. As he ended the call and stalked toward her, she slipped off the stool. "I should go."

Curling an arm around her waist, Knox pulled her to him, staring into azure-blue eyes. Images of her naked, moaning, taking every inch of his cock had haunted his dreams and thoughts. His demon had practically sulked over Knox's refusal to seek her out, and it clearly wanted her more than it had ever wanted another female. As both his body and his demon lunged for her, Knox urged, "Stay with me."

Although it would be dumb, she wanted to, especially while her body was humming with the need to feel him in her. She was pathetically weak when it came to him, and it would be so easy to fold under the weight of the sheer unadulterated need he roused in her. But . . . "I told you on the jet—"

"Yes, you did." He nipped at her pulse, making her jolt. "And I understand. You're forgetting something, though." He sucked on her earlobe. "You already know my demon doesn't form attachments. It loses interest too quickly, it doesn't want a relationship or a mate. And neither does yours or it would never accept humans as sexual partners – it would be searching for more. The last thing I'd do is hurt you. We'll soon be linked on a level deeper than any demonic attachment." He held her gaze as he stated firmly, "When we bond – and we will, Harper – we'll be psychically linked. That means I'm never going to leave your life. Never."

She was starting to believe him. In fact, no, she already did believe him.

"Stay with me."

She nodded once. His mouth slammed on hers and his tongue boldly thrust inside like he owned her. It was no teasing, practiced kiss. It was raw desperation and a devastation of her senses. His mouth dominated and possessed hers – licking, biting, and consuming. One hand fisted in her hair while his other hand palmed her ass and plastered her body to his. All she could do was grab his shirt while he took her over. No one kissed like Knox Thorne. He poured every ounce of himself into it, making it just as erotic as sex itself.

Whipping off her blouse, Knox backed her into the wall. She tasted so fucking good, it almost made his head spin. Tasted of sin, honey, and coffee. All he wanted was to lift her, rip off her pants, and shove himself balls deep inside her; feel her hot, wet, and tight around him as he took her with a fury that would sate the relentless need riding them both. But he wasn't going to rush this, he wanted much more than a quick fuck against the wall.

Sliding one hand under her thigh, he curled it around him and ground against her. "I want in you," he rumbled. "And I'll have you." But not yet.

Harper gasped at the sudden sensation of psychic fingers whispering over her clit, causing a tremor to ripple through her. Despite being ice-cold, those fingers gave off nothing but heat as they parted her slick folds and slid through them. "What are you doing?" *How* was he doing it? She inhaled sharply as cold fingertips circled and plucked at her clit. "Fuck."

"You taste better than I thought you would." Knox licked his way down her neck, over the slope of her breasts, and down to her nipple – biting it through the black lace of her bra.

The sharp bite made her moan, and that was when the psychic fingers thrust inside her. Fuck, she'd never felt anything like it; never felt pleasure like it. They filled her, stretched her, and touched her just right – so cold, yet they burned and created a blazing ache deep inside her that made her pussy quiver. It was almost as if they were branding her with every sensual thrust.

"Knox, I don't know how long I can take this." She was totally serious. Harper didn't have a quick trigger, but *shit* this felt so good that she was very close to coming.

"You'll take it," he told her, scooping out her breast and sucking the nipple deep into his mouth. When she started writhing, he slipped a hand around her throat. "Be still."

"I can't," she breathed. The icy fingers disappeared, and she kicked at him. "No!" He stilled, and then his head slowly lifted until his burning predatory gaze met hers. There was such a calm, dominant, assertive energy about him, yet his sensual features were alive with menace and caution. He clearly didn't like her giving orders of her own.

"You want them back?" he rumbled.

She merely nodded.

"Fine. But you can't come yet."

She would have cursed his controlling ass if ice-cold fingers didn't dip inside her, giving her a shallow, teasing thrust. Just when she was about to demand more, they thrust hard and deep. Later, she'd most likely slap herself for being a sexual mess thanks to invisible fingers. Hating that she seemed to be the only one caught in a frenzy, she slid her hands down to tackle his fly. His cock – heavy, thick, and long – sprang into her hand. She gripped him tight as she pumped, swirling her thumb over the head.

"Harder," he gritted out, tugging down her bra so he could suckle on her neglected nipple. As he scored the tight bud with his teeth, she jerked and moaned. He loved the little sounds she made – raspy and breathless. As she stroked him with a perfect grip, his cock swelled and throbbed.

Tangling a hand in her hair, he tugged slightly. "On your knees, baby." He *had* to feel that fucking luscious mouth around his cock. Her glazed eyes shot to his. Narrowed. "Don't fight me, Harper. You knew what you were getting into." She'd known he'd be dominant and demanding and rough. She wanted this, even needed it.

He licked along her bottom lip. "I want to see my cock in your mouth. I have to know what it's like to slide in and out of it. Show me, Harper." He tightened his grip on her hair as he pushed her to her knees. "That's it." The sight of her there with her eyes defiant, her breasts out, her nipples hard, and bites all over her neck made a sense of masculine satisfaction unfurl inside him. Bracing one hand on the wall, he used the other to guide her mouth to his cock. "Open."

Harper glared at him, not necessarily annoyed with him but annoyed that a part of her *liked* what he was doing. He was right when he'd said she couldn't desire a guy she could control. Knox wasn't someone who would ever dance to her tune, and her strong personality didn't make him hesitate to demand what he wanted from her. That didn't mean she'd just—

A third psychic finger slid inside her. Her mouth fell open in a silent gasp of pure bliss and she gripped his thighs for purchase. That was when his cock thrust inside. She should have remembered the dominant fucker was also a sneaky fucker.

Her mouth was so damn hot it was almost too hot. Just seeing those plush lips wrapped around him was enough to make him groan. As her tongue rubbed the underside of his cock, he growled. "You have the most fuckable mouth I've ever seen." And he was going to enjoy it.

As the icy fingers alternated between driving inside her and teasing her clit, Harper helplessly moaned around the thick cock that literally fucked her mouth. All the while, he told her how good it felt, how much she was pleasing him, how her mouth was made for this. She probably would have panicked feeling him bump the back of her throat, but she was just too far gone with the pleasure whipping through her.

"Come for me."

As more icy fingers pinched a nipple, Harper shattered. Knox lunged deeper as he erupted into her mouth. She swallowed it all, unable to do anything else. At the same time, the fingers inside her dissipated, leaving her tingling and burning.

He didn't pull out, just stayed there . . . and she quickly realized it was a message. He was making the point that he'd move when he was ready, not before, and she'd have to wait and let him lead. She wasn't sure she liked the sound of that. But she'd started to notice a pattern here; when she gave him what he wanted, he gave her what she wanted. It made more sense to be still. So she did.

"Good girl." Withdrawing from her mouth, Knox lifted her carefully and carried her through the house, stopping when they reached his bedroom. He laid her on the bed, unable to take his eyes off the swollen mouth that had made him come so fucking hard he was surprised his knees hadn't given out. He tackled the fly of her pants before slowly peeling them off, revealing toned, shapely legs that he fully intended to have wrapped around him. Leaving on the little scrap of lace that covered her pussy, he removed his own clothes.

Harper swallowed hard as his dark, slumberous gaze roamed over her. His powerful body was all smooth, sculpted muscle and sleek skin that seemed to hum with an untamed masculinity. It was a body that was designed to deliver pure carnal pleasure. She had every confidence that it would. "Can everyone fuck with psychic fingers?"

Knox narrowed his eyes. "If you're thinking you've been

missing out because this is what it's like for everyone, think again. Not all demons can do it." And he did *not* want her thinking about fucking other demons. She actually rolled her eyes at him. Rolled. Her. Eyes. He was pretty sure no one in his entire life had done it before Harper.

"Easy there, Thorne. It was just a question." Although he'd guessed right – that was exactly what she'd been wondering, because she'd have to reconsider keeping demons off her sexual diet if it was this good all the time. "There's no need to . . . oh no, wait, I can't take any more teasing." But it was too late; his tongue was already lapping at her pussy through the lace. His teeth grazed over her clit and folds, almost making her jump out of her skin. "Knox, seriously, no more. I don't want to come again until you're in me." His head lifted slightly as his eyes, flaring with heat, finally met hers. Yes, she had him, she . . . But then the fucker shook his head.

"I'm not done."

He ripped off her panties, spread her folds with his thumbs, and proceeded to drive her insane. His tongue licked, lapped, and stabbed. His mouth clamped around her clit and suckled gently. She tried pushing his head away and wriggling from under him. Suddenly, psychic hands shackled her wrists and pinned them above her head. "Oh, you motherfucking bastard!"

He didn't seem at all offended. He simply held her hips in place as he continued to feast. So she cursed him and threatened him and swore she'd never suck his cock again. That actually made him chuckle. And, oh God, that low velvety rumble shot up her pussy, vibrated through her body . . . and then she was coming. Hard and fast and he lapped up every drop.

She literally melted into the mattress, but her pussy still burned and contracted – as if only the feel of his cock in her would give her the satisfaction she needed. She heard the ripping of a foil wrapper and then his body settled over hers. She opened one eye. "Go away. I don't like you anymore."

Knox smiled. "I'm still having you. And you'll take it." Tilting her hips, he began to smoothly sink inside, making her eyes snap open as they swirled from azure blue to pure gold. She was so fucking hot and slick and *his*. Demons were possessive beings, but he'd never in his life been possessive of another person until Harper. There was a primitive satisfaction in knowing he had rights to her. No one had ever belonged to him before. But this female was *his*. Nothing anybody did would ever change that. Not even she could.

Harper shuddered at the delicious pressure of his cock pushing inside her. The psychic fingers – the same ones still restraining her hands – had left her so seriously sensitive that she was aware of every ridge and vein, and every thick long inch of him as his body stretched and filled hers. Her pussy fluttered and clamped around him almost possessively, and a groan slid between his clenched teeth.

Finally balls-deep in her, Knox took a moment to revel in the fact that he was the first demon to possess her. "I've needed to be in you since the second I first saw you." And now he had her exactly where he wanted her. He fucked in and out of her like he needed her pussy to survive. She was small but she'd taken all of him, fit perfectly around him.

Harper moaned as he sucked hard on her pulse, but when he followed it up with a hard bite, she growled, "Stop leaving marks all over me!" She tensed as Knox stilled, his eyes bled to black – *oh shit* – and a hand clutched her breast in a tight, possessive hold. It shouldn't have hurt, but the flesh beneath its fingers began to prickle and burn. The pain somehow became pleasure; a pleasure that was intensified by the demon's rough, hard thrusts. "I want Knox," she told it nervously.

The demon smiled, as if that was what it had been waiting to hear. Then it retreated.

Knox got to his knees, hooked her legs over his shoulders, and powered into her. She arched into his thrusts, making those husky little moans that played over his skin and made his cock throb. "Make me come, Harper. Now." Her pussy spasmed and tightened around him as a scream tore from her throat. He exploded with a harsh curse as her body milked every ounce of come from his cock.

His body was still shaking from the force of his release when he slipped out of her and rolled onto his back. In the time he'd taken to get rid of the condom, she still hadn't moved. He didn't realize why until she spoke.

"Knox, can I have my hands back now?"

Smiling, he released her from his psychic hold.

As Harper rubbed and flexed her arms to get rid of the stiffness, she caught sight of something odd. And she bolted upright. "What's that?"

"Don't panic."

It was like some kind of tattoo – a black swirly tattoo that circled her breast and had thorns on it. "Your demon *branded* me?" Knox just nodded, like she'd asked if he wanted a cup of coffee. Branding was something inner demons did when they felt very possessive of something.

"From what I understand about brands, they fade once the inner demon withdraws from the person it branded."

"You don't sound sure."

"I'm not. My demon's never branded anyone before."

"It doesn't bother you that it did it now?" He didn't look the least bit irritated.

"Why would it?" Pushing her onto her back, Knox draped himself over her. As he traced the brand with his finger, he found that he liked the look of it on her skin. "Why does it bother *you* so much?"

She arched a brow. "And you would have been totally okay with my demon rising during sex and branding you without your permission?"

"You know what I think?" he said softly. "I think you don't like the idea of anyone laying any sort of claim to you. And I think that's not because your pride balks at it, but because no one's ever really laid a claim to you before" – not even her parents, the fuckers – "and so you don't know how to deal with it." Maybe somebody else would have denied that, refused to admit any kind of weakness, but he knew Harper wouldn't.

"Okay, I'll admit it is a little weird and I'm not sure what to do."

"I'll tell you how I think you should deal with it. I think you shouldn't panic about it. This brand means my demon respects, wants, and is incredibly possessive of you and your demon – that's not something we didn't already know."

As she considered that, she nodded once. "You're right. We knew this. I could just think of it as a temporary tattoo."

"You could." He traced it with his tongue, liking it more and more.

"This is part of why I fight the anchor bond too, isn't it?" She hadn't seen it before, but he was right. Having an anchor was having someone who'd laid a claim to you, and she was just . . . fucked up.

"Yes, I think so. But we're not going to talk about the bond tonight."

She frowned. "We're not?" It was usually her who avoided the subject.

"No, because if we come to an understanding on this here and now, you'll always wonder if I fucked you to make you give in to me. When you agree to form the bond, it won't be when we're in bed."

While she was confident that sex couldn't muddle her thoughts and decisions, she knew he made some sense.

"But we *will* talk about it soon, Harper. I'm not going to walk away from you. And I think you're coming to believe that now." Satisfaction slid down his spine when she nodded in admission. "Good. Now relax and spread your legs. I want in you again."

Like she'd argue with that.

CHAPTER SEVEN

"Your bodyguard's pretty intense, isn't he?" commented Khloë as she, Harper, Devon, and Raini joined the long queue for the nightclub that led to the Underground. To the humans, it was simply a VIP queue. In truth, it was a line exclusive to demons that intended to head to the Underground.

"He's also an asshole," hissed Devon, adjusting her little red dress. Tanner did seem to enjoy taunting her by calling her 'kitty.' He'd also ogled her impressive cleavage when the hellcat wasn't looking.

"I'm surprised he isn't following us inside," said Raini, looking as alluring as always. Despite that most of her body was covered by her black, chiffon catsuit that made her look like a jewel chief, the males stared more at her than the indecently dressed humans.

"He has to meet one of the other sentinels for something," explained Harper. "I don't know what, I don't ask about sentinel business." And they probably wouldn't tell Harper anything without Knox's permission anyway.

As memories of the previous night flickered through her mind, Harper's body began to heat. He'd fucked her so hard and so many times that she'd fallen asleep. Then he just woke her up and took her from behind. She'd left his home early that morning with her inner demon curled up in a ball of satisfaction.

"Why isn't Ciaran coming?" Devon asked Khloë, who looked quirky and cute in her neon pink dress. Harper was wearing a sleeveless dress that was so sleek it looked like liquid silver. Raini had picked it out.

"He's spending time with his new girlfriend," Khloë replied. She was close to her twin brother. "She doesn't like me much. Says I'm too hyper. Personally, I don't think that's a fair assessment."

Raini snorted. "I do."

"It's good then that I just don't give a—"

"Harper Wallis?" interrupted a new, gruff voice.

She turned to see a dark guy built like a linebacker. One of the doormen. "Uh, yeah?"

He unclipped part of the red rope acting as a barrier and tipped his chin toward the entrance of the club. "Go on through."

Harper blinked. "You mean skip the queue?"

Khloë elbowed her hard. "Obviously, Harper, jeez."

"Don't make me hit you, Khloë." Giving the doorman a grateful smile, Harper led the three she-demons inside the club, ignoring the scowls of the other people waiting behind the ropes.

"He must have recognized you as Knox's anchor," Raini said.

"Well, Knox has been sure to parade me in front of as many demons as possible." Descending the stairs on her right, Harper led the girls into the basement. At the rear of the dark room was a door that was manned by two burly demons. Each gave her a respectful nod.

"Miss Wallis," one greeted as he led them through the door and over to an elevator. He punched in a code, and the elevator doors opened. "Enjoy your evening."

"Okay, this getting-recognized-by-everyone thing could get weird fast," said Harper as the doors closed and the elevator descended.

Khloë snorted. "Who cares?"

Finally the elevator stopped and they entered what was essentially a demonic playground. The strip of bars, nightclubs, casinos, restaurants, shows, strip clubs, hotels, and many other things always heaved with people. Each building had no front wall, so that it was easy to see just by walking down the 'road' exactly what was going on inside each place.

As the girls headed to their favorite bar, people either greeted Harper like they knew her or nervously gave her a wide berth. It wasn't all that unexpected when the bartender told her that their drinks were on the house.

"From now on, you come here with me at all times," Khloë told her, delighted as they claimed their usual table.

It was then that Harper noticed the flyers on the table. She picked one up. "What's this? 'Vote Isla.'" She glanced around, noticing they adorned each table. "There are flyers everywhere."

"And posters too." Raini gestured to the walls as she drank some of her cocktail through her straw. "Dario and Malden have plastered some up as well."

Khloë, bopping her head to the music, spoke to Harper. "Jolene said you had a little scuffle with Isla."

"She told you this, or you overheard it?" Harper asked before taking a sip of her cocktail.

"Does it matter?"

"My demon and her demon had an extremely minor confrontation."

"What did she do to piss off your demon?" asked Raini.

"Isla believes Knox is her anchor." Harper gave them all a rundown of everything that had happened at the meeting.

"I'll bet the rumors are coming from Isla," said Devon.

Harper stirred her drink with her straw. "What rumors?"

"Some people are saying that they heard you're not really Knox's anchor; that you're just his newest side piece and you're spreading the anchor rumor to protect yourself."

"Do people believe it?"

"No. A lot of people have heard him call you his anchor; they know he has no reason to lie."

"I don't think you need to worry about the rumors," said Raini. "You wouldn't be getting special treatment if they were having any effect."

Devon gently elbowed Harper. "Hey, who's that bitch glaring at us?"

Harper groaned at the sight she found. "That would be Kendra, Knox's ex . . . bed-buddy, I guess is the best description. See the guy with her? I think his name is Brandt. Anyway, she's using him to try to make Knox jealous."

Raini rolled her eyes. "How very mature." She tilted her head as she studied Harper. "You know, there's something different about you tonight. You seem more . . . relaxed. Like you've . . ." Her eyes widened. "You've had sex."

"No, I haven't."

Devon pointed at her when she blushed. "You *so* have."

"Who was it? Tell me," Raini pressed. "Wait, it wasn't Royce, was it? Please say no."

"It wasn't Royce."

"Who, then? You've been spending so much time with Knox that I don't know how you could have . . ." Raini gaped. "You slept with Knox."

"No, I didn't."

"You *so* did," insisted Devon. "What happened to your 'I don't get involved with demons' rule?"

Harper sighed. "I kind of broke it."

Khloë hugged her tightly. "I'm so happy. It means you're finally accepting that male demons aren't so bad and you won't make the fuck-ups that your primary blood relations made."

It simply meant that Knox was too fucking hot to turn down.

"Honestly, I don't know how you could get in his bed," said Devon. "I mean, he's seriously gorgeous. But he's also incredibly intimidating. And so detached and reserved."

"He's not reserved in bed."

Devon smiled. "I'll bet it was good."

Harper smiled back. "Oh, it was."

Raini groaned. "Uh-oh, here comes Mona."

Bracing herself, Harper twisted to see Mona approaching with her regular group of friends. She stopped in front of the table, her eyes on Harper. But she didn't seem pissed or looking to cause shit. "Can I help you with something?" asked Harper.

Mona cocked her head. "That thing you did to me in the combat circle . . . it hurt like a bitch."

"It was supposed to."

Mona actually smiled. "If I'd known you could cause soul-deep pain, I'd have made sure I kept my distance." She shrugged. "No hard feelings on my end. I respect power. You have plenty of it."

She turned to leave, but stopped when Khloë called out, "Hey, hey, hey, what about me? Where's my respect?" It was obvious Khloë didn't particularly give a crap. Mona threw her a scowl but it lacked any hostility.

"Well that was unexpected." Devon sipped her vodka and Coke. "I mean, if she was going to call a truce, I would have thought she'd only do it because you're Knox's anchor."

Khloë drained her cocktail and put her empty glass on the table. "I say we forget about anchors and bitches and just have fun. Shots! We need shots!"

Harper shook her head. "No shots for you, missy. Your system can't handle them." Khloë was one of those people who not only got wasted easily but thought it was fun to do crazy shit when they were wasted.

"Ye have so little faith in me. We need shots!"

So they had shots. And Khloë quickly got so wasted it took the combined strength of Harper, Devon, and Raini to keep her from dancing on the table.

"I'm hot." Khloë fanned her face. "Isn't it hot in here?" Then she tried to take her dress off.

"No, no, no," said Harper firmly, who had deliberately drank less than the other she-demons so that she could keep a handle on her cousin. "Right, enough shots for you."

"I'm not drunk." Khloë seemed sincerely affronted. "I have a high alcohol tolerance level. God, I love this song!" She started bouncing in her seat. "You're totally my favorite cousin. Did I ever tell you that?"

Harper smiled. "Yes, you've told me at least eight times since you had your first shot."

"Well, it's true. I love you. I feel like we're bonding right now. Don't you feel it?"

Raini and Devon were laughing so hard – at nothing, from what Harper could tell, they were just trapped in a fit of laughter – they couldn't seem to sit upright.

Khloë grabbed Harper's arm. "Listen, listen, are you listening to me? You're not listening to me. This is important. I love you. Like for realsies."

"That's great, Khloë, I love you too."

Her cousin groaned as the song changed. "I hate this one. It makes me think of my ex. He's such a bastard. I should text him. Text him and tell him he's a bastard."

Raini managed to get out through peals of laughter, "Khloë, we *never* text our exes when we're drunk."

"But I'm not drunk. Just a little buzzed, that's all."

Raini wagged her finger. "No talking to exes when we've had shots."

Khloë huffed. "Fine, I don't want to speak to him anyway. I've moved on. So has he. But we're friends. I can text a friend, right?"

"To tell him he's a bastard?" chuckled Devon.

"Exactly." Khloë suddenly frowned. "I need to go pee. Want to come pee with me?" she asked Harper.

"No," replied Harper, "but I will, because I have to protect you from yourself and stop you from getting into shit."

Of course, the moment Khloë stood, she almost fell on her ass. When Harper moved to help her, Khloë held up both hands and declared, "I got this, I got this."

Unreal. Harper kept her hand on Khloë's elbow as she led her to the restrooms.

"I'm sorry," Khloë whined.

Harper frowned. "What are you sorry for?"

"I don't know. Isn't that weird?"

With a sigh, Harper shoved open the door and guided Khloë to a stall. "Do *not* try to wrap yourself in toilet paper so you look like a mummy."

"Why would I do that?"

"I don't know, I asked you that last time you did it, and you didn't know then either."

With a haughty sniff, Khloë slammed the door shut. And burped.

It was only as Harper turned to check her face in the mirror, strongly – and correctly – suspecting that she had Khloë's lipstick all over her face after the girl's dramatic display of affection earlier, that she noticed the two she-demons by the hand dryers watching her warily. "Hey," Harper said as she wiped off the lipstick.

They smiled shakily as they both greeted, "Hi." One looked as if she'd say more, but then her eyes widened as the door opened.

Turning, Harper found none other than . . . Kendra. How fabulous. Dressed in a long emerald green dress, her hair up in some elaborate do, she slowly advanced on Harper wearing a wide, patronizing smile. Her inner demon rolled her eyes, finding the bitch pathetic. Harper asked, "Something you want?"

Kendra seemed taken aback by her bored tone. "I simply thought I'd say hello. How are things down your end? And by 'end' I mean the bottom of the social ladder."

To people like Kendra, who clearly prized social status, that comment would probably be offensive. Harper found it nothing but petty. "I see someone got up on the wrong side of their pigpen this morning."

Kendra ground her teeth. "I'd imagine you can't believe your luck that Knox Thorne is your anchor."

"You're having a little trouble dealing with that, huh?"

"Trouble?" Kendra laughed. "Of course not. I pity him, having not only an imp but a Wallis for an anchor."

Harper batted her eyelids. "Well, aren't you sweet to care."

That was when Khloë came striding out of the stall, fixing Kendra with a hard look. "I'll never understand why people can't just let their exes go." This was coming from a girl who had only moments ago considered texting her own ex. "But I guess Knox doesn't really count as an ex, since you two weren't in an actual relationship. That's gotta hurt."

Harper's inner demon didn't at all like the reminder that Kendra knew Knox intimately.

"Kendra," interrupted one of the she-demons by the hand dryers. "I really think you should leave. If Knox hears you're bothering his anchor, he won't take it well."

Kendra looked at Harper speculatively. "Yes, I've heard he's quite protective of you. Still, it won't last long, because his demon simply doesn't attach itself to people."

Harper heard the bitterness in the latter words. "And that just eats at your pride, doesn't it?" It also satisfied Harper's demon.

"Does it bother me that I have to watch him with others? Yes. However, I'm used to it – Knox doesn't believe in being exclusive. But the good thing for me is that I can move on. I can keep him out of my life and out of my thoughts. You can't, can you? So you'd better hope you don't come to care for him or your life won't be fun watching the man you want flit from woman to woman."

A hurt that was deep, concerning, rose in Harper as the prospect fluttered through her mind. "It's true that I might find it hard on some level. I mean, anchors are possessive of each other, right? But that means Knox is in the same boat. He'll get pissed watching me with other guys. Whereas you . . . well, he doesn't give a shit what you do. Making him jealous isn't working out so well, is it?" Harper pouted. "How sad for you."

Just as she and Khloë moved to pass, Kendra gripped Harper's arm tight and hissed, "You can't possibly—"

"You should let go of me, Kendra." The bitch really, really should . . . because her behavior had triggered a primal reaction in Harper that could mean very bad things for Kendra. Her familiar dark power had rushed to her hands, ready to protect and defend Harper. In addition, her demon was on high alert, raring to take control. Harper urged it to remain calm, assured it that she'd take care of this. "I'd like to say that I don't want to hurt you, but I do. You make it really hard to like you." She put her face close to Kendra's. "So don't tempt me."

"What are you going to do, imp?"

Khloë grinned. "I love it when this happens."

"I'll probably just poke you in the forehead, which I'm fairly sure is pretty empty."

Eyes glittering with malice, Kendra tightened her hold. Warmth shot up Harper's arm and filled every part of her. But that was pretty much all that happened. Judging from Kendra's dumbfounded expression, more *should* have happened. Whatever she'd tried to do hadn't worked.

Harper sniffed. "That all you got?" Then she did exactly as she'd threatened: she poked Kendra's forehead, and the power prickling the pad of her index finger forced its way inside Kendra; past skin and bone, attacking the soul within. Having a dualism to her soul meant that not only did it hurt Kendra, it hurt her demon.

Her eyes widened as she tangled her hands in her hair and cried out, dropping to her knees. Then, sobbing and moaning, she scrambled into the corner, eyeing Harper like she was Lucifer himself. Yeah, that wasn't an uncommon reaction.

"We'll be going now." Taking a gleeful Khloë by the arm, Harper led her out of the restrooms ... and slammed into a solid, familiar body that made her inner demon go from pissed to happy in a nanosecond. She frowned at Knox. "What are you doing here?"

"Are you all right?" he demanded. Levi, Devon, and Raini were behind him.

"Knox came and asked where you were," explained Raini. "We were a little worried that you guys were taking a while."

"Who's crying?" Knox asked.

"I'm surprised you need to ask," said Khloë, "since you've probably made her cry out a few times yourself. In bed, I mean."

Knox pushed his way into the restrooms, causing Harper and Khloë to back up. That was when he saw Kendra huddled into a ball in the corner, whimpering and clearly in pain. It was easy enough to guess why, but it wasn't clear what Kendra had done to provoke Harper. He arched a brow at his anchor. "What happened?"

She shrugged. "Kendra was just saying hello."

Face hardening, he repeated, "What happened?"

Harper sighed. "It's been dealt with."

Knowing his anchor was so stubborn she could keep that up all night long, Knox turned to the she-demons from his lair that were standing off to the side. He didn't even need to ask them what happened; the entire story spilled out of them in a rush. Hearing the things Kendra had said and done, it was really no wonder that Harper retaliated.

"Levi, get Kendra out of here." Knox turned to his anchor. "You come with me." Amber eyes glared at him for that order.

"Look, I get that you want to talk about this, but I'm here with my cousin and my friends – I don't ditch people."

He looked at the three she-demons lingering in the doorway. "Follow us to the VIP section. It's where you *should* have been anyway, Harper." Little squeals of delight came from her companions but, of course, his anchor didn't look all that impressed.

Harper found it strange walking through a busy bar with Knox Thorne holding her wrist. He didn't need to push through a crowd, it parted for him. Respect, fear, awe, and – in the case of some females – desire was in the eyes of many. The respect mostly extended to Harper but, unsurprisingly, the ogling females didn't like her much.

When they reached the VIP section with its comfier furniture, and its separate bar and waiters, Knox gestured for Harper's companions to sit in a booth before he then pulled her into a corner.

She raised a hand. "Before you say anything, let's just be clear that you can't be pissed at me for this. All I did was defend myself, and I'll do it again."

Knox shook his head. "I'm not pissed because you defended yourself. I'm pissed because you were put in a position where you had to defend yourself. It never should have happened. Kendra knows better."

"I dealt with it."

"You think it will end there because you fought back? I'm responsible for policing every single one of my demons. If they cross a line, they're punished – it's as simple as that."

"Don't kill her, Knox." Harper could see that he wanted to. "Demons are known for crossing lines. We do it all the time. Kendra behaved stupidly, yes, but whatever she tried to do didn't work and I dealt with it *my* way. You need to respect that and you need to be *seen* to respect it. Because if you don't respect me and my ability to protect myself, neither will anyone else."

He couldn't deny that was true . . . which only served to piss him off even more.

"Besides, she didn't try to kill me, she tried to hurt me. She was just picking a fight because she's jealous."

"I gathered that from the things she said." What worried him was that those things might have taken him back a step with Harper. He'd made a lot of progress with her, and he'd thought she would agree to bond very soon. Kendra could have fucked it up. "If any of what she said bothers you, let's discuss it now." He knew Harper would tell him the truth.

"Was she right about you not being exclusive? Because I have to say, I'm not a girl who's good with that whole 'seeing other people' thing. I don't like the idea that I could be with someone who was fucking someone else only five minutes before. It's just icky for me."

"I don't share. I always demand exclusivity." He wasn't sure why Kendra implied differently, unless she suspected that there was more to him and Harper than them being anchors.

"She made a good point when she said it'll be hard for us not to interfere in each other's sex life since prying into personal lives is what anchors do, and the possessiveness makes that harder. But I'm told it's worse in the beginning and it gets better."

She was talking as if it was a given that they would bond, and that relaxed him and his demon.

"When your demon withdraws and the sex comes to an end, we'll both move on and you'll be fine with it, because you've had your fill of me."

Okay, neither he nor his demon were relaxed any longer. He gripped her jaw. "Don't talk like you're just a convenient body to me."

"You know what I mean."

Yes, he did. And she was right. They would move on. The problem was that just the thought of her with another male made him feel very dangerous. His demon was so enraged by the idea of it that Knox knew for a fact that if another male was to touch Harper, they'd very simply die. His demon was still too fixated on her.

Harper frowned. "What's wrong?" He just seemed so . . . intense all of a sudden. In response, his hand fisted in the back of her hair, angled her head how he wanted it, and then Knox took her mouth with a ferocity that alarmed her. She tasted anger, possessiveness, and a dark greedy hunger.

His hands slid around to frame her face. "Give into me, Harper." He needed to feel that she was his on some irrevocable level. It wasn't enough to know she was his anchor. He needed to form the bond to solidify his claim on her.

"This isn't exactly the time or the place."

"If we go somewhere private, I'll fuck you, Harper. We both know that's exactly what will happen. Let's do it here and now, where I can't take you how I want to and then you'll never one day wonder if I used sex to convince you." She sighed, averting her eyes that were swirling from amber to forest green. "You're ready for this. I know you are." When she finally returned her gaze to his, she nodded. Satisfaction thrummed through his veins. "Good girl."

From a little place inside Harper, a voice screamed not to do it; that she would be giving him the power to hurt her. But she ignored it, letting herself believe that just fucking maybe this was someone who wouldn't let her down. And if he did, well, she'd ensure he regretted it.

Watching her shift nervously from foot to foot, Knox took her wrist and soothingly circled her skin with his thumb. He didn't blame her for being nervous. It was a life-altering moment. There was absolutely no going back. "Let go. That's all you have to do."

He was right. She'd held firm against the magnetic pull, keeping a tight hold on her own psyche. Now all she had to do was let go. Hoping it wouldn't turn out to be a big mistake, she did.

As their minds slammed together, Harper's knees buckled. Their psyches fused together with a snap, not becoming one mind but intersecting just enough for her to feel Knox's darkly sexual presence; to feel his strength and personal power. There was a psychic 'taste' to him: almonds, dark chocolate, and red wine. It all 'fed' her somehow, strengthening her. Her demon lapped it all up, stabilized in a way it never would have been without this bond.

Just as Jolene had assured Harper, having an anchor wasn't an invasive feeling. Still, it was intimate and a little strange, and it would take some getting used to. She looked up at Knox, who was cupping her nape, looking concerned.

"You okay?" Knox asked, not knowing what to expect from his anchor. *His anchor.* She was finally officially, irreversibly his.

"Yeah, I'm okay."

"Good." He'd touched her mind many times, but this was so much more. He could now *feel* her psychic presence; it rang with her fire, her sensuality, her iron-will, and the gentle streak she tried to hide. And her psychic 'taste' . . . honey, coffee, and truffles. All of it invigorated and steadied both Knox and his demon. This bond would stabilize his demon in a way that Knox never could have done, despite his strength and power. Only Harper could have given it this. There was one thing left for Knox to do.

Harper watched determination flash in his eyes as the hand cupping her nape slid around to collar her throat, placing his thumb at the hollow of her right ear. A hiss escaped her as the skin beneath his thumb suddenly began to burn and throb. It only lasted seconds, but she still scowled. "You could have warned me."

Tilting her head to the side, Knox looked at the mark he'd left in the very place that every anchored demon was marked. Each mark was a tattoo of an infinity symbol with a slight, personal difference. Not much bigger than the pad of his thumb, the glistening infinity symbol was made of a thorn branch. And it told the world that she was anchored; that there was someone who would wreak vengeance on anyone who dared harm her.

"Your turn." She pressed her thumb against the hollow beneath his right ear and imprinted her mark there, which seemed to satisfy him rather than pain him. *Awkward fucker.* The infinity symbol had a sphinx perched in the center of the loops. Her demon relaxed at the sight of it.

"It's done." He found that he couldn't release her, and in fact had to resist tightening his possessive grip on her throat. "Now you can't ever again deny you're mine." Every few seconds or so, her mind idly brushed against his – a psychic touch that could be for reassurance or to offer comfort or maybe it was both. He didn't know. He just knew that he liked it. "Open your mouth for me." The moment she parted her lips, he thrust his tongue inside to tangle with hers. He tasted, feasted, and breathed her into him. "Come home with me tonight."

She swallowed hard. "Okay."

Satisfied, Knox kissed her again. He'd have her as many times as he could before his demon began to get bored. It could take days, it could take weeks, but it would happen. It always did. Even so, Harper would always be his on some level.

CHAPTER EIGHT

Ready to lock up the studio, Harper was slipping on her jacket when Royce walked inside. Groan.

"Who is the guy who's always hanging around outside the building?"

She blinked, startled at his brusqueness. Royce generally didn't have the balls to speak to anyone like that.

"He takes you to work every morning and hangs around outside most of the day. Why?" he demanded.

"I'm confused by the fact that you believe this is your business."

"He works for Knox Thorne, doesn't he?" Royce stepped closer, pissing off her demon. It wanted to claw his face right off his skull. "I saw him come in here with Thorne once." He spoke like there was some kind of conspiracy and he was on to it. "Are you fucking Thorne? Is he why you won't come back to me?"

What a fucking asshole. "Royce, I won't come back to you for a number of reasons – primarily because you seem to think that monogamy is a shade of brown."

"I apologized for that. She meant nothing to me."

"Which is exactly why it should have been easy to turn her down. But you didn't."

"So let's shout this out so we can move forward. Slap me. Kick me. Call me a dog."

"Why? Dogs are loyal."

"Look, I know I did wrong. Believe me when I say I hate myself for it. We can work this out. I miss you, Harper."

She grabbed her purse and keys. "Well, as you can see, I'm drowning in a river of tears." She ushered him out of the studio. "Now if you're done, I have things to do."

Outside, he continued speaking even as she locked the front door. "I've told you over and over, I'm sorry and I hate that I've hurt you. What do you want me to do?"

She faced him. "Honestly? Stick your cock in a bee hive. Call me and let me know how that goes." Flashing him a sweet, acidic smile, she then made her way to Tanner, who was holding the car door open. "Hey, Tanner."

"Problem?" He flicked his gaze to Royce.

She sighed. "I just don't understand your gender. Do you?"

Tanner held up his hands. "This isn't a conversation that could go well for me."

Smiling, she slid into the car. "So true." Within seconds, they were driving en route to her apartment. She hadn't seen Knox for four days, since he'd been on a business trip. In that time, though, he'd contacted her telepathically every night.

The days apart had given her a little time to get used to their psychic bond. It was true that it was impossible to ever feel alone when you were anchored. His mind constantly stroked hers, instinctively yet idly. It was comforting. She could feel him and was always aware of him on some level, yet she couldn't sense him or his feelings as the bond wasn't intrusive.

As he was returning from his trip today, they had made plans to see each other tomorrow. He wanted to talk about the gathering for the whole Monarch business that was occurring in one of his Underground hotels in just two days. The time running up to the gathering had flown over fast, and during that time Knox had taken her to his home every night, had fucked her hard and long with an urgency that told her he was taking advantage of what time they had before his demon withdrew from her on a sexual level. The demon would accept her as its anchor, but it wouldn't wish to keep her as anything more.

Up to now, his demon wasn't at all bored. She knew it because the brand on her breast hadn't faded. She could admit that she checked it each morning and evening, wanting to be mentally prepared for the demon's withdrawal. Considering how obsessed her own demon was with Knox and the predator that lived within him, Harper was pretty sure that her demon would want to burn shit down when his lost interest.

Forcing her mind off the matter, she spoke to Tanner. "I'm surprised you don't sometimes give yourself a break and let either Keenan or Larkin take over."

He glanced at her in the rearview mirror. "Surprised? Why?"

"You must get bored of babysitting me." Her life wasn't exactly exciting.

"You're important to Knox, which makes you important to me."

"This babysitting gig still has to gall you on some level. You're a sentinel." He was meant for more than this.

"Knox would never trust anyone but a sentinel with your safety. I volunteered for the position."

"Dear God, why?"

He chuckled. "I knew I was the best choice. Levi has always been Knox's personal guard and it would be better for it to remain that way. Keenan and Larkin wouldn't have been good guards for you. Keenan would have flirted with you, and Larkin would have conspired with you to do crazy shit just because she's weird like that. Both would have driven Knox insane, which is never a good thing."

She nodded. "Got ya."

"Sometimes I think—" He grunted as his whole body seemed to jolt. Then he slumped in his seat a mere second before the car flipped in the air once, twice, three times and landed upside down. Then it was sliding along the ground, making the metal hood screech. Eventually, it ground to a halt. *What the fuck?*

Coughing, she called out, "Tanner! Tanner!" Nothing. Her inner demon was at serious risk of freaking out.

Instinctively, she spoke to the one person she knew would come. *Um, Knox, we've got a problem here.* Okay, maybe that was understating things a little, but she didn't want him to lose his shit.

What sort of problem? His voice was tense, hard.

Undoing her seatbelt, she awkwardly fell to the ground. Ow. *Well, the car kind of flipped over a few times, like a huge wind caught it up and hurled it. That was after Tanner suddenly lost consciousness. And . . . oh shit.*

What?

Well, a black SUV is heading right for us.

Where are you? It was a rumble of danger.

It's hard to tell. Scanning her surroundings as best she could, she realized . . . *We're in an alley. Tanner had only been driving for maybe five minutes or so; the alley can't be far from the studio.* And as the alley was blocked off on one side, it meant there was no way out. But she wouldn't have left without Tanner anyway.

I'll come for you.

She knew he would. She also knew he was beyond pissed and there was a very good chance these people would die. Grabbing Tanner's arm, she shook him. "Tanner, wake up!" she hissed. Noticing the blood trickling out of his ears and nose, she suspected he'd taken a psychic blow to the head.

Harper stilled at the sound of car doors swinging open. Then there were urgent footsteps crunching on the gravel. *Two* sets of footsteps, she sensed. The door on her right was abruptly yanked open. A hand closed tightly around her arm and snatched her out of the vehicle. That same hand shoved her toward the blond muscular asshole now rounding the Bentley; both males reeked of something which made both her and her inner demon tense: magick.

So she was up against dark practitioners. That wasn't good.

She didn't scream or fight. That would only tempt them to deal her a psychic blow to the mind that would render her defenseless. For them to have not already done so, they believed she would be easy to handle. How silly.

The blond smiled at her, looking cool and smug. It was the smugness that irritated her the most. It also irked her demon, who saw it as a challenge to prove what it could do – to demonstrate just how badly they had misjudged their target. Unfortunately, neither of the practitioners were close enough to touch; if she dived at one, the other would attack her.

"You'll come with us," the blond stated, scratching at his goatee.

"Um, actually I won't."

"You should—"

"You don't want me to go with you," she said in a compelling voice. He blinked repeatedly. "You don't want to hurt me." Sphinxes didn't befuddle people with riddles as mythology stated, but they did have the natural ability to confuse people. She'd much rather stab them with her blade, but they couldn't die until Knox had interrogated them.

"What are you doing to him?" demanded the other practitioner.

"You don't care about that," she told him in that same compelling voice. "You don't remember who he is. You don't remember why you're here."

The dark-skinned male stumbled. "What's happening?"

Harper looked back at the other practitioner ... only to see that he was doing some kind of silent chant. Something heavy and solid slammed into her head. She swayed and staggered, blinking repeatedly. Her vision began to darken around the edges as she fell back against the car and slid to the ground. But she fought the fog and the darkness closing in on her, and she somehow held onto consciousness.

His eyes widened as he struggled to his feet. "That's not possible."

A growl made everyone freeze. Then the Bentley shook as if something was struggling to get out. *Tanner.* By the sounds of it, he'd let out his inner demon.

A mere moment later, the demon was out; launching itself in the air and over the car to land in front of Harper, growling at the practitioners. Hellhounds were like wolves on steroids, yet they had a majestic air about them. They had fur as black as coal, eyes as red as blood, and they brought with them the scent of burning brimstone.

Gripping the hound's fur, she struggled to her feet, her head still throbbing with pain. "Motherfucking motherfuckers need to motherfucking die."

In full agreement with that, her demon barged its way to the surface just as it whipped out the stiletto blade and infused it with hellfire. Loving the fear that wafted from the practitioners, it spoke as it petted the hellhound. "You cannot win this. Of course, you could try. You could attempt to take out myself or the hellhound. It might even work. But while you spend precious time doing a little chant, the other of us will be on you. That means that at least one of you will die."

Harper retained control then with a hiss. "But I won't."

A roar split the air. A roar of fire, she realized a moment later. The fire hissed, cracked, and popped. The flames died away, revealing . . .

"Knox?" He could teleport using fire? Shit, no wonder he'd gotten to her so quickly when Silas paid her a visit.

His dark eyes roamed over her, absorbing every detail, noting the cut on her forehead. Then those eyes fixed on the practitioners, who were backing up. "I'm afraid I can't let you leave." Fire shot out of his palm like it was a flamethrower, enclosing the practitioners in a circle. It might have looked like a rope of fire . . . if it didn't have the head of a dragon and wasn't slithering along the ground, hissing and spitting at its prisoners. And that wasn't weird at all.

He stalked toward the two males, the image of absolute composure. But he looked *too* composed, *too* calm – so much so that it was terrifying. "You deliberately targeted my anchor. Why?" The question was spoken very steadily, yet it was coated in menace.

The blond swallowed hard. "I didn't know she's your anchor."

"I find that very difficult to believe. My anchor would be a prize for any dark practitioner. But such a practitioner would need to be either mindless or desperate for death. Which are you?" He sounded genuinely curious, but Harper knew he was playing with them – like a predator toyed with its prey.

"I'm telling the truth," the blond vowed, "we didn't know who she was to you. Someone wants her, but we weren't told why or what for. Just that we'd be paid well."

"And who is this someone?"

"We can't tell you."

Knox stuffed his hands in his pockets, seeming both casual and bored. "Ah, let me guess. You're under a compulsion."

Both practitioners nodded, flinching as the fire dragon hissed at them.

"I think I'll see for myself if that's true."

The blond, groaning in agony through clenched teeth, probably would have fallen to his knees if his friend hadn't caught him. After a moment, he calmed and it was clear that Knox had withdrew from his mind. Then it was the other practitioner that cried out in pain, knees shaking. He sagged when it was over.

"You're telling me the truth. That's good." Knox nodded his head. "Very good. But . . . there's something you weren't planning to tell me. You didn't know she was my anchor, that's true. But you suspected it." The blond shook his head wildly. "Yes, yes you did. You heard the rumors, and when you saw my sentinel with her you wondered if just maybe those rumors were true. And that made you excited."

Shaking his head again, the blond blurted out, "No, we—"

"You thought draining my anchor of power would somehow drain me also. You decided to keep her for yourselves instead of handing her over to someone else. You planned to drain her using sex magick. She would have been a sexual sacrifice."

Sick fucking bastards. Her inner demon was now pretty eager to watch Knox destroy them.

"That excitement died down when she fought back, however." As the blond opened his mouth to speak, Knox shot him a hard look. "I don't accept excuses. They mean nothing to me. *You* mean nothing to me."

"We can show you where we were supposed to take her, you'll be able to see who hired us! You can use us!"

"I've been in your mind. I already know where you were told to take her. There would be no sense in me going there, however. You were both psychically bugged."

The blond exchanged a confused look with his friend. "What does that mean?"

"Someone has been listening to your every thought, watching your every move," Knox told them. "They know you failed. I've destroyed the bugs, which means they won't see what happens next. I think it will be better to let them guess."

"Wait, we—" He cut himself off as Knox's eyes bled to black and the demon glared out at them. Even from where Harper stood, she could feel the air chilling.

It bared its teeth. "Harper is mine. You hurt her. That means you don't get to live." Spoken like the matter was a mathematical equation.

The blond glanced at Harper. "Doesn't it bother you that he's just going to kill us?"

She tilted her head. "It did . . . for about two seconds. Then I remembered you're a couple of pricks that knocked Tanner unconscious and would have raped me."

"And now they die," said the emotionless voice of Knox's demon.

There was a sudden buzz in the air, like something was charging, building, gathering in power. The ground began subtly vibrating, making the car tremble and the litter flutter. A chill snaked down her spine, and every hair on her body rose.

There was so much power, she could feel it hum and purr against her skin; it slithered between her fingers, stroked over her face, burned her eyes, and made her teeth rattle. A slight ringing sound filled her ears, and her chest suddenly felt so tight it hurt a little to breathe. It was *too* much power. No one and nothing should harness that kind of power. No one should be expected to control it.

Then the practitioners screamed as flames erupted from the ground at their feet and swirled around them. The flames were at least ten-feet high and were a beautiful intricate mix of gold, red, and black. And they gave off a heat that burned so hot she wouldn't have been surprised if her skin blistered. And she instinctively knew . . . *the flames of hell*.

They didn't burn the practitioners, they swallowed them, leaving behind only ashes. Spotting the red residue in the ashes, Harper knew she'd been right. The flames of hell were said to leave behind such a residue. Which meant Knox really could call on them. He really was a threat to not only every demon, but every single thing that existed on the planet. *Well, shit*.

The buzz in the air died away as the power seemed to return to where it came from, and it no longer hurt to breathe. Knox held out his hand, and the fire dragon was sucked back into his palm. As Knox closed his hand tight, smoke puffed out of his fist.

That was when he turned to face her, and she saw that the demon was still in charge for the moment. It prowled toward her, its gaze unblinking. The hellhound moved aside, as if it didn't dare try to come between her and the demon. Harper put away her blade, not wanting to seem a threat.

Coming to stand in front of her, Knox's demon studied her closely. "Now you know the truth."

"I won't tell."

"You fear me now."

Kind of. It wasn't necessarily Knox or his inner demon that she feared, it was the power they had . . . and what they could do with it. "You won't hurt me."

That answer seemed to please it, and it fluttered its fingertips along the cut on her forehead. How could something so dangerous, so capable of cruelty, be so gentle? "They made you bleed."

She gave a casual shrug. "It will be healed within the hour." As if satisfied, the demon retreated. Knox cupped her nape and pulled her flush against him; he held himself stiffly, and she got the feeling he was expecting her to pull away. So she relaxed into him.

"I'm proud of you for fighting back."

"It was good that she did, since I was unconscious for most of that."

She turned to see Tanner, having retained control over his demon, zipping up a pair of jeans. He obviously kept fresh clothes in the car in case he had to let his demon out. "You would have done what it took if Knox hadn't turned up and stole the show." She couldn't help but be impressed as Tanner effortlessly righted the Bentley.

"It'll be safe to drive, it's just a little banged up." Tanner was right. None of the windows had been smashed.

"Is it demonically protected?" she asked Knox.

"Yes," he replied. Then he frowned. "You're hurting." How he'd sensed it, she didn't know. "Where?"

"It's just a headache." Okay, that was understating things a little – it felt like someone was stabbing her in the eye while pounding a hammer on her skull. The pain was making her feel nauseous. "They tried to knock me out the way they did Tanner. But I fought it."

"Bonding with me has made you stronger."

She peered up at him, smiling despite herself. "By the way, the fact that you can travel using fire is really, really awesome."

"I'm glad you feel that way, because that's exactly how we're getting home."

Wait, what?

"Tanner, you can come with us or you can wait here for Larkin and Keenan. I've already spoken to them. They're on their way." By that, Harper guessed he'd called them telepathically.

"I'll stay here and help them with the clean up," said Tanner.

Knox locked both arms around Harper. "Ready?"

Um, no. It *sounded* fun to pyroport, but as she remembered the raging fire, she wasn't so eager to try it.

"The flames will cover you, but it's just normal fire, it won't hurt you," Knox assured her. "Trust me."

A fire suddenly roared to life around them and, fuck, it was one of the weirdest things she'd ever experienced. The heat was unbearable for a millisecond as the flames engulfed her entire body, licking every inch of exposed skin. Then the flames parted and the heat vanished, and she realized they were in his living room. "Well, fuck."

Hearing a deep rumbly laugh, she turned to find Levi on the sofa. "That was my thought the first time he pyroported me somewhere." His brow crinkled. "You okay?"

"Been better," she mumbled tiredly as she flung herself on the sofa. "I'm seriously tired."

"You used a lot of psychic energy fighting to stay conscious after the practitioner dealt you a psychic hit," said Knox. "Of course you're tired."

Using too much psychic energy was like being given a sedative. Lethargy was creeping over her, making her sleepily curl up into a ball. Unfortunately, the pounding headache had the potential to keep her from resting peacefully. Something in her expression must have given away the amount of pain she was in, because Knox sat beside her and used the pads of his fingers and thumb to massage her temples and scalp. It felt so good, she pretty much melted into the soft leather. "I really wish I'd killed Frick and Frack myself."

"Frick and Frack?" echoed Levi.

"Dark practitioners," Knox explained. Levi listened quietly as he told the tale. Sensing Harper had fallen asleep, Knox ended his massage and brushed his fingers through her hair; it was like liquid silk and he loved the feel of it against his skin.

When he'd received her frantic telepathic call, he'd almost lost his fucking mind. It was a dangerous thing for someone like Knox to be without the control that kept his demon and his abilities in check. Knox knew without a doubt that if Harper had been killed tonight, his demon would have taken over and expressed its anger on the world. It cared for nothing other than its own survival and pleasure. But Harper belonged to it, and someone had tried to take her away. That wasn't acceptable to it.

In the alley, Knox had stepped aside and given his demon supremacy, knowing it needed to be the one to punish the practitioners if it had any chance of calming. Its anger had already subsided. Although its rage was always cold, it was also always fleeting.

"The more I think about everything, the more I believe this isn't a case of different camps of people targeting her," said Levi. "I think the dark practitioners were put up to this by the same person that sent Silas."

"You think it's Isla," sensed Knox.

"I think it's very likely her," confirmed Levi. "She's got more reason to target Harper than anyone else. To her, Harper's trying to take a place that rightfully belongs to Isla."

"But she didn't know about Harper until the Manhattan conference," Knox pointed out. "Silas visited her studio before that."

"How are we sure that she didn't know before the conference? She *looked* shocked, but Isla's always been a good actress. The news of Harper's connection to you spread far and wide. It's extremely possible that Isla heard. Maybe she believed it, maybe she didn't. We know Silas was sent to test your reaction. But what if the real reason someone was interested in that reaction was because it would tell them whether the rumors were true? I think Isla heard and she sent Silas to confirm it." Levi leaned back in his seat. "The only other enemies Harper has are Kendra and Carla."

"The practitioners said that someone wanted rid of Harper. What reason would her mother have to do that?"

"Carla got rid of her once before," Levi pointed out.

"Abandoning your child and killing your child are two different things."

"Stop thinking of them as mother and daughter. From what I can tell, the only thing Carla Hayden ever did for Harper was give birth to her. She didn't want her, she dumped her onto someone else, and she didn't look back. Yes, there are many parents out there who've given up their children for one reason or another. But Carla did it coldly. She's had no relationship at all with Harper since then, despite them not living all that far away from each other. And didn't Harper tell you that whenever they've crossed paths Carla dismissed her?"

The more Knox considered Levi's words, the more his theory sounded very, very plausible. "Carla got rid of a baby she viewed as a mistake and then built a new life in which she pretended Harper didn't exist; then she could forget what a fool she'd been to believe she could trap Lucian," he mused aloud. "But now she can't pretend Harper doesn't exist any longer. Harper now has a certain fame among our kind."

"Yes. People are curious about her. Carla could worry that someone will find out she's her mother. Other than for Kendra and Carla, our lair feels naturally protective toward Harper because of who she is to you. They were seriously pissed with Kendra for what she did. So imagine how they'd feel about Carla.

I don't think her mate and sons know about Harper. Bray loves kids; he has two from a previous relationship and he's been a constant, steady presence in their lives."

"It still seems farfetched for Carla to try to kill Harper. It's not as if Harper wants Carla's recognition, is it?"

"It doesn't matter. Carla's carefully constructed world could very well fall apart if people find out the truth. Bray might be unable to understand and forgive her. Carla might feel it's a lot easier to get rid of the threat to her world than to risk it. She dumped Harper coldly. Why couldn't she end her life just as coldly? Some people are just callous through and through."

Knox knew that well. "The day Carla came to my office, she painted the picture of a woman who made a mistake, regrets it, and would love nothing more than to fix it. But it's possible that what she was really doing was making herself seem the least likely person to cause Harper harm so that no one would suspect her."

"Yes. And that's why she needs monitoring closely."

"Get some of the Force on it."

"As for Harper's other enemy . . ." Levi sighed. "I don't think Kendra would put herself through all the trouble of compulsions and hiring practitioners. She's too lazy."

"But she's jealous of Harper. And it's not just because Harper's my anchor."

Levi narrowed his eyes. "What don't I know?"

Glancing down at his anchor, he lowered his voice. "It's possible that she and Kendra are sisters."

Levi gaped. He wasn't a man who was easily shocked. "Are you shitting me?"

"You know I always do a background check on demons who request to join my lair. So when Kendra joined two years ago, I had one done on her. She comes from a high profile family in a lair in Alabama, though she very quickly shed that accent when she came here. It turns out that there was a scandal many years ago; her mother, Beatrice, got pregnant with Kendra by a demon who later left her for a much younger female, a sphinx. That female sphinx turned out to be Carla. It would explain why Kendra seemed to dislike Carla on sight."

"How can you be sure Lucian is the demon who got Beatrice pregnant?"

"I wasn't sure, I hadn't originally asked Tanner to dig that deep. But when I realized Harper's father was Lucian, I had him do some more digging. He confirmed it was Lucian." Knox paused as Levi cursed. "If Kendra knows Carla lured her father away, she knows who her father is – a father that also played no part in her life. Yet, in his way, he raised his other daughter and, in fact, Harper's the only living being he seems to have any true regard for. That can't make Kendra feel good."

"It's a shame you can't punch your way into her mind to find out if she's responsible."

It was a shame. But Kendra was a breed of demon known as a 'nightmare.' There was only one thing he would find if he invaded her mind: his worst nightmare.

"You could still invade Carla's mind. I mean, I get that if the lair thought you'll happily go around forcing your way into people's minds, you could lose their trust and loyalty. But you have good reason here. They would understand if you explained the situation."

Knox curled a strand of Harper's hair around his finger. "There would be no point. I lightly touched Carla's mind when she came to my office. It seems that Harper inherited her unusual shields from her mother."

"Unusual?"

"They have the psychic equivalent of steel barbs. No one

could get through them without doing major damage to their own psyche."

Levi winced. "Then I guess we'll just have to keep an eye on both Kendra and Carla. Have you told Harper that Kendra could be her half-sister?"

"Not yet."

"Why?"

"Because I know Harper. Maybe better than even she does. And she already had plenty of reasons in her pretty little head to not form the anchor bond. I didn't want to give her another. Now, it could be that it wouldn't have bothered Harper to know that her anchor had an extremely brief fling with a half-sister she doesn't even know. But anchors can be very possessive of each other, and it does apply in our situation. So there was a chance it *would* have bothered her. In any case, she would have undoubtedly grasped onto it as another reason to avoid bonding."

Levi gave him a knowing look. "And you didn't want to give her a reason for it to maybe feel a little weird to get in your bed."

"No, I didn't."

"When are you planning to tell her?" There was a hardness in Levi's voice that told Knox the reaper fully expected Knox to do so and would be thoroughly pissed if he didn't. Knox arched a brow at his sentinel's tone.

Levi shrugged. "I like her. I don't want her upset."

Neither did Knox. "I'll tell her tomorrow. Hopefully she won't make me pay too harsh a price for keeping it from her."

Levi grinned. "Oh, she'll make you pay."

He was probably right. As Harper's body shifted restlessly, Knox sighed. "I better put her to bed before she rolls off the couch." She didn't fuss when he scooped her up and cradled her against his chest, but her mouth did settle into a cute pout that he wanted to kiss right off her face. Four hours. He'd give her four hours to recover, and then he'd take her the way he'd wanted to for the past four days. He'd developed an addiction for her hot little body, and he fully intended to indulge it.

CHAPTER NINE

Wake up for me, Harper.

Harper's eyes snapped open as a hot tongue licked at her. She wasn't sure whether it was the telepathic call that woke her or the talented tongue that was now swirling around her clit. A moan slipped out of her, earning her a growl of approval from the male settled between her thighs.

"For four long days, I've thought about this pussy, about how it tastes." The thickly spoken words rumbled against her slick folds. The tip of Knox's tongue flicked at her clit just before his teeth gave it a light nip. She bucked, and his hands firmly pinned her down by her hips. "Be still."

"It's a little hard not to move when—" A gasp flew out of her as ice-cold fingers pinched her nipple. "Shit." Like last time, the fingers made her flesh burn and tingle in the best way. They pinched, tweaked, plucked, and circled her nipples while Knox licked and sipped at her pussy like it was some kind of delicacy. Then he plunged a finger inside her; every thrust was slow, deliberate, and a taunt that made her pussy ripple and clench.

It was a sensual assault, and she couldn't take anymore. "Knox, I need to come."

"Not yet."

"Then you need to get in me fast." She shuddered as he blew over her clit while his psychic fingers plucked at her nipples again. "Motherfucker." Chuckling, he rose above her . . . and his hot mouth landed on her taut, cold, tingling nipple. "Oh, fuck." Making it worse, two icy psychic fingers slid deep in her, burning her from the inside out as her pussy began to blaze and quiver.

Knox suckled on the hard bud, watching as she trembled beneath him from the onslaught he was subjecting her to; she writhed and arched, curving her restless, delectable body into his. She was so fucking sensual and responsive. So fucking *his*. He bit the curve of her breast, sure to leave a mark. Her head shot up as her eyes swirled from a soft violet to an electric blue.

"Enough teasing!"

"But I *like* teasing you."

"If you expect to ever fuck me again, you'll get inside me *now*." Harper stilled as Knox's demon suddenly took control. It was hard to read those eyes, but she could swear the entity was pissed. "Um . . ."

A hand clamped possessively around her pussy. "Mine. Mine to fuck whenever I want it."

Then she felt a familiar prickling beneath the hand as her skin began to heat, and she knew exactly what it was doing. She shook her head. "No. Not there." The flesh under its hand suddenly felt like it was on fire. Yet, what should have been sheer agony was sheer pleasure; she arched into the hand, so damn close to exploding.

The icy psychic fingers pumped hard and fast as the demon pressed down on her clit with its thumb. "Come. Come for *me*."

Her release crashed into her, ripping a scream from her throat. The psychic fingers dissolved, and the demon seemed happy enough to then subside. "It did it again," she told Knox. She inhaled sharply as he ground against her sensitive newly branded flesh, sending a shockwave of pleasure sizzling through her.

"I know." Knox licked his lips as he donned the condom he'd placed on the bedside drawers. "You taste better than I remembered. Let's see if you feel better than I remembered." He flipped her onto her stomach, pulled her to her knees, and slammed into her. She was swollen from her last orgasm, but he forced his way inside until he was balls-deep. He groaned through his teeth as her inferno-hot pussy tightened and contracted around him. "You do feel better."

"Fuck, fuck, fuck." She was so sensitive inside that it was almost painful to have his cock filling her. But even if she'd wanted to move away, she couldn't have; his fingers bit into her hips as he held her still and took her with brutal, powerful thrusts. His pace was feral and unrelenting, and Harper could only fist her hands in the bedsheet as he became absolute male domination.

As ice-cold fingers began to toy with her clit, she almost sobbed. "Knox, no, I can't take anymore." Her pussy was filled to bursting, her nipples still tingled, and her branded flesh was throbbing. Having him play with her clit on top of all that . . . It was too much sensation.

"You'll take it," he said into her ear before licking over the wing marks on her back. "You'll take it because I want you to, and you want to please me." He ferociously hammered into her slick, tight pussy, the way he'd needed – craved – to do for four long fucking days. He had to face that he was as obsessed with Harper as his demon was.

A sharp tug on her clit made her whimper. "Seriously, I'm gonna come."

"Fight it."

"I can't. I really, really can't. I'm too close."

He knew that, because her pussy was fluttering and squeezing him. "Wait." Raking a hand into her hair, he pulled her face to his and dominated her mouth; swallowing her whimpers as she fought her orgasm. "Good girl." He cupped her pussy, rubbing the heel of his palm over the new brand there. "That's it, come."

She didn't come, she went up in flames – screaming and milking Knox, who slammed home with a grunt and pulsed deep in her. When his body finally left hers, she sagged forward so that she was lying fully on her stomach. She'd felt a little refreshed after waking up from only a short sleep, but now she was completely boneless. "I'm not sure if I can move again."

"Then I'll move you." Knox gently rolled her onto her back and pressed a light kiss to her mouth.

As he slid down her body, she guessed his intention. Groaning, she threw her arm over her face to cover her eyes. "I'm not going to look."

Knox chuckled. "I like it." The V of her thighs was now a triangle of intricate black swirls. Of course, the swirls featured thorns. He followed the swirly thorn branches with the tip of his tongue, smiling when she helplessly bucked beneath him.

Her curiosity got the better of her. "Fine, let me see." Bracing herself on her elbows, she studied the brand. "Your demon doesn't do anything by halves, does it? It's not funny."

"I'm not laughing."

"Not out loud." But his amusement was right there in his eyes.

"What does your demon think?" he asked, snaking a hand up her soft thigh.

"The brands don't bother it. Your smugness, however, pisses it off."

He smiled. "Can I help it if I like it?"

"Don't you realize I can't ever again go to a spa for a Brazilian? *It's not funny.*"

After they'd taken a shower during which Knox had fucked her hard against the tiled wall with her luscious legs locked around him, they sat down for the evening meal. Once they'd finished, Knox leaned back in his seat. *Truth time.* "There's something I haven't told you."

Harper froze with her glass halfway to her mouth. "What's that?"

Bracing himself for her anger, he said, "There's a possibility that Kendra is your half-sister."

She blinked. "Oh. Yeah, I already knew that."

And for what was probably the millionth time, his anchor had managed to surprise him. "You knew?"

"Well, I wasn't *sure.* She doesn't look anything at all like a Wallis." Harper sipped at her wine. "If you think I'm the only kid Lucian's fathered and abandoned, you're wrong. There are plenty of 'possible' offspring of Lucian Wallis. If Carla hadn't handed me over to Jolene who then forced him to play a part in my life, he wouldn't have."

Knox was looking forward to the day he finally met Lucian; he fully intended to give the selfish prick a well-deserved lecture.

"I don't know the names of the others he could have fathered," continued Harper, putting down her glass. "But I knew about Kendra. I heard my family talk about how although Lucian left Carla while she was pregnant for another she-demon, they had no sympathy for her – they said she'd gotten a taste of her own medicine after luring him away from Beatrice, who'd been pregnant with Kendra."

"So … from minute one of meeting Kendra, you knew she could be your half-sister?"

"No, I didn't make the connection." Harper crossed her legs beneath the table. "To be honest, I hadn't really thought about her much over the years. It was Jolene who figured it out. When I called to tell her that you and I had formed the anchor bond, I mentioned my little encounter with Kendra in the restrooms. She asked me to describe her. When I did, Jolene told me it was possible her mother was Beatrice."

"You never said anything."

"Neither did you."

Fair point. "I thought you would find it strange to be—"

"Yeah, I get it. For a few minutes, I did find it a little weird knowing I'd slept with a guy who had also fucked someone who could be my half-sister. But then I thought, 'So, what? It doesn't change anything.' And if she and I are related, it's not like we're sisters in an emotional sense. We don't know each other, and believe me when I say that Kendra hates me. I could see it in her eyes."

"If she is your half-sister – and I think it's probable that she is – her jealousy of you probably runs very, very deep. Lucian publically acknowledges that you're his daughter, he did his own poor version of raising you, and even now he remains in contact with you. Kendra, however, has had none of that."

Harper sighed, feeling bad for her. "It's no wonder she's pissed."

"Don't feel sorry for her. Being upset about her situation with Lucian doesn't excuse her taking it out on you. It's understandable if she wants his recognition and attention, but in that case it should be *him* that she expresses her anger on. Not you."

"I guess her distaste for imps is more about her distaste for

Lucian. But despite hating him, she's jealous of me. I don't understand that."

"Why?"

"Carla has two sons. I'm not jealous that they had her and I didn't."

Knox leaned forward. "Because you and Kendra are totally different creatures. You're not capable of bitterness." Harper wasn't what anyone would term pleasant or cheerful, and she could often be rude and aggressive. But he'd come to realize that beneath all that was a kind, loyal, accepting person who loved from the soul.

"You suspect she might be behind the attack earlier," Harper deduced.

Knox shrugged. "It's a possibility that I'm not willing to rule out. Look at the facts: she's jealous of you and she resents you, which is enough. Add in that she's probably embarrassed by how you reduced her to a puddle of misery in the restrooms, and she certainly has plenty of motive to hurt you."

"Any other suspects?"

Her expression told Knox she had a good idea of who else he suspected. "Levi and I talked about it earlier. We came up with three possible suspects: Kendra, Isla, and Carla." Shadows entered her unusual eyes that were currently a soft plum in color. "I'm sorry, baby, I know it has to hurt to know your own mother might wish you harm. I'm not convinced it is her, but I won't take chances with your life. That means keeping an open mind. I agree with Levi that the person who hired the practitioners is the same person who sent Silas to test me."

"I get why he might then suspect Kendra and Carla, but how could it be Isla? Silas came to my office before she . . ." Harper trailed off as understanding hit her. "You and Levi think it's possible that she already knew about me before the meeting in New York."

"Isla prides herself on 'being in the know.' I was very vocal about the fact that I'd found my anchor, and I ensured that you and I were seen together all over Vegas. The news could have reached her if it traveled outside of Vegas."

"But she seemed genuinely surprised at the conference when I introduced myself as your anchor."

"Maybe she was so surprised because, until that moment, she'd believed it couldn't be true."

"Yeah, but if she *is* the one who sent Silas, he would have reported back to her. You made it very clear to him that I'm your anchor. Wouldn't she have accepted that?"

"Isla and I have known each other a very, very long time. In all that time, she's fully believed that I'm her anchor; has convinced herself that one day I'll finally see this and that I'll then bond with her. It would take a lot to shake such a fixed deep-seated belief, especially for someone who thinks of herself as superior to most people. In Isla's mind, others couldn't possibly know better than she does."

"You could be right. Devon told me that someone's spreading rumors that I'm not really your anchor; just your newest side piece who's claiming to be your anchor to protect myself. If that's Isla, it's clear she believes I'm simply a bed-buddy to you. It suits her to believe that."

"Recall her departing words. She said, 'You can't change the truth, Knox, whether you choose to accept it or not.'"

Harper snorted. "We could say the same to her."

"While I hope it isn't Isla, considering how dangerous she is, I also don't like the thought of how it would hurt you to know your own mother or half-sister was responsible." She'd already been let down enough by her family. "I really do doubt that it's Carla."

"It's all right, you don't have to reassure me. Parents are just people, and people can be shitheads. I know that well. You've never talked about your parents."

Knox tried not to tense. "No, I haven't."

His tone didn't welcome further questioning. Harper folded her arms across her chest. "You know, it's shitty of you to do that. Since the first day we met, you've done nothing but quiz me about my family, my life, and my past. I didn't ask you many questions, because I wasn't planning to form the bond, so I didn't see the point in getting to know you. We're officially anchors now. Don't you think it's only fair for me to get to know you too?"

Picking up his glass, he swirled it a little. "You do know me."

"I know you're a dominant control freak who likes to always have his way."

"You know many of the rumors about me are true. You also know that I spent a lot of my childhood in a children's home for strays."

She tilted her head. "What about your parents?"

"They're dead. Have been for a very long time."

She frowned. "Why didn't you stay with your lair when they died?"

"I wasn't part of a lair then." He'd been part of something pure evil.

Harper sensed that to probe further into his childhood would make him shut down. She wanted to hear more about his life. "What happened when you left the children's home with the sentinels? Did you all join a lair?"

"No. We considered ourselves strays, integrated ourselves into the human world."

"A world you more or less conquered."

He drank a little of his wine. "I suppose you could say I've achieved many things."

"Ruthlessly."

He smiled, admitting, "Yes."

He'd gotten where he was through his own efforts and determination. Harper could respect that. "And the fact that you were seen as a power in your own right made demons gravitate toward you."

He nodded. "Then, before I knew it, I was the Prime of a lair. A lair which has grown over the years."

He was so uncomfortable talking about himself that it was almost amusing. "You can relax. I'm done." She smiled. "For now."

His eyes narrowed, glittering with humor. "So very tenacious."

"Why, thank you."

Knox? It was Keenan.

Yes?

I've got news you're gonna want to hear. Call the others. I'll be twenty minutes.

"I'm guessing there was some telepathing going on," said Harper. "I felt the echo of the conversation because our minds are connected, but I couldn't make out the words." It was weird.

Knox raised his brows, once again surprised. "Strange. Apparently, Keenan has information. I have a feeling I'm not going to like it."

By the time Keenan arrived at the mansion, Larkin, Tanner, and Levi were already waiting in the living area with Knox and Harper. "Tell me," said Knox.

Keenan flopped on the sofa next to Larkin. "You know all the missing strays? They've been found."

"Found?" echoed Levi. "Alive?"

"Yes."

Tanner leaned forward. "When?"

"A few hours ago," replied Keenan. "They were all in a warehouse in some kind of induced coma."

"Are they awake now?" asked Larkin.

Keenan nodded. "But it seems that they don't remember a single moment of their capture. The last memory each of them have is of what they were doing just before they were taken."

Harper spoke then. "Wait, who found them?"

Keenan's smile had a cynical edge to it. "Isla." He looked at Knox. "And you can imagine just how grateful and indebted the strays now feel toward their savior, who managed to find them when no one else could."

"If you ask me, she was the one to take them in the first place," said Larkin. "She's not dumb; she knew that no Prime would wish to give up power. She knew that to get what she wanted, she'd have to include every demon in America in the voting. Finding the missing strays will certainly earn her some votes."

Levi nodded. "I agree. Isla planned this. It's part of her scheme to win the favor of the demon community."

"How successful have Isla, Malden, and Dario's campaigns been so far?" Harper asked, suspecting the sentinels would have kept a close eye on things.

"People are dubious," replied Tanner. "But that could change when the three Primes present their cases this weekend."

Larkin looked at Knox. "What's the itinerary for the weekend?"

Knox took the seat beside Harper. "Malden will present his case on Friday. Isla will present hers on Saturday. And Dario will give his on Sunday. Each statement will be recorded live so that the demons outside the hotel can watch it on various big screens around the Underground."

"What promises do you think they'll make to the public?" Harper asked Knox.

"Plenty of very appealing ones. But I strongly doubt they would intend to keep any of those promises. Let's hope the public see that."

CHAPTER TEN

Glancing around the reception area, Harper saw that the Underground hotel hosting the gathering was just as ritzy and luxurious as Knox's hotels on the Vegas strip. The only difference was that the demons didn't have to hide their true natures here. It was simple things, like they didn't have to pretend they were physically struggling to carry their luggage, to big things like the doormen/sentries could be in their hellhound form.

As Jolene and the receptionist went through the check-in rigmarole, Harper noticed Beck discreetly stuffing his pockets with complimentary mints. Imps never turned down freebies. Meeting Tanner's amused gaze, she rolled her eyes. As usual, he was acting as her bodyguard.

Returning to her apartment after work, she'd found Jolene, Martina, and Beck waiting for her. They'd said they wanted to spend some 'quality family time' with Harper before the political games began. In truth, they had wanted to update her on their 'findings' on Kendra. Translation, they ripped into her life . . . confirming that Lucian was, in fact, Kendra's father. Her upbringing hadn't been great, since her mother was an alcoholic and her stepfather was quite simply a dick. If she fantasized that her life would have been a bed of roses if Lucian had taken responsibility for her, she was wrong there.

Jolene had been pissed to hear about the practitioners attacking Harper. She shared Knox's suspicion that Isla was most likely behind all the recent problems. When Harper mentioned that Carla was a suspect, she'd expected Jolene to scoff and say that Carla wasn't intelligent enough to pull off any of it. Instead, Jolene had said, 'Someone who can hate a tiny little baby is capable of anything.'

Studying the hotel map, Martina excitedly said, "Oh my God, this place has a spa, fitness center, nine swimming pools, eighteen restaurants, a casino, and a shopping mall."

Harper smiled at her aunt. "I'm glad you like it so much. Hopefully that means you won't burn anything."

"It's certainly very impressive," allowed Jolene. "Where are you staying, Harper?"

"The same floor as Knox. He has a whole floor to himself and his sentinels."

"And he wants you to sleep on the same floor for your protection," said Jolene with a nod. But she wasn't dumb, she suspected something was going on between Harper and Knox. It was really only a matter of time before she brought it up.

Harper hadn't seen him since the previous night. He'd had a business meeting that morning with his human colleagues. After that, he'd been busy ensuring everything was in place for the gathering.

"Here you go." The receptionist handed Jolene several keycards before flashing Harper a shaky smile.

A bellboy appeared. "Can I take your luggage?"

Beck raised a hand. "Not necessary, we can carry them just fine. I don't see the point in bellboys," he told Harper as they made their way to the elevator, luggage in hand. "We've got arms, we've got a map, and why would we want to tip someone for something we can do ourselves? It's just laziness."

Harper snorted. "You just don't want to part with your money." Beck was one of the stingiest people she'd ever met. Turning to Tanner, she said, "You can take the case up to my room. I'll need the two store bags; I'm getting ready in Jolene's suite." She held out her hand, but he didn't hand them to her.

Knox is expecting you, Tanner reminded her as they stepped into the elevator.

Yes, she knew Knox intended for them to share the same suite. *And I'll see him soon enough. But I want to spend some time with my family. I don't see them often.*

Tanner's mouth curved. *It's nice being around someone who doesn't bow to his every whim.*

Only because you like watching his face turn purple.

When they reached her family's designated suite, it was to find Keenan waiting outside the door, wearing a boyish grin. "Hey, sphinx."

"Keenan's going to take over while I go change," Tanner told Harper, handing her the two store bags, as Keenan introduced himself to her family. "I'll be waiting out here within the hour. Be ready."

Harper saluted him before closing the door. As she'd expected, the three-bedroom suite was just as lavish and grand as the rest of the hotel.

"It's more like an apartment than a hotel room," Martina said excitedly. She was right.

"I very much doubt we'd have been given such a suite if we weren't your family, Harper," said Jolene.

Beck read over the pamphlet they had been given by the receptionist. "The itinerary says that there's a reception dinner taking place in an hour."

"Knox said he wanted everybody to be as relaxed as possible before hearing out the first candidate," explained Harper.

Jolene smiled. "Then let's get ready."

Approximately fifty minutes later, Harper entered the living area of the suite to find the others congregated there.

Beck was fidgeting with the top buttons of his shirt. "Don't you laugh," he grumbled. For some reason, he never looked right in a suit, but Harper held her hands up in a gesture of peace.

"Sweetheart, you look beautiful," Martina said to Harper as she fingered her silk dress – it was a gentle blend of cobalt and jade.

"Thanks. Raini picked it out. You look great." Her aunt was dressed like a sixties pin-up girl with her red and white polka dot dress and matching head scarf.

"Are we ready to go?" asked Jolene, looking as elegant as always in a violet evening suit.

"If Tanner's here, yeah." As promised, the hellhound was waiting outside the suite in a dark gray suit. She smiled. "Well, don't you look dashing."

He cast her a mock glare before leading them down the elevator and straight to the restaurant, where the reception dinner was taking place. Halting at the entrance, she consulted the seating plan and saw that she would be at the same table as her family, Knox, and Raul and his anchor.

"Some of the Primes witnessed the little exchange between you and Isla in Manhattan, so they might try to talk to you and ask questions," warned Tanner. "Just keep moving. Okay?"

She nodded, keeping stride with Tanner as he led them through the restaurant. Some demons were polite and respectful as they greeted her while others were either distant or snarling in outright jealousy – the latter was mostly the females. A few Primes did attempt to begin a conversation with her, but she kept moving just as Tanner had instructed.

Their table was in front of a dais. Like the other tables, it was set up beautifully and elegantly. Raul and his anchor were already there, and they stood with a smile.

"We haven't officially met," said the Prime. "I'm Raul. You're Knox's anchor."

She nodded. "I'm Harper." He then went on to introduce himself to her family, so Harper offered a nod of greeting to the dark-skinned she-demon at his side, who was astonishingly beautiful.

"I'm Tanya," she told Harper and her family as she lifted her chin; a princess peering down at a bunch of peasants. It wasn't bitchiness, it was more like Tanya just believed herself to be superior to pretty much everyone.

After helping Harper into her seat, Tanner melted into the shadows near the wall, on guard. A waiter quickly appeared and served them champagne, to Martina's delight. Glancing around, Harper noticed that Larkin and Keenan were on either side of the room, their perceptive gazes missing nothing. Levi was no doubt with Knox, who currently was nowhere to be seen.

At the rear of the restaurant, a camera was set up directly opposite the dais. It would record the discussions live and allow the demon public to watch them on the TVs scattered around the Underground. One was actually in the dome while others were in the bars, casinos, and restaurants. The footage would also be shown in each and every hotel room.

Feeling eyes on her, Harper turned to find a particular she-demon staring at her with contempt. *Isla.* She looked amazingly beautiful yet so very, very cold.

Following Harper's gaze, Jolene leaned into her. "She's definitely not a happy bunny." She took a sip of her champagne. "Good."

Harper's inner demon agreed that it was, in fact, good; that anything that annoyed the bitch claiming she had rights to Knox was good.

Raul must have noticed Isla's glare too, because he said, "I didn't actually witness your dispute with Isla at the conference in New York. What was it about?"

"This and that," Harper replied.

He grinned. "Given that you're an imp, I suppose I should have expected an evasive response."

"This is going to be a lovely dinner," said Martina, reading the menu. "It's a shame it will be spoiled with political crap."

Yeah, their lair wasn't much into politics. They were like one huge family and that, in Harper's opinion, was why there were so few issues within their lair.

Knox's mind stroked hers just as a door near the dais opened. Dressed in a black, tailored designer suit, he walked inside with that innate animal grace that never failed to take her breath away. Levi slipped out behind him and took up a position beside Tanner.

Silence fell across the room as the guests all turned their attention to Knox. Halting in the center of the dais near the stand, he spoke. "For many years now, demon lairs have kept to themselves. The U.S. has had no Monarch or power structure except within our own individual lairs. It has worked well. Yet, as you know, three Primes in this room have proposed a change. They believe it would benefit the U.S. to have a Monarch that oversees the other lairs.

"During the course of this weekend, each of the three Primes will put forth their case, present you with reasons why we should not only have a ruling Prime but elect them as said Monarch. Two weeks from now, the U.S. demon population will be asked to vote whether they are in favor of a change – if they are in favor, they will also be asked to state which candidate they wish to elect."

His face hardened slightly. "I would like to make it clear that although I have agreed to host this gathering, I am not in favor of the change. I believe that power structures simply don't work for demons. The extent of power that a Monarch would be given never fails to corrupt and bring chaos. But you each have to make up your own mind on that, and that's why we're here today."

Menace slithered into his voice. "There are rules that must be followed in order for this to be an effective democracy. Firstly, there will be no dueling between Primes, no threats, and no ultimatums. The decision made two weeks from now will be based on votes alone. If you wish to win those votes, you will need to present a civil case. Secondly, there will be no destruction of property – I will take it *very* personally if someone should violate that."

Harper gave Martina a meaningful look, who smiled reassuringly.

Knox scanned the room. "Are the rules clear?" There was a chorus of 'yes.' He nodded. "Good. The first Prime will put forward their case two hours from now. In the meantime, enjoy your dinner."

Stepping off the dais, he headed straight for Harper, looking very predatory in that moment. Following the lead of the others at the table, she politely stood to greet him, and his gaze roamed over her in a way that made her feel naked. When he reached her, he brushed his mouth against her cheek – not uncommon behavior between anchors.

"Harper," Knox rumbled. For the first time that day, his inner demon relaxed. It had obsessed over Harper every minute of every hour, which Knox would have snorted at if he hadn't been doing the same. It was like her scent, her taste, and the feel of her was all imprinted on his system so that he couldn't get her out of his head. *All I want to do is back you into the wall, flip up that dress, and fuck you so hard you can't walk.*

She smiled, knowing that her face was heating. *And they say romance is dead.* "Knox," she greeted in return.

Raul went to speak, but his anchor beat him to it. "It's a pleasure to meet you, Mr. Thorne. I'm Tanya." Going by the respectful way she spoke to him, Harper figured that Tanya considered Knox an equal. She also seemed to consider him fair game, if the sultry smile she gave him was anything to go by. Harper's inner demon hissed.

The woman was waiting for a reaction, Knox realized. She was used to males admiring and wanting her, and she was waiting for him to cast an appreciate eye over her. She was a female who knew how to play the seduction game – a game he hadn't realized he was so weary of until Harper came along. She outshone Tanya by far, and he wondered if either of the females knew it. Knox simply said, "Ah, you're Raul's anchor."

Tanya's face tightened, her cheeks turning pink. It probably made her more annoyed that Knox greeted the others by name.

No sooner had they sat down than the starters were brought out. Between each delicious course, various Primes came to their table and talked briefly with him. They wanted him to know that they fully agreed that electing a Monarch would be a bad move, and they were interested in his opinion on whether or not the demon public would feel the same.

All of them had heard that the missing strays were found, and it seemed that most of them suspected Isla had kidnapped them as part of a campaign tactic. The woman wasn't fooling these people; they knew her too well. They confirmed that she was the source of the rumors that Harper wasn't Knox's true anchor, and they were clearly hoping he would explain why Isla seemed to have such an issue with Harper. He didn't, though. His private business wasn't theirs to know.

Isla's very unhappy, Levi told Knox. *She's been watching you and Harper closely. Every time you introduce Harper to people as your anchor and they give her the respect and acknowledgment that she's due, Isla snarls at them.*

Watch her. Warn me if she approaches.

Quick question: Are you so on edge because Isla's nearby or because a lot of males are sending Harper admiring glances?

Both. The males were subtle about it, as if fearing it would trigger Knox's possessiveness as her anchor, but it still pissed off Knox and his demon. Tanya didn't appear to like it either, obviously feeling that all male attention should be focused on her. Whenever his anchor caught Tanya glaring at her, she'd glare right back until Tanya looked away. Then Jolene would cackle.

"The Primes are like a bunch of old women looking for gossip," Harper whispered when there was a lull in the visits to their table.

"Yes," he agreed, discreetly placing his hand on her knee beneath the table. For a moment, she froze. But then she relaxed under his hand, and his inner demon smiled in satisfaction.

There weren't many people who were relaxed around Knox. They were always on their guard to some extent, and it was wise of them to be wary. But the one person he'd never harm was Harper, and it pleased him and his demon that she believed that. No one could have blamed her for fearing him after witnessing what he could do, but she still trusted him with her safety. She probably had no idea what that meant to him.

"They're also looking for a weak spot in Isla," he told her, admiring the sapphire color of Harper's eyes. "We wouldn't be here today if she hadn't pushed for it. They don't want her to succeed."

"Why don't you just tell them that she's suffering from delusions?"

"I don't explain myself to people." He drew circles on her inner knee with his thumb, loving the velvety feel of her skin. "They seem to be drawing their own conclusions anyway. And no one appears to believe her lies about you."

She sipped at her champagne. "I got a call from Lucian earlier."

"He's heard about all this?"

"No, he's in Australia right now. He doesn't have a clue what's going on in the U.S. He probably wouldn't care anyway. Being a nomad, he doesn't consider himself to be a U.S. citizen."

"Did you tell him?"

"Nah."

"You didn't tell him about me either, did you?" Knox involuntarily clenched his hand on her knee. "That's why you didn't mention the election. You don't want him to come here."

Harper sighed. "I didn't tell him because I'm not yet sure if having him near Kendra is wise. If she *is* behind what happened to me, then I've no doubt she could target him too. And, I admit, I'm really not looking forward to him having a shouting match with you."

"He'll be that opposed to me being your anchor?"

"He's protective in his own way. He'll think I'm not safe with you."

Like Lucian was a stable presence in her life. "But you know differently. You know I'd never harm you."

"I know," she confirmed, watching as his eyes warmed.

"Good evening, Knox," said a familiar voice that made Harper inwardly roll her eyes. *Dear ole Malden*. He nodded at Harper before smiling at her grandmother. "Jolene, it's good to see you."

Jolene smiled, twisting in her seat to face him. "Oh, hello . . . um . . ."

Harper leaned into her grandmother. "It's Malc—"

"*Malden*," he stressed, a tic in his cheek going crazy again.

Smiling brightly, Harper clicked her fingers. "That's what I was going to say."

I'd feel sorry for him if it wasn't for the fact that I know he wants you, said Knox. Malden wasn't quite as subtle about it as the others, but Harper didn't seem to sense his interest any more than she sensed the interest of the others.

"Is it time for you to present your case already?" asked Jolene.

"It is." Turning to Knox, Malden said, "I hope I can change your stance on electing a Monarch."

Knox shook his head. "No one can do that." Malden just smiled enigmatically before disappearing. "He must think he has a convincing argument if he believes he can change my mind."

"Or he's just as delusional as Isla," suggested Harper.

The chatter died down as Malden walked onto the dais and leaned on the stand. Harper thought he looked oddly amused. "I never thought there'd be a day that I'd agree with Isla Ross on anything." That got some laughs, which hopefully irritated the bitch. "But she's right about one thing – we need better order. Knox Thorne also has a point, though. Our kind has never done well with power structures. It's in our nature to seek power, not to share it. And that urge to seek it is stronger in some than it is in others. But that is the very reason why we need an authority above others; we need a Monarch that keeps the peace.

"The other candidates will tell you that a hierarchical structure would work best." He shook his head. "There is no 'best' form of power structure for demons. There is only a solution to the problems we face. A Monarch – a demon that has power above all others – can provide that. And that is the only change I intend to make. I don't wish to introduce a structure, simply a Monarch."

Well, that's different from Isla's proposal, began Harper. *He probably thinks it will bring the Primes on board.* Knox gave an almost imperceptible nod.

"My wish isn't to rule you all. Demons aren't creatures to be ruled; we're free and wild, and we wish to stay that way. My intention is to guide, protect, and defend. The only thing I ask of you is this: You trust me to provide our kind with what we need. And what do we need? Quite simply, we need order. And we'll never have that as long as we're allowed to war with each other without consequences. We'll never have it as long as we don't know exactly what the general public wants, because that only breeds strife, unhappiness, and resentment."

Malden zoomed in on the camera, addressing the public. "Every decision shouldn't be made by your Primes with your best intentions at heart. You should all have a voice, all have a say in your own lives. That is what I am promising every demon out there in exchange for your trust: A voice.

"Should any of you have an issue that your Prime is not addressing, you can report to me. If any of you wish to complain of injustices committed by your Prime, you can report to me. If a lair is having problems because of another, they can come to me – avoiding disputes and wars. And if in the future I feel that changes need to be made, it would go to a vote; each and every one of you would be part of that decision. So if you want a voice, if you want peace and protection, vote for me."

Jolene drank some of her champagne. "Smart of him to promise a voice. To have a voice is to have an element of power. Every demon will find that an attractive idea."

"I don't think he wrote that speech himself," said Raul. "He isn't smooth enough."

Beck nodded. "Politicians rarely write their own speeches."

"Any questions?" Malden asked.

One of the Primes called out, "You don't want the lairs to exist on levels of power?"

"No. Such a hierarchy wouldn't work in the long run. It's too strict." Malden smiled as he added, "Demons don't like laws, they like loopholes. All I'm proposing is that I'm elected as Monarch – a demon with influence and authority above all Primes of the U.S."

"But is any kind of Monarch truly realistic?" asked Raul. "You're powerful, Malden, but there are Primes more powerful than you. How do you intend to exert authority over them?"

"If the demon public of the U.S. elect me as Monarch, they have given me that authority," replied Malden.

"Yes, but how would you *exert* it?" Raul persisted. "Knox Thorne has clearly stated he'll never answer to another. I don't think anyone's in a position to force him to do anything he doesn't wish to do."

Malden inclined his head. "I'd hope the other Primes, Knox Thorne included, would respect the opinions of the public enough not to dismiss my authority. Dismissing it would be a betrayal of every American demon."

Ooh, that was a clever answer, Harper told Knox. It would make her anchor the bad guy if he stood up to Malden, not the more powerful of the two. But she doubted that would bother Knox, since he didn't care for the opinions of others.

Raul turned to Knox as he said loud enough for everyone

to hear, "Honestly, what would you do if someone was made Monarch and tried interfering in your business?"

Knox replied coolly, "Ensure they reconsidered ever doing it again."

A Prime on a neighboring table spoke to Malden then. "Here's what I think will happen if you're made a Monarch. The demons scattered around the U.S. who are unhappy with the decision will request to join the lairs of Primes that they believe you can't overpower, thereby stopping you from having any say in their lives."

Malden considered it for a moment and then shrugged. "That would be their decision, and I would have to respect it."

"But don't you see the consequences of that?" asked the same Prime. "The lairs of the more powerful Primes would therefore grow. Knox Thorne already has a large lair. It would get bigger and bigger and bigger with every fuck up you made. And you *would* fuck up – all leaders do it sooner or later, because you just can't please everyone."

"He has a very good point," Jolene said to Harper quietly.

A Prime near the back of the room called out, "Think of what would happen if you started pissing off the Primes, Malden, or if they found they couldn't take being under the rule of someone else. They would all unite to overpower you . . . and then we're right back to where we are now. Sure, our kind has problems the way things stand now. But there will always be problems. To elect you *might* solve some of our issues, but it would just bring us new ones."

Murmurs of agreement spread around the room. A few more questions were asked before Malden stepped down and returned to his table.

"I have to say, Malden surprised me." Raul leaned back in his seat. "I didn't think he was taking this all that seriously."

"I thought he just wanted to avoid answering to another demon, but now I'm thinking he's very interested in being Monarch," said Beck.

"I don't believe any of the Primes will support him," began Knox. "None of them are interested in having a leader. But I think that if placed in a position where they felt forced to answer to someone, they would rather it was Malden, since he doesn't want to make many changes."

Jolene nodded. "The rest of the U.S. demon population, however, might very well be in favor of him."

And that was a scary thought.

CHAPTER ELEVEN

"Harper, if you don't want me to break the dog in half, you need to get him away from me *now*," Devon warned.

Sighing, Harper glared at Tanner, who sat further along the bench beside Devon, sniffing her. He'd accompanied Harper, Raini, Devon, and Khloë around the Underground while they went shopping before finally stopping at a restaurant . . . and he'd done nothing but taunt Devon the entire time. "*Tanner*."

"She doesn't need your help, Harper," said Tanner with a smile, his eyes on Devon; there was a challenge there. "She can take care of herself. Can't you, pretty kitty?"

"He's trying to rile you because he wants to know what you can do," she told Devon. It was a stupid move on his part, since Devon could seriously hurt him if she wished to do so.

Devon's smile was a little feral. "You want to know what I can do, pooch? I can shove my foot so far up your ass, you'll feel it in your throat."

"Now you're just lying." That got him an exasperated hiss.

Harper shuffled along the bench, making room between her and Khloë, whose attention was fixed on her BBQ wings. "Devon, come sit here." The hellcat did so with a huff. Harper turned back to Raini. "Now . . . you were telling me about everyone's response to Malden's speech last night."

"Like I said, most people don't like him much – he's got a real smarmy way about him." Raini paused to drink some Coke through her straw. "But his promise of a voice *really* got people's attention."

Devon nodded. "A lot of demons are mistreated by their Primes. They don't wish to leave their lair because it would mean leaving their home and family, but they also have no one to go to for aid. Malden is offering that."

"And the fact is that he's right – our Primes make our decisions for us," continued Raini. "We don't have a say whenever there are debates among the Primes, even though the results of the debates affect us. It doesn't bother everyone, but it does bother most."

Swallowing a bite of her steak, Harper frowned. "Does it bother *you?*"

"No, because I trust Jolene to always look out for us," replied Raini. "But not all Primes have the best interests of their lair at heart."

"And there are times when the other Primes overrule Jolene," began Devon, "which means that even though her actions benefitted us, they came to nothing simply because the other Primes didn't support her. If *every* demon had a voice, things like that wouldn't happen."

"Yeah," agreed Harper, "but I don't believe Malden would truly act on votes."

Devon's brows drew together. "What do you mean?"

"Seriously, why would someone in such a high position of

power leave major decisions up to 'the little people,' huh? He wouldn't. He would hold a vote, sure, but he wouldn't count the votes and base his decision on them. It would just be for show."

"Giving people the illusion of power so they didn't feel controlled when, in fact, they had no say whatsoever," Devon realized. "You're right. But I don't know if the public will see that and – *oh my God, stop sniffing me!*" She whirled on Tanner, who had moved so that he was once again beside Devon.

Wiping her hands with a napkin, Khloë stared at him curiously. "Why are you sniffing Devon?"

He smiled. "She smells like candy."

"Yeah? What kind of candy?" Khloë sounded genuinely interested.

"*Don't encourage him*," hissed Devon.

Khloë raised her hands. "Fine. Hey, Harper, how come Knox didn't join us for lunch?"

"Just because he's my anchor doesn't mean we're together 24/7."

"Yeah," said Khloë, "but you guys have been doing the hunka-chunka."

Devon's face scrunched up. "Doing the what?"

"You know . . . Riding the flagpole. Roasting the broomstick. Going deep into the bush. Pounding the punanni pavement."

"Stop, stop," laughed Raini, her hand on her chest.

Khloë rolled her eyes. "Prudes." She looked at the chuckling hellhound. "Come on, don't pretend you didn't know."

"I knew." He shrugged at Harper. "You wear his scent."

Harper wasn't sure she liked the sound of that. "I, what?"

Devon explained, "It happens sometimes when demons are—"

"Playing a little how's your father," supplied Khloë.

"—intimate for a while." Devon threw Khloë a look of exasperation. "But only if the intimacy exists on more than one level. You guys are anchors, so you're intimate on a psychic level. Having sex means you're also intimate on a physical level." She took a sip of her lemonade. "It'll wear off when you stop sleeping together."

"*If* they stop sleeping together," said Raini.

Khloë frowned. "Why would they stop sleeping together?"

"Knox's demon gets bored easily." Harper veiled the dangerous disappointment that knowledge caused her. The brands hadn't begun to fade yet, but they would soon enough. "Speaking of boredom, I'm done shopping, let's—" She cut herself off as four shadows fell upon them. Looking up, her stomach sank. Her inner demon went from laidback to infuriated in a heartbeat.

Harper knew who they were, but it was the small, nervous she-demon who had most of Harper's attention. She hadn't been this up close to Carla since she was a baby, hadn't realized just how very little they looked alike. Maybe it was petty, but she was grateful for that.

"We just wanted to stop and introduce ourselves," said the cheery male beside Carla. "I'm Bray, and this is my mate, Carla. It's a pleasure to meet Knox's anchor."

Harper forced a smile. "The pleasure's all mine." *He doesn't know,* she said to Tanner. *Carla hasn't told him I'm her daughter.*

That's why she looks terrified. She's afraid you'll blurt it out right in front of them and ruin the fabric of her little world.

I irritate her enough purely by existing, I don't need to go to extra measures.

"And these are our sons, Roan and Kellen," continued Bray.

It was so much harder than she'd thought it would be to look at her half-brothers and pretend she didn't know who they were. "Good to meet you both."

Roan, who greatly resembled Carla, nodded. "And you."

The younger brother looked more like his father. "Yeah, you too," said Kellen, eyes narrowed. There was a knowledge in his gaze that shouldn't be there. He knew something. What, she wasn't sure. *How*, she wasn't sure.

"This is Raini, Devon, and Khloë," said Harper. "And, of course, you know Tanner."

Carla stiffened at Khloë's glare. She knew the she-demon was a Wallis, and that seemed to increase the panic she was already feeling.

"We'll leave you to finish eating your lunch. We just wanted to formally introduce ourselves." Bray gave Harper one last bright smile and then headed for a table; his family followed, though Kellen was slow in removing his gaze from her. Only then did Harper's demon relax slightly.

"That kid knows something," whispered Raini.

Harper sighed. "I was thinking the same thing."

"I swear, I could disembowel that bitch and not blink an eye about it," Khloë practically growled. "I don't know how anyone can just stand there and treat their own daughter like she's a perfect stranger."

Harper moved to sit by Khloë and curled an arm around her. Her cousin's parents were fabulous; worshipped the ground their children walked on. Khloë knew from experience what a real parent was. She genuinely couldn't understand how Carla could have abandoned Harper. "She's not important, Khloë."

"That doesn't mean I can't visualize ramming a chicken wing up her ass."

Harper smiled. "No, it doesn't."

"How about we get out of here?" proposed Raini.

Devon rose to her feet. "Great idea. I'm done and – *stop sniffing me!*"

* * *

Knox had just finished a phone call with a difficult human business associate when there was a knock at the office door. He hoped it was Harper, since splaying her delectable body on his desk would go a long way to improving his mood. Instead, he found that it was none other than . . . "Isla." His inner demon snarled, not at all happy to see her despite their history.

Her smile was pleasant and gracious. "Good afternoon, Knox."

"Something I can help you with?"

She glanced around his office. "I've been at the hotel for almost two days and we've spent no time together at all. You always made time for me in the past."

Yes, he had. Whenever he'd looked at her, he'd remembered the child who had been dumped at the children's sanctuary, bruised and bleeding; it was almost a month before she'd spoken a single word. Whenever he looked at her now, however, he remembered finding Harper in an alley with two dark practitioners.

Isla took a step toward his desk. "How about we go get a drink? You can tell me what I've missed since we last spoke in New York."

"I don't have time for that." The words came out harsher than he'd intended.

"Why the cold shoulder?"

Why? Because Knox didn't trust her. She was quite possibly the person responsible for what happened to Harper. "I'm not what anyone would call 'warm.'"

Her eyes narrowed. "Is this because of the tiny confrontation I had with your imp?" Her tone insinuated that such an explanation would be dramatic.

"It certainly didn't win you any points."

"You've known her two weeks. You've known me—"

"How do you know how long I've known her?" No response.

"Shall I tell you what I think, Isla? I think you heard about Harper before the New York conference. I think you sent Silas—"

Her brow furrowed. "Silas?"

"—to test me. And I think there's a very good chance that you're the one who sent dark practitioners after Harper."

Isla appeared suitably offended. "I may not have any regard for the imp, but I wouldn't betray you by targeting someone in your life. And if you truly believed I *had* betrayed you in some way, you would have tried to kill me by now. I say 'tried' because, let's be honest here, you couldn't have killed me. You couldn't have brought yourself to do it."

"Is that what you think? You believe you can fuck with me and I won't retaliate?" His demon released a dark laugh at the idea. "I'm a lot of things, Isla – merciful isn't one of them."

She cocked her head. "You are quite fond of your little imp, aren't you? It's a shame for you that your demon won't form that same attachment. It means you'll have to give her up soon enough. So sad." Her voice hardened as she added, "If I wanted to hurt the imp, I wouldn't have 'sent' anyone. I would have gone after her myself. I don't use minions, and you know that."

"Yes, I do . . . and that would make you an unlikely suspect, wouldn't it? Maybe that's exactly what you're counting on." His next words came out in a dark rumble. "Hear me when I say this, Isla: If I do discover that you targeted my anchor, I'll destroy you."

"You truly believe she's your anchor?"

"I'm positive that she is. So do the wise thing and let this go, concentrate on the election." Her confidence crumbled, and she suddenly looked lost, reminding him of the terrified, injured child she'd once been. "Has it occurred to you that just maybe you convinced yourself I was your anchor back then because, at the time, you felt you needed one? That you felt you needed the assurance that someone would always be there for you, always protect you?"

Affronted, she argued, "I need no one to protect me."

"Not now. But back then, you weren't as strong."

She spoke in a low voice. "You always protected me in that place."

"I did. But not because I ever believed you're my anchor."

She was silent for a few minutes. "If you're so very certain the imp is your anchor, I will accept that. I obviously confused your protective behavior for being something more. It was my mistake. I apologize." She studied his face. "You don't believe me."

"You're a very accomplished liar, Isla."

She smiled. "That is true. You will just have to trust me."

"That's the thing: I don't."

Her smile widened. "You always were smart. Be assured, however, that your imp is safe from me." With those words, she strolled out of his office.

It was really no surprise that Levi, who had been guarding the door, waltzed inside. "I don't know about you, but I'm not buying a word of what she just said."

Knox sighed, sinking into his chair. "I can't say I'm all that convinced either."

"You know, I've always wondered . . ."

"What?"

"When we were in the sanctuary, Isla used to talk about going to live on a farm, surround herself with animals. You remember?"

"Yes."

"Instead, when she left us because she was pissed that you wouldn't accept her as your anchor, she joined a lair. She later became Prime of that lair, she took over human businesses, she enlarged her lair, she sought more and more power – even going as far as to have a vampire attempt to convert her in the hope that it would make her more powerful. Which it has."

"I know all this. What's your point?"

Levi folded his arms across his chest. "If Harper had denied being your anchor, would you have believed her?"

"No. I *know* she's my anchor." He knew it with every fiber of his being.

"And Isla believes you're *her* anchor. Let's say Harper had walked away from you instead of forming the bond."

"I wouldn't have let her walk away. I would have made her face the truth and accept reality."

"Reality . . . That can be different things to different people. For a very long time, Isla's 'reality' has been that you're her anchor but you just wouldn't accept it. I saw her face the day she left all those years ago. There was a lot of rage there. Rage, resentment, and spite. To her, you were rejecting her. '*Are you saying I'm not good enough for you?*' she asked. Remember?"

Knox drummed his fingers on the desk as he thought back on that day. "I remember."

"I can't help but wonder if Isla became a Prime, took over all those businesses, enlarged her lair, and made herself into something unique all in an effort to be your equal. I think she thought that being your equal would make you want her as an anchor. Only it hasn't, has it?"

Knox considered that for a minute. "It's possible that was her plan. But if that's true, I think she long ago abandoned that plan. She does the things she does now because she's become obsessed with gaining power. Anyone can see that."

"Yes, because power corrupts. The more power Isla got, the more she got a taste for it. But I don't think she wants to be Monarch of the U.S. out of greed. I think she wants to have control over *you*. Either to force you to accept the anchor bond or to punish you for *not* accepting it. She may not know why, but she knows that the one thing you can't tolerate is anyone controlling you. This would hit you where it really fucking hurts, just like you hit *her* where it really fucking hurts."

It made some sense, but . . . "I don't know, Levi. There are a lot simpler ways to let someone know you're pissed at them."

"Demons hold grudges, Knox – especially she-demons. Isla's got a big one. Not only did you deny her, you then declared another she-demon is your anchor. That would have sent Isla into a rage." Levi shrugged. "I could be wrong. Isla could be telling the truth. But I still believe her motivation behind becoming a Monarch is to punish you for turning your back on her. After all, wasn't that what her mother did when she killed herself? We know how much hatred she harbors for her mother."

Knox thought on how Harper had been abandoned by both parents, yet she wasn't filled with hate and bitterness. Oh, there was some righteous anger in her system, thanks to what she called with a roll of her eyes 'textbook abandonment issues,' but nothing corrosive. She still had the inner strength to bond with him and trust that he wouldn't do what her parents had done. Hell, she was stronger than most people he knew. And he wouldn't let her down. "Then it looks like Isla's our prime suspect, doesn't it?"

As he exploded inside Harper, Knox sank his teeth so hard into her nape it was a wonder he didn't taste blood. She slumped on the bed beneath him, tremoring with little aftershocks. She'd just gotten out of the shower when he entered the hotel suite, and he hadn't been able to resist bending her over the bed and fucking her into oblivion.

Knox licked over the fresh bite. His demon wasn't the only one who liked to mark what was his. It had been two weeks since the first time he'd had Harper in his bed, and boredom hadn't even begun to set in for either him or his demon. How could Knox possibly get bored of her? He liked her company. Liked having someone who was capable of surprising him, who didn't fear speaking their mind to him, and who wouldn't obey his every order.

When she'd dressed in Jolene's suite the previous night instead of coming straight to him on arriving at the hotel, it technically should have pissed him off a little. Instead, although he hadn't liked that she hadn't come to him, he'd found himself smiling. Even his demon found it amusing. Their little sphinx had her own mind and no one – not even him, except for maybe in bed – would ever control her. The frustration she caused him actually invigorated him.

"Now I'll have to get another shower," she grumbled.

Slipping out of her, he stood upright. "You can shower with me."

"If I do that, we'll end up fucking again."

"Of course we will."

"Which means we'll be late for dinner."

"Not if we get dressed quickly." He spanked her ass, making her shoot to her feet and whirl on him. "Shower. Now."

"Bastard."

His gaze roamed over her naked body, and his demon rumbled its satisfaction at the sight of the brands. "You'll still let me fuck you."

She snorted as she strode past him, chin up. "Don't be so sure." But she did, in fact, let him take her again.

Half an hour later, they were both ready to leave. And the sapphire strapless dress that had a slit which ran from knee to mid-thigh made all sorts of fantasies swirl around his head. "I'm not sure what I want most – to flip up the dress or to whip it off altogether while I fuck you fast and deep."

"Well, I might let you do one of those things. *Later.*"

"Before we leave . . . " He dipped his hand in his pocket and pulled out a square, velvet jewelry box that made her tense.

Harper's eyes widened when he opened it, revealing a white gold necklace that had diamonds hanging from it like raindrops. She'd never seen anything that beautiful. "Holy fuck. Are those real diamonds?" His expression said 'Don't insult me.' She blew out a breath. "I can't accept this."

"Of course you can."

"I told you I didn't want you buying me expensive things."

"Yes, you did. But I didn't tell you that I'd listen. If I want to buy you things or spoil you, I will." It was almost cute how awkward she looked. He got the feeling no one had ever spoiled her. "Turn around."

She grimaced, twisting her fingers. "What if I lose it or break it?"

"You won't," he chuckled. "Turn around." He chuckled again when she stiffened her shoulders like she was going into battle. Slowly, she turned and he put on the necklace before trailing his finger down her spine. With a shudder, she turned to face him again. "Beautiful." He cupped her hips and pulled her flush against him. "You'll leave it on later when I have you again. Maybe just wear that and the heels."

She laughed. "Let's go get this dinner over with."

He sucked on her earlobe. "Tanner said you saw Carla today."

"Only for a few seconds."

"What did she say to you?"

"Not a single word." His eyes flashed demon. "Don't get mad. It doesn't matter."

It did fucking matter, but Knox wasn't interested in darkening her mood. Clutching one breast, he plumped it up to get another glimpse of the brand.

"Do you know how hard it's been to find dresses that don't flash this brand?"

Knox licked over it. "People would just think it's a tattoo."

"Right," she drawled. "It has *thorns* on it. Anybody who saw it would have known what it was. Then they would have wondered if just maybe Isla's little rumor about me being your new bed-buddy is true."

"Anchors sometimes have sexual relationships."

When he pressed a kiss to her neck and followed it with a nip to her pulse, she moaned. "Come on, we've got to get to this dinner thing."

"I'd rather eat you."

"You can't say stuff like that when we have to leave," she whined.

"Nothing tastes better than you do," he rumbled in her ear, his hand proprietary as it splayed over her breast.

"You're doing this on purpose."

"And nothing smells better than you do."

"Tanner said I smell of you."

He arched a brow, tightening his hold on her breast. "That a problem?"

"I kind of thought it might bother you."

"It doesn't."

As his hand snaked under her dress and cupped her, she gasped. "Don't even—"

"Be still." He slipped one finger inside her panties and thrust it inside her. "Nice and slick for me." Withdrawing his finger, he sucked it clean. "Now I feel better."

She shook her head at his crooked smile. "You're such a bastard." But she didn't pull away when he closed his hand around her wrist and led her out of the suite. With Levi and Tanner as guards, they made their way to the restaurant. It wasn't until

Knox took his seat that the food was served. They sat at the same table as the previous evening; once again, they were joined by her family, Raul, and Tanya.

"Nice necklace," commented Jolene, eyes narrowed.

Harper cleared her throat, feeling awkward again. "Thanks."

"I take it Knox bought it for you."

"Yep."

Don't think I don't know something's going on between you two.

Harper had known this was coming. *Grams, leave it alone. It's no big deal.*

It is, sweetheart. Jolene's telepathic tone was soft, understanding. *In the early days before I met your grandfather, Beck and I were . . . close. It didn't last long and it wasn't serious, but it made things complicated when we both met other people. He was jealous of your grandfather for a long time. I'm not telling you to break things off with Knox. That's your business. But I want you to be prepared for how hard things will be for a while. It passes with time, but it's still hard. Don't kid yourself into thinking that it's 'no big deal.' That's all I ask.*

Harper nodded. *Thanks for the advice, Grams.* Sensing Knox's stare, she realized he was looking curiously at her. "Everything okay?"

He leaned closer, bringing them into their own little cocoon. "Who were you talking to?"

"I was just chatting to Jolene." His expression turned expectant; he was clearly waiting for her to repeat the conversation. "You're so damn nosy." His smile was unrepentant.

Like yesterday, the food was amazing. It was mere moments after the tables had been cleared that Knox went rock solid at her side. "What is it?"

"Hello, Knox," said a pleasant voice. *Isla.* How delightful.

"Isla," he greeted simply.

Her lips briefly thinned before breaking into a polite smile as her gaze swept along everyone at the table. "I hope you all enjoyed your meal. I must say, Jolene, I was surprised that your family joined us this weekend. I wouldn't have thought your lair would particularly care about the election. After all, you haven't bothered much with political events in the past."

Jolene's smile was all teeth. "How could we miss this? We're looking forward to watching you crash and burn." Yeah, her grandmother had no tolerance for Isla, since she believed the bitch sent the dark practitioners after Harper.

Isla's pleasant act disappeared. "You would do well to remember that there's a high chance I'll soon be an authority over you."

"'High chance' might be overstating things a little."

"I suppose you believe you can offend anyone without consequences now that you're linked to Knox through his anchor."

"At least you're acknowledging that I'm his anchor," said Harper, not entirely convinced Isla genuinely believed that.

"As I said to Knox when we spoke earlier today in his office, if he's so very certain that you're his anchor, it must be true."

Harper nodded. "Yeah, *he's* not the delusional type."

With one last fake smile, Isla headed for the dais.

Lifting her champagne flute, Harper quietly said to Knox, "You didn't mention Isla paid you a visit."

"I was distracted by . . . other things."

Picking up on his insinuation, she snorted.

"Are you still wet?"

She nearly choked on her drink. "Of course not, I'm bone dry." He just chuckled. "Do you think she's honestly accepted that she's not your anchor?"

"I doubt it."

"It seems it's time for Isla to have her moment," announced

Jolene as the vamp-banshee leaned on the stand. Silence descended, but it was a wary silence.

"Good evening, everyone," said Isla with a courteous smile. "I have long believed that it should be a basic right for each demon to have a say in their own life, which is why I have fought hard to have this election and enable every demon to have a say in this matter." She looked at the camera as she continued. "Many of you will already be aware of my opinion that it will benefit our kind to implement a pyramid hierarchy of power within the U.S. Malden will tell you that a hierarchical system will never work." She chuckled. "But this is the same person that said the Underground would never be a success, and look where we all are now."

To be fair, that was a good point.

Gratification lit her face. "There is no stronger preternatural species than ours. None. We can pride ourselves on that, and we do. Yet, our kind suffers more deaths than any other species. Why? Because we have no laws, we have nothing at all in place that gives us any protection – not from outsiders, and not from ourselves.

"Lairs target each other in the hope of expanding their power. In doing so, they cause suffering to their own. How is that beneficial for us? How many of you have lost people you cared for? How many of you have suffered because of such greed? I do not feel I can allow that to continue, and I find it difficult to believe that any of you can overlook this."

If I didn't know what good a liar she is, I might have bought that devastated look on her face, said Knox. His concern was that many others would buy it.

"It is not simply strays and small lairs that are vulnerable," she continued. "Each and every one of us are in a weak position when it comes to the matter of our main enemies – dark practitioners. Do we unite against them? No. Primes are so busy keeping power for themselves that they are blind to the truth. We have made ourselves easy prey. Demons are not built to be prey. We are predators through and through. Still, this is what we have done to ourselves. Apart, we are vulnerable. Together, we are strong."

She focused on the camera. "If I am elected, I will put in place a pyramid hierarchy that is similar to the layout of authority that exists within each lair. A constitution will be formed that stipulates and restricts the power and influence of each level within the hierarchy. Primes will still have power, but they will also have regulations that prevent them from warring with each other. This will protect all of you."

Her hand balled into a fist. "Our kind needs a Monarch that will bring changes, will find solutions, and will give equal rights to every demon. Malden promises us all a voice, yet his lair stole my campaign materials and removed them from every establishment within the Underground." Whispers traveled around the room, and an angry flush marred Malden's cheeks. "That not only takes away my voice, it takes away your right to have an unbiased opinion. He doesn't promise you a voice. He promises you the illusion of a voice."

Even Harper could admit that much was true.

"What do I promise you? Security. A guarantee that no one will ever again target you, no matter who you are – a stray, an average demon, a Prime. If you elect me, I will build a Force that will protect us against dark practitioners; a Force that will hunt down and punish those who have taken our friends or families. I will provide protection for strays, who have the right to be without a lair *and* still have the protection that every other demon is granted. I will ensure that lairs are no longer able to terrorize others.

"This is not just about electing a Monarch, it is about choosing how our kind would like to live. None of us want our species to remain prey. You can change that. How? By electing a Monarch; by electing me. I hope you make the right decision."

"That was a clever speech," allowed Jolene. "And that worries me."

Isla smiled, spine straight. "If anyone has any questions, I will be happy to answer them."

A female Prime called out, "What makes you think a hierarchy will be better than simply having a Monarch?"

"Look at your lairs. You have a hierarchy within each one, do you not? It helps maintain order. It makes people feel secure, because they know exactly where they stand. It helps the demons on the lowest level of that hierarchy feel secure, because they have the knowledge that they are protected. Rules and regulations keep things running smoothly. At present, we do not have those."

There was a small silence before another voice asked, "How would you choose where each Prime exists within such a hierarchy?"

"The decision would depend upon their individual level of power. They need to be strong enough to hold their position."

"Why?" a different Prime asked. "You're promising a future without war. Why does it matter if they can hold their position?"

"Demons respect power," she replied as impatience very briefly flickered across her face. "A Prime on a high level would need the respect that ensures Primes on levels below them take their authority seriously."

"But what about the Primes *you* decide should be placed on the lowest level?" called out Malden. "They would have no real power at all. It would only be a matter of time before they started challenging Primes on higher levels in an attempt to overthrow each other."

"They would need my permission to battle; such a rule would be in writing."

Jolene scoffed. "And we're supposed to wave that piece of paper at any lair who bothers us and hope it makes them go away?"

Isla's jaw clenched. "If a Prime did such a thing, they would be severely punished."

"But the damage would already be done," Malden pointed out.

"Yes," allowed Isla, "but once they were punished, the rest of our kind would be very hesitant to do so again."

"You say that small lairs are vulnerable now," began another Prime. "Your plan – which would include placing us on lower levels – would simply make us even more vulnerable."

"You would have the protection of the higher levels."

That same Prime addressed everyone as he asked, "Can any Prime in this room say they haven't punished one of their Force or sentinels for abusing their power over the other lair members? The same would happen to each Prime if a hierarchy was implemented," he told Isla. "That power would be abused, and the vulnerable would pay for it."

Isla shook her head. "If we implement my hierarchy, there would be better order, less demons being harmed, and safer streets. In addition, we would not have divides. We would effectively be united. It would put us in a good position if somehow our existence was exposed to humans."

Someone from the back of the room snorted. "It's been exposed many times to humans, and we've dealt with it each time."

"Yes," agreed Malden. "One point I want to make is this: if you really had such faith in your own plans, you wouldn't try to attack my character and my promises by fabricating stories about me stealing your materials."

She regarded him with disappointment. "You and I both know it's the truth."

Raul spoke then. "I asked Malden this question yesterday, and I'll ask you the same thing. How do you think you can exert your authority over Primes who are more powerful than you?"

"There are few Primes more powerful than me," replied Isla, her tone arrogant. "In any case, I don't need to be more powerful than someone to exert authority."

Raul snickered. "How else could you keep someone like Knox Thorne in check? If you tried to punish him, he wouldn't stand there and take it. He'd retaliate."

"Knox would never harm me."

Harper turned to Knox. "I think she truly believes that."

"He and I go back a long time," Isla went on. "We have too much regard and respect for each other for him to harm me."

Raul raised a brow at Knox. "Is that true?"

"I wouldn't *like* to harm you," Knox told her. "But that doesn't make you safe from me. And I'll never give you or anyone else any power over me." Never in his life would anyone ever control him again.

That response had Raul smiling. "Let's pretend you've been elected, Isla. You're Monarch. He's refusing to do what you want. So, what do you do?"

Face hard, she responded, "Punish him, of course."

"How? How can you be expected to take him on?"

"All of us here would stand united against any crime committed. That means we would unite against him. I doubt even Knox could defeat us all as a unit."

"And what if we don't want to join you in standing against him?" asked the Prime directly behind Harper. "What if we'd rather mind our own fucking business?" Some chuckled at that.

"That would be considered a betrayal."

Raul sighed, waving a dismissive hand. "Maybe the public might be in favor of your hierarchy. But as far as I'm concerned, there's nothing realistic about it. Like Malden, you'd be biting off more than you can chew."

She licked over her front teeth. "I'm sorry that's how you view things, Raul. It's true that we can keep our ways as they stand. But then our problems will also remain. Think on that."

CHAPTER TWELVE

There were certain types of people who were only interesting when they were drunk. Dario was one of those people. Sadly, he wasn't drunk.

As he did his best to convince Harper that electing a Monarch would benefit the U.S., she got the feeling he was hoping that if he could get her onside, he could thereby get Knox onside. Snort. No one had that kind of influence on Knox. The idiot should know that.

Glancing at the reception desk, she saw that Knox was still there; flicking through papers with the concierge, who had rushed to him as they exited the restaurant not long after Isla's speech. Knox had left her with Tanner while he quickly helped his staff deal with something. Dario must have seen it as an opportunity to speak with Harper without any interference.

"Isla was correct when she said that electing a Monarch could bring some form of order," said Dario. "But, like Malden, she wants to be Monarch for all the wrong reasons."

"Is that right?" Harper's disinterested tone didn't faze him.

"What they want isn't order. It's power. Nothing more, nothing less."

"Hmmm."

"They're not interested in the well-being of our kind. Surely you see that."

She sighed. "Let me just save you some time, Dario, and make it clear that nothing will warm me to the idea of having a Monarch."

"Then you're failing to see the bigger picture." He stepped close to her, *too* close. Beside her, Tanner growled, but Dario didn't seem to notice. "You're a smart girl, Miss Wallis. I can see that sharp mind right there in your eyes. You have to know that electing a Monarch is the way forward." He held out his hand. "How about you and I go to the bar, discuss this further?"

"Why would we do that?"

Knox's mind brushed against hers, bringing a shocking vibe of black jealousy. *Why is Dario so close he's practically touching you?*

He's just trying to get my vote. And she didn't appreciate the accusatory tone of Knox's voice . . . like she was flirting with the asshole or something.

"Dario," Knox drawled as he and Levi joined them. Knox didn't return to her side. He moved to Dario's side instead, but his focus was on Harper – his brooding eyes glittered with jealousy, possessiveness, and anger.

As Dario turned to face Knox, he immediately stepped back at his dark expression. "I was just talking with your anchor."

"I see that." And it took everything Knox had not to gut the prick, especially while his demon's predatory possessiveness was whipping through him. It wasn't just because Dario had edged into Harper's personal space. It was because not only was there a covetous glint to his eyes, a greedy desire to possess, but because Dario was telepathically broadcasting that desire loud and clear.

Knox was powerful enough to pick up stray thoughts and images from people's minds if their shields weren't solid. Dario was very clearly imagining Harper naked beneath him, her legs wrapped around him while he fucked her hard. *Not* a picture Knox wanted in his head.

He could understand Dario's urge to have her. Harper was beautiful, unique, without guile, and so aloof that it was a challenge to any male demon worth his salt. Knox had picked up that challenge. But she was also *his* and . . . and now Dario was fantasizing about her sucking him off.

"I suggested that she and I could go to the bar for a—"

"That won't be happening," Knox rumbled. "And neither will the shit that's going through your head."

Dario paled. "We were just going to discuss the election, that's all."

Knox could sense Dario doing his best to clear his mind, to keep a firm grip on his fantasies, and to focus totally on Knox. But, as if the pressure was simply too much for him, Dario's fantasies all burst out of that mental grip and flashed through his head like a flicker pad: images of him fucking Harper, tasting her pussy, tying her up, sucking on her nipples, having her ride him, and forcing her to suck his cock . . . It was too much for Knox, and it was far too much for his demon.

Harper inwardly cursed as Knox's eyes bled to black. Head tilted, the demon slowly advanced on Dario like a predator closing in on its prey. The rage emanating from it sent apprehension prickling down her spine. Hey, just because she knew it wouldn't hurt her didn't mean it wasn't a scary fucker – especially when she had seen for herself exactly what it was capable of doing to someone that pissed it off.

To Dario's credit, he stood his ground against that chilling presence. She had no clue what was going on, but she could sense that Knox's demon was seriously unhappy.

"I see what you want," it told Dario, who swallowed hard. "I see it all." It slowly shook its head. "You can't have her. She's mine."

Clearing his throat, Dario nodded. "Understood."

Yeah? Well she was glad *someone* understood, because Harper was still a little confused here. She looked from one male to the other as Knox's demon retreated. "I really hope that wasn't about me. We were only talking about the election."

Knox turned to her. "Really?"

"Yes, he thinks that—" Harper nearly jumped out of her damn skin when an ice-cold fingertip flicked her clit. No, he *hadn't* just done that in public! He hadn't just—

She jerked as the same fingertip circled her clit, making it heat and tingle. Oh, the bastard.

Dario frowned at her. "Are you all right?"

"You don't look too good, baby," commented Knox, ensuring he looked the image of concern. "Your cheeks are flushed. Must be all the champagne."

An icy finger slid through her folds, and Harper had to lock her knees to stay upright. *Stop it*, she hissed. Knox didn't. As he and Dario talked, the finger casually slid through her folds over and over, pausing now and then to play with her clit. She didn't know how something so cold could give off so much heat. *I will kill you for this*. The psychic finger sank inside her, and she couldn't hold in a gasp.

Brow creased in worry, Knox moved to her. He stroked a hand over her hair and down her back to rest on her ass – an unmistakable display of masculine possession. "Maybe you should go upstairs and lie down."

I'm going to rip your cock off and—

A second finger joined the first; they scissored, stretched, and swirled. Despite her best efforts to withstand the pleasure, her knees buckled. She had to grab onto Knox's shirt for support.

He curled his arm around her. "Seems like the champagne's definitely gotten to you. Dario, enjoy your evening." There wasn't an ounce of sincerity in the latter words. Knox guided her to the private elevator that would take them straight to the top floor. All the while, those icy fingers continued to pump.

You'reamotherfuckingcocksuckingpsychopathicsonofabitch!

A hard thrust of those fingers wrenched a gasp from her. At this point, her pussy was flaming and throbbing – *needing* him so badly it was all she could do not to sob. But he was being a dick.

When Levi and Tanner went to step into the elevator, Knox shook his head. "Take the stairs." The sentinels nodded, giving him a knowing smile.

The moment the doors closed, she whirled on Knox with a growl. Before she could say a word, his mouth crashed on hers and his tongue shot inside. The kiss was dominant, possessive, and devastating. He forcefully backed her into the wall, making the breath slam out of her lungs. His hands shackled her wrists and held them high above her head – the entire time, the psychic fingers continued to drive her to the brink of insanity.

Knox kicked her legs apart and used his lower body to pin her in place. "Look at me." As she did, her eyes changed from amber to gold; they blazed with a raw need that made his gut twist. He fucking burned for her. He was hard and hurting, aching to be in her, to feel her pussy clenching and squeezing him. But not yet.

As the fingers picked up their rhythm, Harper moaned and bit hard on her lip. Being unable to move, unable to arch into the thrusts, only increased her frustration. But she didn't fight him, knowing from experience that the sadistic bastard would slow down to punish her if she didn't let him lead.

"Good girl, take it." Upping the pace of the thrusts to reward her, Knox sucked on her earlobe. "Did you know that if I stopped now, you'd stay like this? You wouldn't be able to finish yourself off. It wouldn't matter how hard or how many times you fucked yourself with your fingers, it wouldn't matter if you turned to someone else – which you wouldn't, or I *would* fucking kill them for even daring to touch what's mine." He stared into eyes that were glazed over with lust. "Only I can take that ache away once I put it there, Harper. Only me."

"Knox, I'm really, really close to coming." At that moment, they reached the top floor. His hand shot out and punched the emergency button before the doors could open. Then the cold, tormenting fingers dissolved, making the blistering ache inside her even worse. "No!" she sobbed.

"Tell me you want my cock in you." Defiance flared in her expression. He arched a brow. "If you want it, you have to tell me."

She licked her lips. "I want your cock in me."

He peeled up her dress, hoisted her up, and unbuttoned his fly as she curled her limbs around him. "Are you protected?" he rumbled.

She nodded. Demons had invented contraceptive pills before humans.

"Good. I want to shoot my come inside you. I want you dripping with it." He plunged inside her, groaning as her pussy clamped around him like a vise. "I love that you get so fucking wet for me." He drove into her again. "And I love being in this pussy. Tight. Hot. Slick. And mine."

Harper clung to him as he brutally powered into her at a furious pace – taking everything, demanding everything. She was so hot and hypersensitive inside and he was so big that it should have been painful, but nothing had ever felt better than his cock stretching her, filling her to bursting.

"Tell me you belong to me, Harper," he growled. Her eyes narrowed. "Say it."

She snarled. "Now you're pushing it." He stilled, pinning her with his dark sensual gaze that suddenly glittered with danger and caution. She froze instinctively.

"Say it," he rumbled, his tone dominant and implacable.

"I'm your *anchor*, so you have rights to me," she conceded. "But I belong to me." He smiled crookedly, but it didn't relax her – there was nothing reassuring about that smile.

Knox punched his cock inside her once, twice. "Oh, you're so wrong, baby." The words were soft yet insistent. "You belong to me."

She shook her head. "You'll give me up." He'd have no choice once his demon lost interest. But resolve was suddenly etched into every line of his face.

"No." He drove deep once more. "I won't."

"Your demon will make you do it." She swallowed hard as his eyes bled to black.

"No, little sphinx," countered that familiar emotionless voice. "You're ours."

It began ruthlessly ramming into her at a feverish pace. For a few moments Knox regained control, groaning about how hot she was, how her pussy was made for him. Then the demon was back, driving so deep inside her she knew it was in her womb. Again and again they switched, so that she was being ferociously fucked by both Knox and his demon. Neither gave her any reprieve.

As her pussy tightened and fluttered around his cock, Knox knew she was about to come. "Wait," he ordered.

"I can't," she sobbed.

But he knew she would; she always did. Even when he shifted his angle, hitting her sweet spot, she held back for him. "Good girl. You can come now." He growled low in his throat as her blazing hot pussy squeezed and rippled around him when she came, screaming. "Fuck." He jammed his cock deep and exploded, shooting jet after jet of come inside her.

Eyes closed, she slumped over him as tremors racked her body. Knox hit the emergency button to release the elevator and then pyroported into the bedroom of their hotel suite. His little sphinx was so wiped out that even the lick of flames against her skin didn't disturb her.

Carefully, he laid her on the bed and removed her clothes before removing his own and settling beside her. Shudders were still rocking her, but her panting had eased. As his arm slipped around her and pulled her against him, she opened eyes that were now a jungle green.

"Why do I get the feeling that the public psychic finger-fucking incident was brought on by Dario's thoughts?" she asked.

"Because it was."

Her brow furrowed. "I'm confused."

Toying with her necklace, he explained. "I didn't like seeing him so close to you. It was bad enough that he'd been watching and ogling you all night." Her frown deepened. "You never notice when males are staring at you, but trust me, they do." He smoothed his hand down her back. "But I picked up some of his thoughts. He was imagining you and him in some very—"

"La, la, la, don't tell me, I don't want to know." She juddered, not at all turned on by the idea of Dario touching her in any way. "So, why did I get sexually tormented?"

"I was reminding you that you're mine." He buried his hand in her hair, loving the fruity smell and silken feel of it. "I'm not used to being possessive of another person. It's also very new to my demon. Neither of us are good at processing it yet. Downstairs, I wanted to disembowel Dario. My demon was leaning more toward burning him alive on the spot. The only reason it held back was that Dario didn't dispute its claim on you."

"Its claim on me?"

"You haven't worked it out yet? It wants to keep you. It wants to take you as its mate."

It was only right then, as happiness threatened to burst through her, that Harper realized she'd gone and done what she'd always feared doing: she'd fallen for a demon. Fallen hard. Technically, it should have made her want to run. It didn't, though, because she wanted him more than she wanted to protect herself. So why *didn't* happiness fill her at the thought that he felt the same? She generally distrusted any situation where she got what she wanted. In her experience, if it seemed too good to be true, it wasn't at all true.

"Always so wary," Knox mused with a smile.

"See it from my point of view. You were very clear that your demon would soon lose interest. Now you're saying it wants me to stick around."

"Not just 'stick around.' It wants to keep you. Collect you. Own you." The entity inside every demon was incapable of caring for others; it didn't have the emotional capacity for that. But when it became as firmly attached to a person as Knox's demon now was to Harper, it wanted to own them – and it never let them go. "It has always been possessive of you. So possessive that it branded you. Twice. But downstairs, the depth of its possessive fury surprised me. Then I sensed what had built that possessiveness to such a level, what fueled it. And I understood."

"Good, 'cause I have no idea what you're talking about."

"You gave it what no one else has ever given it: total acceptance."

"But your sentinels—"

"Are loyal to me, but there's still that wariness of me and my demon. And there should be. They're smart to fear us. But you . . . you believe it will never harm you, you *trust* it to never do so, and you accept it despite your fear." She'd watched it call on the flames of hell, watched it destroy two practitioners. But she hadn't backed away, even though there had been fear in her eyes and scent. The demon usually liked the scent of fear, but it hadn't liked the taint of it in Harper. "And even though it spooked you a little downstairs with its jealousy, you didn't reject it just now. In doing all that, you sealed your fate. It's keeping you."

"You know, it's possible that this is because I'm your anchor. The demon could be a little confused—"

Knox shook his head. "It doesn't think of sex on the same level that it thinks of anchors. To the demon, the first is a basic need, and the other is a psychic need. This attachment it formed to you isn't about needs, it's about *you*." He tucked her hair behind her ear. "My demon's so powerful that it considers everyone prey. That's part of what makes it very easily bored, but that also makes it lonely.

"When the demon pursues a female, it's more about the conquest. It doesn't think of any woman as unique, they're interchangeable to it. And it reads people so well that it sees everyone as predictable. But you . . . it never knows what you'll do or say next. You not only pretty much snort at my forceful personality, you stand up to the demon if you think it's pushing you too hard. You intrigue it and accept it. Like I said, you sealed your fate."

It was all very well that his demon wanted to keep her and

take her as its mate, but . . . "What about you? What do you want?"

"I'm not a good choice for you, Harper." He wouldn't lie to her. "I don't have a lot of good in me." When she looked like she might argue, he said, "I'm not a self-loather, I'm a realist. The truth is that I'm as cunning and calculated as they say. I manipulate, I hurt, and I destroy to get what I want. You've seen what I'm capable of. You can imagine what damage and pain I can cause. I'd never harm you, but I have and I will harm others if and when I have to. I'll always be ruthless and controlling. You can do better. But . . . it's too late for you. I told you before, you belong to me. I won't let you go."

It wasn't because she was his anchor, it was because she was Harper. He had always considered himself too emotionally disconnected to ever want a mate. Especially since he was so restless and discontented despite having everything he wanted . . . or maybe it was *because* he had everything he wanted. The fact was that he was just as attached to Harper as his demon was. Neither he nor the predator within him was willing to give her up. "There's no going back."

As he bent to lick over the brand circling her breast, she asked, "You're not going to ask me what I want?"

"No." He latched onto her nipple, sucking hard. "It's not relevant."

"What do you mean *it's not relevant*?"

Her prickly tone made him smile. "You know how our kind works. They never give up what's theirs. Do you honestly think that anything you say would make me walk away?"

"Did it occur to you that I might not want to walk away?"

Not really. His little sphinx had a lot of issues. "Are you telling me that, for once, you're going to accept a claim on you without a struggle? That you want me as your mate?"

"Well, yeah. I can't exactly struggle when me and my demon are just as gone for you and yours, can I?" The crooked smile that always heated her blood surfaced on his face.

"No, you can't." He rolled her onto her back, hiked up one leg, and drove himself deep. "All mine."

If there was one thing capable of shitting on Knox's mood, it was coming out of the shower to hear Harper arguing with an irritating fucker via her cell phone. 'Royce the Rodent' Khloë called him. Knox thought it was an accurate description. The human persisted in sending Harper apologetic text messages that she pointedly ignored. But the silent treatment didn't seem to be working, because he was bothering her again. The human definitely needed dealing with.

As she ended the call and turned to Knox, her expression inscrutable, he growled, "The human?"

Harper nodded. "I told him he has to be mistaken but . . . he said there are snakes outside my apartment."

Nothing she said could have shocked Knox more. "There are, what?"

"I gotta go there."

Minutes later, Levi drove them and Tanner to her apartment. As they pulled up outside and she caught a glimpse of exotic-looking snakes slithering over her front door, she shuddered. "That's just freaky."

Royce, who was leaning against what was presumably his car, came rushing over as they exited the Bentley. "I told you I wasn't lying. Do we call pest control?"

Knox dismissed the human with a look. "We can take things from here. You can go."

Royce bristled. "I'm staying."

Knox ground his teeth. If they had the time for this shit, he would be happy to deal with the fucker. Right then, they had more pressing matters. "Go, Mr. Yardley."

"Don't think you get to tell me what to do." Royce clenched his fists. "I'm not stupid, I know you're sleeping with Harper. But I also know it won't last. You've got a reputation for being a player. He's not serious about you, Harper. Everything I've read about him says he's never been in a real relationship and he doesn't want one. He's just using you."

Tanner growled. "Okay, you really need to leave."

"No, Harper's—"

"Mine," stated Knox silkily, pushing into the human's personal space until they were nose to nose. "That means you are no one to her, and she is no one to you. Are we clear?"

Harper went to speak, to tell Royce to leave, but Levi gave a quick shake of the head. She understood. Knox needed to deliver his warning. It was a guy thing.

"You'll throw her aside within a week. I'm the one who loves her." Ignoring Harper's snort, Royce went on, "If I hadn't messed up and she hadn't left me—"

"I'd have taken her from you," finished Knox. He wasn't lying. He'd have pursued Harper whether she was single or not; he'd have done whatever it took to lure her away from the human in front of him. "Like I said, she's mine. You *will* stop calling her, stop texting her, stop bothering her at work, and stop turning up at her apartment. Or life could get very, very hard for you."

"Are you threatening me?"

"I don't like rhetorical questions." Knox's demon was dangerously close to the surface, stirred by both the human and the immediate threat to Harper. The demon's ire slipped into his tone and expression as Knox added, "In simplistic terms, if you don't leave now, I'll make your life hell in a way you can't even comprehend. Trust me, you don't want that."

Whatever Royce saw in Knox's eyes made him blanch and take a step back. Knox slanted a glance at Levi. Understanding, the sentinel urged the human to his vehicle. Royce ranted a little about being manhandled, but he eventually sped away in his car. Knox threaded his fingers through Harper's as he led her toward her apartment. "He's a waste of skin, Harper. I don't understand what you saw in him."

"Me neither. But I'm more confused by *this*." As they came to stand in front of her door, she said, "I mean, what the fuck? Why would—?" A snake coiled and launched itself at Harper with a speed that shocked her. "Shit!" A hand shot out and caught it before it could reach her. Hellfire rushed from Knox's hand to engulf the snake's body. Then it was gone; completely vanquished. "Um. Thanks."

"I've seen this before. The snakes aren't real. We can touch them, and they can bite. But they're not animals, they're part of a spell. Unravel the spell, and they disappear."

"Dark practitioners at work again," Tanner growled, radiating more protective energy than usual as he stood beside Harper – probably because Knox had announced to him and Levi in the Bentley that he'd taken her as his mate. Neither sentinel had seemed all that surprised.

Harper turned to Knox. "You said this is a spell. What kind of spell? I mean, what is its purpose? To stop me from going inside?"

"The intention isn't to keep you out of your apartment," said Knox, 'feeling' the energy of the spell and 'reading' it. "There are more snakes inside. All poisonous and in an aggressive state. Their venom is preternatural, and it has one purpose."

"What does it do?" asked Levi.

"Corrupts," replied Knox. "Whatever they bite will decay, rot, and degenerate to ash."

Harper gaped. "Are you saying that if their venom touches any of my stuff, it'll basically crumble to nothing?"

"Yes. But their target is *you*."

As if to prove it, another snake launched itself at her. Tanner caught that one and sharply folded it backwards, snapping its neck. Ooookay.

"Oh my God!" exclaimed a female voice behind them as Levi destroyed the last two snakes with small balls of hellfire.

Turning, Harper blinked. It was obviously a day for surprises. Knox and his sentinels all positioned themselves in front of her.

Knox asked suspiciously, "What are you doing here, Carla?"

The woman clasped her hands in front of her as she slowly walked forward, dancing her alarmed gaze from Knox to where the snakes once were. "I, um, I wanted to talk to Harper. Larkin wouldn't tell me where she was – only that she wasn't in the hotel. I thought she might have gone home."

Knox narrowed his eyes. "Is that so?"

"Where did the snakes come from?"

"Now that's a very good question."

Carla stumbled before coming to an abrupt halt. "You suspect me?"

More interested in the little matter of a spell being put on her home, Harper asked Knox, "Can you unravel the spell?"

He shook his head. "Only another practitioner or an incantor can do that." Incantors were demons that could use magick.

"I know a few incantors," said Levi. "I can call one, have her come down here. She should be able to understand and untangle the threads of the spell."

"You do that." Knox curled an arm around Harper. "Come on, let's go."

As Tanner opened the rear door of the Bentley, Carla stepped forward. "Wait, Harper, I – I was hoping we could talk. Just for a minute. Please?"

Harper cocked her head. "Why? You want to make nice with me to be sure I don't ask Knox to cast you out of the lair? Or are you panicking that I'll blab about our sharing of DNA to your family?"

Carla's shoulders slumped. She looked defeated and hurt. "I should have known there was no point in this. The imps have all turned you against me."

Harper snorted. "Oh no, Carla, you did that all on your own." Harper hopped into the Bentley, puffing out a long breath. What a fucking day.

Sliding close to her, Knox combed his fingers through her hair as the car began to move. "You okay?"

"No, I'm pissed. As if it's not bad enough that someone wants me dead, I had a lot of sentimental stuff in my apartment from all the places I've been. It's a good chance that most of it is ashes now. I'll have to buy new furniture and—"

"No, you won't. You'll be living with me."

Her eyebrows flew up. "Is that a fact?"

He curled his hand tight around her jaw. "If you think I'll let my mate live apart from me, think again."

"Such charm." She ignored Tanner's snicker.

Knox slid his hand from her jaw to her throat. "There's no sense in us living apart."

"Hm."

"And you love the mansion."

She forced a snort, even though it was totally true. "Where did you get that idea?"

"You relax when you're there."

That was also totally true. She felt safe there. Not only because it had top security measures, but because there was an unexpected restful atmosphere to the place that allowed a person to wind down. Meg's merry nature and fantastic cooking probably helped with that, just like Dan's innate positivity. Harper couldn't help but soak it in. Still, she shrugged, trying to seem casual. "You have a nice bathroom." A very decadent bathroom that contained a large, circular bath made of black granite that had Jacuzzi jets.

Knox went to speak again but stopped as Levi told him, *Carla's crying. I think she expects me to hug her.*

Ignore the 'poor me' routine.

I am, but there is something she said that you might be interested in hearing. She claims that Kendra drove past her as Carla was making her way here. Now what would Kendra be doing down these parts?

Yes, what *would* Kendra be doing there? *I'll have Keenan bring her to me.*

"Was that Levi? Is Carla being a pain in the ass for him?" Harper asked with a small smile.

Knox looked at her. "Yes, it was Levi."

His tone was . . . off. "Something wrong?" His hesitation made her tense. "Don't lie."

"Carla told Levi that she passed Kendra on her way to your apartment." *Keenan, find Kendra and bring her to the boathouse.* The building was on the same grounds as his mansion.

Will do, Keenan replied.

Harper frowned thoughtfully. "Odd that Kendra would be in North Las Vegas. She considers the place and everyone in it to be very much beneath her. But if you're thinking she had something to do with those snakes, I really doubt it."

"Why?"

"I've been thinking a lot about the things that have been going on, and about just how each of the suspects operate. Kendra has a serious issue with me – there's no denying that.

And she seems to think we're competing in life somehow. But that's exactly why I think that if she did something, she'd want me to know for a fact that it was her. She'd want me to know how smart she is, that she won. I don't think she'd hide behind compulsions and dark practitioners."

"She'd have to if she wanted to live," Knox pointed out. "She knows that killing you is a death sentence simply because you're my anchor." He wondered how Kendra would take hearing that Harper was now also his mate.

"Maybe. But I wouldn't put it past Carla to lie about seeing Kendra just to shift the suspicion onto someone else. Don't overlook that possibility."

"I won't," he assured her. Still, Carla was the least likely suspect to him. Harper was undeniably a threat to Carla's world, and there was a possibility that the people so curious about Harper would uncover Carla's connection to her. But there were easier ways for the woman to deal with this than to get rid of Harper. She could instead do damage control and make peace with Harper so that if the truth came out, Carla could act the regretful mother who did love her child. It did appear that, by approaching Harper, it was in fact her plan.

Isla and Kendra had more reason to want Harper dead. Both resented her because both believed she had something that should have been theirs – in Isla's case, her anchor; in Kendra's case, her father. Isla was cold and cunning, and she would think nothing of ridding the world of Harper. Kendra was angry, jealous, spiteful, and bitter; that was a bad combination that could drive someone to do cruel things, including kill her half-sister for having everything she didn't.

One thing was for certain: Whoever was targeting his mate would soon know a pain like no other.

CHAPTER THIRTEEN

Harper was surprised when Tanner pulled up at the mansion, since she'd expected them to go straight back to the Underground. As usual, Dan gave Harper a big smile as he opened the front door. "Good to see you again, Miss Wallis."

"Thanks." She still wasn't all that great at dealing with the courteousness. "One question," she said to Knox as he guided her through the mansion. "Why did we come here instead of going back to the hotel?" Dario would be giving his speech later.

Knox led her into his bathroom, and she gasped. "I asked Meg to get a bath ready for you." Meg had clearly taken it upon herself to add jasmine-scented candles and a glass of red wine.

"Not that I'm not eager to hop into that thing but . . . Why?"

Pulling her flush against him, he pressed a lingering kiss to her mouth. "You're upset." She didn't show it, but he knew well that she was hurting at the idea that her own mother might want her dead. "As I mentioned before, you relax here." And he wanted to take care of her. But she was so damn self-sufficient, so used to having only herself to depend on, that she always turned a little awkward when he tried to take care of her. She didn't quite know how to handle it. He watched an array of emotions cross her face as she held back the awkwardness, rolling back her shoulders to push away her tension.

"Thank you," she finally said.

He smiled in amusement. "Hard, wasn't it?"

She gave him a mock scowl that turned into a grimace. "Shit, I didn't bring any clothes with me."

"You have clothes here."

"You mean all the expensive designer stuff you bought that I told you to take back?"

"They're just clothes, Harper." Before she could rant, he sucked her bottom lip into his mouth. "Hear me now, because this is important. I know you feel uncomfortable about this and I understand why, but I *am* going to buy you things. I *am* going to spoil you. I *am* going to take care of you when you need me to. Because I want to. Because you deserve it. Because that's what mates do. Rejecting the things I do or give you is much like pushing me away."

"You know that's not what I'm trying to do."

"I do know that, which is why I'm not mad. You wouldn't like it if anything I did made you feel that I was holding you at a distance."

"You *do* hold me at a distance. You're very tight-lipped about your past and what you are. I get it," she quickly assured him. "I really do. It's nothing personal to me, it's just that you're so used to keeping secrets it's uncomfortable for you to share, and it's not like your secrets are small. *But* you can't call someone your mate and keep important things from them. I'm not saying you have to spill your guts here and now. I wouldn't ask that of you. But if we're really going to build something, you're gonna have to do a little sharing."

It sounded so simple, yet Knox knew it would be far from it. His past was as dark as the truth of what he was. She was strong enough to handle both, but he didn't want her to have to – and he didn't want to run the risk that she'd leave. Still, she was right; there had to be honesty between them. "I'll try sharing if you try accepting things from me."

"Compromise," she drawled. "All right, I'll try."

"Good girl."

Knox, began Keenan, *we're here.*

I'll meet you in the boathouse.

"Levi again?" she asked, sensing a telepathic exchange. "Has the incantor arrived to undo the spell?"

"No, it was Keenan." With one last kiss, Knox released her. "Enjoy your bath, I'll be back soon."

"Remember that little conversation we just had about secrets and compromises?"

His demon chuckled, oddly delighted by her astuteness as opposed to irritated by the fact that they'd never get anything past her. Knox sighed. "I asked him to bring Kendra here. They're in the boathouse."

"You're going to question her."

"Of course."

"But you don't want me to be there."

"Once Jolene pointed out that Kendra was probably your half-sister, did you feel bad that you'd caused her soul-deep pain?" He already knew the answer. Harper had a tough exterior, but she was soft on the inside.

"A little," she admitted. "We're not emotionally sisters, we don't have a bond. But . . ."

"I might have to hurt her, Harper. I don't want you to see that."

Harper ran a hand through her hair. "I really don't think she's behind all this."

"You might be right." But he wasn't willing to risk it.

"Okay, I'll stay." She was too damn tired emotionally to deal with Kendra in the same day she'd dealt with Carla and yet *more* dark magick bullshit.

Knox kissed her. "I won't be long."

Strolling into the boathouse, he found Keenan leaning against the wall as he stared at the she-demon squirming in a chair. She haughtily lifted her chin as Knox moved to stand in front of her. Despite her efforts to appear cool and collected, her nervousness was easy to sense. But . . . was she nervous because she was the culprit they were looking for? Or was she nervous because being brought in front of her Prime was never a good thing?

"What's this about?" she finally asked.

"I'd start with the question, 'Where were you tonight?' But I already know the answer to that. And I find it confusing."

The squirming stopped, but she didn't speak.

"You knew people were watching you, didn't you, Kendra? You slipped away so they wouldn't know where you were going. Why would you do that? More to the point, what reason could you have for being in North Las Vegas?"

"There's no law against going there."

"That doesn't answer my question." He took a single step forward, letting his rage show in his expression. She blanched. "My patience has been tested too many times tonight, Kendra." The words came out a dark rumble. "You don't want to push me. Or did you enjoy your last punishment so much that you want a repeat?"

Fear glimmered in her eyes; she was no doubt recalling being forced to swallow a ball of hellfire for confronting Harper in the restrooms – it had burned her mouth, throat, windpipe, lungs, stomach, and intestines before fizzling away. Merciless, sure, but he'd been through worse at five years old.

"I was meeting someone at a bar there," she admitted.

"Why?"

"It's personal." She jolted when he conjured an orb of hellfire. "They know the location of a demon I'm trying to find," she said in a rush.

"By any chance, would Lucian Wallis be the person you're trying to locate?"

Her face went slack. "You know . . . ?"

"That he's your biological father? Yes. That you hate him for having no part in your life? Yes. That you hate Harper for having what you didn't? Yes." Casually, Knox repeatedly bounced the orb of hellfire in his hand. "Do you hate her so much that you want her dead? That you would use dark practitioners to help achieve that little dream?"

She gasped in sheer horror. "What? No! I won't lie and say I have any pleasant feelings for Harper Wallis. I don't. Never will. And since I value my life, I wouldn't risk it for someone who means nothing to me – attempting to kill your anchor would indeed put my life at risk. And I find the idea that you believe I would ever associate with dark practitioners very offensive." The woman was haughty through and through.

"You do? I find the fact that someone tried to kill Harper very offensive."

"You should have thought of that before you declared she was your anchor. In doing that, you put a target on her back. It's true that it keeps her safe from the majority of the demon population. But you have many enemies. They see her as a way to get to you. Most of them will never act on that out of their fear of you. But some will be too stupid or simply too hungry for vengeance to care."

He knew that. It was why he'd assigned Harper a bodyguard. In a world so brutal, she was still far safer being known as his anchor than as a she-demon of a small lair.

"If she's in danger, it's because of *you*."

"Or maybe it's because of *you*, Kendra." Knox crushed the orb of hellfire in his hand. "Maybe it's because you despise her for having everything you wanted."

Kendra laughed. "You think I'm jealous that she had *Lucian Wallis* for a father?"

"You speak of him with such contempt," observed Keenan. "Yet, you're trying to find him. Why?"

"I want to confront him. I want to tell him what a bastard he is for leaving my mother so broken that she turned to alcohol for a comfort that it was never going to give her."

"One way to strike out at him would be through the daughter he acknowledges – the only person he has any real regard for," Keenan pointed out.

"I don't want him to hurt because *she's* hurt. I want him to hurt because the truth hurts. He needs to hear the truth of what he did to my mother."

"Maybe that's true," said Knox. "But not for one second do I believe that you don't hate my Harper with a passion."

"*Your* Harper?" Her upper lip curled as bitterness wafted from her. "So you *are* fucking her. I wonder how long it will be before your demon tires of this one. I suppose it won't be long, since she's an imp and a W—"

With a snarl, his demon shot to the surface. "I thought you value your life," it said.

She shrank in her seat, eyes wide. "I – I do."

The demon had no pity. "Never insult what belongs to me."

"I'm sorry," she whimpered.

Knox resurfaced, but she didn't calm – most likely due to the fury thickening the air and making the floor tremble. "Hear me when I say that if I discover you had anything to do with the attacks on Harper, I will destroy you, Kendra. Not fast. But slowly. Very, very slowly. The pain will be far worse than you can ever imagine. So agonizing that you'll beg for death. But I wouldn't give it to you. No, because that would be merciful. And we both know I'm a cruel, ruthless bastard. You might be a nightmare by breed, Kendra, but I'm everybody's fucking nightmare."

She licked her lips. "It wasn't me, I swear it wasn't me."

"Then you'll get to live the life you claim to value. If not, you die."

Who would ever need so many clothes?

Wrapped in the softest towel ever, Harper puffed out a long breath as she browsed through the things in the huge closet, forcing herself not to check the price tags. The clothes ranged from casual stuff to evening dresses. The lingerie in the drawers were all pretty raunchy, as were the sheer, scraps of lace she was assuming were nightgowns.

Hearing footsteps, she turned to see Knox striding into the room. "Well?"

He fingered her wet locks. "Kendra claims it wasn't her. Unsurprisingly. She says she met with someone who could give her Lucian's current location. Apparently, she wishes to confront him."

That didn't sound good. "Do you think she means to hurt him?"

"Physically? I don't believe so."

"She'll get a shock if she does. He's got abilities that freak even me out. And I have eyes that frequently change color – there isn't much stuff weirder than that."

Knox looked into eyes that were presently mercury. "Do you get that from Lucian?"

"Nope. I don't know if it's a trait that's in the genes somewhere or just a real freaky defect."

Knox nipped at her bottom lip. "They're not freaky or a defect. They're unique, just like you." He smiled at her mumbled 'Whatever.' "Feeling better?"

"Yes, actually." Her eyes sharpened. "In fact, you look tenser than I was. I guess it's always a shitty thing to have to interrogate a member of your own lair. What?" He had the oddest look on his face.

"You referred to the lair as mine."

She gave him a pitying smile. "It is yours, sweetie. Did you hit your head?"

He ignored the tease. "But you're my mate, which means you're part of it now."

Shit, she really hadn't considered that. And it presented her with a problem, since . . . "Knox, I don't want to leave my lair."

"I know that you don't. And I know that trying to demand it of you would gain me nothing but frustration. So we'll compromise and say you're part of both lairs."

"Wow." She'd expected an argument. "You're good at this whole compromising thing."

He brushed his mouth against hers. "I'm someone who chooses his battles wisely."

"You sound like a parent who's letting their child win the little battles so the poor thing has the illusion of control and independence." But she couldn't be annoyed, because he flashed her that lopsided smile that made her stomach clench.

Knox glanced at the closet. "Have you picked anything to wear yet?"

"Do you realize there are three times more clothing in here than there are in my wardrobe? Of course, there's a chance that most of the stuff in my wardrobe has been destroyed by the snakes," she added glumly. Sure, they were only clothes. But a lot of them were from various places around the world, they carried good memories.

"We can go to your apartment to check the damage after Dario's speech, if you want."

"Yeah, I'd like to see what survived the spell." Casting another frown at the full closet, she asked, "Can't you just pyroport us straight to the hotel suite where my dress is?"

"No. I was seen leaving, so I need to be seen returning."

"Ah, you like to keep people guessing about what abilities you have."

He shrugged. "They don't need to know."

"Fine." She grabbed underwear, socks, a pair of blue jeans, and a white shirt. "Notice that I am snapping off the tags without checking the prices. I will just pretend they aren't designer clothing and you got them from thrift shops."

He smiled. "If that makes you feel better . . ."

Knox? called Levi. *We need to talk.*

Now?

Yes. It's important, he added with an urgency in his voice that made Knox tense.

I'll be at my office in the hotel in ten minutes, said Knox. *Meet me there.*

Don't bring Harper. I'll explain when we meet.

"Now you're even tenser than you were before," commented Harper as she pulled on the jeans.

She was too observant for her own good. "Levi has something

he wishes to speak to me about. In private." She regarded him with a blank expression, and Knox expected her to bristle. Instead, she shrugged.

"Fair enough."

Knox arched a brow. "Fair enough?"

"I'm not a sentinel, so I get that there are things I won't always hear about unless you okay it first. I don't expect to be told everything – unless it's related to me, in which case it's *totally* my business."

That truly *was* fair enough, but he had to meet her halfway here. "I won't keep secrets from you unless they're not mine to tell."

Buttoning her shirt, she gave an approving nod. "I can work with that."

On arriving at the Underground hotel, Knox sent Harper and Tanner upstairs to their suite while he headed for his office. Levi was already waiting near the door, jaw clenched and eyes hard. It wasn't until they were both inside the office, door closed, that Knox spoke. "Tell me."

"The incantor came to Harper's apartment and unraveled the spell. Ella said it was quite an advanced one. The practitioners that we're looking for would have been expensive to hire."

That information helped, but . . . "You didn't need to speak with me privately about that, so I'm guessing there's more."

Levi toed the chair in front of the desk around and straddled it. "Carla was leaving when Ella arrived. Ella recognized her, said she'd never forget the face of 'that heartless bitch.' She knew Carla from a long time ago – a time when Carla had once been pregnant."

Knox stiffened, instinctively knowing he really wasn't going to like this. "Go on."

"Apparently, Carla wasn't just angry back then that Lucian

left her while she was pregnant. She was angry that he got her pregnant. She tried to abort Harper."

Knox cursed as anger rose sharply within him. His demon snarled, just as enraged.

"But it didn't work, obviously. So Carla went to an incantor and asked for a spell that would kill the baby."

"You're fucking kidding me," he growled, the anger of both him and his demon spiking.

Levi shook his head. "I shit you not. She told the incantor, Dawn, that she didn't want any part of Lucian inside her – that she was looking forward to telling him and his family that his child was dead. Dawn didn't want any part in killing a baby, and she doesn't believe that magick should be used for such a thing. Making it worse, Carla had even asked if there was any way of trapping the baby's soul in a container, so that she could taunt Lucian that his child would never have peace."

This time, his demon roared its anger. It took every single ounce of Knox's control to keep the entity from reaching for dominance and exacting that anger on its surroundings. He knew his eyes had briefly flashed demon when Levi stilled. "I'm fine," Knox told him. "Tell me the rest. I need to know."

"As I said, Dawn didn't want any part in it, but she knew others would do it for a price. So she placed a protective spell on the baby instead. Then she went to Jolene and told her everything."

Shock froze Knox's thoughts for a moment. "Jolene knows about this?"

"Jolene paid Carla to carry the baby to term and then hand it over. And that's exactly what Carla did." Levi's gaze turned speculative. "So I'm guessing you'd really like to rip Carla Hayden apart, limb from limb."

Knox's demon thought it was a fucking fantastic idea, but in

Knox's opinion . . . "That would be too lenient." His voice had come out guttural. If Carla's plans had been successful, his mate would never have lived.

"I agree. I don't judge people who seek abortions, although I don't like the idea of them. But I *do* fucking judge someone who wants to trap a child's soul." Levi crossed his arms over the top of the chair. "Are you going to publicly announce that Harper's your mate?"

Knox sensed that Levi was trying to calm him by changing the subject, so he went with it. "I won't make an official announcement, I'll simply let the news spread." He'd only need to mention it to one person for it to reach everyone. "I want the demon population to know she's taken. And there's a chance that just maybe it will shift the anger of who's targeting her to me."

"You think so?"

"Whoever's after Harper is carrying a lot of rage, but they didn't act on it until I made it public that she was my anchor. There could be two reasons for that. One, they don't want good things happening in her life, maybe even resent it; if that's the case, hearing she has a mate will infuriate them. Or two, the fact that *I'm* her anchor set them off; if so, they really will be pissed to hear I'm now also her mate. In both cases, it's the fact that *I've* entered her life which has changed things. That might redirect their anger onto me."

"You do realize Harper will know what you're doing, don't you? She won't like you setting yourself up as a target."

"Tough," Knox snapped, "she'll just have to fucking deal with it. Why are you smiling?"

"I like that you're not so divorced from your feelings when it comes to her. She makes you happy. Nothing's ever made you happy. Things have pleased and pleasured you, but that's all." Levi cocked his head. "What's it like? Having a weakness, I mean."

"She's not a weakness."

"Of course she is. It's not a bad thing. Before, you kept yourself alive purely because of self-preservation. Now you live for her. There's no better reason to live than for your mate. But we both know that you and your demon would lose all control if you ever lose her – it's the one thing that could truly hurt you. That makes her a weakness as well as a strength."

Knox knew that Levi was right. He could remember the rage he'd felt when he found her in the alley with the dark practitioners; could remember almost losing the control that kept him and his demon in check. Would Knox care about the damage his rage caused everything around him if he lost Harper? No.

"But hey, maybe we don't need to worry so much. Let's face it, if you lose her and lose your control, you could destroy the fucking world. Only someone who wants to die, start a war, is a rogue, has a tiny IQ, or who is simply completely insane would harm her when they learn she's your mate."

Since insanity wasn't exactly rare among their kind and there were plenty of rogue demons out there, Harper still had threats to her safety.

"Have you told her what you are yet?"

"Not yet." His hesitation was clear in his tone.

"Harper doesn't scare easily."

"No, she doesn't. But my kind aren't supposed to walk the Earth. You know what they say – what's born in hell should stay in hell." Contrary to what humans believed, there were much worse things in hell than Lucifer.

"You'll have to tell her soon. You'll also have to tell her the truth about Carla. I wish she didn't have to hear this shit, I really do. But it's better if she's on her guard around Carla, if she doesn't buy the 'please let me talk with you' routine."

"I can't talk to Harper about it until I've spoken to Jolene and

I have all the facts. But I *will* tell her." He could never keep a secret like that from her, especially after his assurance that he wouldn't withhold anything from her that concerned her.

"How do you think Harper will take it?"

"*That* I don't know. She always manages to surprise me."

Figuring that it was likely that Jolene was in her suite, getting ready for the dinner that would start in an hour's time, Knox and Levi headed straight there.

Jolene, already dressed in a lilac suit, looked surprised to see him. "I was expecting Beck and Martina. Come in." She peered around him. "No Harper?"

"No," replied Knox as he closed the door, leaving Levi outside to guard the suite. "I thought it was best that she wasn't present for this conversation."

One of Jolene's brows slid up, making him think of Harper. "Oh? She won't like you deciding what's 'best' for her."

"She won't like learning you've lied to her all her life either."

Jolene narrowed her eyes. Realization appeared to dawn on her quickly, so she obviously knew this could only be about one thing. "I really don't believe this is any of your business."

"Harper's my—"

"Anchor, but that doesn't entitle you to know everything."

"It does when I'm her mate."

Jolene sighed. "I suppose I should have expected that." Taking a seat on the sofa, Jolene crossed one leg over the other. "She's one of a kind, isn't she? Special."

Yes, she was.

"It's hard to imagine that this might have been a world without her in it. Suck some of that rage back in before your demon takes control."

"Why the lies, Jolene?"

"How did you find out?"

"A friend of Dawn recognized Carla and mentioned it to Levi," replied Knox. "Why didn't you tell Harper the truth? Or, if you were so set on lying, couldn't you have told her a kinder one?"

"You think I should have told Harper that her mother sought magick that would end her life and trap her soul just to have vengeance on her father?" Jolene sniffed. "That would be hard for anyone to handle, and it could have made her reject both parents. Yes, I could have told her a kinder lie. But that would have risked Harper one day making the decision to seek out Carla. And at least this way if Harper ever discovered the truth, it wouldn't be too much of a shock. She already knows Carla's selfish and cruel."

"You know another thing I don't understand? Why you gave Harper to Lucian. You could have raised her yourself. She deserved better than what she got."

"Do you think I wanted to give her to him? I cried for days. But it wasn't easy for her being the only Wallis who wasn't an imp – it made it worse that her parents weren't around. I needed her to realize that the problem wasn't her, it was them. If that meant she lived with Lucian to find that out for herself, so be it. And it worked. You can't deny that."

No, he couldn't. It didn't mean he had to like it.

"Are you going to tell her the truth about Carla?"

"We're *both* going to tell her." Knox opened the door and swept out a hand. Jolene didn't move. "If it doesn't come from both of us, the truth will hurt her even more. I won't have that." After a long silence, Jolene grabbed her purse and followed him out of the suite.

Once in the elevator, Knox told her, "Tonight, someone put a death spell on Harper's apartment."

Jolene's face hardened and the elevator began to slightly

rattle. Quick enough, the rattling stopped. "She's fine." It was a 'she'd better be fine' statement.

"Of course," he said. "Shit would be burning down if she wasn't. That's twice now that dark practitioners have targeted Harper. So it would seem that the culprit likes to use magick to get what they want, especially when what they want is vengeance. A little like Carla."

"You think she could have sent the practitioners?"

"You don't?"

Jolene's expression turned pensive. "She tried to kill Harper once before. I guess it wouldn't be a shocker if she tried it again."

"Don't play dumb with me, Jolene. You're an astute, shrewd woman. I don't believe for one second that you haven't already considered it might be Carla."

"I have her watched, much like you. But she'll be expecting that, so she's not going to do anything incriminating. She'll be very careful about who she's seen to associate with. But you don't have to *see* someone in person to associate with them, do you?"

"You're monitoring her calls and emails, aren't you?"

"Of course. But she'll be expecting that too. She's telepathic, so it's possible that she's communicating with unsavory people that way." Jolene pointed a finger. "Don't let this blind you to the fact that it's equally possible that Kendra or Isla is the mastermind."

Reaching the top floor, they exited the elevator and headed for Knox's suite. "Kendra went to North Las Vegas last night."

"Yes, she's looking for information on Lucian's whereabouts."

He smiled. "Her informant works for you, doesn't he?"

"Imps are liars and cheaters by nature. But we don't betray our own. He'll send her on a wild goose chase, which will hopefully get her away from Harper."

Tanner, who was guarding the door, frowned at Knox.

"Everything okay? You have some serious anger radiating from you."

Of course he did. "Levi will fill you in on the details. I need to talk to Harper." With that, he left his sentinels outside and led Jolene into the suite. They found Harper in the living area, talking on her cell phone. Knox picked up Raini's voice, but he didn't hear the words. He was a little distracted by how stunning Harper looked in a pastel blue dress.

Looking up, she smiled. "Hey, Grams. Raini, I'll call you later." Glancing from Jolene to Knox, she said, "All right, what's going on?"

Jolene sat on the sofa opposite Harper. "I won't begin this by saying *'there's something you should know,'* because honestly, sweetheart, I don't think you need to know this. It will only hurt you. But Knox insists that you should have the truth. So if that's what you want, you can have it."

Harper again looked from Jolene to Knox, who was now sitting beside her. "The truth about what?"

When Jolene didn't respond, Knox spoke. "Carla."

Harper twisted her mouth. "Let's hear it."

Jolene flicked her hair away from her face. "She didn't dump you on my doorstep. I've had you in my care since the day you were born. I was actually at the birth." She paused. "I paid her to carry you to term and hand you over."

"You paid her?" Harper easily read between the lines. "She wanted to abort me." Her grandmother nodded. While that didn't exactly make her feel warm inside . . . "I could have handled that, Grams. Why not just tell me?" But there was only one reason Jolene would have kept it to herself. "It gets worse, doesn't it?"

"Carla sought out an incantor's help when the abortion didn't work. She didn't just want you dead, she wanted to trap your soul."

Nice. Her inner demon curled her upper lip, ready to hunt down the bitch.

"It wasn't to hurt *you*," Jolene quickly added. "I don't think she even saw you as a person. She's so self-centered that she couldn't see past her own desperate need for vengeance."

"I was a pawn she was hoping to use to hurt Lucian."

"It wasn't a story I wanted you to hear as a child. But I had to give you a story that was close to the truth – close enough that you would never wish Carla was in your life, that you knew you were better off without her."

"You could have told me everything when I grew up."

"You'd been hurt enough. I didn't think telling you the rest would serve any purpose other than to hurt you more."

While a part of Harper was pissed that Jolene had withheld the truth, she understood. She also understood something else. "I was wrong."

"About what?" Knox asked, waiting for Harper to start ranting. She seemed too calm.

"I always thought Carla hated me. But I wasn't a person to her."

Jolene sighed. "When you were eighteen months old, we came across Carla in a store. It was one of the times Lucian came to visit. He was holding you, laughing at something you'd done, when Carla rounded the aisle." Jolene looked at Knox. "Whatever you might think about Lucian, he loves Harper. He truly does. And right then in that store, Carla saw that. She hated it." Jolene moved her attention back to Harper. "She started yelling that children should be with their mothers, she tried to grab you. You slapped her hand. And then she was sobbing on the floor."

"I used my ability?" Her inner demon was seriously smug about that.

"At eighteen months old, you reduced the bitch to tears. That day, she was *forced* to see you as a person – a powerful child that couldn't be manipulated and used against Lucian. A child even more powerful than she is. She wanted to hurt *your* soul, and instead you were able to hurt *hers*. Ironic, really." Jolene paused. "You understand why I didn't tell you?"

"I'm not mad at you. I get it. I would rather have known the truth, but I get why you didn't tell me." She gave Knox a half-smile. "Thank you for ensuring I knew the truth."

Knox frowned, once more surprised by his mate. She wasn't crying, she wasn't yelling, she wasn't condemning Jolene, and she wasn't vowing to see Carla dead and buried. She just wasn't normal. "I expected tears. A little ranting."

"Why? It's not like I didn't already know that Carla's twisted. Am I upset? A little. I mean, no one wants to hear that their mother tried to abort them, do they? But honestly, I always thought it was kind of odd that she *didn't* abort me, considering that would have hurt Lucian more than dumping me on Jolene's doorstep. It made no sense to me that she went through the birth. So I'm not really that surprised by all this."

"You're not upset about the soul-trapping part?" Knox fucking was.

"Well, yeah, but how can I take it personally when she didn't *see* me as a person? The fact is that a demon that's lost its mate is a very dangerous thing. She considered Lucian her mate, and he rejected her. He didn't even want her as his anchor. Everything she did as a result of that wasn't about me, it was about her. And look, it's all backfired on her, hasn't it?" So much so that her inner demon was smirking.

Gazing at his mate, Knox shook his head, musing, "So unpredictable."

Harper shrugged. "I just think that if someone has a problem with me, well it's their problem to deal with. Why should I feel bad about it? I'm not responsible for what other people do or don't feel. Carla didn't want a child – that's not my fault. She craved vengeance – also not my fault. So why torment myself with it?" As her cell phone started ringing, she grabbed it from the table in front of her. "It's Devon." No doubt Raini had told Devon and Khloë that Harper had taken Knox as her mate. Harper hadn't wanted them to find out from the grapevine. "I'll be back in a second."

When Harper shut herself in the bedroom, Knox turned to Jolene. "She has a very unique way of looking at things. I like that."

"Lucian's partly responsible for her outlook on life, you know," Jolene told him. "He's aloof to anything that doesn't directly affect him, he isn't personally threatened by the opinions or actions of others, and he doesn't take life too seriously."

Knox growled, "He's an asshole."

Sighing tiredly, she shook her head. "You insist on seeing him as this evil person. Harper didn't have a terrible upbringing, it was just different. He passed on a lot of good traits to her – the independence, the confidence, and even the directness."

"He's selfish and ignorant."

"He is."

"He put his own needs before hers."

"In some ways, yes. You've heard all about Lucian the partying playboy. His playboy-ways stopped the moment he took Harper to live with him. He also stopped doing drugs and partying too hard. Yes, he dragged her around the world with him. But Lucian *loves* traveling – it's the only thing in life other than Harper that brings him any joy. Sharing that with her was really the only thing he could give her.

"He honestly believed that exposing her to different lifestyles and cultures would be good for her. If at any point I'd thought she was unhappy, I'd have insisted he return her to me. But she liked to travel, even though it had its ups and downs. She has little knickknacks from all over the world. They're all important to her, because they all have good memories attached to them."

"She deserved better," he insisted.

"But she might not be the person she is today if it wasn't for the upbringing she had. There are so many people out there who've had horrific childhoods filled with abuse and neglect and cruelty."

Knox knew that too well.

"Harper never suffered any of that. Lucian is self-centered and has the emotional age of a kid. But he never hurt her. Never will."

Knox leaned forward. "Jolene, if I thought for even a second that he had, he'd be dead by now."

Jolene actually cackled. "I really do hope I'm present when you two meet."

"When who meets?" asked Harper as she reentered the room.

"Lucian and Knox."

Harper's nose wrinkled. "Yeah, I can't say I share your anticipation."

"I do," said Knox.

"He'll be here for her birthday in two weeks' time," Jolene told him. "You'll see Lucian then."

When were you going to tell me your birthday is approaching? he asked Harper.

Oh . . . never. I don't like fuss.

Get used to it fast. He'd already warned her that he intended to spoil her; he meant it. She'd just have to learn to love it.

CHAPTER FOURTEEN

Raul, Tanya, Martina, and Beck were already at the table when Knox, Harper, and Jolene arrived. As Raul started to make small talk, Knox quickly realized that he was looking for clues as to whether or not Harper and Knox were more than anchors. Knox had known of course that his sexually possessive display in the reception area would spread throughout the Underground. It had been his plan. He wanted everyone to know Harper was taken.

What they couldn't know was that he and Harper were mates, and he was positive that no one would consider it was possible. Everyone knew how detached he was. They wouldn't imagine he would ever take a mate. Knox hadn't seen it coming either. But then, he hadn't seen Harper coming.

"Some anchors have sexual relationships," Tanya reminded Raul irritably. "Big deal. Why are you hung up on the subject?"

Knox already knew the answer to that. So did Tanya. Hell, probably everybody at the table knew – except for Harper, because she seemed to miss male demon flirting cues. Probably because she was used to human males. "Harper's off-limits, Raul," Knox said as he played his fingers possessively through her hair. "I don't share. And I'd never let anyone touch my mate."

"Mate?" Tanya echoed, stunned.

Smiling, Raul whistled. "Can't say I blame you."

Martina whined at Harper, "You took Knox as your mate and you never told me?"

Harper sighed at her. "A lot has happened in the past twelve hours, okay." And she really didn't want to relay it all right there and then.

"I'll explain everything," Jolene told Beck and Martina. "But not here."

Harper mouthed 'thank you' at her grandmother, who winked. *Thanks so much for blurting that out to Raul when I haven't even told all my family yet, Knox.* The gossip would quickly spread. The culprit would no doubt be pissed at Harper and potentially even at Knox. Understanding hit Harper like a slap; she'd come to learn how Knox's mind worked. *You're hoping it will piss off the culprit so much that they might even come after you.*

Knox had to smile at her astuteness, even though it was a pain in his ass. *I want to flush out the person targeting you, yes. If they're angry enough about this, they might act rashly.*

I'll act rashly if you get hurt, you dumb bastard. The vibe of male amusement that stroked her mind only served to irritate her more. At that moment, waiters arrived at the table with their meals. Each course was as delicious as the one before, and she felt her tension slowly drain away. As always, the dessert was her favorite.

Feeling Knox's hand lightly squeezing her knee, Harper snapped her gaze to his. He looked her dead in the eye, laser-focused on her in that way he often was. It sent a shiver of anticipation down her spine, though she still maintained he was a dumb bastard.

"I'm still hungry. You going to feed me when we get back to the suite?"

She knew he wasn't talking about food. She could have said 'Maybe' and played aloof, but that would have gotten her another psychic finger-fuck. She wasn't going to allow that to happen while her grandmother was sitting next to her. "I can do that."

He tapped her ear gently. "Come here."

"I am here."

"I want you closer. Come here, Harper."

"I think you should meet me in the middle," she said. A crooked, sexual smile curved his mouth.

Cupping her chin, he leaned in as he pulled her toward him. "I love that dress on you." He moved his mouth to her ear. "The trouble is . . . it's keeping me from what's mine. That just makes me want to slip my hand up your dress and find out if you're wet for me. Are you, Harper?"

Well she was now. He didn't need to whisper, he could talk to her telepathically. But he knew the whispering in her ear thing *totally* did it for her. "Don't get me too wet. I'm not wearing panties."

Knox's cock twitched. He was hard and heavy, and he wanted to fuck that mouth that was pursed in an impish yet sensual smile. "One less barrier between me and what's mine."

She chuckled. "I guess so." The sound of a throat clearing had her looking up to see Dario, stiff as a board. Knox didn't move, and she realized his focus was still on her face. Oh, he knew Dario was there. Had probably sensed the guy approaching – Knox was always aware of everything around him. "Speech time, huh?" she said.

Sliding his hand from her chin to her nape, Knox finally looked at Dario. He wasn't broadcasting any fantasies tonight, which meant he could live.

"Before I give my speech, I just wanted to thank you for your hospitality this weekend, Knox. The entire event has been peaceful and enjoyable. I doubt it would have been so if you hadn't been the host." The Primes might have risked pissing off another host, but not him. After Knox gave him a simple nod, the demon headed for the dais.

"I have to admit," began Harper, "I'm interested to hear what he promises."

"You would consider voting for a Monarch?" asked Raul, shocked.

She snorted. "Not even in an alternate reality. What I mean is that he'd have to offer something different from Isla and Malden, and I can't think of much else anyone could possibly suggest that would appeal to our kind."

"Good, because then there's a high chance his proposal will be dismissed," said Jolene.

Dario's smile was wide and pleasant. "Good evening, my fellow demons. If you're listening after two days of speeches, you're obviously not as bored as I'd expected. I'll try to keep this short to minimize the risk of boredom, so listen carefully.

"I do believe the idea of a hierarchical system has merit. But I also believe it will not work for every Prime or every lair. Some demons simply aren't built to submit, and I do not believe it would be fair to punish them for being who they are."

"I didn't see that coming," muttered Jolene.

"And let's be honest," continued Dario, "it isn't realistic to assume that we can punish every Prime. Some are simply too powerful to be forced to do anything. Any attempts to punish them would only result in them retaliating which, in turn, will soon lead to a war. Or being swallowed by the flames of hell, if that is indeed an ability Knox can boast to have, and I'm not eager to know what that's like." Chuckles spread around the room.

"If I am made Monarch, all Primes will have the right to choose whether or not they wish to be part of the new structure and, as such, whether or not they answer to a Monarch. If they choose not to join, their decision will be respected, not punished."

"Well that's different," said Harper in a low voice.

"I am not tempted by the idea of a hierarchy where Primes of small lairs are automatically denied the influence and power that Primes of large lairs would have." Dario shook his head. "Just because a demon has a small lair does not mean they shouldn't have the same rights, respect, and say in their lives as other Primes. That is why I am proposing that, in addition to having a Monarch, we should also form a council.

"The Prime of each and every U.S. lair will have a place on that council – providing, of course, they accept me as their Monarch. This does not mean, however, that only the council will have power over decisions. It means that we can work together. Any major changes proposed will, like now, be put to a vote by all U.S. demons – other than for those who have a Prime that chooses not to answer to a Monarch."

Dario's gaze swept the room before concentrating on the camera. "There is one final issue I wish to address. Right now, we have lairs that span cities and even entire countries, but we do not have territories. Demons from different lairs can easily intermingle, and this is part of what results in conflict between lairs. I am proposing that each Prime be given their own territory – a territory that outsiders can only cross with permission. This would not only avoid many disputes, but it would make demons within their lairs feel much safer as they will be better protected."

"Shit, that might just tempt a lot of people," said Harper. Demons loved to own things. Having territory of their own would seriously appeal to them.

"As for the Primes that do not wish to answer to a Monarch," began Dario, "however far their lair expands will be considered by those who are part of the new system to be their territory. They will have the right to punish anyone who crosses it, and no one will seek vengeance for such an act. It also means, however, that they will need to in turn respect the boundaries of other territories so as to avoid feuds.

"I truly believe this is a system that can work. Why do I believe that? Because it would benefit everyone, and it would inconvenience no one. The public will have a vote in each decision. No Prime will be considered more influential than any other as only the Monarch would have any authority. All lairs will have territorial boundaries that keep them safe. And any Primes that do not wish to be part of the new system are free to continue as they do now; I only ask that they respect the boundaries of other Primes, just as we would respect theirs. If you want a system that works for all of us, vote for this – vote for me." He exhaled heavily. "Any questions?"

"You said that any Prime who doesn't wish to be part of the new system can opt out," called out a Prime on their left. "What if none of the Primes here wish to join?"

"It's a very good question, since there is a possibility that it will happen," allowed Dario. "All I would ask of those Primes is that they respect the boundaries of my territory – nothing more, nothing less. I will form a council from the demons within my own lair, and each future decision I make will depend on votes."

"So you intend to implement some kind of system, even if it's only within your own lair?" asked another Prime.

"Yes, because I believe very strongly that it can work; that all demons should have the right to have a say in their lives."

"When you say that all Primes would be given their own territory, how would you measure the boundaries of that territory?" There was a disturbing amount of interest in that voice coming from the back.

"Let's say, for instance, that the demons living within a Prime's lair covers half of Manhattan. That will be their territory. If it covers the whole of Manhattan, all of that will be their territory. In other words, it will only expand as far as those living within their lair currently reside."

"But what if a small number of the lair live among demons that belong in a separate lair?" Malden asked. "It's extremely rare, since lairs like to stick together. But what if that was the case?"

"I would say the simplest answer would be for those demons living away from their lair to move closer to it. However, they could also request to switch to the lair they currently live among, or simply ask permission from the Prime of that territory to live in that area without having to join. As you say, it's an extremely rare situation, so it will hardly affect anyone."

"Okay, but what if demons want to relocate to a location that is within the territory of another lair?" persisted Malden.

"My answer to the previous question would also apply here. They would need to either switch lairs or request permission from the Prime of that territory to reside in that area without joining that lair."

There was a short silence before another voice called out, "The problem I foresee here is that although many of the public may like your system, they won't benefit from it if their Prime chooses not to join you."

"They are always free to join my lair or another that is part of the new system."

"That could mean *a lot* of demons join his lair just to have more rights," Harper said to Knox. He nodded.

"I have a question," declared Raul. "There are places in the U.S. that demons don't inhabit. What if Primes suddenly decide that they want to claim those territories? Wouldn't that lead to war?"

"No," denied Dario. "The issue would be discussed by the council and myself. An agreement would be reached."

Raul's brows raised. "Without the votes of the public?"

"It's not a decision that would directly affect the public. Asking them to vote on every little thing would eventually bore them." That was actually true – something Isla and Malden hadn't considered.

"All right, here's something to consider," said Raul. "We all know how much our kind love Las Vegas. This is where most of Knox's demons reside, which means it would then be considered his territory. We couldn't cross that territory without permission, could we?"

"No. But I can't imagine that Knox would wish to keep us away. If nothing else, it would affect his businesses."

"What about the Underground? He created this place, he runs it, so that would also make it his territory."

"Yes, so you would need his permission to come here. Again, though, I don't foresee him preventing outsiders from coming. He created the Underground for our kind, not for himself."

"Let's ask him." Raul turned to Knox. "Would you let demons from other lairs cross your territorial lines? Would you let us come here the way you do now?"

"That would depend," replied Knox.

"On what?"

"Whether or not having territories causes demons to see outsiders as enemies," said Knox. "It's true that lairs intermingling can cause conflict. But if Primes start claiming territories, that will effectively create divides. Suddenly lairs will consider other lairs to be potential enemies. I won't have the Underground or Las Vegas suddenly becoming a battle ground."

A Prime to their right spoke. "Knox has an excellent point. You say your system will unite us, Dario. Instead, it could just divide us more."

"I see how Knox may view it that way." There was no judgment or hostility in Dario's tone. "But I truly believe this system could work. The Primes would be working together, all demons would have equal rights, and we would be united. It would make us stronger. That can never be a bad thing."

As Dario left the dais, Beck spoke. "I thought that the only demon who'd present a reasonable case would be Isla, since the other two just want to avoid answering to someone else. But all three of them have presented proposals that just might appeal to the public."

"Worse, Dario's proposal might appeal to the Primes," commented Martina.

"I think that if the Primes start worrying that the public will want a Monarch, they'll prefer it was Dario, because it would gain them territory – more power. Even Isla can see that." Jolene tipped her chin toward the she-demon in question; she was currently glaring at an unsuspecting Dario, clearly seething.

Knox whispered into Harper's ear, "I have to say a few words and remind everybody what happens next." The moment he walked onto the dais, the attention of the room settled on him. "Over the course of this weekend, you've heard all three proposals, and you've heard the opinions of many Primes during the Q&As. Now it's time to form your own opinion.

There are pros and cons of having a Monarch, and there are pros and cons of each proposal. A vote will take place in the Underground two weeks from now. Anyone who votes will only be able to do so once, and each vote will be anonymous. If you vote in favor of a Monarch, you'll need to also specify which candidate you wish to elect. So think it through, and choose your fate wisely."

It was as Knox reached Harper that the Primes began to head to his table. Gently pulling Harper to her feet, he spoke briefly to each demon as they thanked him for hosting the event. Knox was sure to refer to Harper as his mate, wanting the news to spread fast.

When Malden approached, he was wearing a very smug smirk. Knox had the feeling that he believed his proposal would be the most favored. "It was good seeing you, Knox. Where's Raul?"

"He already left with his anchor," replied Knox.

"I had hoped to say goodbye. Never mind. Jolene, it's always a pleasure. And Harper, you take care."

She nodded, smiling. "You too, Malcolm."

To her amusement, the tic in his cheek did a crazy dance as his smirk fell. "It's *Malden*."

She smacked her forehead with the palm of her hand. "That's right, sorry."

As the Prime marched away, Knox smiled against her mouth. "Such a tease." He inwardly groaned as he sensed a very unwelcome she-demon approaching. *Isla's coming.*

My evening is complete.

"Hello, Knox." So deceptively pleasant.

Knox lifted his head. "Isla."

"I just thought I'd say farewell. We'll talk again soon. Oh, and do reconsider electing a Monarch. I could improve so much for our kind."

His smile was as forced as hers. "Your plea is wasted on me, Isla."

"You always were stubborn." Her tone was full of nostalgia. Turning to Harper, she held out a small, black velvet bag. "I wanted to give you something, Harper. Call it a peace offering."

Dubious, Harper raised a brow. "Yeah? What is it?"

"Open and see."

Curiosity alone made Harper take and open the little drawstring bag. Inside was some kind of silver chain. She pulled it out, realizing there was a silver pendant hanging from it. It was engraved with a triquetra and had a gold dragon attached to it. It also fairly buzzed with power.

"It's a protective amulet," Isla explained. "Be sure to wear it."

The genuine concern in the she-demon's voice made Harper look up. With a regal nod, Isla turned away and left. "I'm guessing this thing is cursed or something, because there's just *no way* that that woman wants me protected."

Knox took the amulet and closed his hand around it. "There's power in this."

"I know, I felt it. But it didn't feel bad."

"It isn't."

"You're saying Isla wants to protect Harper?" Levi was clearly skeptical.

"No," replied Knox. "I'm merely saying there's no negative power attached to the amulet."

"Maybe she wants to *appear* concerned for Harper, hoping it will make us think she's innocent in all the shit that's been going on," theorized Tanner.

"That seems more likely than her giving Harper some kind of lucky charm." Martina scowled at Harper. "Don't think I haven't noticed that you don't wear the necklace I gave you with the fishbone charm on it. It's for good luck."

Harper frowned. "How can it give good luck? Things didn't exactly go well for the fish."

Beck's laugh earned him a glower from Martina.

"Well, sweetheart, I'm afraid we have to leave." Jolene gave Harper a tight, one-armed hug. "Come visit me soon, bring Knox. And Tanner and Levi can come along." She smiled. "It's always nice to have things around that are pretty to look at."

Once she'd said her goodbyes to Martina and Beck, Harper turned to Knox. "After we've picked up our luggage from upstairs, I'd like to go to my apartment and see what survived the spell."

Having returned the amulet to the velvet bag and placed it in his pocket, Knox took her hand. He'd shove the amulet in a drawer somewhere later. "I'll have Keenan take the luggage to the mansion while we go to your apartment. It's going to be a mess, baby. Be ready."

It turned out he was right. One step inside the apartment, Harper halted with a groan. The place looked like an abandoned house – the furniture still standing was stained with the ash of the items that had been destroyed by the venom. It was dark, damp, and smelled like a morgue. Like rot and decay.

"You know, it makes no sense to me that the practitioner would perform a spell that put so many snakes *in*side and then only a few *out*side," she told Knox. "The snakes slithering on my front door were a huge fucking warning that there could be more inside. Why give me that warning?"

"I don't think any were supposed to get outside. But a few escaped through the letterbox, something the practitioner obviously hadn't considered would happen."

"Maybe. But why not just do a simpler spell that hid a few snakes inside – they could have taken me off guard and easily bitten me. At first, I couldn't understand it. But now, looking at this mess, I'm thinking that they put all the snakes inside because they intended to do this much damage. They wanted to destroy my stuff to hurt me, and to help vent their anger. If it's a reaction to finding out you and I are mates, the news obviously didn't shift their anger to you."

And that pissed Knox the fuck off. "Come on, let's see what's still intact, box it up, and get out of here."

So that was what they did. With so much dark energy filling the space, it was a relief to get out of there. The smell seemed to cling to her flesh and clothes. She scrubbed at her skin in Knox's shower, trying to wash it away. But it was as though the scent of rot had clogged her nostrils. Settled on the sofa in the living area, dressed in her sweats, she inhaled the coffee Meg – bless her soul – had made, hoping it would chase away the horrid smell that seemed to haunt her. According to Levi, it would take a little more work from the incantor to remove the stains of the spell from the apartment.

Beside her, Knox was leaning over the box on the table that contained the things Harper had rescued from the apartment. Meg had washed each one before placing them in a different box, ridding them all of the scent of decay. She really was fabulous.

"What are all these?" he asked.

"They're just knickknacks. You know, sentimental stuff." She lifted out a hand-painted skeleton-shaped trinket box. "I got this from a market in Mexico. We didn't live there long, but I loved it there." Returning the little box, she pulled out a tiny, beautiful piano replica. "This is from Switzerland. We didn't stay there long, either. Lucian got me this when I told him I wanted a piano – his idea of a joke." She carefully put the piano back and pointed to a wooden, carved model of the Colosseum in Rome. "He bought me this when we were in Italy. We stayed there for over a year. I loved it there."

Knox turned in his seat to face her, propping his elbow on the top of the sofa. "Jolene was right."

"About what?"

"You have good memories of your time with Lucian."

"I've told you before that I enjoyed the traveling, and that I wouldn't change my upbringing."

She had, but Knox hadn't seen how that could be possible. He hadn't seen how she could have enjoyed years of having no real say in basic things like where she lived. Knox tucked her hair behind her ear. "Tell me more about Lucian. I need reasons why I shouldn't kill him."

She shot him a mock scowl. "Lucian isn't cruel. Self-centered and absentminded, yeah. At the core of all that, he's very lonely." All demons were plagued by loneliness, and Lucian felt it acutely, which made him seriously restless. "But he doesn't have the emotional maturity to do anything about it or to connect with others. So he lives with a hole inside him. Once upon a time, he tried to fill it with drugs, alcohol, women, gambling, and all kinds of dangerous shit. He's past that phase now, but he can't fill that void. I'm not sure if he even knows exactly what he's looking for in life, but he's always searching for it, and he's always searching in all the wrong places."

Knox got it then. "Someone so lost can't concentrate on the needs of another person."

"That's exactly it. Demons aren't built to be alone. But he's been alone for a very long time."

So had Knox, but he didn't see that as an excuse for the selfish behavior Lucian had shown. "He had you."

"That's not the same as having a mate, though, is it? And to be fair to him, he never tried to use me to fill that void. He could have clung to me the way some lonely parents do, could have held me tight to him to make him feel loved, cherished, and important. But he never did. I think that by raising me to not need anyone or anything to complete my life – to only enhance it – he was trying to make sure I didn't turn out like him."

While that made sense, Knox didn't *want* it to make sense or he'd have to let some of his anger at Lucian go. He couldn't deny one thing, though. "He does care for you."

"I believe he does. When I first went to live with him, he told me that he'd done me a favor by leaving me with Jolene; that I was better off without having him around permanently. He warned me that he was going to screw up, and he apologized in advance for it. He really isn't a bad person, Knox. Just unable to meet the needs of others, because he can't even meet his own needs. So please don't kill him," she added with a smile.

Knox sighed. "It's important to me that you were happy. I just need to be sure."

Harper regarded him thoughtfully. "You didn't have a great upbringing, did you? Ooh, he tenses," she chuckled. "Come on, you can give me something. You once said you didn't belong to a lair before you moved to the sanctuary. Where were you?"

Knox threaded his fingers through her damp hair; everything within him recoiled at the idea of revisiting that time in his life, but this was Harper. "People would nowadays describe it as a cult. Back then, it was just a group of demons that detached themselves from their lair and formed a Prime-less group, pooling all their resources and claiming a plot of land."

That answer certainly threw Harper. "Why did you all leave the lair? Was the Prime a bastard or something?"

"I don't remember a lot about the Prime, but I remember that everyone feared him. So some of them left as a group, but they didn't join another lair, because they all rejected the idea of having a Prime. They didn't want to be ruled, they wanted peace. They wanted to be free."

"But they didn't get that peace," she guessed. He didn't answer, just stared at her with eyes that gave away nothing. "You promised you'd try sharing," she reminded him.

He sighed heavily. "From what I can remember, it wasn't so bad in the beginning. The females and the children were treated like royalty. Everyone was happy and close and felt free."

"What changed?"

"One of them, Riordan" – the name alone infuriated Knox's demon – "appointed himself as a sort of messiah. He preached about the corruption of lairs; calling all Primes power-hungry authoritarians who didn't care for the safety of those under their protection." The bastard could have been talking about himself. "In effect, he was actually making himself their Prime. And they didn't see it."

When moments went by and he said no more, she asked, "How old were you when the 'cult' was formed?"

"Three. By the time I was five, it was an isolated totalitarian society. Little by little, Riordan took over. He introduced a dress code, a job chart, a timetable, and guidelines that placed a lot of restrictions on everyone and made them reliant on him. In addition, he cut everyone off from the outside world."

"Keeping them all isolated and inducing dependency would have made it easier for him to brainwash and control them." It was little wonder that Knox was such a control freak and had such a total aversion to relying on others. Someone had once ripped control away from him. He'd taken it back, but it had made him determined to never lose it again. "Didn't anyone speak up?"

"Not many, because he and his helpers punished any form of insubordination. Riordan did whatever he had to do to keep his power." Manipulated. Intimidated. Exploited. Oppressed.

As usual, Knox's exterior was calm and his tone was even. But she'd come to know him so well that she could sense his buried rage. And she just knew that the answer to her next question would be bad, but she had to ask, "What did they do to you?"

He leaned toward her. "Maybe your question should be . . . what did I do to them?"

CHAPTER FIFTEEN

The menace that had slithered into Knox's voice made even her inner demon freeze as Harper watched him warily. He'd spoken so softly, so steadily. But the danger was there, sending a trickle of trepidation through her system. It was an instinctive reaction that she couldn't escape, despite trusting that he wouldn't exact that menace on her. He was the ultimate predator, and she could never overlook that.

"Aren't you going to ask?" It was a dare that carried a taunt.

She swallowed, veiling her apprehension. "Not until you answer my question."

"He punished anyone who wouldn't give him the unquestioning devotion and submission that he demanded."

Harper didn't need to ask if Knox had rebelled. "Punished how?"

"Lots of ways." Knox tangled a hand in her hair, watching as her jade green eyes swirled and changed into an entrancing cobalt blue. "He liked to keep people locked in a closet for a week or so. In that time, he wouldn't let them eat, he wouldn't let them sleep, and he'd beat them frequently." His demon snarled at the memories. "Many of his followers helped. They got a taste for it, and they enjoyed it."

Her apprehension was swiftly replaced by fury. "Then the bastards deserved whatever they got."

"How can you be so sure when you don't know what they got?"

"They hurt you, so I really don't care."

Her response warmed him and settled his demon. "I never said they hurt me. I said they punished people who refused to submit."

"You refused."

She was right. Knox and his demon had resisted Riordan's control, refused to submit, no matter what he or his followers did. But the rage hadn't really hit Knox until he left and got his freedom; that was when he'd realized what the outside world – one he'd been brought up to believe was bad and dangerous – was truly like, and he'd understood exactly what the bastards had stolen from him.

It had been difficult to adjust, but he'd worked hard to properly develop the sense of self that the bastards had tried to break down and take from him. In the sanctuary, he'd soaked up knowledge of every kind. When he left, he'd used that knowledge to gain all the things he'd been deprived of. And he'd vowed that he'd never again let anyone have any form of control over him.

"Didn't your parents ever help you, ever try to stop him?"

"Not until the people who questioned or defied Riordan developed a habit of disappearing. That made them wary and suspicious. So when I was twelve, they tried to leave and take me with them."

"He killed them," she guessed. "You tried to protect them."

"No, baby," he said softly. "I avenged them." Riordan had forced him to watch as he slit his parents' throats. Knox had struck back, taken his vengeance out on everything around him. "You've seen what destruction I can cause. You can guess what I did. I warned the innocent ones to run, but most of them wouldn't leave Riordan – they'd become too dependent on him, were utterly brainwashed. So they died with him. But I didn't care. I was too eager to see him suffer."

"Stop trying to scare me."

"Scare you?" Knox cupped her chin and breezed his thumb over her bottom lip. "Baby, I'd never do that. But you have to understand that the answers you want to the many questions in your pretty little head will very often not be what you want to hear. They might shock you, they might disgust you, and they might even frighten you. I don't want to scare you, but I won't lie to you. Don't ask for the truth unless you can deal with it."

She *could* deal with it. So she asked the one question that might just have the potential to terrify her. "What are you?"

"You're not ready for that answer yet." And Knox wasn't willing to tell her until he'd managed to make her so attached to him that she wouldn't want to leave him, no matter what. It was ruthless, yes, but he was too determined to keep her to care about that.

Harper bristled. "I get to decide what I'm ready for."

"No, you don't." He fisted his hand in the back of her hair, angled her head how he wanted it, and brought his mouth down on hers. Loving the taste of her, he plundered her mouth with his tongue, just as he wanted to plunder her body with his cock. He bit down hard on her lip, and she snapped her teeth at him.

"You think the answer will scare me so much I'll leave," Harper sensed.

Too. Damn. Astute. "I won't let you leave."

"If I wanted to go, I *totally* could."

His demon chuckled, always entertained by the fire in her – its temperament went from grim to relaxed in an instant. Only she seemed able to do that. Knox was just as amused by her 'spunk,' as Tanner often referred to it.

"You're not supposed to smile at me like I'm a little kitten that stupidly thinks it's a jungle cat." Secretly, she was happy she'd lifted his mood.

Knox pulled her onto his lap to straddle him. "How can I not be a little entertained? You're in the den of the big, bad wolf – caught and claimed – but you think you can take him on."

"Hey, you might be a powerful bad ass, but I'm not helpless here. I could still hurt you if I wanted to. Why are you still smiling? You're supposed to fear my mighty wrath."

His shoulders shook with silent laughter. "In case you can't tell, I'm petrified."

"You will be if my mighty wrath is ever unleashed. Stop laughing!"

As the door of the studio closed behind Harper's client, Raini made an exasperated sound. "If I have to hear another demon talking about how 'cool' Malden's proposal is, I might just hurt them."

Harper began tidying her station. "I had hoped they'd realize his promise of a voice is just bullshit."

"A lot of people like Isla's proposal," Khloë told them, spinning in her chair. "Mostly because she promised to create a Force that would fight dark practitioners; that kind of thing would avenge demons who had died at the bastards' hands."

"According to Knox," began Harper, "Dario's proposal has

appealed mostly to Primes, though the majority of them are still against having a Monarch."

Raini leaned against the wall by Harper's station. "When is Knox back from his business trip?"

"Tomorrow." It had been a little weird being in the mansion without him for four days, but he'd occasionally pyroported there to see her – and fuck her like a guy possessed. But she didn't tell her friends that, respecting his wish to remain mysterious about what abilities he had.

Khloë stilled her chair. "What's he like to live with?"

"A lot easier than I expected. Although he's very dominant and can be bossy at times, he's not a dictatorial 'I'm man of the house and you'll live by my rules' kind of guy. He gives me space when I need it, doesn't treat me like a lodger. To him, it's my home and I have free rein to do whatever I want to it or in it." That had to be hard for any demon, since they were territorial creatures.

Raini smiled. "He makes you happy."

"I guess he does."

The door swung open, and Devon came waltzing in with four Starbucks coffees. Her cheeks were flushed with irritation. "Harper, you need to do something about that bodyguard of yours, because he's getting on my goddamn last nerve."

Glimpsing out of the window, Harper saw that Tanner's arm was hanging out of the front window of the Bentley . . . and there was a cat collar dangling from his hand. It was pink and had a little bell. "At least it's pretty."

"My demon wants to claw his face off. Can't you ask Knox to assign someone else?"

"Devon, don't expect me to feel sorry for you – you're just as bad as he is. For God's sake, you brought him a bag of dog biscuits yesterday."

Devon chuckled to herself. "Yeah, that was fun. Anyway, what are we talking about?"

Raini accepted the coffee cup that Devon handed her. "The fact that Knox makes Harper happy."

"Unfortunately, I can't see that placating Lucian when he finds out Knox is your mate," said Devon, who took her own cup.

Harper sighed. "Me neither. He'll go nuclear."

Khloë frowned, crossing the room to grab her coffee. "Fuck Lucian. That negligent bastard doesn't get to have a say in this."

"Maybe he'll fear Knox enough not to aggravate him," suggested Raini, though she didn't appear convinced.

"Lucian's not smart enough to experience fear," scoffed Khloë. Pausing, she took a swig of her coffee. "So . . . just how scary a breed is Knox? I'm not asking *what* he is, just how scary it is."

Harper cleared her throat. "Well, um . . ."

Her cousin easily saw the truth. "He hasn't told you what breed he is? Seriously?" She shook her head, perplexed. "Why aren't you pissed? Doesn't it bother you that you don't know what *your own mate* is?"

"It bothers me, yes, but I get that it has to be hard for him to part with such a big secret."

"That's my point, though," said Khloë. "There *shouldn't* be secrets that big between mates." Raini and Devon nodded in agreement.

"I'm sure he'll tell me when he's ready. I can wait. Why are you looking at me like that?"

Khloë stepped closer. "Want to know what I think?"

"No. I want you to answer the phone like you're paid to do."

Khloë waved a dismissive hand at the chiming phone. "I think the reason you're not riled by him holding back something so important is that deep inside – maybe so deep you don't even sense it – you're not taking this relationship seriously, because you're expecting him to leave you. Not because you don't trust him or because you're insecure. But because you're used to people coming and going."

"I don't think he'll leave." Harper truly didn't.

"But what we think and what we feel deep inside – not always the same. Life has conditioned you to believe that people don't stick around. It's sort of an emotional reflex for you to subconsciously expect them to leave at some point."

Devon and Raini nodded, as if it made perfect sense.

Harper snorted. "That's just a load of psychological bullshit."

Khloë straightened, affronted. "Well that's not very nice."

"Answer the damn phone."

With an exasperated sigh, Khloë headed to the reception desk.

"Khloë has a point," said Raini. "You do automatically assume everyone you meet will be a fleeting presence in your life. It makes you hold back from people."

"I don't hold back from Knox. Hell, I moved into his goddamn house."

"Yes, but let's be fair, moving into a new house is something you've done a million times throughout your life," Raini pointed out. "On an emotional level, it's not a huge thing for you. It doesn't scream 'permanence' to someone with a past like yours. Be honest, did it *feel* huge?"

"No," Harper confessed. "But I took him as my mate; that's huge."

"Sure it is. And it tells me that you really care about him. But if you – a person who doesn't take bullshit from anyone – aren't seriously hurt and pissed that your mate is holding back something so significant, it's because you're not expecting this to last. In your head, you're still in a 'we'll see how it goes' phase. You haven't quite accepted that it's permanent yet."

"Psychological bullshit," Harper repeated.

Devon patted her hand. "We're not trying to needle you, we just want you to be aware of this, so you can deal with it in your head."

The sound of the door opening was quickly followed by Khloë's voice. "Sorry, kid, you're too young."

"I'm not here for a tattoo. I want to talk to her."

Harper had only heard that voice once before, but she easily recognized it. Pivoting on the spot, she forced a smile for the teenager who also happened to be her half-brother. He was casting nervous glances at the other three she-demons, who were all staring at him. They obviously also recognized him. "If you're looking for Knox . . ."

Kellen gave a fast shake of the head. "No, I . . . Can we talk in private?"

Harper faked nonchalance. "Is there a problem?"

"Maybe." His eyes held a knowledge that could turn everything to shit.

Great, just fucking great. She gestured at the diner across the street. "Let's talk over there. I won't be long," she told the girls before escorting him out. After informing Tanner – whose eyes sharpened at the sight of Kellen – that she'd be in the diner, she hurried over there. Only once the waitress had poured them each a coffee did Harper ask, "So . . . want to tell me what this is about?"

"I know who you are." His expression was mutinous, daring her to deny the truth. What she didn't know was just how much of the truth he knew.

She ripped open two packets of sugar, sprinkled the contents into her coffee, and stirred it with a spoon. "And who would that be?"

He didn't appear to like her aloof act at all. "Don't treat me like I'm stupid and delusional."

She sighed at the determined glint in his eyes – he wasn't going to let this go. "It's Kellen, right? Kellen, there are some stories that are best not to hear."

His eyes flashed demon for a brief moment. "You're my sister. Don't say you're not." He made a visible effort to calm himself. "I won't tell anyone, I just want to know."

"I'm your sister," Harper acknowledged. She blew over the rim of her cup before taking a sip. "Carla won't like you talking to me."

"She doesn't know." He lifted his own cup. "She has a picture of you."

Okay, well that almost caused Harper to spit her coffee all over the table. "A picture?" she asked disbelievingly.

"I found it in a box she keeps hidden in her closet."

Harper smiled. "Let me guess . . . she keeps a stash of cash there."

His cheeks reddened. "I just needed enough to—"

"I grew up with imps, I can't judge."

"In the photo, you're in a graduation outfit."

Carla was at her graduation? No fucking way.

"It's not a close-up shot, you're laughing with someone, but I know it was you."

"Why would that make you think I'm your sister?"

"It didn't. Sometimes, I *know* things when I touch stuff." He frowned, looking a lot like his father in that moment. "It doesn't always happen. And sometimes, it's not very clear. But when I held the picture, I *knew* you were her kid, I *knew* she gave you up, and I *knew* she was scared of you."

Harper blinked. "Scared?"

"Why is she scared of you?"

"I don't know." Harper doubted it was related to what happened when she was a toddler. Instead, it was likely that Carla wasn't necessarily scared of Harper; she was scared of the truth getting out.

"Yes, you do."

Harper had to smile. "Persistent little shit, aren't you?"

He shrugged, returning her smile, though it was a little strained. "I just want to understand."

"The only person who really understands it is Carla. All I know is that she didn't want me, she handed me over to my paternal family, and she wants nothing to do with me." Harper paused as they both sipped their coffee. "And I know she despises my father for leaving her."

"She's not . . . normal. She can be really nice, kind. And it's not an act, it's real. But the strangest things can make her angry. I think she finds her demon hard to control and it wears on her. Roan said she's twisted up inside but that it's not her fault. I don't know what that means."

"Maybe she had a shitty childhood or something."

"She got angry when she heard you and Knox are mates."

Ho, ho, ho, that was just fabulous. Her inner demon chuckled in delight, happy about anything that would rile the woman. "Did she?"

"She didn't do or say anything, I could just tell."

"I'm her dirty little secret, Kellen. It's hard to pretend you don't have a dirty little secret if it's now the mate of your Prime," Harper explained.

"My dad will be seriously mad when he finds out about this."

"I have no intention of telling your dad or anyone else."

Kellen seemed shocked. "You don't want anyone to know? But what she did was wrong!"

"But if she could never have brought herself to care about me, giving me up was the best thing she did for me. I'm not bitter about what she did. If you ask me, holding bitterness inside will just destroy a person from the inside out."

There was a long silence before he asked sheepishly, "Can I come see you sometimes? I mean, I want to know you."

Harper smiled. "Okay. I'd like to know you too."

"I don't think it would be a good idea to tell Roan. He wouldn't keep it from her. He does his best to please her all the time. He might as well be lodged up her a . . . butt."

She almost laughed at his attempt not to curse in front of her. He'd soon learn she cursed like a drunken sailor. "Then it's best if we keep it between us." They talked for a little longer, discussing everyday things. When Kellen left, she crossed over the road to the studio.

Tanner poked his head out of the open window of the Bentley. "He knows, doesn't he?"

"Only that Carla gave me up. He doesn't know the rest, thankfully." She gave him a quick rundown of everything Kellen said. "He's smart enough to have kept it to himself so far, and he's promised me he won't tell anyone – not even his dad or brother."

"Do you really think you two can have a relationship without Carla finding out?"

"I've no idea." Entering the studio, she puffed out a long breath. "That was hard."

"What happened?" asked Raini. "What did he say?"

"She has a picture of me." Harper still couldn't quite grasp that. "She went to my graduation, but she stayed out of sight. She took a picture while she was there."

Khloë double-blinked. "I'm not understanding that."

Harper sighed. "Me neither."

Devon was the image of compassion. "What did he want?"

"To know what happened, why Carla did what she did. In his place, I'd want to know too." Hearing the door open, Harper turned. And smiled as her nerve endings and her demon shot to life. "I didn't expect you until tomorrow."

Knox's mouth curved as he stalked toward her, radiating a raw sexuality that always made her body hum. "I got back early." Locking his arms around her, he pressed a lingering kiss to her mouth. But then he frowned. "What's wrong?"

"It's just been a weird afternoon."

"You can tell me about it in the car."

They rode with Levi, since it seemed that Tanner had already taken off – apparently he had 'something to get ready for,' whatever the hell that meant.

Knox twisted to face her. "Tell me."

So Harper did. He didn't interrupt her. He just listened as he soothingly threaded his fingers through her hair.

Once she was done, he said, "Strange that she should have a picture of you."

"I can't even begin to make sense of that."

"Then let's not try." He combed his fingers through her hair once more. "She isn't important. You're important. Forget about her, so you can enjoy yourself."

That sounded interesting. "Enjoy myself how?"

"I haven't spent any real time with you in four days. Before that, things were intense with fucking politics. So tonight, we're going to the Underground to wind down and have time together." Knox licked over her bottom lip. He loved her mouth. Loved the sensual shape of it. Loved the feel of it wrapped around his cock. Loved knowing that it was *his*.

Knox kissed her again. He would have done a whole lot more if Levi wasn't in the car. Knox had been hard since the moment her eyes met his in the studio. Although he'd had fleeting moments with her over the past few days, it hadn't been enough for him. He'd learned that he wasn't just addicted to her body, but her mind, her laugh, her unpredictability, her ever-changing eyes, and the way she teased him. Every time someone had jumped to obey him in the past few days, he'd thought of the way Harper snorted at his orders. He'd . . . missed her.

His demon, too, had missed her. She probably had no idea just how deeply attached the demon was to her. She was its sole source of satisfaction; the only person that entertained, impressed, and delighted it. It had been bored out of its mind without her, which had made it intolerant of everyone around it.

"Yeah? Wind down how?" she asked.

"You'll see. And you'll get to see Tanner run, too."

Her brow crinkled. "I don't know what that means."

"You will soon."

A little while later, Harper was gaping through the protective glass of a VIP box in a hound racing stadium in the Underground. And Knox's words made sense. She spun to face him. "Please tell me Tanner isn't going to race here."

Knox arched a brow. "You didn't know hellhounds liked to race?"

Well, yes, she'd known about it. The tracks were located near the casinos, and as Harper wasn't much into gambling, she hadn't visited them. It looked like any normal dog racing stadium. There was a spectator area, grandstands, and private boxes that all gave a perfect view of the oval track. "I've heard it can be pretty brutal."

"It can be," he confirmed. "Almost as brutal as the hellhorses."

That was bad, Harper knew. Normal horses could be sweet and placid. Hellhorses? Not so much. They were not only as predatory as every other demon, they were fucking wild. You didn't ride a hellhorse unless you were crazy. "How often does Tanner do this?"

"Pretty often. Just as Levi likes the combat circle, Tanner likes the track."

She was about to ask what Larkin and Keenan liked to do when a bell rang and eight hellhounds slowly prowled onto the track. The crowd cheered, their excitement evident. She was a little too nervous for Tanner's demon to share in their excitement. Yes, it was most likely ironic that she was protective of the demon who protected her.

She recognized Tanner's hound by the scar on its muzzle. It was more powerfully built than the others, but she was worried all that bulkiness would slow it down. Each of the hellhounds got into position, growling and snarling at each other . . . and then things turned fucking weird. Oily pits, small fires, and puddles of bubbling, boiling water abruptly appeared in random places on the track. "Well, fuck."

Knox chuckled. "Don't be so nervous. He'll be fine."

A bell rang a second time, and the hellhounds bolted – Tanner's hound instantly fell into sixth place. Damn, they were fast as they leaped over the obstacles. Tanner's hound was totally focused, and its pace was steady and swift, but she had the feeling it was holding back a little.

It was no shock to discover that the hounds had no problem with cheating. They liked biting, clawing, and body slamming their competitors in an effort to take the lead. One locked its jaws around the back leg of another hound and spun it off the track – a move that lost it time as other hounds raced ahead of it. One howled as it was knocked into a puddle of boiling water by another hound.

Within fifty seconds, Tanner's demon was in third place. A competitor bit into its flank – bad decision. Tanner's hound slammed it into a pit; the oil kept the hound stuck in place.

The crowd was going crazy – yelling names, words of

encouragement, and also some threats. Every time a hound was taken out of the equation, people who'd clearly bet on them began stamping and cursing and even turned on their friends.

Tanner's hound soon shot into second place. All was looking good until ... "Someone just shot him with a fucking orb of hellfire!"

Knox locked his arms around her from behind and nuzzled her neck. "The spectators are allowed to do that in the last section of the track."

"*What?*"

"That's why the race is pretty much anyone's race. It doesn't matter how fast a hound is, they can be hurt and slowed down in the last section if they're hit too many times."

"Tanner's hound must be pissed." She worried her lower lip as another hound came close. "Come on, faster!" Hearing Knox chuckle again, she glanced at him over her shoulder. "I'm aware that it can't hear me. That doesn't mean I can't offer moral support."

"Of course it doesn't."

"Shit, it's slowing down . . . and that fucker just raced ahead of it." She cursed. "And now it's been hit again." This time on the leg. "Oh God, they're nearly at the finish line. Well, third place is pretty—" She gasped as Tanner's hound put on an impressive burst of speed. It shot straight into first place and right over the finish line. She found herself bouncing up and down in Knox's arms. "Tanner's hound won!"

"I see that."

"Okay, it's a little exciting," she allowed. "And I *might* have enjoyed it. Can we eat now? I'm starving."

"Not yet." Knox bit her earlobe before sucking on it. "Put your hands on the glass."

She stilled at the dominance and authority that rung in his

voice. She knew exactly what that tone meant. Her body knew what it meant, began to melt and ready itself for him. Harper's knees buckled as an ice-cold finger slid through her folds right as Knox snaked his hand beneath her shirt to cup one breast. "*Shit*. Tell me no one can see me."

"No one can see you . . . unless I flick that switch on the wall over there."

"Don't."

"Why? Don't you want them to see me taking you? Don't you want them to know you're mine, that every inch of you belongs to me?" He whipped off her t-shirt and bra. "Shoes."

She kicked them off while he quickly unbuttoned her fly and shoved down her jeans. Her panties went with a snap just as two icy fingers drove into her. The first cold thrust was always a shock, but the heat emanating from the fingers made her pussy blaze and spasm.

At his urging, she stepped out of her jeans. That was when his psychic fingers began pumping into her, making her body melt against him. Anticipation sent a tremor down her spine as she heard his zip slowly lowering. The bastard was dragging it out on purpose. The psychic fingers dissolved, leaving behind a flaming ache that was all too familiar.

"Hands on the glass, Harper. That's my good girl." Knox grabbed her hips, angled them just right, and slammed home. Her hot, slick pussy squeezed his cock almost to the point of pain. Too. Fucking. Good. Clutching the breast his demon had branded, Knox powered into her. "This is what I need."

Harper's back arched like a bow as he pounded into her, his fingers digging so hard into her breast and hip that she knew she'd have bruises. She caught his reflection in the glass. Eyes hooded, mouth set in a harsh line, there was savage need stamped into his features.

Hand bunched in her hair, Knox yanked her head back so he could suckle and bite her neck. Her taste and scent assaulted his senses, making his cock swell even further. Nothing felt better than her tight muscles greedily clamping around him, as if trying to hold him deep in her body. He growled low in her ear. "Do you know how hot it is to see the reflection of the brand on your pussy?" It stroked the possessive streak in him that came violently alive around Harper. "Every time you see it, do you remember how it felt when my demon put it there? Do you remember that it means I own you?"

She gasped as his fist tugged her hair hard, bringing her face to his. He didn't kiss her mouth. He devastated it. Biting on it, licking at it, and softly sucking on her tongue. The kiss repeatedly alternated between hard and rough to teasing and sensual. She felt off balance, couldn't think. She only knew she needed to come so bad it hurt.

Feeling her pussy begin to tighten around him, Knox knew her orgasm was close. "You know you can't come until I tell you, baby."

"I can't help it," she hissed.

"Yes, you can. You will." Releasing her hair, he collared her throat as he hammered into her at a feverish pace that dared her to defy him. She didn't, just like he knew she wouldn't. "Beg me to let you come."

Motherfucking asshole. Knowing better than to curse him out loud and risk him stopping – he'd done it a few times before – she begrudgingly ground out, "Please."

"Good girl." He slid his other hand down to tug on her clit. "Come, Harper." A scream tore from her throat as her pussy quaked and squeezed his cock. Biting out a harsh curse, he exploded in her, his hand tightening around her throat. Forcing himself to loosen the hold, he stroked her neck as she slowly came down from her high.

"How can you still be hard?"

Knox ever so slowly withdrew, causing her pussy to close around his cock and try to suck him back in. "Don't worry, baby, I'm not done yet." He drove deep with a grunt. "This time, scream my name for me."

CHAPTER SIXTEEN

After a long, boring conference call, Knox left his office and sought out Harper. He found her in the living area, legs crossed yoga-style on the sofa . . . and doing something he never would have expected. She had a box at her side that contained a collection of gems, crystals, sequins, rhinestones, beads, lace, sash, and other appliques. And she was sewing and gluing some on her collection of jeans. Designer jeans.

"Hey." She only spared him the briefest glance, preoccupied with sporadically attaching tiny, silver skeleton heads to a pair of black jeans.

Most of the other pairs that were folded on the sofa had already been 'decorated.' She'd even slashed at some with a razor, sewn white flowery lace on the back pockets of others, and . . . "What happened to *them*?" One particular pair of blue jeans were now a whitish blue from mid-calf downwards.

"Oh, I dipped them in bleach," she said, her tone absent.

"You dipped them in bleach? I buy designer clothes, and you—"

She did look up then. "I told you, *they're from thrift shops.*"

He couldn't stifle a smile. "Thrift shops. Right." He poured himself a gin and tonic, and then settled beside her, admiring her steady hand. "Do you do this a lot?"

"I like personalizing things. When I lived with Lucian, I traveled pretty light. We couldn't always afford to buy new clothes, so I'd revamp the ones I had." She gave him an impish smile. "Whenever he pissed me off, I'd glue pink sequins to his pants."

Knox tapped her bottom lip. "Cruel."

"I thought so." She sounded pleased by that.

"And here I thought Meg bought a new coat. You put rhinestones and crystals on it, didn't you?"

"She made me muffins in exchange. I thought it was a good deal."

As something occurred to him, he narrowed his eyes. "You haven't sewn or glued anything to any of my clothes, have you?"

Her smile widened – it was a taunt. "Not yet."

Knox returned the smile. He couldn't recall many people ever teasing him. People were generally wary of offending him. Harper didn't hold back, and it was yet another thing that showed that she was comfortable around him. This back and forth they did . . . It was intimate. And he liked it.

He put his glass on the table. "Come here." Knox slipped a hand around her throat and sipped at the mouth he was obsessed with. Then he kissed her hard, dancing his tongue along hers. The taste of her burst through his system, making him groan. He knew he'd always crave it, always crave her. "Later, I'm going to fuck this mouth." A hint of defiance sparked in her presently ice-blue eyes. Knox flexed his grip on her throat. "I'll have it, Harper. It's mine. Mine to taste, mine to use any way I want."

And he *had* used it any way he wanted. He knew he was

dominant and rough in the bedroom, that she wasn't used to being led or pushed to her limits. She probably had no idea what a turn on it was to teach her what he liked, to show her how it could be between demons. She was used to humans, so she'd had no idea just how intense and satisfying sex was with her own kind. "So let's try this again. Later, I'm going to fuck this mouth."

As the hand collaring her throat slid into her hair and gripped just hard enough to make her scalp prickle, Harper hissed. He did that sometimes, let her feel the bite of pain to warn her not to resist. But he never hurt her, never did anything he thought she wouldn't like or couldn't take. In doing that, he'd earned her trust in the bedroom. However, that didn't mean she'd ever be totally compliant. "You can fuck it," she began, shrugging, "if you can catch it." His sensual mouth curved into his panty-dropping smile.

"So defiant."

"But you like that, because having everyone obey you 24/7 has gotten old, hasn't it? And . . . you like to punish me." Those punishments usually went in the form of sensual assaults, prolonging foreplay, making her wait what felt like hours to come, or simply shackling her with psychic hands so she couldn't touch him.

He spoke against her lips. "I do like to punish you. I especially like seeing you shaking with the need to come . . . and cursing me in several languages for not allowing you to."

Harper laughed. "Well that's—" She stopped at the sound of footsteps approaching. All four sentinels then strolled into the room, and all looked grim; Keenan more so than the others.

Larkin's expression brightened a little when she saw Harper's handiwork. Blinking, she said, "Wow. You did all this?"

As Knox released her hair, Harper nodded at the female sentinel, who then sat opposite her. "Revamping stuff is always fun. And I'll tell you all about it after Keenan explains why he seems ready to burn shit down."

Keenan hesitated, glancing at Knox. The incubus wasn't yet used to including anyone other than Knox or the other sentinels in conversations concerning their lair.

"You can always speak freely in front of Harper," Knox told him. "So unless this is something very personal to you or someone else that can't be shared, explain now."

"It relates to me," Harper said with total surety. She could tell by the odd look that Keenan kept shooting her. Still, he hesitated. And that just pissed her off. "Keenan, do you like your clothes? Because I have a needle, thread, glue, and sequins – and I ain't afraid to use them. Tell me what's going on."

Keenan sighed. "You're right, it relates to you. It's just weird discussing lair business with outsiders."

"She's my mate, which makes it her business," Knox stated. "It also makes her part of this lair as well as her own."

Inclining his head, the incubus sat next to Larkin. "I called the other sentinels here, because I thought we all needed to discuss this."

Levi, who was leaning against the wall, asked, "Discuss what?"

"It's about Kendra," said Keenan.

Harper put aside the jeans she was working on. "Yeah, what about her?"

Keenan pulled a flask out of his jacket. "I got a call from the demons we've had watching her – she's missing. She slipped her guard again."

Knox twined a lock of Harper's hair around his finger absentmindedly. "It's possible that she's gone searching for Lucian using the information she was given by the imp she met with."

"I thought it was likely after what I heard in the boathouse," said Keenan. "So I went to Kendra's apartment to see if any of her stuff was missing – that would have told me if she'd taken a little trip. Nothing seems to have gone, and I couldn't help but notice there was nothing personal there at all. Not a damn thing. It bugged me. I can't explain why, it just did. Anyway, I went looking for her, and I asked people if they've seen her. No one has. I wondered if she'd gone to visit the mother she cares so much for that she feels obliged to avenge, so I paid her a visit." Keenan took a long swig from the flask. "Imagine my surprise when the young woman who invited me inside introduced herself as Kendra."

"Kendra?" echoed Tanner, who was lounging on Harper's left.

Keenan nodded. "Yep. I spoke to her, I spoke to the mother – Beatrice – and I can tell you that Kendra never left Alabama to come here. I don't know who the she-demon is who's been staying in our lair, but she's not Kendra Watson." He dropped the news like a bomb.

A short silence reigned before people began to curse.

"You're certain of this?" Levi asked Keenan.

"Absofuckinglutely certain. What I don't understand is why that bitch has been posing as Kendra."

Knox didn't have the answer to that, but he'd find it. "Did you tell Beatrice and Kendra that someone had been passing herself off as her?"

"No," responded Keenan. "That's lair business. I made up some bullshit reason for turning up and then I left."

"Did the real Kendra look anything like the fake one?" asked Tanner.

"A little. Same hairstyle. Same height. Same weight. Same eye color. But I don't think they're related. More like someone's been using Kendra's identity because they conveniently look alike."

Larkin folded her arms across her chest. "Why would someone join our lair, posing as someone they're not?"

"She could be a plant," said Knox, anger beginning to thrum through him. "There are plenty of demons who'd like to know our lair's personal business."

"That's true," agreed Levi, moving away from the wall. "She made an effort to get to you. She could have been sent here to seduce you, to find out your secrets." Levi snorted at the ridiculousness of it.

Keenan took another drink from his flask. "It wouldn't surprise me if Isla sent her."

"Why would . . . whoever she really is . . . be looking for Lucian if her job was to spy on you?" Larkin asked Knox.

"You have a point," conceded Knox. "'Kendra' went to the meeting in North Las Vegas. Jolene confirmed she met with an imp there, asking about Lucian."

Levi shrugged. "It could have been a cover, a story to give you in case someone saw her near Harper's apartment that night."

"You know," interrupted Harper, "it's possible she's not hiring dark practitioners at all; that *they* are hiring *her*." When no one spoke, she added, "There are plenty of demons for hire out there – they'll work for the enemy for a price."

Tanner frowned, pensive. "You could be right. Practitioners probably see you as a way to get to Knox, to weaken him."

"She really does hate me, though," insisted Harper. "I felt it in the restrooms."

"Maybe she just has an issue with your family or with imps in general," suggested Keenan. "And bear in mind that she's a real good actress, Harper. In the boathouse, she had me completely fooled about her hatred for Lucian and her distress over her mother."

"So we can agree that 'Kendra' is a plant," said Knox. "We're just not so sure who sent her."

"I'd say it's Isla," declared Keenan. "She always seems to know too much about what's going on. She could have put a plant in every lair, not just ours."

"It could just as easily be one of the other Primes doing a little spying," said Larkin. "Knowledge is power."

"Maybe," said Levi, "but I think Harper's right. I think dark practitioners hired her. It really would explain a lot."

"If that's true, she's a lot more dangerous than we thought." Larkin crossed one leg over the other. "She'll have many connections to many of our enemies."

"The way I see it, we have two options." Tanner leaned forward, bracing his elbows on his thighs. "We can put a bounty on her head or we can act like she's still fooling us."

Knox thought about it for a few moments. "We'll try the latter, see if it brings her home. If she doesn't appear in a couple of days, we resort to the first option. In the meantime, find out who the goddamn bitch really is."

Once the sentinels left, Knox turned to Harper, twisting fully in his seat to face her. "You okay?"

She exhaled heavily. "It's a relief to know that I haven't been warring with my half-sister. But I don't exactly like the alternative – dealing with dark practitioners isn't fun, and they seem to want me dead."

Knox tugged her closer. "They're trying to get to me . . . which means Kendra – or whoever the hell she is – is actually right; you're being targeted because of me."

"I'm being targeted because they're thick as pig shit and probably have a crazy idea that if they can weaken you enough, they can contain you and then use you to fuel their spells," she corrected.

Maybe. They wouldn't be the first to assume they could capture and use Knox for something.

"You didn't start shit with them. *They* came at *you*."

"And they're using you to come at me, which isn't at all acceptable to me." They thought that hurting her would hurt him. It would. He wasn't sure when she'd become so important to him, but she was so deep under his skin there was no getting her out. When a demon fell, it was quick and hard and intense. He'd never thought to experience it. Hadn't imagined it was possible for another person to be so vital to him. He didn't fear it, though. He welcomed it. Knew he'd forever want this little sphinx with him.

He'd always thought that to need someone would make him vulnerable. Now Knox knew differently. Yes, Harper had power over him, but he knew she'd never abuse that power. He could trust her with it, just as she trusted him with the same power he had over her. He'd tried to lure her to him using various manipulation tactics, and all the while he'd been unknowingly falling for this she-demon. "Levi's right; you're my weakness."

Harper frowned, confused but knowing one thing: "I don't like the sound of that."

"Control is essential to me, Harper. Essential for many reasons. If anything happened to you, if you were taken from me, that control would be gone. What I did to Riordan and his followers . . . that would be nothing compared to what I'd do if someone took your life."

If he thought he was scaring her, he was wrong. "You think I wouldn't seek vengeance if anything happened to you?" Harper fisted her hand in his shirt. "I'd make sure the bastards got whatever they deserved."

He cocked his head. "You would, wouldn't you?"

"Duh." How could that surprise him?

"That's the thing, though, baby. You'd track down and punish the person or people responsible, and you'd give them what they deserved. But you'd stop there. Even with your demon riding you hard, you'd hold back."

"You have enough control to hold back your demon."

He smiled wanly, refusing to lie to her. "Baby, I wouldn't want to. I'd make them all pay. But I wouldn't stop there. It wouldn't be enough. Not for me, not for my demon. So many would die, so much would be destroyed." It had to be a hard weight for her to carry. "You need to live."

As his gaze held hers, Harper sensed that – maybe only subconsciously – he expected some level of rejection here. Maybe he thought his admission would spook or repel her. Hell, maybe it should have. But although it left her a little off balance to know she was so important to someone, it also thrilled her. He said she'd given him one thing no one else ever had: total acceptance. Well, he'd given her something no one else ever had: the feeling of being indispensable to someone.

When Harper straddled him, curled her arms around his neck, and melted into his chest, Knox tucked her head under his chin. She fit right there, like it was exactly where she belonged. He smoothed his hands up and down her back, sensing she was offering the reassurance that she still accepted him and his demon just as they were.

He was a dark breed that had no right to walk the Earth. But he didn't hate what he was. Quite the opposite, Knox *liked* the power, the rush, and the added strength. He liked the control that it allowed him to maintain. Liked that he never felt vulnerable. He accepted the creature inside him that had protected and saved him when no one else would. Knox hadn't expected that anyone else would ever accept the entity, though. He'd never thought they *should*. He hadn't asked it of Harper, but she'd done it anyway. She'd also accepted Knox, brutal bastard though he was. She was a total wonder to him.

"You could beg me to let you go, but I wouldn't." He'd told her before that he didn't intend to give her freedom, but he needed her to understand how utterly serious he was. If she chose to leave, he'd find a way to make her want to stay.

Harper pulled back to look him dead in the eye. "Okay, first of all, I only beg in the bedroom – and that's on rare occasions. Don't think I'll ever do it under any other circumstances. Second of all, I'll never be anyone's captive; no one can keep me anywhere that I don't want to be." She was an imp for all intents and purposes, she could escape from anywhere. "Lastly, if you majorly fuck up and hurt me badly – like cheating on me, for instance – I'm gone, Thorne. But if you mean you still expect me to go based purely on what breed you are, I'm pissed that you think so little of me."

For a moment, Knox couldn't speak. Her reactions threw him every time. "Let's address all those responses, shall we? It's true that you beg in the bedroom occasionally. I happen to enjoy it. However, I'd never expect you to beg me for anything; if you ever want something, you'll have it. Except, of course, your freedom. As for your next point, it wasn't a good idea on your part to use the word 'captive' – that has all kinds of sexual fantasies running through my head. So be prepared for the consequences, and remember you only have yourself to blame."

When she would have spoken, Knox put a finger to her mouth. "Thirdly, I'd *never* betray you or purposely hurt you. You're mine to care for, and you'll never be anything *but* cared for. And the idea that I might ever want another woman is just plain fucking stupid anyway. Lastly, I *don't* think little of you. If I did, I wouldn't want you as a mate, would I? But the fact is that I'll be a difficult person to be with. Controlling, possessive, selfish, highly sexual, inexperienced with emotional intimacy, and I always want what I want exactly *when* I want it. I've told you before, I don't have a lot of good in me. You're not getting a very good deal here, baby."

"Oh, and I'm some kind of innocent, perfect maiden?" She'd be bored if she was, to be honest. "Let's look at a little thing called 'reality.' Everybody has flaws, Knox. No one is easy to be with. I don't think you actually realize just how crazy I'm going to make you. I'm impossible to control, I have a bad temper, I curse like nobody's motherfucking business, and I'm – quite often deliberately – annoying. I'm also stingy with trust, and I'm uncomfortable when people buy me shit or even just be nice to me. Even *I* know that's just weird. I don't exactly have a lot of experience with emotional intimacy either. But you accept all my shit just like I accept yours. That's how it works."

She sat up straighter as she added, voice hard, "And if you *are* still paranoid that I'll leave when you finally pull your big boy pants up and tell me what you are, I'm gonna get cranky. It won't matter because I care about you, and whatever breed you are doesn't change *you*. And now I'm blushing because I blurted out the last part. I blame you for that."

Knox pressed a soft kiss to her mouth. "I already knew you cared. You wouldn't have taken me as your mate if you didn't. Demons don't take mates unless they care."

She folded her arms over her chest. "That's a real poor way of saying you care about me too, you know."

It was. "You won't hear pretty words from me often," he felt compelled to warn her.

"I know that." He was charismatic, but he wasn't a flatterer when it came to feelings that had any depth. He suffered from emotional poverty almost as bad as his demon. "I don't expect to hear them and I'm not going to crave them. Compliments and pretty words make me blush, which I don't like to do, because it's just embarrassing. All I'm asking is that you don't pretend that you don't care out of some kind of masculine pride."

He could have taken the out she'd just given him, vowed to simply not put on a façade, but that wasn't who he was. She deserved better. "I've been around for centuries. I became jaded, empty, lonely – but at least they were feelings of some sort. Over the past year, I was growing . . . numb. There wasn't much that truly mattered to me anymore. You changed that. You matter. So much that you're a vulnerability, a weakness. But I'm keeping you."

Knox framed her face with his hands. "Nothing is more important to me than you. And I'll kill anyone who tries to take you from me. What you have to live with is that you have more control over my demon than I do, because it will annihilate everything in its path if anything bad were to happen to you. I wouldn't be able to hold it back even if I wanted to." He waited impatiently for her to speak, for her blank expression to give away something of what she was—

"Is this the part where I flee in terror? I'm not sure. Give me a hint." With a snort, she rolled her eyes. "I think you're forgetting just how much control *you* have over *my* demon. You're its mate, which means that if you're hurt, it won't give a flying fuck about anything but avenging you. And as much as I'd like to say my conscience would speak up and I'd then try to rein in the demon, I'm not so sure I would. I'd be a wreck at the time, because you're just as important to me. I don't like having a weakness, it's actually pissing me off. But you're stuck with me."

For a moment, there was utter silence. She opened her mouth to speak, and suddenly she was being kissed like he needed her taste to survive. He plundered, consumed, dominated. She felt herself getting wet, felt her nerve endings all—

They broke apart at the sound of someone clearing their throat.

"Mr. Thorne," called Dan, "I believe the fax you're waiting for has just arrived in your office."

Knox inhaled deeply. "Thanks, Dan." Brushing her hair away from her face, Knox kissed her once more. "I'll be back soon."

She couldn't help but ogle his epic ass as he strode out of the room. Her demon wanted to bite it, and the idea truly did have its appeal. Maybe later. She picked up the jeans she was working on and went back to revamping them.

"Skeleton heads? Nice."

The unfamiliar and unexpected voice made her jerk in panic and instinctively strike out with a punch to the jaw. They hit the ground with a thud, out cold. As she realized who it was, she winced. "Oh, shit."

"Um, Knox. I kind of just knocked the Devil unconscious."

Knox's head snapped up from the fax he was reading to stare at Harper. "Repeat that."

"He surprised me," she said defensively. "My power rushed straight to my hands, so when I sucker-punched him, he fell like a sack of spuds."

Knox strode out of his office and into the living area with his mate in tow. And there was Lucifer himself, sprawled on the floor. Harper's power delivered at close range with such a harsh impact had obviously struck his soul so hard, his mind had clapped out.

"It is him, right?" asked Harper, chewing on her thumb. "I mean, I haven't seen him since I was a kid."

"It's him," Knox confirmed. "You saw him when you were a child?"

"He came to Jolene's house to yell at her for something, so

she fed him some cookies as an apology. Of course, they were drugged and made him high as a kite. He stripped down to his boxers and sang 'Baby Got Back'."

Knox couldn't help but smile. "Is that why he loathes your grandmother?"

"No, but that incident kind of fed the hate. Although I think, on one level, he actually admired the cunningness of it." Seeing him as a child, she'd been taken aback to discover it was Lucifer. Like now, he'd been dressed in casual, almost scruffy clothes and a baseball cap. "He's gonna be pissed at me."

"Even if he is, he won't hurt you."

"He won't?" She wasn't convinced.

"No, because he'll have to deal with me if he does." According to many human religions, Lucifer ruled hell. Not really. Lucifer moved to hell after he left heaven, he brought some order to the place, and he issued an open invitation for any soul to enter upon their death. There were many worse things in hell than Lucifer.

A slight psychic slap from Knox was enough to wake him. Eyelids fluttering, Lucifer groaned. "That hurt." In a blink, he was upright, looking at Harper curiously. "Soul-deep pain, huh? Never got hit by that before. I like to try new things."

"Why are you here?" Knox asked bluntly.

Lucifer blinked at him. "I heard you'd taken a mate. I'm too cynical to believe it, but I was curious." He smiled. "I like her. She surprised me. That doesn't happen a lot."

Knox snickered. Lucifer didn't like anyone. Abrasive, blunt, and offensive, he was a social nightmare. He was also psychotic and came with a child-like sense of entitlement, a love of sarcasm, and a propensity to constantly switch from one emotional state to another.

Lucifer turned back to Harper. "I didn't even catch your name."

She gave him a nod. "I'm Harper."

"Call me Lou. You remind me of someone." He clicked his fingers several times, deep in thought. "Are you a Connell?"

Harper couldn't help grinning, anticipating his reaction. "No. I'm a Wallis."

His cheeriness died away as his jaw clenched. "A Wallis?"

Retaking her seat, Harper nodded. "Jolene's granddaughter, actually."

He shuddered. "That woman. Sneaky. Scheming. Vicious. Qualities I usually admire."

"She snorts when you give her orders, doesn't she?" asked Knox.

"Every time," growled Lou.

Knox could understand his frustration. "It's in the genes."

Lou studied Harper closely. "You're a sphinx. I'm guessing then that you're Lucian's daughter." Lou sat beside Harper and began nosing in her box of appliqués. With a muffled curse, he started moving some of them around.

She frowned. "What are you doing?"

"You're getting them mixed up." He sounded genuinely agitated. "See, you've got rhinestones over there with the sequins."

Oh, yeah, Jolene had once mentioned he was a little OCD. "Does my grandmother still send you chain letters?"

He growled again. "Yes. She knows I can't break them. It's bad luck."

Harper shook her head. "Not really. It's called OCD and—"

"Yes, yes, so my psychiatrist tells me."

"You have a shrink?"

"Apparently, I have some repressed anger and unresolved abandonment issues after my experiences with God." An element of vulnerability entered his tone as he continued, "You know from your experiences with Carla and Lucian – that kind of thing leaves its mark on a person, doesn't it? It hurts right to the core."

This conversation was becoming way too surreal for Harper. "I really don't know how to process you."

With a grunt, Lou looked up at Knox. "Have you told her what you are yet?"

Knox narrowed his eyes. "Not yet."

Lou rubbed his hands together, suddenly excited. "Ooh, the suspense."

"*Lou*," drawled Knox, not trusting the guy to not simply blurt out the truth.

"Fine, fine." And now he was back to somber. "So, I heard your mate here is having some trouble."

Knox explained the recent goings on. "We're either dealing with dark practitioners, Isla Ross, or Carla Hayden."

"I don't like Carla." Lou grimaced. "She's very mercurial, it's annoying."

Pot, kettle, black, thought Harper. "I think dark practitioners are responsible." She looked at Knox. "You still think there's a good chance it's Isla, don't you?"

Knox shrugged. "She's twisted enough to do all this."

"That's true," agreed Lou, nodding a few times.

"I've heard rumors about her renting out demons from her lair to dark practitioners," Knox told him. "Only someone losing their hold on their demon or just sick in the head would do that."

"Maybe she smokes crack," Lou suggested.

Ignoring that idea, Harper spoke to Knox. "I can't understand why she'd take the risk of renting them out like that, knowing her own kind could turn on her for it. Something must be fucking with her head."

"Could be crack," said Lou.

Knox also ignored him. "I know it makes little sense; that's why I've always doubted the rumors," he told Harper. "But, like I said, she's cold and power-hungry enough to do it. She wasn't always like that. Something changed her."

Lou swept out a hand. "Adding support to my 'crack' theory."

Exasperated, Harper burst out, "*Oh my God*."

Lou frowned at her. "Can we leave him out of this, please?"

Knox blinked in surprise. "You said 'please.' Snappy or not, you used manners."

"I decided to branch out from cold and pure evil."

Harper was sure she'd never met anyone as whacked as this guy.

Lou stretched his legs out. "There are some whisper campaigns going on. The candidates for this whole boring election extravaganza are spreading rumors about each other to make themselves look better."

"Yes, there's a rumor that Malden long ago made a point of banishing every harpy from his lair out of racial hate." It had pissed off Larkin.

Lou sniffed. "I have no tolerance for racism. I find it offensive."

Harper arched her brows. Who'd have thought the Devil had morals? "Does it bother you that Isla might be doing horrible shit to her lair?"

"She hasn't violated any of my rules."

Knox knew she'd always been careful not to. Lou's rules were pretty simple: don't get caught breaking human laws, don't reveal their existence, and don't hurt any child of any species. Yes, he was protective of children. The Devil was no more one-dimensional than anybody else.

"Dario allegedly engages in voodoo sex rituals with his harem that's constructed of one of every breed of demon, male or female," said Knox.

Lou's expression was one of distaste. "Rituals . . . I'm not really into that."

Harper just had to ask. "So all those humans who play with what they believe are satanic rituals—"

"Purely irritate me. It's like having a phone that constantly rings, and each caller is a telemarketer wanting to deliver an annoying spiel and then ask for something in return. And what do they promise me in exchange for whatever I may give them? Their souls. I already have their souls for the simple reason that they just sacrificed a virgin and drank her blood." He shook his head incredulously, rising to his feet. "Anyway, now that I've satisfied my curiosity, I'm heading back. Think you could put some of those skeleton thingies on the collar of my jacket next time I stop by?" he asked Harper.

Surely he had to be kidding . . . but he didn't look like he was. "I guess so."

He grinned, happy again. "Excellent." Then he was gone.

She stared up at Knox, knowing she had to appear as stunned as she felt. "He's like a psychopathic child with bipolar and OCD."

Knox sighed. "That about describes him."

"Is it wrong that I find him a little morbidly fascinating?"

Knox loomed over her, resting his hands on the sofa either side of her head. "If you're going to find anyone fascinating, it should be *me*."

She smiled, running her hands up his chest. "You're a different kind of fascinating. And hot. Seriously hot. Your ass is epic. And you have the best voice – velvety and smoky and rumbly. Did I mention you're hot?"

He nipped her chin. "Good save."

"Aw, you two are kind of cute."

Knox closed his eyes. "*Lou.*"

"Okay, okay, I was just bringing the jacket." He slung it on the sofa. "One minute you're perfectly civil, and the next minute you're growling at me. I don't know where I am with you." He disappeared again.

Harper found herself chuckling. "I don't know how to process any of what's just happened." It just felt too surreal.

"You know what, baby . . . it's probably best for your mental health if you don't."

"Yeah, you're probably right."

CHAPTER SEVENTEEN

"Got the info you asked for. Wasn't easy."

Harper leaned back in her office chair, sighing at Khloë. "I'm not going to like this at all, am I?"

"Not one little bit."

Jolene had taught Harper to 'always know your enemy.' So weeks ago, Harper had contacted her sources and done some research on Isla. But all the different stories she'd heard had contradicted each other, and she'd quickly suspected that Isla had fabricated those stories to keep people from knowing the truth. So Harper had gone to the one person who could find out anything: Khloë.

Her cousin settled in the chair opposite Harper. "It took so long to dig up info because her inner circle is utterly devoted to her in a way that's just creepy ... like she's some kind of goddess."

"What did you find out?"

"In short, Isla's an ambitious, greedy, power-hungry bitch who rose to her position by blackmailing, intimidating, framing, and jumping in bed with people."

Harper blinked. "It's hard to imagine her jumping into bed with someone. She's never struck me as a sexual person – she's too robotic and apathetic."

"Yes, but sex can often be a way to control people, can't it? She probably uses it as a weapon."

That sounded more like Isla.

"She has no limits and believes herself to be untouchable. She also flies into rages that could put fear into even Lucifer."

"Rages?" It was hard to imagine that happening. Isla just seemed so composed all the time. Even when she'd been pissed at the conference in Manhattan, she hadn't lost control.

"Oh yeah. Behind that collected exterior is a paranoid, deranged, corrupt woman. She also has a little secret that she mistakenly thinks is well-guarded. She thinks that only her inner circle of demons – who believe she can't do wrong, and who'll do whatever she asks of them, because they worship her – are the only ones that know."

Harper leaned forward in her seat. "What is this little secret?"

"It seems that Isla has a little thing for sexual sadism."

Okay, that was a shock. "Seriously?"

"Personally, I don't view what she's doing as sexual sadism. I just call it plain twisted. She ties up unwilling women and does everything short of killing them. When she gets bored of a woman, she has one of her inner circle kill her. It's odd that she doesn't do that herself, considering she has absolutely no problem doing other sick shit."

"The women she's been hurting . . . are they from her lair?"

"Yes. The other lair members know she's punishing the women, they just don't know *how* she's punishing them. Apparently a lot of those punishments are for imaginary crimes."

Khloë's upper lip curled. "In my opinion, she's not punishing them, she's doing it because it's how she gets off."

"Before, you said *sexual* sadism."

"She sexually assaults them."

Harper cursed, scrubbing a hand down her face. "I feel sick."

"According to my source, she seems to *hate* her own gender."

"Any idea why? Was her mother abusive or something?"

"No, but her father was; her mother committed suicide. That's as much as my contact knows about her past."

Harper shrugged. "Then maybe it's something else. Maybe she hates herself and she's projecting that onto other women – especially if those women are confident, happy, and have things that Isla wants."

"Could be."

"There isn't a way we can help them. Lairs don't interfere in each other's business." Harper exhaled heavily. "Sadly, she's not the only Prime who hurts her lair. It goes on all over the world."

"Yep. And Malden's promise of a voice will appeal to all those victims," Khloë pointed out.

"He won't live up to his promises."

"*We* know that. But I have a feeling that most of the public don't. And that's not good."

Harper sighed. "No, it's not." The polling would take place in two days' time in the same Underground hotel that the speeches were held. "The whisper campaigns have done some damage, though not the damage the Primes had intended." Instead of making the public choose one Prime over the others, it had made them too confused to trust any of the candidates. As such, a lot of demons weren't so keen on making any changes.

"I gotta tell ya, Harper, I'm no longer so sure that it's dark practitioners behind the attacks on you. At first, I thought you were right. But now that I know what Isla's capable of, how good she is at hiding her true self from anyone, I'm thinking maybe Knox is right and Isla's the culprit."

"She'd certainly get off on it. But that doesn't necessarily mean it's her."

"Speaking of another possible culprit . . . Has Knox or his sentinels figured out who the Kendra impersonator really is?"

Harper shook her head. "They can't find her either. Not even with a bounty on her head."

"She's probably stolen another person's identity, hiding in plain sight."

"That's what I'm thinking."

Khloë braced her elbows on the desk and began playing with Harper's stapler. "Enough of all the depressing shit. What are you doing for your birthday tomorrow?"

Harper happily went along with changing the subject. "Knox is being very mysterious about it. All I know is that he's taking me somewhere." Demons didn't do the whole card and gift thing like humans, but they did celebrate their birthdays. Some liked to indulge in a good ole adrenalin rush, others might prefer a night in the Underground, and – in the case of imps – some might be more attracted to the idea of breaking into a bank vault for fun.

"What about Lucian?"

"He called me yesterday. It'll be a few days before he can make it here. He said he can't find anyone to take care of his emu while he's gone."

Khloë gaped. "An emu? That guy is just warped."

Harper chuckled. "I'm actually glad he won't be here for another few days. I'm not at all eager for him to meet Knox."

Putting down the stapler, Khloë smiled. "Knox is gonna verbally kick his ass. You know that, right?"

"I know." Harper sighed. "I've tried to explain that Lucian's not as bad as he thinks, but I'm not getting through to Knox."

"He's your mate, he's protective of you. That's a good thing. So . . . has he told you what he is yet?" Her tone warned that there would be repercussions if he hadn't.

"Don't interfere. He'll tell me when he's ready."

"But—"

"*Khloë*."

"Fine, fine, whatever. I suppose we can't really be upset with him for holding back from you, since you're keeping a whopper of a secret from him."

"I am?" This was the first Harper had heard of it.

"Yes . . . unless you've finally told him that you love him."

Harper spluttered. "I didn't say that I love him."

"Be honest, you do." When Harper didn't speak, Khloë groaned, her expression a plea. "Come on, you can tell me, Harper. I know I'm an irritating bitch, and I know I'm full of advice that you don't want to hear, but we've always shared shit."

She made her confession quickly. "Yes, I love him. No, I haven't told him."

"You don't want him to know you love him until you're sure he loves you right back," Khloë guessed.

"I'm honestly not sure if 'love' is on Knox's emotional scale." It wasn't something she begrudged him for. He was the way he was, and she had to accept that.

"At least you're not denying that you love him."

"Now that you have your answers, can we move on to another – and much more casual – subject?"

Khloë gave her an apologetic smile. "I just want you to be happy."

"I am, doofus."

Harper? Knox's velvety voice slid over her skin.

Yeah?

I need you to go with Tanner. He'll bring you to me. A vibe of frustration accompanied the words.

What's wrong?

Carla's secret . . . it's out.

Well, shit.

A short while later, she and Tanner were entering Knox's Underground office above the combat circle. He stood near the window while Keenan and Levi lounged on the sofa.

"What's happened exactly? Who blabbed?" She wondered if it was Kellen, but—

"We actually don't know." Knox came to her, every muscle in his body tense, as if he was coiled to spring. As usual, he looked totally calm, despite the anger pulsing in the air. "Like with the whisper campaigns, the news seemed to come out of nowhere. It has spread around the Underground like wildfire."

Harper cursed. She'd known it was highly likely that the truth would one day come out. She just hadn't expected it to be so soon. As Tanner had led her to the office, people had stared and whispered. The fact that everyone knew . . . she hated that.

Tanner leaned against the wall. "There's a great deal of anger brewing down there."

"A lot of people aren't happy," said Levi.

Harper frowned. "Why? I mean, I know she did wrong, but my family already knows about it. Who else would care?"

"Our entire lair cares," replied Levi. "You're Knox's anchor *and* his mate, which automatically makes them protective of you. People see you at his side, supporting him at meetings and gatherings. To support him is to support all of us. Larkin had to pull Carla out of a mob of pissed-off demons ready to kick her ass."

He had to be kidding. "Mob?"

Knox, twining her hair around his finger like he was apt to do when pissed or in deep thought, said, "Mona was leading it."

Harper snorted a laugh, which appeared to further anger him. "Come on, you don't find it funny that a she-demon who once dueled with me down there is now my biggest supporter?"

Keenan pursed his lips. "There is an amusing quality to the situation."

"Nothing about this situation is humorous," countered Knox. Moving closer to her, he placed his hands on her forearms. "I can't cut this rumor off. It's already spread too far, too fast. That means we have to ride it out."

"Has Carla denied the truth to everyone?" Harper asked him.

"Oddly enough, no."

She'd have thought the woman would have maintained her innocence, given that she'd have to know full well that Harper would just as happily deny the rumor was true. "Does her mate know yet?"

"Yes. He called me earlier, asking where Carla was."

Levi cocked his head. "He didn't ask you if there was any truth in the whispers?"

"No."

"Maybe he wants to hear it from her," suggested Harper. Hearing her cell ring, she dug it out of her pocket. "It's Jolene."

As Harper moved to the other side of his office to take the call, Knox turned to his sentinels. "Whoever released this information did it practically anonymously. That tells me they're adept at this sort of thing . . . maybe as adept as those who have been part of the whisper campaigns."

"Like Isla, you mean," concluded Keenan.

For Knox, it was becoming more and more likely that Isla was the culprit.

"Someone went through the trouble of digging deep into Harper's life," said Keenan. "Why? What's the point?"

"It'll distract people from the election," Levi pointed out. "But I don't think that was the motivation. Releasing the secret has hurt Harper, hasn't it?"

Knox glanced at her. She was trying to talk Jolene down from turning Carla's home to rubble. Harper didn't look at all like she was hurting, but he knew she was, and he hated it. Although he didn't like that his mate was, in her words, 'Carla's dirty little secret' and he didn't believe it was fair that she was kept as one, he also knew that Harper was a private person who wouldn't want her personal business up for public consumption. It infuriated him that he couldn't protect her from this.

"Whoever's been trying to hurt her hasn't been successful," continued Levi. "Maybe they've accepted that and they're settling for making her suffer in other ways."

Keenan shrugged. "What do we do?"

"The only thing we can do: damage control." At the knock on the door, Knox called out, "Come in."

Larkin walked inside, dragging a reluctant Carla with her. His inner demon snarled. Knox prided himself on being good at reading people, but he'd never been able to discern Carla's true feelings about Harper. He'd known one thing, though: Carla's part in every conversation about or with Harper had always been an act. As he stared at Carla now, he could see that her façade was gone. Maybe it was the shock of the situation, but the mask had finally fallen. There was none of her usual graciousness or timidity. She looked terrified and devastated. And it was real.

Larkin guided a pale, trembling Carla to the chair opposite his desk. "She doesn't know who started the rumor," the female sentinel told him. "I can't find out either."

As Carla spotted Harper, grief and longing briefly glimmered in the woman's eyes. But then it was gone. It wasn't even that she was trying to hide it. Instead, it was as though there was a part of Carla that possessed those feelings, but it was too small a part to make any difference.

"What exactly is the rumor?" Knox asked Larkin.

"Just that Carla gave Harper up to Jolene when she was a baby."

Well, Jolene's fictional version of events was a lot better than the full truth. "Nothing more?"

Larkin's brows drew together. "*Is* there more?"

Knox looked down at Carla. "Much more. Isn't there, Carla?" The woman gulped.

"Jolene's pissed," announced Harper as she sidled up to Knox, briefly glancing at Carla – the woman wouldn't meet her gaze. "She's trying to find out who started all the whispers. So far, she's having no luck with it."

"The mob has separated, but people are still unhappy," said Larkin.

Knox glared down at Carla. "It galls me to have to protect you. In my opinion, you deserve to be fucking verbally crucified out there. You deserve *worse*. But I won't have warring going on within my lair. That means taking steps to calm the situation."

"I could make a statement that I'm not upset," suggested Harper.

Larkin shook her head. "That won't be enough; they're upset on your behalf."

"So maybe I could be seen to escort her out of here."

Knox turned to Harper. "You're not protecting her. She didn't protect you. Did you, Carla?"

"No." It was spoken so quietly, it was a true wonder that anyone heard it.

"In fact, the only thing that kept Harper alive during the pregnancy was a damn spell, wasn't it?"

"*Knox*," Harper cautioned. It was bad enough that people knew as much as they did. She didn't want him blurting out the rest.

"You can't have any idea how much I'd like to end you," Knox rumbled at Carla. "The only reason you're breathing is that Harper doesn't want vengeance. Oh, I thought about ignoring her wish to let you be. I thought about making you suffer the way you wanted her to suffer."

"I didn't want her to suffer," Carla objected quietly.

"You wanted Lucian to suffer. Do you think that excuses what you did?"

"No." Again, her voice was low.

A frantic knock was followed by Bray's voice asking to be let inside. Knox wouldn't have thought it was possible, but Carla's face paled even more. Knox summoned him in, but Carla didn't turn to face her mate. His hair was ruffled, as if he'd dragged his hand through it several times. His eyes were wild and desperate – most likely, he was desperate for her to deny what he'd heard; for her to decry that it was all lies.

Bray looked briefly at Harper before moving to stand in front of Carla. "Is it true?" His voice was like gravel.

Carla didn't meet his gaze. "Yes."

Bray's jaw hardened. "How could you not tell me? *How?*" he demanded with a growl.

"I was ashamed, Bray!" she burst out, finally looking at him. Her words all came out in a rush. "I hate myself for what I did! She was an innocent little baby who hadn't done anything to anyone. But I was hurting and angry when Lucian left me, so wrapped up in my own misery and pain that I wasn't thinking straight. He was my anchor *and* the person I'd wanted as a mate, *but he left me.* My head was a mess, my demon was demanding the bastard while all I wanted was for him to hurt the way I hurt. A need for vengeance was the only thing keeping me going!"

There was a whole lot of truth in that, Knox sensed. If Carla had felt for Lucian even half of what Knox felt for Harper, he could understand how that would have twisted her so much inside; how it would have left her so overtaken by rage and despair that nothing and no one else seemed to matter. But to Knox, it would never fucking excuse what she'd done to Harper. Never.

"*She* should have kept you going," insisted Bray, pointing at Harper. "*She* should have mattered more than vengeance."

"Yes," whispered Carla. "By the time I realized that she did, it was too late." She turned to Harper. "I tried to take you back once."

Harper would have snorted, except there was some genuine emotion there. "Only because you saw with me Lucian and realized that I was a potential weapon to use to hurt him."

She shook her head. "I was jealous. He had you, and I didn't. I tried not to think about you after I gave you to Jolene as a baby. But that day, I had to face that you were real. That I'd done something so very, very cruel. You used your ability on me. All the while, your eyes were changing colors. You get that trait from my baby sister, you know. She died. That was my fault. I pushed the swing too hard and she fell . . ." Carla inhaled deeply. "In the store, I saw you both staring at me, condemning me as I felt a pain I had every reason to feel."

"So you just went back to pretending she didn't exist after that?" asked Bray, disgusted.

Carla continued speaking to Harper. "I went to see you sometimes, whenever you came with Lucian to visit Jolene. Not up close. Just . . . from afar. I just wanted to see you." She didn't even seem to know why.

"Yet, you dismissed her when you saw her in the street," Knox reminded her. "That part I just don't get."

"I bumped into one of your aunts once," she told Harper. "She gave me one hell of a lecture about leaving you on Jolene's doorstep when you were a baby, and I realized that Jolene hadn't told people the whole version. I was worried that if you came to me, Jolene would be mad enough to tell you everything so that you stayed away from me. I didn't want you to know just how cruel to you I really was. So I made sure I seemed unreceptive."

Bray ran both hands through his hair. "You should have told me, Carla."

Carla flicked a glance at him. "I was worried you would leave me."

Bray looked at Harper, perplexed. "You don't seem upset."

Harper shrugged. "I had a good life. Maybe not a normal life, but it was good. I was happy. If your mate was really such a mess at the time I was born, I doubt she could have given me that. We were both better off without the other."

"But she's your mother."

"I traveled a lot over the years. I've seen a lot of places. Some weren't good. I saw suffering that would make all this seem like a damn fairytale. One friend I had . . . her mother did the opposite of what Carla did. She kept her daughter, but she hated her. Hated her and was cruel to her while doting on the other kids. I would rather not have lived that life."

Bray was silent for a few moments. "You're very mature and wise for your age." His face hardened as his attention returned to Carla. "We're going home, and you're going to tell me everything. *Everything*."

"I will." Carla got to her feet.

"Larkin and Keenan will escort you out," Knox told them.

On reaching the door, Carla glanced at Harper over her shoulder. "I really am sorry I couldn't be the mother you needed." With that, she left.

Knox turned to Harper, concerned by her blank expression. "You okay?"

"I want to go home." She knew she probably sounded a little lost, but she felt off-kilter.

"Then we go home."

Sitting across the dining table from Harper, Knox watched as she absently shoved the food around the plate with her fork. When he brought her home earlier, she'd claimed she just wanted to lounge around for a while. Although she'd settled comfortably on the sofa, she hadn't really been watching the T.V. Her expression had been vacant, her eyes faraway. She'd been quiet for hours now. Pensive. It wasn't like Harper to overthink things. "Eat, baby."

Her brow wrinkled. "I'm not really that hungry."

"Eat or Meg will be offended." When she shoved a piece of pasta in her mouth, he arched a brow. "You'll do it for Meg, but not for me?"

"She might stop making me muffins."

He would have smiled if she hadn't dropped her fork with a clang and sighed. Knox moved to sit beside her. Forking some pasta, he held it up to her mouth. Casting him a sour look, she ate it. "Good girl. Tell me what's bothering you so much that you can't eat."

Swallowing down her pasta, Harper sipped at her wine. "It's stupid."

"If it matters to you, it matters. That means it isn't stupid. Tell me."

"In my head, I've always had Carla in a box safely marked 'selfish and unfeeling.' She was the baddie, and so I didn't have to care what she did. The things she said earlier . . . they still make her selfish, but not exactly unfeeling. I don't know how to see her differently. I don't *want* to see her differently." Because if she wasn't bad, Harper might have to care. To care meant to be hurt by what had happened.

Knox gripped Harper's chin. "She should have put you first, no matter what shit was going on in her life, but she didn't. She doesn't deserve your forgiveness, so don't expect it of yourself. Carla fucked up royally, and she never once tried to fix it." He forced Harper to eat more pasta before he continued. "You can concede that just maybe things weren't as clear-cut as you thought, but that doesn't mean you have to be understanding." He certainly fucking wasn't. "Nothing can excuse what she did."

"I guess I just don't know what box to put her in now."

"No one can be firmly marked anything, baby. No one's all good, and no one's all bad. Everyone has different dimensions to their personality, and everyone has different things that drive them. People can change, sometimes for the better and sometimes for the worse. A person's nature is a fluid thing."

He was right, she realized. "I love you." And now he was gaping at her, which wasn't surprising. "I know it's a really weird time to say it. I get that. But it occurred to me before that I grew up never really knowing for sure if the people in my life loved me. I don't want you to wonder."

Knox snapped out of his stunned state as she rose from her seat. He grabbed her wrist. "Baby, you don't get to say something like that and then walk away."

"I *so* do." She slipped out of his hold and headed to the bedroom, close to laughing at the fact that she'd managed to shock the unshockable Knox Thorne. She hadn't waited for him to return the sentiment, because she'd known he wouldn't. She wasn't fanciful, she was practical. As she'd told Khloë, she didn't think 'love' was on his emotional scale. Even if it was, he'd been solitary for too long for him to suddenly be alive with feelings other people took for granted. It was enough that he cared for her.

Sitting on the bed, she removed her shoes. He appeared in the doorway, brooding and unnerving. "You're looking at me funny. Yeah, I know blurting that out and then walking away was kind of weird. But we both know *I'm* weird, so give me some space to do strange stuff without judging me." She huffed. "You're still looking at me funny."

He glided into the room in that predatory way that he had. "You told me something that was difficult for you to say. I know it was hard, because I know you don't like to be vulnerable to people. And the best way to guard yourself is to not let them see you, and to not let them see how much you care."

"Just for the record, I don't like that you're so perceptive," she griped.

"It would be selfish and spineless to not give you some honesty in return. Selfish? I'm that. But I'm not spineless."

She stilled as a buzz vibrated in the air . . . much like that time in the alley with the practitioners. As though something was charging up, gathering in power. And she knew then that he was going to tell her what he was. No, he was going to show her. Her inner demon went on high alert, both curious and wary.

Just as it had in the alley, the power purred against Harper's skin and made her eyes burn, her teeth rattle, her ears ring, and her chest tighten. His predatory stare was wholly focused on her, danger in every line and curve of his face. He didn't look like Knox then, he seemed like a total stranger. Her heart slammed against her ribs. And suddenly, she wasn't so sure she wanted to know what he was.

With a roar, flames erupted from the ground. Gold, red, and black, they swirled around Knox, engulfing him until she couldn't see him. What the fuck? No, not even *he* could survive them. She moved toward him desperately, but the heat was just so blistering and she—

And then she saw it: a figure of raging flames stood inside the fire. She couldn't help but gawk as her heart pounded so frantically it hurt. Her inner demon was shock-still. There was only one thing that could withstand the flames of hell . . . because it was the only thing that was born from the flames of hell. Her breath caught in her throat. "Archdemon."

Just as archangels were born in heaven and served God, archdemons were born in hell. But they weren't there to serve Lucifer as many religions believed. They were there to serve hell itself. Born from the flames, their purpose was to command, control, and destroy.

That was when it occurred to her . . . She'd thought he was charging up before. No, the power hadn't been building – it was straining to get free. And he was repressing it. She couldn't understand how anyone could repress that level of power. But then, he was an archdemon.

A fucking archdemon.

The flames calmed, slowly easing and lowering until all that was left was a figure of pure fire. Then the fire . . . it was like it peeled away from Knox's flesh. His clothes were surprisingly still intact.

He cricked his neck, his dark eyes glittering with danger. "I don't just call on the flames of hell, Harper. I am the flames of hell."

CHAPTER EIGHTEEN

What the fuck was she supposed to say to that?

Harper wasn't sure she even *could* speak. Shock had her rooted in place, gawking unattractively. Since meeting Knox, she'd come up with dozens of theories of just what breed he could be. None of those theories were all that inventive, but she still considered them much more realistic than the guy being an archdemon. Even her inner demon was in shock.

Considered too powerful to live on Earth after a rogue archdemon almost destroyed it, the decision had long ago been made to keep them in the very place they were born. Yet, here Knox was. An archdemon. A motherfucking archdemon.

No matter how many times the word circulated through her mind, she couldn't wrap her head around it. She couldn't reconcile the Knox she knew and cared for with creatures that, according to everything she'd been taught, were almost as cold and conscienceless as the inner demons they carried.

"You never suspected, did you? Nobody ever does. Poor, poor Harper's not sure she likes the reality of what I am."

Harper narrowed her eyes at the deliberate bite to his words. He was taunting her, meant to scare her. He was pushing to see if she'd run. Her demon didn't like it any more than Harper did.

"Ignorance is quite often bliss, isn't it?" He cocked his head. "Your heartbeat sounds something like a rabid racehorse."

Well forgive her if she was just a little spooked to find out her mate was part of the fabric of hell.

"Look at you. Eyes wide. Body frozen in place. Like every good, well-behaved prey."

Okay, now he was just pissing her off. "I'm nobody's prey," she snapped.

One brow slid up. "Oh?"

"And you're being an asshole." Going on the attack as a form of defense. She understood why, of course. He was expecting disbelief, terror, and finally rejection. And she realized now that he hadn't withheld the knowledge from her because he thought little of her. It was because of just how dark and frightening the truth really was.

"Asshole?" His chuckle was humorless, almost bitter. "I'd say I'm much worse than that. Wouldn't you?"

"Yeah. You're also a dick."

His face hardened. "What am I, Harper? Admit it." It was a demand and a dare. "*Admit it.*"

"You're an archdemon." A breed that was malignant, callous, pitiless, and unforgiving. But . . . "I don't care. Big motherfucking deal."

Knox prowled toward her like a panther, eyes unblinking and locked on her. "I was born in the flames of hell . . . and you don't care?" Pure skepticism.

She shook her head. As he reached out to touch her face, she knew he was testing her. So she held still. Of course, she almost jumped when small flames played over his fingertips. Again, he was testing her. "Pretty. Any more tricks?"

He circled her. "I can smell your fear. My demon doesn't like the scent of it at all."

"I didn't say I wasn't scared." Only someone with the IQ of a crumb wouldn't be afraid. "I said I don't care." Whatever he was, whatever he could do, he was still Knox. Even the entity inside her, rattled though it was, would accept it.

"You don't care, despite your fear?"

"You'd never hurt me."

He stopped in front of her. "How can you be so sure?" Another taunt.

"I trust you."

A pause. "Maybe you shouldn't."

"Stop being an asshole!" And now her temper was kicking in. "I told you I don't care. If you don't believe me, fuck you! I'm going to watch some T.V!" Her regal march was hampered by the arm that curled around her and yanked her back against a solid chest.

"You never, ever react how I expect you to," he said into her ear, a smile in his voice. "I like that." He held his other arm up in front of her. There was the slightest hum of power in the air . . . and then his lower arm was in flames.

Whoa. Involuntarily, she stiffened as self-preservation kicked in and the urge to flee hit her hard. But she didn't move away, didn't recoil. This was still Knox, *her* Knox. And the hand that was currently flaming had touched her a thousand times but never once hurt her.

She hadn't thought it was possible for fire to be beautiful, but it was. In fact, the red, gold, black flames were almost mesmerizing. Yet another example to prove she wasn't at all smart, Harper reached out to touch his arm. She balled up her hand instead.

"The flames can't burn you, Harper. Because they're me. And you're right, I'd never harm you."

Ignoring the scorching heat radiating from his arm, Harper skimmed her fingers over a golden flame. It didn't hurt, didn't even burn. It was like touching hot, liquid silk. She was about to ask if the heat burned his skin but then she remembered that, hey, he *was* the flames.

"You do trust me," Knox marveled. He honestly didn't know how the fuck she was taking it so well, or how she could let him hold her despite her fear. But then, he was still stuck working out how her fascinating little mind worked. He eased the fire, putting out the flames. "It really doesn't make any difference to you, does it? Even though you fear what I am, you don't care."

She turned to face him, smoothing her hands up his chest. "You're still you."

Like that was all that mattered to her. With those words, she fucking owned his soul and she didn't even realize it. He threaded his hands through her hair, gripping it tight. He wished he had pretty words to give her, but it wasn't in him.

When she'd said she loved him, Knox's first reaction had been disbelief. He was a realist, was well aware of each and every fault he possessed. He'd never considered himself a loveable person and, honestly, it had never bothered him. Why? For the same reason that panic had quickly set in at her words. He didn't believe he had the emotional capacity to feel it.

There were times when he'd picked up the emotion from others as they stared at their mates or relatives, so he knew exactly what it was. And he knew he'd never experienced it himself. If he *couldn't* feel it, what did he have to offer Harper in return?

The only thing he'd had to give her was a truth he'd withheld – a truth that had the potential to kill whatever she felt for him, considering he literally *was* everyone's worst nightmare. But he'd taken the risk, because it was all he had to give her.

He'd expected her shock and fear, had expected her to struggle to accept the dark reality of what her mate was – who *wouldn't* struggle with it? So none of those things had come as a surprise to him. But he really hadn't known what to expect after that, because he could never predict Harper's responses.

Some possibilities had entered his head: Maybe she'd try to flee. Maybe she'd ask for time alone to think. Or maybe she'd be too terrified to speak.

What he wouldn't in a million years have suspected was that she'd give him attitude. When he'd pushed her, she'd called him on his bullshit. She'd refused to let him intimidate her, just as she always did. And when he wouldn't believe that the truth genuinely didn't make any difference to how she felt, she'd cursed at him. His inner demon had chuckled.

There was no one like her. She was totally unique. Delightfully complex. And now he had to have her.

He took her right there on the floor, where there was no give and he could bury himself as deep inside her delectable body as it was possible to be. It was fast and hard, and she came screaming his name while he pumped every bit of his come in her.

They migrated to the bed. As he lay on his back with her draped over him, he smoothed her hair between his fingers. "I'm almost disappointed that you didn't try to flee. It would have been fun having you as my captive. Helpless. Vulnerable. All at my mercy."

She propped her chin up on his chest. "Such a kinky bastard. Is it an archdemon thing?"

He smiled. "Not that I know of." He sobered as he said, "You know you can't tell anyone, Harper, don't you? Not even Jolene, not even your friends."

"I know. If your secret got out, our kind would probably unite to go up against you."

"Most likely." It wouldn't do them any good – he could destroy them all with minimal effort. But he had no desire to wipe out the demon population.

"I'm curious. If archdemons are born from the flames, does that mean you don't have genetic parents?"

"Yes. My kind live in hordes. The adults all share in the care of the children."

"So when your horde moved to Earth, they took you with them?"

"Yes. The horde separated – some traveled, some joined lairs," he explained, watching as her eyes swirled from apricot to a smoky gray. "I stayed with a mated couple who joined a lair."

"You were effectively their child."

"They warned me not to tell what we were. To hide what I could do. Back then, I was nowhere near as powerful as I am now. An archdemon's power grows with age." It never stopped growing; that was part of what made them so dangerous.

"Lucifer knows what you are, doesn't he?"

"Yes."

She frowned. "I thought he agreed to keep your kind in hell."

"He did agree to it, and he *does* keep my kind in hell. But he didn't agree to round up the archdemons that already lived on Earth and return them to hell."

Now that she'd met Lucifer, she could imagine just how smug he was about the loophole he'd found. "I understand now why you hide how truly powerful you are and keep everyone guessing about what you can do. You don't want anyone to suspect the truth."

"I'm trusting you to keep it to yourself, Harper. I know women like to talk and share with their friends, and I know you're close to yours. They'll no doubt ask you what I am. I understand you'll find it uncomfortable to have secrets between you and them, but you can't tell them. They can't know."

"I admit, I don't like keeping things from them – especially big things. But your safety is more important than that. You come first." And even though she didn't believe her friends would fear him so much that they'd betray him by revealing his secret, it would put them in danger to have information like that. Noticing Knox's odd expression, she asked, "What?"

He didn't have words for her. Nobody had ever put him first before. Nobody. He couldn't explain the tumultuous emotions running through him. Among them were relief, incredulity, contentment, and adoration. So he told her how he was feeling the only way he knew how. He rolled her onto her back, slid down her body, and ate her until she came so hard she almost lost consciousness.

"Why can't you just tell me where we're going?"

"I explained it was a surprise. I didn't realize that required any elaboration for you to understand." Knox had to smile as Harper practically bounced in her seat on the jet, glowering at him. No one else would dare scowl at him that way, and no one else could possibly entertain him as they did so. His demon loved seeing her riled. "Enjoy the anticipation."

"I'm too impatient by nature to experience positive feelings of anticipation." The teasing glint in his eyes was pissing Harper off. He didn't want her to feel excited. He wanted her to feel agitated by the wait. "Just tell me."

He took a swig of his gin and tonic. "No."

"Mean."

"Of course."

"It's my birthday; you're supposed to let me have my way." She'd woken just as he thrust deep in her . . . then he'd wished her a happy birthday before riding her so hard that her scream got trapped in her throat.

He arched a brow. "Is that so? I'm distraught to say I can't give you that."

She huffed. "Really, you could have just pyroported us to wherever it is we're going. You've taken me on this long-ass flight just to drag it all out and drive me insane."

Of course he had. "We *are* going to pyroport to where we're going."

"Are we going to hell?"

"I don't think I've heard those words uttered with excitement before."

"I just like to do things I haven't done before."

"I know."

The wicked curve to his mouth both aroused and worried Harper. "Put me out of my misery and either tell me what the big mystery is or take me wherever we're going."

"All right, I'll take pity on you." He stood upright and pulled her to him. *Tanner, Levi – we're leaving now. We shouldn't be any longer than an hour.* Both sentinels were in the other cabin.

As he curled his arms tight around Harper, he kissed her softly. She stilled as the heat of fire enveloped them, burning her without hurting her. Then the flames died, and they were suddenly standing alone on a large stretch of land. And . . . "That's a volcano." Definitely not what she'd expected to see.

"It is." Taking her hand, he walked her toward it.

"I've never seen one this close." It was a scary yet beautiful sight. And seriously big.

"We'll be getting closer. Much, much closer."

She tensed, coming to an abrupt halt. "I don't like the way you said that."

"Ever bungee jumped before?"

Her heart slammed against her ribs. "Say what?"

"I'll take that as a 'no.'" Knox smiled. "Don't worry; you'll enjoy it."

She gaped. "Wait, you want to bungee jump . . . into that?" Was he insane? Apparently so. It could be an archdemon-thing. She should probably look into that.

"*We* are going to jump into it. Not into the magma chamber. We'll stop several feet above."

He said it casually . . . like it was just a bus ride as opposed to a death-defying experience. "How? There's no equipment or—" She cut off as wings suddenly snapped out of his back, fanning out behind him. "Oh. My. God." The feathers were gold, red, and black . . . and on fire. Touching one of the wings, she realized they weren't quite substantial; it was more like they were constructed of magma energy or something. Jealousy crept in as she suddenly felt the absence of her own wings very acutely. The guy never ceased to amaze her. "Do all archdemons have wings?"

Nodding, he flapped his wings once. "Come on, let's go."

"Whoa there, Thorne . . . You're going to fly us over there?"

"Yes. Then, while I'm holding tight to you, we're going to drop."

"Seriously?"

"You're excited, admit it."

Okay, yeah, an element of excitement was trickling through her. It was a terrifying idea, but it was also thrilling – she was a demon, her kind thrived on adrenalin rushes. But Harper also thrived on being alive. "Whole cities have been destroyed by eruptions of lava, gas, and ash from volcanoes. And you want to jump into one? Have you done it before?"

"A few times. Come on, you'll enjoy it. This one only erupts at night," he reassured her. "And it's not like the lava or the heat coming from it can burn you." Their skin was impervious to both. "Come here. Trust me."

"I do." So she stepped into his arms, both of which came around her. Then they shot into the air like a bullet. He was scaring her on purpose. "You're an asshole!" He just chuckled. She kept her eyes closed as, still holding her tight, he flew in a horizontal position. It wasn't long before he came to a halt, still in the air. Forcing open her eyes, she saw that they were soaring above an ash cloud.

"We're going to drop down the throat of the volcano," he told her.

He slowly lowered them to hover just under the cloud, and the breath left her lungs at the sight below her. *Fuck.* She fisted her hands tight in Knox's shirt, locking her legs around him.

"Look."

Oh, she was looking. She wasn't liking. There was really nothing quite like hovering above an active volcano. As if the view of the descent into the crater wasn't bad enough, there was the bubbling pool of red-hot, molten lava.

"You ready?"

Not really. Her heart was in her mouth, and she was pretty sure it belonged in her chest. Steeling herself, she took a long breath.

"I won't let you fall, you know that." He spoke into her ear. "The first time, we'll jump feet first."

"The *first* time?" Shit, what was she doing up here? Why was she putting her life in the hands of a clearly insane archdemon?

Her heart was pumping rapidly, her teeth were rattling, and her hands were shaking.

"You don't have to look down. You can just look straight ahead."

"Get on with it. The more I think about it, the more aggravated I'm getting." Her demon was totally up for this; it didn't find fear an unpleasant sensation, so it wasn't at all ruffled.

"After three."

Why was he doing this to her?

"Three."

Would her friends miss her at all?

"Two."

No, she wouldn't fret anymore. She'd meet her death with dignity.

"One."

His wings snapped around her and they dropped. It was like time just stopped. There was absolute nothingness for one single moment. And then they were falling.

Falling.

Falling.

The wind whipped up her hair, and her stomach rolled like it did on a rollercoaster ride. Oh shit, that red-hot lava was coming at them fast. "Knox, stop!" But he didn't. "*Knox, stop!*" They just kept falling and falling and—

Abruptly, his long, smooth drop halted just a few feet above the bubbling lava. "You fucking bastard!" But she was laughing. As they shot back above the ash cloud, she knew she had a wide, stupid-ass grin on her face. She had to admit the drop had been kind of exhilarating. Her hands were still shaking from the adrenalin.

His wings kept them floating. "I told you that you'd enjoy it."

"Okay, it was a little fun."

"If you liked that, you'll love this."

And then he was tipping them. "Oh no, not upside down," she groused, gripping him even tighter. "Why do you hate me?" The view was even worse this time. Another shot of adrenalin pumped through her, making her demon almost high as a kite.

"On the count of three." He tightened his arms around her. "Three. Two. One."

And then they were falling again. Plummeting head-first into the crater. She would have screamed, but the sound just wouldn't come out. And here was her good friend, lava, again. "Stop! Stop! Stop!" But of course, he didn't. Because he was evil. She was totally seeing that now. "*Knox!*"

He stopped.

The lava was *way* too close for comfort, and she was staring right into it. "Sooner or later, you've gotta sleep. Then I'll kill you." His laugh did not improve her mood at all.

Rocketing them once again above the ash cloud, he said, "You enjoyed that." She huffed, but he could see the excitement in her ocean blue eyes. "Again? There are lots of ways to do a drop like this. I won't let go of you . . . unless you want me to."

"No, don't let go."

"I won't."

"You said you wouldn't let go."

Knox did his best to stifle a smile. She'd been glaring at him since they returned to the jet. And now she was opposite him, shaking with fury. Yet, she still made him think of a hissing, spitting kitten. He thought it best not to say that aloud. "I caught you," he reminded her.

"That's not the point."

"Falling's not the same when someone else has hold of you. I wanted you to experience what it's like to just fall." He shrugged one shoulder. "And you did say you'd like to know how it felt to fly."

"I hate you."

He chuckled. "No, you don't. Come here, I'll apologize."

She snorted. "No, you won't. You'll feel me up."

"That too," he admitted with a smile. "Come here."

The dominant, authoritative rumble made her stomach clench; she knew that tone too well. "You know what? I don't think I will." She jolted as an ice-cold finger flicked her clit. "Don't."

"Then come here." His mouth curved as her eyes narrowed defiantly. "If that's the way you want it."

Her mouth opened in a silent gasp as the psychic finger slid through her folds – so cold, yet it produced so much heat. It stroked her again. Over. And over. And over. Occasionally, it stopped to swirl around her clit, making her pussy spasm. Holding tight to the armrests as if they could anchor her, she locked her muscles in place, resisting the urge to squirm. But it was so hard when her flesh was burning and prickling, desperate for more. "*Stop*."

"You know what to do if you want it to stop, baby." She couldn't have any idea how fucking hot it was to watch her eyes glaze over and her cheeks flush with need. Her breathing turned shallow and uneven as a climax slowly began to build. So hard it hurt, Knox undid his fly. His cock sprang out, heavy and pulsing. He fisted himself. "Do you want it, Harper?" He pumped once. "You look like you do." Her slumberous gaze was fixed hungrily on his cock. "Come here, and you can have it."

A moan slid out of Harper as the icy finger drove inside her. She couldn't help arching into the slow thrusts, so wet and on fire. Her thighs trembled as the friction built, threatening to tumble her into an—

The finger dissolved, leaving her pussy throbbing. She felt red-hot inside, and so unbelievably empty it hurt. She barely held back a sob.

"Only I can give you what you need, Harper." He'd put the ache there, and only he could take it away. "Come to me."

Harper might have cursed the dominant fucker, but that would only make him torture her a little more. There was only so much defiance he would allow, and she'd learned just how far she could push.

As she rose and moved to stand between his thighs, Knox praised, "Good girl." Snapping open her fly, he shoved down her jeans and panties. Once she'd kicked them and her shoes aside, he gripped her hips and lifted her, positioning her right where he wanted her. "The brand on your pussy is one of the hottest things I've ever seen. Be still." He lashed her clit with his tongue.

Her fingers knotted in his hair. "Knox." His tongue eased the burning as it slipped between her folds, licking and lapping, but it also began to build the friction once again. As he suckled her clit, her head fell back. "I'm gonna come."

Knox moved her to straddle him. "Not until I'm in you." He draped his arms over the back of his seat. "Fuck yourself on me, Harper." She took him inside with one slow, downward, spiral thrust that almost made him come. "Give me your mouth."

Gripping his shoulders, Harper kissed him just as she began impaling herself on his cock, loving how it stretched her oversensitive pussy just right. He forced his tongue inside her mouth, made her taste herself as he devoured and dominated.

He bit her lip hard. "You want me to come in you, Harper?" She moaned her assent. "Then work for it." Their mouths stayed locked as she increased her pace, slamming herself down on him. They shared breaths, pants, and groans. He sensed exactly when her orgasm was close. "Wait."

"Will you just let me come this one damn time?" she griped, digging her nails into his shoulders.

"Wait." He grunted as she clenched her inner muscles around him in revenge. His demon was both amused and irritated by that.

Harper froze mid-thrust as Knox's eyes bled to black. The demon didn't look pissed, but it definitely looked a little piqued. Shit.

"Sneaky little sphinx," it commented.

"I get a free pass on my birthday, though, right?"

It chuckled, and it was an odd sound; flat, yet not humorless. Then Knox was back. She was about to speak, but he arched a displeased brow.

"Who told you to stop?" he demanded, smacking her ass; her pussy clamped around him and soaked him in a rush of cream. "I said wait, not stop. Ride me." She mumbled a curse, but he let it slide – mostly because she was frantically impaling herself on his cock. The feel of her so slick, burning hot, and almost painfully tight around him was too much. He knew he wouldn't last much longer.

"Make me come, Harper. Do it," he bit out. "Then you can come." Her movements turned erratic and her hand slid to his nape as she kissed him hard. Her hold wasn't tight, but his nape began to heat until it was burning and it felt like tiny needles were stabbing his flesh. The bite of pain instantly became pleasure. He opened his eyes to see that hers were black – her demon had branded him, he realized.

"Fuck." Just as Harper resurfaced, Knox cinched her hips and repeatedly slammed her down on his cock. His climax barreled into him, making his fingers dig into her hips as he thrust deep and filled her with everything he had. As she came hard, she bit his neck to muffle her scream. Sated, she then sagged against him, arms flopping to her sides. "Your demon branded me."

"Yep. Does it bother you?" she asked cautiously.

"Of course not." The demon had every right to brand him. And it was a huge fucking turn-on. He liked that Harper and her demon were possessive of him. "I'm intrigued about what the brand looks like."

Once they were both cleaned up and had their clothes back in order, Harper took a look at his nape. "I'm not so sure you're gonna like it."

"Describe it."

"Well, it's sort of tribal. Has solid black lines and pointed curves." She'd done tattoos similar to the brand. "One of the curves has wings and the head of a sphinx – which looks uncannily like me. Hang on a sec." She snapped a picture with her cell phone. "See."

Knox turned to look at the photo. "I like it."

"That's a relief, because you're kind of stuck with it . . . unless you're planning to get rid of me at any point. Then I'll just carve it into your flesh out of spite."

He chuckled, sliding his arms around her. "I consider myself warned. So, what does the birthday girl want to do next?"

"I need to visit Jolene. I promised."

"Then I'm coming with you."

"Okay, but" – she grimaced – "just know in advance that my family is kind of crazy."

"They're imps, of course they're crazy."

"I'd like to use the excuse that it's *because* they're imps, but . . . well, you'll see. Just brace yourself."

Standing in Jolene's kitchen a few hours later, Knox had to wonder if this was what a mental ward was like. Over the past few hours, every member of the lair had appeared at one point or another to wish Harper a happy birthday. Some had remained, some had left. With the exception of Jolene, Beck, Martina, and Harper's co-workers, all had looked at him like they thought he was imagining sticking their severed heads on a flagpole.

They thought *he* was insane, yet they could accept the strange behavior going on around them. One imp was wearing nothing but a kilt, blue face paint, and a pink Hawaiian flower necklace. Another was dressed up as Harry Potter and occasionally blurted out meaningless spells for no apparent reason. There was also the imp who was carrying a hedgehog and losing patience with the creature because, 'You're not listening to me; you never listen to me.' Then there was the group taking bets about whether the teenager currently eating a raw onion would vomit.

"Are you really Harper's mate?"

Hearing that sweet, tinkle-like voice, Knox looked down to see the most angelic looking child he'd ever laid eyes on. Long white-blonde ringlets, aquamarine eyes, and rosy cheeks. She couldn't be much older than four years. "I am."

"You're really tall," she said shakily, worrying her lower lip.

He squatted down to meet her level of height, so he didn't seem so intimidating. "That better?" Her smile was all dimples as she nodded shyly. "I'm Knox."

"I'm Heidi. Harper calls me Heidi-ho."

"It's good to meet you, Heidi."

"I'm gonna be five in four months. You can come see me on my birthday, if you want."

"Thanks, I—"

"Heidi-ho," drawled Harper. "Give him back his wallet."

Blinking, Knox frowned. "Wallet?" He watched in bemusement as the child's innocent expression morphed into a put-out snarl that called Harper a traitor.

"Don't be fooled by those angelic looks, Knox," Harper told

him as he stood upright. "That kid is a plotter. She's as manipulative as Jolene, and she can cry on cue."

Handing Knox his wallet, Heidi burst out into very convincing tears. Then she smiled brightly. "Good, aren't I?" Heidi wrapped her body around Harper's leg.

His inner demon was chuckling, impressed. He turned to Harper. "She does that 'you're really tall' thing in that trembling voice to make people bend down, doesn't she?"

"Yep. Then she robs them blind."

Hearing a new voice behind them, Knox guessed another lair member had arrived. But when sharply Harper pivoted on the spot just as Heidi released her with an 'Uh-oh,' Knox had a pretty good idea who it was. He turned just in time to see a tall male imp with salt and pepper hair hold his arms out to Harper with a wide grin.

"I thought you couldn't make it," said Harper.

Lucian wrapped his arms around her. "Happy birthday, baby girl." Pulling back, he told her, "I sold the emu. I couldn't miss this, could I?"

There was no way Knox could fail to see the genuine affection Lucian had for Harper. It was in his eyes and the tone of his voice. While Knox wished for her sake that it would be enough to cool his anger at the imp, it simply wasn't.

He gave father and daughter a few minutes to catch up before he sidled up to Harper. Lucian gave him an assessing look. "You must be Lucian," said Knox, conscious that a silence had fallen. "I'm Knox Thorne."

"I know who you are," said Lucian. "Can't say I ever expected to see you at my mother's house. What's she done this time?"

"I'm not here to see Jolene. I'm here with my anchor. She also happens to be my mate."

Lucian's brows flew up. "Really? Who—" He paused, taking

in just how close Knox stood to Harper. His face reddened, his lips thinned, and his nostrils flared. "Anchor? *Mate?*"

"That's right."

Lucian actually stamped his foot as he looked at Harper, his emotional immaturity quite evident at that moment. "You mated with *him*? Do you have any idea how dangerous he is? Do you not value your own life?"

With a silent groan, Harper stated firmly, "Knox would never hurt me."

"You can't really believe that! You must have heard all the stories about him! He's ruthless, brutal! He doesn't have an ounce of mercy in his system!"

"Very true," confirmed Knox. "In fact, most of the stories about me are true. I'm a danger to every demon out there ... except for Harper."

Lucian sniggered. "Forgive me if I don't find the words of an evil, conscienceless bastard comforting."

Harper raised a hand. "Lucian, I don't want to argue with you – I really, really don't – but Knox is my choice, and I *won't* have you insult him." But she knew her words would fall on deaf ears. Lucian was wearing his 'I'm ready to rant' expression.

"I don't understand *why* he's your choice! It's not like you could be short of male attention! Why *him?*"

"Isn't it obvious? I care about him."

"But does *he* care about *you*? That's the question! Don't tell me he does! That demon cares for no one but himself!"

Knox's chuckle was empty of humor ... and the dark sound made everyone freeze. "Isn't that a case of pot, kettle, and black? Oh, and you really do need to quit talking to her that way. I won't have it." His demon wanted to gut the bastard for it. "This is all a surprise for you, I get that. But then, if you were a *real* part of her life, you'd have already known."

Lucian's eyes narrowed. "If you've got something to say to me, just say it. No sly remarks."

"Fine." Knox stepped into the imp's personal space. "You're a selfish, irresponsible, juvenile, self-indulgent asshole. In fact, scrap 'juvenile' – you're not quite that advanced."

"You son of a—"

"Harper had already been abandoned by her mother. Did you make up for that? Did you make sure that she at least had one parent take care of her from the start? No. You left her with Jolene, and you continued with your self-centered, nomadic lifestyle. And let's be honest, you wouldn't even have visited Harper if Jolene hadn't insisted on it."

Clenching his fists, Lucian lifted his chin. "She was with me from the age of four—"

"Because Jolene forced you to take responsibility for your child, which was something you should have done from the beginning."

"What, you think I should have taken a baby around the world with me?"

"No, you should have *stayed with her.* But that would have required you to put another being before yourself. And you just can't do that, can you?" Knox shook his head. "It amazes me that Harper is the person she is today after having you and Carla for parents."

Lucian snorted dismissively. "You think you know all about our lives? You know nothing."

"Wrong, Lucian. I know everything."

"Then you know I took care of her—"

"No, Lucian, *she* took care of *you.*"

The imp's jaw hardened. "You've no right to judge me."

"She's my mate, I have every right."

Seeming lost for words, Lucian turned to his mother . . . like a small, petulant child. "You don't care that he's speaking to me like that?"

Jolene shrugged. "You need to hear it, Lucian. I've tried to make you see yourself as you really are, but you never listen to me. Maybe you'll listen to him."

Eyes clouded with uncertainty, Lucian turned to his daughter. "We didn't have a bad life, did we?"

"No, we didn't," replied Harper.

"But it wasn't a life that gave her stability and security, was it, Lucian?" said Knox. "It wasn't a life that began from the moment she was put in the care of this lair. You should have put her first, quit traveling, and given her what she needed. You didn't. And for that, I'll never, ever like you. I'll accept you're a part of Harper's life, because I'd never ask her to choose, but that's as good as it will ever get between you and me." His inner demon, however, would never accept Lucian.

Harper slipped between the two males. "Look, you've both taken your shots at each other; let it go. Let it go," she repeated when Lucian went to speak. Predictably, he stomped off in a huff. He was still wearing that sulky expression when she and Knox left half an hour later.

"You're upset with me for insulting Lucian," assumed Knox as Levi drove them home in the Bentley. Tanner rode shotgun.

"No," she denied. "Don't get me wrong, it wasn't a fun moment. But I know that if it was the other way around, I'd smack the shit out of whoever I believed let *you* down."

The protectiveness in her tone made him smile. "I couldn't help but notice that Khloë enjoyed the dispute."

Harper shrugged. "She's never liked Lucian."

Knox's phone beeped, halting what he would have said next.

"Is everything ready for the voting poll tomorrow?" she asked, watching his fingers adeptly flying over the screen of his cell.

"Almost," he replied.

"Which way do you think the wind will blow?"

"It's hard to say. Each of the three candidates made appealing proposals. One thing in our favor is that demons, as a rule, aren't fond of great changes. The whisper campaigns also did a lot of damage."

"The question is: Just how much damage did they do?"

There would be no knowing the answer until tomorrow.

CHAPTER NINETEEN

Knox arranged for the polling station to be open from 6am to 10pm in the same Underground hotel that held the speeches. Demons voted using an electronic polling system that had been used in the past. In short, each demon entered a polling booth and voted using the computer inside – one that was designed to ensure the demon couldn't place more than one vote.

According to Larkin, many demons claimed they wouldn't be voting, since they were undecided. Still, it seemed that the entire U.S. public had come to the Underground to witness the result of the election. As such, everybody was no doubt waiting impatiently for the Primes to finish their five course meal.

The restaurant's táble-seating arrangement was the same as it had been for the speeches. Beside him, Harper was as stunning as always in a fuchsia halter-neck dress that dipped near her cleavage enough to flash some of his demon's brand. The sight was enough to make him hard, despite that he'd exploded inside her only an hour ago. He thought about the brand he now wore on his nape and felt masculine satisfaction rise in him. His mate had marked him, made it clear that he was taken. His inner demon was pretty smug about it.

Knox watched, totally rapt, as Harper licked chocolate sauce from her spoon. She was such a sensual creature, and so very unaware of it. He put his mouth to her ear, speaking quietly. "Every time your tongue flicks out to catch that sauce, I remember how it feels to have your tongue lapping at my cock."

"You should get that put in a Hallmark card or something."

A low chuckle rumbled in his chest.

She pushed aside her plate and spoon. "Looks like almost everyone is done with dessert. How long until you announce the result of the poll?"

"A few minutes." Sweeping his gaze around the room, he studied each of the candidates. Isla looked smug, seemingly confident that she would be elected. Dario seemed composed, but he was chugging down wine like a man dying of thirst. Malden's expression and posture betrayed nothing.

Neither Knox nor his inner demon was comfortable having Isla in the same room as Harper. So far, Isla had done nothing more than greet him from a distance with a simple nod. It was difficult to imagine that the cool, collected she-demon was the same one that enjoyed sexually assaulting and torturing the women within her lair.

When Harper informed him of Khloë's findings, his initial reaction had been shock. Dismay had quickly followed – dismay at the fact that the vulnerable, abused child he once knew had grown into an abuser herself. That such cruelty existed within her only gave him more reason to suspect she was responsible for the things that had happened to and around Harper. If so, the Prime was living on borrowed time.

"Why do you look like you've just swallowed something

bitter?" Harper asked him. Her eyes were presently a bright gold that fairly mesmerized him.

Knox lightly touched one of the two jeweled, metal hair sticks she'd inserted into her bun. "I don't like you being in close proximity to Isla."

Harper wasn't so keen on it either. Although she didn't share Knox's belief that Isla was the guilty party, it didn't mean that Harper was comfortable around such a twisted bitch. "Any news on the mysterious Kendra impersonator?"

Knox shook his head. "We still haven't been able to find out her location or her true identity."

"In terms of whether she's a likely suspect, it doesn't look good for her that she's disappeared."

"No, it doesn't," he allowed.

"You've crossed Carla off the list of suspects, haven't you?"

"I don't believe she wants you dead."

Neither did Harper. "Lucian's pissed that I found out the whole Carla story. He thought it was best that I just believed the woman was an evil heifer, nothing more."

"Can we not talk about that negligent, childish, self-absorbed bastard?"

"Can't you come up with a pet name for him that's a little less offensive?"

"How about I shorten it to just 'bastard'?"

Harper sighed heavily. "Forget it."

"What's wrong?" asked Jolene.

"I don't like to admit defeat, but it's possible that I'll never get Knox and Lucian to like each other," replied Harper.

Her grandmother shook her head. "Lucian will never like *any* male in your life. And Knox will never stop imagining new ways to kill him. It's a hopeless case." Jolene patted her hand. "But I'm sure Knox wishes he could put his dislike of Lucian aside for your sake. I'm sure he wishes your feelings on this matter could come before his. I'm sure he—"

Knox cut her off. "Don't try to manipulate me, Jolene. It won't work." He kissed Harper's cheek. "It's time. If the result causes any kind of uproar, Tanner will get you out of here." Before she could bristle and tell him she could take care of herself, Knox pushed away from the table and walked onto the dais.

Harper frowned, confused, as Isla moved to stand beside the dais . . . as if she was expecting to be called up there. Dario and Malden followed her lead.

"Have you noticed all the scowls that Isla has received tonight?" Jolene asked her. "There are many unhappy bunnies in this room, and they seem to hold her responsible for their misery."

Yes, Harper had noticed. "I don't know what she's done, but whatever it is has pissed off a lot of people."

Knox spoke then, filling the silence that his mere presence had commanded. "As you all know, the polling station closed two hours ago. The votes have all been entered into the polling computer software, and in just a few minutes the software will count the votes. Before we get to that, I want to make it clear that if a Monarch *is* elected, it will not give them any power over me or this place. As such, do not think to issue any orders at the moment of your election. Your authority and your position means nothing here."

"Isla didn't like that remark," commented Jolene as Knox moved to the side of the white screen that was hanging behind him.

Knox nodded at Levi, who was near the laptop situated on a small table in front of the dais. Instantly, the laptop screen was projected onto the large white screen, showing the image of a box that said, 'Count Votes.' After another nod from Knox, Levi clicked it. The words 'Please wait' replaced the box, and under it was a bar that showed the percentage of time left to go.

The silence now seemed weighty, somber. The air fairly hummed with a suspense that brought goosebumps to Harper's arms.

Eighty percent.

She licked her lips, anxious. If the demon public chose to have a Monarch, it would impact everyone, whether each demon accepted that Monarch or not. It didn't matter that Harper would never answer to them. *Others* would have to answer to them. The change would affect so many, alter so much.

Sixty percent.

Harper glanced at the candidates. All three were admirably composed. Isla's gaze shone with an unsettling amount of self-satisfaction. Did she know something they didn't?

Forty percent.

Taking a sip of her champagne, Harper looked at Knox. In spite of her current tension, she couldn't help but note that he was the epitome of self-assurance and untamed sexuality. He was also staring at her.

Twenty percent.

Leave with Tanner if necessary, he reminded her. *Take your family with you.*

She didn't assure him she would leave, unwilling to lie. If things went tits up, she'd be at his side. And he should know better than to think that Jolene would ever walk away from a riot. Hell, the woman was more likely to be in the middle of it.

'Done!' popped up on the screen, along with a box marked 'See Result.'

That was when Harper finally understood the term 'bated breath.' For a single moment, she didn't breathe at all. Then her breathing turned shallow and rapid as she couldn't seem to get the air she needed. So much could fuck up if the wrong decision was made.

"Levi," was all Knox said. After one click on the box from the sentinel, an image of scales appeared. One was labelled 'Yes', and the other was labelled 'No.' Mere seconds later, percentages popped up beneath each scale.

Only forty-three percent of the votes said 'Yes' to a Monarch.

Relief rushed through Harper like a tidal wave. Glancing around, she saw that her relief was shared by almost everyone. *Almost* everyone. Disappointment shadowed Malden's features, but there was no anger; she got the feeling he could take the public's rejection providing no Monarch was elected at all. Dario bit out a few harsh expletives, every line of his body tense. Still, he took the rejection with a little dignity. Isla, however . . .

Her spine snapped straight, her hands balled into fists, and her beautiful face became a mask of anger. "No!" she shouted. "I refuse to accept this!"

Knox shrugged at her, dismissive of her outburst. "It is what it is."

"I demand a recount!" Isla fairly barked, not so composed now.

A deathly quiet descended as Knox's eyes bled to black for a moment. "And who are you to demand anything of me?" he asked silkily, malevolence dripping from every syllable.

To her credit – or utter stupidity, whichever – Isla stood her ground. "I have many supporters, Knox. It makes no sense to me that this is the result of the poll."

"Maybe they weren't as loyal to you as you thought."

"They wouldn't have betrayed me!" she insisted. "The results were fixed! They have to be fixed!" Here was the paranoid streak Khloë had mentioned.

Knox arched a reproachful brow. "That's an offensive claim you're making, Isla. Be careful." The latter words were like blades.

Levi spoke then, overriding what Isla would have said next. "Don't you have enough power, Isla? Why push so hard for more? What is this really about?" No answer. "Is it power you want? Or is it power over Knox?"

Isla's mouth tightened around the edges.

"You had to know that Knox would never answer to anyone," continued Levi. "Being Monarch wouldn't enable you to control him. But it could have put you in a position to take him out. I think you thought that if you ruled over the other Primes, you could force them all to unite against him. Was that your plan? You must be pissed that it didn't work out."

"It *should* have worked out!" she yelled, obviously out of control now that she'd lost everything she'd worked for. "I had loyal supporters! The results have to be fixed!"

"Why is that?" asked Knox.

Harper laughed as realization dawned. "Been up to your old tricks again, Isla? Tell me, just how many people *did* you blackmail, threaten, or manipulate to try to get what you want? Are some of those people in this room?" That would certainly explain the amount of scowls she'd been receiving all night. "I'll bet you were the one to start the whisper campaigns, too."

"I don't believe I was speaking to you," Isla sneered at Harper.

"I don't believe I care," said Harper with a shrug.

"So brave because you have Knox to protect you."

Harper didn't rise to the taunt; she simply stated, "I don't need the protection of him or anyone else." Harper hid behind no one. If Isla wanted to believe she was weak, that was her mistake.

A glint of calculation entered Isla's eyes. "Really? Very confident." A pleasant smile lit her face. "Maybe you and I should take a turn in the combat circle, and we'll see just how strong you are."

Raul almost choked on his champagne. "You want a duel with Harper? Truly? You're *that* crazy?"

Knox crossed to Isla, muscles rippling with danger. "I wasn't aware that you wanted to die, Isla. I warned you that I'd destroy you if you harmed her."

Isla shrugged one shoulder delicately. "It would just be a little fun, Knox."

As Tanner moved to stand in front of Harper, his stance protective, Harper assured him, "It's okay, Tanner, I really don't think she can kill me with her scowl." Harper peered around him and raised her hand. "I have a question. Do you want to duel with me because you still believe you're Knox's anchor? Or is it that you need a whipping boy because you're so pissed off that you didn't get your precious votes? I'm interested."

"I *am* his anchor," she snapped.

Harper shook her head sadly. "Oh, Isla. How you do enjoy your delusions." She sighed. "And here was me thinking it was the second answer. After all, you do like to take your rage out on women."

Isla's eyelids flickered.

"Yes, you find inflicting pain and sexually assaulting the she-demons of your lair to be lots of fun, don't you? You're addicted to the high you get from it."

Isla hissed, ignoring the whispers of disgust that traveled around the room. "Lies."

Harper snorted. "It's not me that prefers the world of fiction, Miss 'Knox-is-my-anchor-despite-all-evidence-to-the-contrary.'"

"Isla, *leave*," snarled Knox. "Or I *will* kill you. That's your last warning."

"Don't you think you're all overreacting a little?" Isla rolled her eyes. "I suggested a duel. Not a battle to the death."

Harper got to her feet. "I think it would be kind of enjoyable."

"Not a fucking chance, baby," Knox ground out. "Tanner, get her out of here."

"Nu-uh. I don't walk away from a challenge." *Knox, I know you're worried for me. I know you don't want to see me hurt. I get it, and I love you for it. But I've told you before, I can't hide behind you. It's not who I am. And people need to see that I'm no easy target. I'm sick to fucking death of people assuming I am one.*

"I know you're strong," Knox told Harper aloud, wanting everyone to hear just how much faith he had in her. "I know you don't need my protection. But you're my anchor and my mate, which means I won't allow anyone to hurt you irrespective of your strength."

Knox stilled as Jolene's voice came then. *Knox, you understand why Harper has to do this. She has to make it known that she's strong in her own right. People see her as your weakness. They have to understand that she can also be a strength for you. That she herself isn't weak.*

In a sense, Knox did understand. But he couldn't, he *wouldn't*, sanction her putting herself in harm's way. Isla wasn't just a banshee, she was half vampire. "Tanner."

Understanding, Tanner went to lead Harper away.

"No! She's mine!" cried Isla.

There was a blur of movement followed by excruciating, stabbing pains in Harper's neck. Harper stared in shock at the she-demon in front of her, who now had Knox's hand wrapped around her throat. "You bit me," said Harper.

"I didn't just bite you, I weakened you." Isla laughed. "That's my vampiric gift, you see. I can steal some of a person's power through their blood. It'll be hours before you get it back."

That was when Harper snapped out of her shocked daze. With her inner demon's rage fueling her, she launched herself at Isla, punching her square in the jaw. Isla howled in soul-deep agony, but Harper didn't get a chance to enjoy it before Tanner picked her up and slung her over his shoulder.

Harper drummed her fists on his back as she screeched, "Let me at the bitch!"

"Many from Isla's lair were watching the voting in the Underground, Harper," said Tanner as they walked out of the emergency exit and into a side alley. "They're going to see Knox make Isla die painfully. Her inner circle worship her. They'll want vengeance. You're weakening fast, so we need to get you out before any of them try to come for you."

He was right. Her entire body felt sluggish, like she'd expended a massive amount of psychic energy, only ten times worse. Already her vision was beginning to darken around the edges. "I really don't know how much longer I can stay awake," she slurred.

"It's fine, we'll—"

At his abrupt halt, Harper looked around her curiously. That was when she noticed that people were coming at them from all sides. "Too late." Then the darkness took her.

Knox glowered at the whimpering she-demon in his grip. It had been damn fucking hard to ignore the urge to simply snap the bitch's neck, especially when his demon was riding him to do exactly that. But that would have been a loss of control; Knox couldn't allow the public to think Harper could take that from him, or his enemies would come at her again and again. In addition, he wanted this to be painful for Isla; wanted it known by the demon public *exactly* what he would do to anyone who went after Harper. Even his inner demon couldn't deny the importance of that.

Isla struggled in his hold, sobbing from soul-deep pain, courtesy of Harper. His mate no longer had to worry about anyone viewing her as weak.

"You can't kill me, Knox. We're too close. We're *anchors!*"

"You're nothing to me," he ground out, his eyes flashing demon as the entity backed him up. "Nothing. Even if you were, *no one* hurts my mate and lives."

Her bottom lip trembled. "My lair will avenge me."

"Ask me if I give a fuck." Conjuring a lethal orb of hellfire, Knox tipped her head back and forced it into her mouth, and down her throat. It lit her body as it moved down her windpipe and into her stomach, growing and growing as it burned her from the inside out. She screamed, clawing at her peeling flesh as the hellfire ate away at it. But Knox felt no remorse, no pity.

She heaved in one final breath before slumping in his grip, dead. Knox released her blistered, melting, steaming corpse with a sneer. His inner demon thought the act was too merciful, and it was rather disappointed by the speed with which she died. But Knox had wanted the world to see just how quick and easy it would be for someone to die at his hands.

"No!" cried one of Isla's companions; a young male demon who had obviously been enchanted by her. Both males dropped to the ground beside her.

"I'll escort them out once the body vaporizes," Keenan told him.

Knox, need a little help out here, called Tanner.

"Did Tanner take Harper out of the side exit?" Knox asked Keenan.

"Yes."

Knox rushed outside and came to an immediate halt at the sight of Tanner standing amidst four dead demons. "What happened? Where's Harper?" Dread hit him fast and hard.

A muscle in Tanner's jaw ticked. "She was taken," he growled.

Several emotions crashed into Knox. Fury. Panic. Helplessness. A need to hurt. A need to make someone *pay*. His demon roared inside his head, smashing its way to the surface. "By who?" it demanded in a rumble.

Tanner's gaze was wary, but he replied, "A demon and some dark practitioners – I could smell the magick on them. The demon teleported her and the practitioners out of here while those fuckers attacked me."

Drawing on every bit of control he possessed, Knox shoved his demon back down. Clear thinking was needed if they had any hope of getting her back. The demon wouldn't think, wouldn't plan. It would just destroy. *Harper? Harper?* No response.

Knox rubbed his fist over his heart, wondering at the ache there. He hadn't experienced helplessness since he was a boy, hadn't felt this level of anxiety since his parents tried to take him away from Riordan and instead ended up dead. It had mostly been a show of power on Riordan's part; a message that he was in control. Then Knox had given him – given all of them – a real show of power. Afterwards, he'd put the reins back on his demon and his abilities. He'd become the epitome of self-control, vowing that nothing and no one would ever take that control from him again. But this situation threatened to snatch it from beneath him.

"Did they say where they were taking her?"

Tanner shook his head, his expression one of self-condemnation. "I put her on the ground behind me while I fought . . ."

"It's not your fault." The words might have sounded genuine if they hadn't been guttural. He didn't blame Tanner, knew the sentinel would have protected her if he could. *Harper? Harper, fucking answer me!* "She's not responding, but I know she's alive. I can still feel her mind."

"She passed out as they surrounded us."

The door swung open and Levi strode out. One scan of his

surroundings was enough for him to conclude, "Someone took Harper."

Tanner scrubbed a hand down his face. "Can you track her through your anchor bond?"

"No." Knox paced, striving to stay calm. "That's not how it works." Flames flickered from his fingertips. The sentinels eyed him warily. He thought of Harper's reaction to the sight . . . *'Pretty. Any more tricks?'* She accepted him in a way no one else ever had or ever would. He couldn't fucking lose her; he just couldn't.

"We'll get her back," Levi assured him.

"You love her," Tanner mused.

No, he didn't. The times Knox sensed that emotion in others, it had been soft and deep. What he felt for Harper was a dark, dangerous, clawing emotion that surpassed that.

"I know she won't like it," began the hellhound, "but you could shove your way into her mind and force her back to consciousness."

"Her shields are extraordinary. I can't get through them without shredding my own psyche." If he did that, he'd be useless to her. *Harper! Harper! Answer me right. Fucking. Now.* Still nothing. His demon was pumping his anger into Knox, trying to goad him into handing over the reins; to surrendering control as Knox had done as a child. But he wasn't that child anymore. He inhaled deeply, digging deep for the strength to fight his rage and anxiety; to think clearly. "Anchored to me, she's stronger. That means she'll rejuvenate from Isla's bite reasonably fast. All I can do in the meantime is repeatedly try to wake her. Then she can tell me where she is." *If* she knew where she was.

The door once again opened. Jolene, Beck, and Martina strolled out. Jolene froze, face hardening as she took in the dead bodies and the grim expressions of Knox, Tanner, and Levi. "Where's my granddaughter?"

It was Tanner who answered. "In the hands of dark practitioners. A demon – probably a stray who had been hired by them – teleported the practitioners here, so they could snatch Harper."

"We have no idea where she is," said Levi, "which means we have no idea how to get her out of wherever they're keeping her."

Jolene snorted, to everyone's surprise. "Do you really think my granddaughter can be held anywhere she doesn't want to be? She may not be an imp, but she's a Wallis through and through. So tuck your crazy back in, Knox. We need you calm. By the time you get to wherever she is, she'll already be out of there. Concentrate on planning what you'll do the bastards that dared to take her."

"That plan is simple," rumbled Knox. "They'll die."

CHAPTER TWENTY

Harper! Harper! Answer me.

If Knox would just shut the fuck up and let Harper sleep, that would be great. Her head felt heavy and her limbs were like noodles.

Harper! Wake up, baby. His voice had softened slightly, sounded almost ... desperate. That made no sense. *I need you to wake up.*

Trying to sleep here, she grumbled.

A vibe of relief stroked the edges of her mind. *Tell me where you are, baby. I can't find you until I know where you are.*

His anxiety made her frown. Knox was never anything but composed. *Why are you so—?*

Memories suddenly flashed before her ... Isla biting her. Tanner carrying her outside. Being surrounded in an alley. Darkness closing in.

Harper snapped to alertness, forcing her eyes open as she tried to bolt upright. *Well, shit.*

What?

I'm tied, spread-eagle, to some kind of table. There was even a rope around her waist to stop her from squirming. Well, at least she wasn't naked. That didn't placate her inner demon – it was totally pissed. Scanning her surroundings, she felt her stomach drop. *Well, double shit.*

Harper, tell me where the fuck you are.

I don't know. It's like some kind of man-made temple. There are candles everywhere, ritual symbols on the walls, and a huge circular ritual marking on the floor . . . and I can smell dark magick. And it seemed like she was secured to a sacrificial table. How delightful. *Looks like it was the practitioners after me all this time. Is Tanner okay?*

He's fine. Do you recognize anything around you?

No. There's a set of stairs at the end of the room, so I think I might be in a basement of some kind. That's all I know. I have absolutely no idea where I am.

He bit out a string of curses.

I can get out of here, don't worry.

Don't worry? You're tied down!

You say that like it makes a difference. You know, you constantly underestimate me, and I've yet to figure out why. In truth, she was glad he wasn't able to come straight to her. There was no doubt in her mind that she was being used as bait. After all, if her kidnappers had wanted to kill her, they would surely have done it by now; they would have taken advantage of her unconscious state. If they thought to lure Knox here, they had to also believe they had a way of containing him. She wouldn't allow that. No fucking way.

Hearing voices approaching, Harper closed her eyes, feigning sleep. There was a loud yet smooth whirring sound . . . like some kind of machinery was being used. Was the door electronically locked or something? The whirring stopped and then footsteps descended the stairs, slowly making their way toward her. She counted four sets of footsteps.

"Odd that she's still unconscious," remarked a very well-spoken male.

I know you're strong, Harper, but—

Shh, I've got company and I'm trying to listen.

"It means being anchored to him hasn't made her as strong as we'd expected," continued the eloquent voice. "Are you sure they formed the anchor bond?"

"Well, he calls her his anchor," replied a coarse voice.

"Yes, Jacques, but that does not mean that they have formed a bond."

"I figured they did," defended Jacques.

"Yet, she remains unconscious."

"That doesn't have to mean anything, Alton," said a female voice. Kendra – or whoever the hell she really was. "We don't know enough about Isla's bite to know how long a victim typically loses consciousness. We have nothing to measure it by."

The bitch is here, Harper told Knox. *Fake Kendra is here. She must have been hired by the practitioners, so it looks like my little theory was right.*

How can you be smug? YOU'RE TIED TO A TABLE LIKE A DAMN SACRIFICE!

I don't appreciate your tone.

"Alton, when do you want me to get a message to someone in his lair?" asked another male voice.

"Soon, Ezra. I need to be sure everything is ready before we give an anonymous tip with her location," said Alton.

"Can I make her scream a little first?" 'Kendra' practically purred.

"Still sore that he chose her over you?" Jacques teased.

"It's not about *him*. She should die for the agony she caused my soul."

"Be honest, Jeanna, Knox choosing her was an ego blow. You treasure that ego."

She huffed. "I'd already walked away from him by the time he met her, remember?"

"Yeah, but you thought he'd chase you. Instead, he pursued *her*. That has to have pissed you off, since you literally have the gift of seduction. Tell me honestly, did you try to seduce her, too?"

"*Her*?"

He chuckled. "Don't give me that horrified look, Jeanna. Whenever a mated guy turns you down, you seduce his mate out of spite."

"I don't seduce them, I just make them want me so much that they beg for me to touch them . . . then I walk away."

Wasn't she just a precious little thing? Her inner demon wanted to crush her skull.

"Like that's any better," snorted Jacques. "Come on, tell me, did you try it on her?"

"Once. It didn't work. She's an awkward bitch."

That could explain the warmth that had briefly bloomed through Harper when Jeanna grabbed her arm in the restrooms.

"Do you really think you can trap Knox Thorne?" Jacques asked.

"Any predator can be trapped with the right bait," replied Alton.

"But can you *keep* the predator trapped? That's the question."

"Your part here is over, demons," said Alton. "You've been paid, and you've been paid well."

"I want to see it through," said Jeanna.

Alton huffed. "I fail to understand why you believe you have any authority here. Ezra, please escort the demons to their vehicle while I check everything is in place."

Someone in your lair will get a call with an anonymous tip on where I am, Harper told Knox as the voices gradually faded. *It's a trap—*

I know it's a fucking trap. His tone said he couldn't give a shit. *I'll be there soon.*

That meant she needed to get *out*side before the dumb motherfucker walked *in*side.

Once she was absolutely certain she was alone again, Harper opened her eyes and called hellfire to her hand. Then she twisted her hands enough to grip the table, infusing the hellfire into the wood. The flames burned away the rope, enabling her to free herself. Thankfully, she was impervious to any hellfire she conjured or she'd be in absolute agony right now.

Honestly, she was insulted that anyone thought rope was enough to secure her. No self-respecting Wallis would be unable to escape ties of any kind.

Harper smoothly slipped off the table. She stood still for a moment, testing the strength of her legs. Maybe it was the adrenalin or maybe it was that being anchored to Knox made her stronger, but her body was no longer physically weak. She knew that she still hadn't psychically recovered from Isla's bite, though.

With the stealth she'd learned at an early age, she silently hurried to the other end of the room. She quickly dashed up the wooden steps, wincing when one of the boards creaked ever so slightly. The sound was like a bomb in the silence of the room, but it didn't appear to have alerted anyone.

When she almost reached the top step, she blinked, totally baffled. Where the fuck was the door? There was barely even a wall. The roof here in the corner of the basement was sloped.

There was only a two foot gap between the top stair and the bottom of the slope. There was literally no door. She might have thought the door had been moved underneath the stairs during renovations or something, but she had clearly heard the others descend the rickety steps.

That was when she recalled the whirring sound she'd heard earlier. Okay, if she was an electronic door, where would she be?

Harper skimmed her fingers along the wall, searching for some kind of switch. Her index finger brushed over something hard and circular. Hopeful, Harper pressed it . . . and the small sloped roof above the steps started to lift. She listened hard for any signs of people approaching, but there was nothing.

Finally, the slope came to an abrupt stop, revealing a doorway. It was only when Harper hurried through the opening that she realized the sloped roof was actually part of a staircase that led to upper floors. The clever bastards had hidden their little temple very well. Clicking another switch, Harper then watched as the small portion of the staircase moved back into position. To look at the staircase as a whole, no one would ever imagine that the bottom section lifted. She couldn't help but begrudgingly admire the design.

Voices in the distance snapped her out of her musings.

Crap. Strongly suspecting that the front and back entrances to what was clearly a massive house were being guarded, she headed silently up the winding staircase. Reaching the top floor, she listened carefully for signs of company. Satisfied she was still alone, she crossed the landing to a smaller winding staircase that no doubt led to the attic. Hopefully it wasn't another damn sacrificial chamber.

Thankfully, it turned out to be a storage room. Quietly, she wound her way through the boxes and pieces of furniture, heading for the side window, which was disappointingly small.

Not that a little thing like that would stop her. Hey, she'd once gotten in and out of a bank vault – she had this.

The window turned out to be pretty damn stiff, so it was a slight struggle getting it open. If it hadn't been for her enhanced strength, she might not have managed to open it. She slinked her upper body through the small space, taking in the nighttime view, and was immediately assaulted by the scents of wet grass and dark magick.

Knox, it would appear that I'm in a house in the middle of nofuckingwhere. Great.

I haven't received the anonymous tip yet telling me where you are. His impatience vibrated against her mind. *I'll be there as soon as I get it.*

She could hear muffled voices, but none were close by. Wanting a thorough view of her surroundings and an idea of where each of the practitioners waited, she clambered onto the flat roof. It seemed like it was one of those eco-friendly builds that was all metal panels, timber, and plexiglass. Instinctively, she froze, knowing she wasn't alone. Then there was mock clapping.

"Clever girl." Jeanna moved out of the shadows. She looked very different. The elegant look was gone. Her clothing was casual, her hair was now red, and her eyes were a pale blue. She was also holding a black, swirly dagger. "I had a feeling you'd get out – you're a Wallis, after all. Don't worry about them down there; they can't hear us through my shield. But they *will* see us while I take your life."

"You stuck around for payback." Typical of their kind. Harper balled up her hands as her familiar protective power rushed to her fingertips.

"That . . . and it will be interesting to see if their spell works. They believe they can trap Knox. Truly. Practitioners are covering each corner of the house, forming a cube shape. Once Knox steps inside that psi-cube, walls will slam up . . . and the cube will get smaller and smaller until it's the size of a closet."

Not good at all. *Knox, when you get here, don't come near the house! The practitioners think they can trap you in some kind of psychic cube. Knox? Knox?* No answer. Was Jeanna's shield blocking the message? If so, this was bad. "You're the one who planted the compulsions."

Jeanna shrugged one shoulder. "I couldn't have people pointing the finger at me, could I?"

"And the snakes?"

"One of the practitioners did that, but it was my idea. I was there." Eyes narrowing, Jeanna asked, "Just how did you survive them?"

"A few escaped out of the letterbox; there might as well have been a neon sign warning me away. Why work for these bastards? Why?"

"I'll work for whoever pays well. Be honest, Harper, our kind is darker than theirs will ever be."

In some instances, that was indeed true. "Do I have *you* to thank for the rumor about Carla?"

"That was a personal hit. Have you ever felt soul-deep pain yourself? It's an experience unlike any other. It hurts every part of you, inside and out. Every nerve ending, every organ, every bone, and – finally – every piece of your soul. You could say it packs an emotional punch."

"You wanted me to hurt like you hurt," Harper deduced.

"Yes. So I did my research on you, looking for dirt. I was annoyed to find that you're not actually an imp. I don't like being wrong." Jeanna tilted her head. "A sphinx without wings. That's a little like a dog without a bark."

Harper kept her expression neutral, betraying nothing. "You think if you piss me off, I'll charge at you? I've heard worse from better." The bitch hissed, clenching her hand around the dagger. "Ooh, temper, temper," taunted Harper.

"I will enjoy killing you."

A frisson of fear slithered into Harper. Shit, what if she couldn't do this? What if she failed and let Knox down? Of course she'd fail! She was weak, pathetic. She wouldn't—

Harper shook her head a little. She'd never thought of herself as weak. Realization dawned. "You can induce fear." Well that wasn't good.

"Let's end this, shall we?"

Harper had no problem at all with causing this bitch a world of pain; her inner demon wanted to gouge out Jeanna's eyes and shove them down her throat. But Harper needed to be away from the house before Knox arrived or he would step inside the cube to reach her. "Think, Jeanna. Knox will come, and he won't come alone. You won't get away from here."

"Of course I will. Jacques is waiting for me in the woods. He'll teleport us away."

"You don't want to do this, Jeanna," Harper said, her voice compelling. "You don't even know who I am."

"So it's true that sphinxes can cause confusion."

Shit, it didn't seem to be working here. Harper could guess why. She was still psychically weak, courtesy of Isla's bite. And she was expending precious psi-energy on fighting the artificial fear that threatened to drag her under and make her forget why it was so important that she win this duel – Knox. She would fight because he needed her to, because she wanted to stay with him.

Resigned that this would come to bladed combat, Harper drowned out Jeanna's next words and studied the nightmare.

Jeanna was obviously comfortable with a blade. Being tall, she also had a long reach. However, her height also meant her legs were exposed.

"Before I kill you, I must ask . . . what is Knox? You must know." When Harper didn't answer, Jeanna smirked. "An amazing lover, isn't he?"

She thought to make Harper jealous? Thought such an emotion would make her lose control? "That's not going to work, Jeanna. You're insulting us both by being so petty." Hearing voices call out to each other, Harper knew she and Jeanna had been spotted. "They see us. They'll come up here."

Jeanna shrugged, unconcerned. "They can't step inside the shield. Nothing can penetrate it."

"If you kill me, Knox will kill you."

"If he finds me, yes he will. But it won't make you any less dead, will it?"

She had a point.

Grinning, Jeanna held up her dagger. "Like it? I bought it from the practitioners."

"That explains why it looks more like a Harry Potter wand."

A scowl that promised retribution. "It's enchanted. The handle is the bone of a demon who died in glorious agony. Each time I strike you with it, you'll hear a cry of his pain."

"Yeah" – Harper smiled tauntingly – "if you can slice me."

Jeanna rushed Harper, pumped full of anticipation. With the swiftness of any sphinx, Harper retrieved her blade from her boot, infused it with hellfire, and parried the blow. The blades clanged as they met. Jeanna danced backwards, eyes wide.

Harper smirked. "You didn't think you were the only one who had a blade, did you?" Apparently so. Jeanna had thought this would be a quick win, an easy method of payback. Wrong. Harper was taught combat and fencing by imps. They fought dirty. They cheated. They were damn bloodthirsty. "You sure you still want to do this?"

Jeanna's expression answered that. Keeping her muscles loose, Harper lunged at her; went for every weak spot, including the face, neck, and chest. She was quick. Precise. Didn't stop moving, kept up the pressure. The blades clanged as they repeatedly clashed.

There was no hesitation in Jeanna. She parried and thrust with ease, all the while careful not to let Harper's hands touch her. It quickly became clear she was confident and, worse, very good with a dagger. She didn't make the error most did and try to hit the blade; she tried to hit her opponent.

Moments later, she was successful. The dagger stung, slicing cleanly through Harper's skin like a knife through butter. For some reason, the first cut was always a shock. What stunned her more was the agonizing male cry that rang through her head. *Fucking enchanted piece of shit.*

Harper heard the practitioners gathering close like vultures. The only thing keeping them back was Jeanna's shield . . . which meant this situation was fucking hopeless, really. Killing Jeanna would feel great and would save her from being impaled on a dagger, but then she'd no longer be protected from the practitioners by the shield.

Determination flooding every vein, Harper went at Jeanna again. She didn't let up, ensuring she was in constant motion, refusing to allow the dead male's cries to distract her. The smell of burning flesh filled the air as the hellfire coating Harper's blade ate at Jeanna's wounds, pleasing her inner demon. "Looking a little like a leper there, Jeanna."

"You *will* die for this." She slammed her open palm into Harper's face.

Shit! Her eyes watered, making it hard to see. Jeanna took

instant advantage and sliced Harper's chest. She winced – both at the pain and the male scream that reverberated through her head. Fuck, that cut was deep; she could feel blood pooling to the surface but she ignored the urge to examine the wound. If she looked away from a smug-looking Jeanna, she was dead.

A tendril of fear curled around her. She was going to lose. Jeanna was too strong, too fast. There was no way Harper could defeat her, there was no—

Pushing aside that artificial fear, Harper swung her hips and kicked her opponent hard in the stomach. Jeanna retaliated with a swipe of her blade. Harper ducked and came up on Jeanna's side, stabbing deep. Blood bloomed, soaking her t-shirt. "Now we're even."

Hissing with anger as her flesh sizzled, Jeanna tossed a succession of hellfire orbs. One hit Harper's leg and another skimmed her temple.

"You like to throw shit, huh?" Adrenalin pounding through her, Harper yanked one of the metal hair sticks from her bun, infused it with hellfire, and hurled it at Jeanna. It buried itself in the bitch's shoulder.

With a shocked, angry cry, Jeanna yanked it out. She snarled as her flesh burned. "That really, really hurt."

Um, it was supposed to.

The taste of trepidation and anxiety suddenly filled Harper's mouth. Jeanna was clearly redoubling her efforts to swamp her in fear. Grinding her teeth, Harper fought it. But it was hard; she could feel her psychic energy waning – she still wasn't fully recovered psychically from Isla's bite. Still ... "It won't work, Jeanna. You won't reduce me to the blubbering wreck you were in the restrooms." She blinked at the bitch's curse. "Something I said?"

Jeanna struck again. As Harper parried each blow, she could

sense the practitioners watching, waiting for her to fail and die at Jeanna's hands . . . or to win and then be vulnerable to them. Either way, Harper was a loser to some extent.

Twisting slightly, Jeanna evaded one of Harper's blows and kicked her hard in the thigh. Shit, that was gonna bruise, and Knox was gonna be pissed.

Ignoring the pain and the sweat trickling down her temples, Harper made an effort to regulate her rapid, shallow breathing. She was running out of steam, physically and psychically. It didn't help that she was bleeding from cuts and stab wounds on her cheek, chest, and arms. Not that Jeanna looked much better. Her flesh was peeling and blistering in several places, thanks to the hellfire. The stench of it was awful. "God, Jeanna, at this point you're just nauseating."

Too deep in her anger, Jeanna began to strike out wildly. She should know better than that. But apparently Jacques was right – she treasured her ego. Harper slammed her foot into Jeanna's knee, causing her leg to buckle. Then she lunged, thrusting the blade deep into the bitch's gut. Seemingly stunned, the nightmare dropped her dagger as she inhaled sharply, eyes wide. Harper twisted her blade before withdrawing it. Then she thrust it into Jeanna's neck just as she slammed her hand into Jeanna's solar plexus, sending soul-deep pain rippling through her.

Her face a mask of agony, Jeanna gurgled, flapping her hands at the knife as blood fairly pumped out of the wound. She stumbled once before dropping to the ground, eyes blank. Harper retrieved her blade and, cold though it was, wiped it on the nightmare's t-shirt. It took a few moments for her to die . . . and that was when the shield winked out.

The practitioners began to circle her, ready to pounce. By then, Harper had already pulled the second long, thin blade out of her hair and infused it with hellfire. Well, if she was going to die here, she'd take at least one of these bastards with her. The six males exchanged knowing looks, and she had the feeling a spell would be coming her way. Had a feeling that—

A mind slid very firmly against her own. *Knox?*

I see you. It was a rumble.

Instinct had her looking to her left. And there he was. Just standing in the field, his body language casual. *Don't come near the house!*

"He's here!" exclaimed someone from below – apparently not all of the practitioners had joined her on the roof. "Get into your positions now!"

The magickal fuckers disappeared. Well, all but one.

The remaining practitioner smirked at Knox. "If you want her, come get—" He cut off with a scream as a huge, black blur leaped onto the roof and barreled into him. *Tanner.* The practitioner screamed over and over as the hellhound tore into him with teeth and claws.

"Hey, sphinx, let's go!" called out a familiar voice.

Harper smiled at Larkin, who was hovering at a standstill with her gorgeous midnight black wings out. "'Bout fucking time you shitheads got here."

Larkin just laughed, gripping Harper around the waist as she flew them off the roof and headed to—

Motherfucker. Slamming hard into a wall, Larkin and Harper fell gracelessly to the ground. But there was no wall, she observed with a frown. She shoved out her hand, hitting something solid that flickered white like a bulb. It was a large energy barrier. They were trapped in the cube that was meant for Knox. Worse, two practitioners headed for Harper and Larkin as the she-demons got to their feet. And Harper's blades had fallen from her grip when she hit the ground. *Shit.*

"We now have your mate and two of your sentinels! Would you like us to free them?"

Knox didn't respond. Just stood still and composed in that eerie way that he had. His dark eyes gave nothing away.

"If you wish for them to be free, you must trade places with them!" continued the practitioner. It was clear that he was nervous. But he was also excited, obviously confident that he would get what he wanted. And that confidence freaked Harper out. The cube had to be particularly strong. "Their life for yours!"

Still nothing at all from Knox. He didn't appear in the slightest bit fazed.

Unnerved by Knox's cool exterior, the practitioner licked his lips. "If you do not give us what we want, we will kill them!"

"No." Knox's tone was so cool yet so menacing. "You won't."

CHAPTER TWENTY-ONE

Seeing Harper there, injured and at risk of being killed right in front of him, the past and the present collided; Knox's hold on his fury slipped a little. He had watched his parents die. He wouldn't watch Harper die, wouldn't allow anyone to take her from him. The demon was raging at the danger to her. It wanted to express its rage in the only way it knew how.

"Surrender yourself, and we will free them!" shouted the bastard now pointing a knife at his mate's throat. "If you do not, she will die!"

More anger pulsed through Knox, mingling with his demon's rage. "Give her to me, or you'll all die."

"We know what you are!" The practitioner wore a self-satisfied yet shaky smirk. "You're Lucifer himself."

Had Knox not been drowning in a fury that bordered on madness, he might have laughed. As it was, Harper and Larkin *did* laugh. "I'm not Lucifer," Knox told him. "I'm worse."

Knox released the power buzzing through his veins; let it fill the air as he called to what birthed him, to what lived inside him. The ground shook beneath him as flames circled his body and licked over his skin. The fire within Knox surfaced, beginning to take over every inch of him. "Now you die."

Oh, shit, thought Harper. Every hair on her body stood on end as a gray, thick cloud began to build directly above Knox, swirling and frothing. It looked alive, aggressive. At the same time, a red haze began to fall, and she quickly realized the moon had bled from silvery white to blood red. Worse, the flames that had circled Knox were now heading for the house, leaving a trail of black and red ashes in their wake. A figure of raging fire, Knox slowly walked toward the building.

"The flames of hell," gasped the practitioner who was pointing the knife at her. He fisted her collar and began dragging her away. Not a chance. She went limp in his hold, causing him to stumble and bend forward. Then she slammed her hand down on his foot, letting the protective power in her fingertips pass into his body and torment his soul. As he cried out, she grabbed her stiletto blade from the ground and thrust it upwards, burying it into his heart just as she infused it with hellfire.

Blood dripped onto her face – *ew* – as she withdrew the blade and shuffled away from him. When he hit the ground like a sack of potatoes, she turned to Larkin . . . just in time to watch the harpy finish off the second practitioner with nothing more than her hands.

Harper might have expressed her admiration for the female's combat techniques if it wasn't for something else. "We're surrounded." Flames at least ten feet high framed the psi-cube that enclosed the house. It was odd seeing fire without smoke. "The cube's still up." That meant no one had managed to escape.

"The practitioners wanted to trap him. Instead, they've trapped themselves." It was almost ironic.

"Do you think the flames will get through the cube?" asked Larkin, wiping blood away from her nose.

"The flames of hell can get through anything. Where's Tanner?"

"Last time I saw him, he was on the roof."

Harper looked up at the roof, straining to see or hear him. It was hard to hear anything over the roar of the flames that battered at the cube. "The practitioners are all gathering up there. They must think they're safer on higher ground." There was no safe place when you were facing the flames of hell.

Tanner? Harper called. *Tanner?* "He's not answering me telepathically."

"Nor me. He must be still in his demon form." Larkin shot vertically into the air, wings flapping gracefully. "I see him," she said, hovering at a standstill. "He's stuck under some kind of energy net, but he's conscious. And seriously pissed off."

"Can you get to him?"

"Not without getting extremely close to the practitioners. They'll attack me."

"I think they have more pressing problems," said Harper as she looked at the energy wall on her right. "Look."

"What?" Larkin tracked Harper's gaze. "The flames are eating the cube." There were holes that looked a lot like cigarette burns. Larkin returned to Harper, landing gracefully. "And they're out of control."

The flames – so beautiful, yet so deadly – indeed looked that way. But Harper shook her head. "Knox wouldn't hurt us."

"That's not Knox."

Through the fire surrounding them, Harper caught glimpses of the flaming figure. "No, it's not." As pot holes began to appear in the ceiling of the cube, she said, "We need to get Tanner."

"I can't leave you." Larkin's voice was firm, implacable. "You're Knox's mate. I'm sworn to protect you."

"That's great and all, but I don't like Tanner being up there with them." The practitioners were now stood in a circle, hand-in-hand, and appeared to be chanting something.

"What are they doing now?" asked Larkin.

"Probably casting counter spells." A pointless exercise, in Harper's opinion. "It might distract them enough for us to get Tanner. If they need to hold hands, I doubt they'll break the circle just to keep him."

Picking up movement in her peripheral vision, Harper turned her head … and found herself staring directly at the flaming figure that was her mate. Even her demon was wary of what he'd become. Only the flames and the disintegrating cube separated them. There were no eyes, no facial features of any kind, but she knew that it saw her somehow.

Knox? Knox, can you hear me? Silence. Nothing she said seemed to penetrate the mental shield of fire that was now between them. The figure took a slow step backwards and was swallowed up by the flames. "Where's Levi and Keenan?"

"They had to stay behind. Isla's demons went crazy, and there was no chance Knox was going to stay there and take care of it while you were here." Larkin peered up at the ceiling of the cube. "The holes up there are getting a little bigger. I'll fly you out as soon as one is large enough."

"Not until we have Tanner," Harper told her. "We're not leaving him behind."

"I can come back for him."

"We leave *together*, Larkin. Now let's fucking go get him. It's risky, I get that. Putting me near the practitioners might tempt them to grab me again, I get that too. But if Tanner's stuck here when those flames get through, he dies."

Larkin growled. "Fine. But if those bastards grab you, I'll kill you myself!"

"You can try, I guess."

With another growl, Larkin flew them both onto the roof. Tanner was thankfully outside the circle that the practitioners had formed. It was as both females struggled to find a way to break the energy net that one of the practitioners saw them.

As he broke the circle and advanced toward them, Harper shot to her feet, blade in hand and glowing with hellfire. "If Knox sees you holding me, you'll be the first person he kills when he gets through the cube."

"What is he?" the practitioner demanded. When she didn't answer, he snarled, "Do you want to die? Look around you." The holes were everywhere, making the cube look like a chunk of cheese. "Tell us what he is. If we know, we can stop him."

"Fuck. You." A growl came from the now free hellhound at her side, causing the magickal shitheads to jump.

"Maybe if we offer to give her back to him, he'll stop," said another practitioner.

A third practitioner responded, "He won't hear us over the flames. He'll just—" The walls of the cube flashed repeatedly, making everyone freeze. Then, with a sizzling sound, they disintegrated. "We're dead."

The flames rushed at the house, making Harper, Larkin, and the hellhound back up fast. Worse, the flames were so tall they were curling over the building, so thick and raging that there was no clear path for Larkin to fly them all out.

An elderly practitioner shrunk away from the sight. "We'll be safe if we get inside," he told his friends. "The house is protected, it will remain standing."

One of the other practitioners shook his head. "No. The protective spell will do no more than buy us time." He turned to Harper. "If you don't tell us what he is, if we don't stop him, you'll die with us. You'll—" He screamed as a single flame suddenly curled and contracted around him like a boa constrictor.

Another flame hooked around the throat of a female practitioner and tossed her into the fire. A black flame then lashed out like a whip and wrapped around the ankle of a chanting practitioner, causing him to fall flat on his face. He screamed for help, scrabbling at the ground for purchase, but the flame dragged him into the fire.

"Harper, we're dead if those flames keep coming!" shouted Larkin, face red from the blistering heat.

She was right, but the figure controlling them didn't appear in a rush to ease them. It stood there, calm as you please, as it watched the destruction around it. The flames were licking along the walls of the large building, ready to devour it. Each time she breathed and took that hot air into her lungs, her chest felt tighter.

"Call to him, tell him to stop! Yell at him telepathically!"

"There's a shield of fire between his mind and mine." Once more, Harper attempted to pierce it, but it held strong.

"If he doesn't pull back, he'll kill us all!"

Harper was about to reassure her that Knox would stop, that he had the control to pull back, but then she remembered something he'd once said. '*If anything happened to you, if you were taken from me, that control would be gone.*' More of his words came to her . . . '*I'd make them all pay. But I wouldn't stop there. It wouldn't be enough. Not for me, not for my demon. So many would die, so much would be destroyed.*'

It was only now – as the flames ate at everything they touched, as the practitioners screamed in agony, and as the building began to creak and weaken beneath their feet – that Harper truly understood the severity of his warnings.

Desperate, Harper psychically battered at the shield between her and Knox. It hurt like hell, but she kept going; slamming her mind against his, crashing her psychically spiked shields into the wall of fire, calling on every single ounce of psychic energy she had and—

Screaming, Harper curled in on herself as the shield cracked and a scorching heat poured into her mind, flooding every crevice, and searing everything it touched. The agony spread like wildfire, making her back arch as it crackled its way down her spine, boiling her skin until it sweltered and sizzled. The pain ate every vertebrae, every nerve, every muscle, and every ligament.

Tears burned her eyes. She was going to die. She was. No one could live through this.

Her demon panicked, fought to surface and somehow help, but it was trapped. Harper screamed again as the scalding pain blasted the space between her shoulder blades, making her bones groan under the strain and her skin peel. She could smell her flesh burning, could hear it sizzling. Then it was like something ripped the skin off her back. A scream slid through her gritted teeth and she—

The pain stopped. Just stopped.

"Oh! My! God!"

Frowning at Larkin's exclamation, Harper went to speak when she suddenly became aware that something was very different. Very wrong? Her demon didn't think so.

"You have wings, Harper!"

Wait, she what? Sure Larkin was wrong, Harper glanced behind her and ... "Oh, my God." She had motherfucking wings. They were ... well, they were gossamer. A striking gold with strands of red and black. Well, fuck.

The building shuddered and creaked once more. It wasn't going to last long.

"Harper, if there's something you can do, do it now!"

There was really only one thing she could do. There was a good chance it wouldn't work, but she was fresh out of ideas. Taking a preparatory breath, Harper jumped to her feet, rushed across the roof, and leaped into the flames – heading straight for the figure of fire. Because there was another thing that Knox had once said ... *'The flames can't burn you, Harper. Because they're me. And you're right, I'd never harm you.'*

She'd love to say she flew, but it was more like she shakily soared through the fire and, fuck, it was *hot!* The flames scorched her skin, zapped every nerve ending in her body, as she headed for him. But they didn't hurt her. Somewhat ungracefully crashing into him, she picked him up, ready to fly them out of the flames. Not yet adept at flying, however, she lost her balance and they slammed to the ground, rolling several times.

As they came to a halt with her straddling him, Harper distantly registered that she might have broken a few ribs and maybe even cracked her skull, but her concentration was on getting the flaming figure beneath her to hear her. "Knox, pull back!" He didn't respond, and the fire continued to rage. "*Pull back!*" Just when she was about to pummel the shit out of him with her fists, the flames seemed to peel away from him, starting from his head and making their way down his body. "Thank fuck."

Eyes of pure black met hers. "Mine," stated the demon, as if that was all it recognized her as right then.

"Well, yeah, but that's not important right now. Knox! Seriously, answer me!"

The demon blinked, and then it was Knox looking back at her, brows drawn together. "Harper." Her name was a guttural growl.

"Knox, pull back the flames. *Now.*" She wasn't sure whether it was as effortless for him as it looked to be, but a single sweep of his gaze at the fire seemed to have it instantly beginning to calm. It wasn't just calming, it was shrinking and thinning out.

An emotional mess, she dropped her forehead to his chest, panting hard. "For a minute there, I didn't think you were coming back from that."

Sitting them upright, Knox pressed a kiss to her temple. "I almost didn't." He'd had one goal in mind: To get to Harper. He'd been willing to destroy everything that stood in his way. His anger had blurred his thoughts, given him tunnel vision until he hadn't spared a thought for anyone but her. Not even for his sentinels.

It had been Harper's touch, scent, and voice that pulled Knox out of that state. But even with her safe in his arms, his demon hadn't wanted to retreat – too caught up in its rage and too drunk on the power it was using. The demon had been born to destroy, and it had continued to do exactly that. Being anchored by Harper in more ways than one had given Knox the strength to reach for supremacy and regain his control.

As the flames finally disappeared, Harper's stomach dropped, and her heart slammed against her ribs. There was no building. No Larkin. No Tanner. Not even a single body. Only black and red ashes. No, no, no, no—

"You both look like shit."

Harper tracked Knox's gaze and saw that Larkin and Tanner, no longer in his hellhound form, were staggering toward them. Relieved to see them alive, Harper wanted to smile. Instead, she heard herself growling, "I thought you were fucking dead!"

"When the flames eased off, I flew us out of there," the harpy explained.

"You're okay?"

Tanner waved a dismissive hand at Harper's concern. "It's not like it's the first time he almost killed us."

Harper really didn't know what to do with that comment.

"Wings, huh?" Knox whispered his fingers over them. "Soft. Hot." His memories were blurred a little by the rage that had consumed him, but . . . "I remember you cracking through the shield. My power spilled through into your mind." And gave her wings whatever push they had needed to finally surface.

"That was a really stupid but ballsy move, Harper," berated Tanner.

Harper rubbed her nose against Knox's. "The flames can't hurt me – not inside, not outside. Can we go home now?"

Knox kissed her forehead. "Whatever you want."

Lying on his side on the bed, Knox watched his mate putter around in just panties and a tank top as she spoke to Jolene on her cell. Maybe another person might have wanted a little private time to assimilate the fact that their life had been threatened and they'd just watched their mate almost destroy everything around them. Not Harper. She'd stayed close to him since they returned to the mansion; had even insisted he join her in the bath. Maybe it was her way of reassuring him that he still didn't scare her – or, at least, not enough to make her leave.

"Grams, I'm fine, I promise. Of course I got out of the house by myself, don't insult me. There's nothing left standing for you to reduce to rubble. According to Levi and Keenan, Isla's demons have left, and the mayhem in the hotel is over." She let out a heavy, put-out sigh. "Fine, put him on." A long pause. "Hello, Lucian. I'm fine. Knox came for me. He's not a deranged psychopath."

She crossed her eyes, making Knox smile.

"I will come see you tomorrow, okay? Then you can see for

yourself that I'm fine. Right now, I'm tired and I need sleep – so do you, if the rumors I heard about you and Raini's aunt are true. La, la, la, I didn't say I wanted to know if it was true. I'll talk to you tomorrow. Bye." Puffing out a long breath, she placed her cell on the drawers.

"Come here." A growl of contentment rumbled up his chest as she slipped under the covers and fit her body snug against his. She was such a little thing, yet she'd robbed him of his infamous control. But she'd also given it back to him when he'd been bloated with power and overtaken by rage.

Harper's eyes fell closed as his hand roamed over her, both possessive and reverent. As if he just had to touch her. "I take it Isla's dead."

"She ate an orb of hellfire." His inner demon smiled at the memory. "I got to the practitioners' house just as you stabbed 'Kendra' through the neck."

Harper opened her eyes. "Her real name is Jeanna. She's very much dead." As something occurred to Harper, she clicked her fingers. "Oh shit, the demon that took me, I think his name is Jacques, was waiting—"

"In the woods. Tanner killed him."

"Good." As he traced a half-healed stab wound, she assured Knox, "I'm okay, really." Most of her injuries had already fully healed.

"But you might not have been. The practitioners could have killed you before I even knew you were gone, if that had been their goal."

"But they didn't kill me. And I'm not easy to kill."

Slipping his hand under her tank top, Knox closed it around her breast. "It would be better if you were much harder to kill."

She arched into his proprietary grip as he cupped and shaped her breast almost idly. "It would." When his hand slid to her back and traced the markings there, she smiled. "Even if I do say so myself . . . my wings are seriously cool." They had sort of melted back into her skin about twenty minutes after they'd returned home. She'd have to get some advice from her relatives on how to control them.

"They are," he agreed. It hadn't escaped his notice that they were the same colors as the flames of hell. What that meant, he didn't know. Maybe it was just a mere reflection of his power. Maybe it was nothing to be concerned about. But while his fear for her was still fresh, he couldn't relax.

"I'm safe now," she soothed when she heard his teeth grinding.

He touched his forehead to hers. "When I realized you were gone, I almost lost my fucking mind." Intellectually, he'd known that he'd lose control if she was ever taken from him, but he hadn't been prepared for the blind fear and sheer panic that tormented him. "I haven't felt fear in a very long time."

Harper pressed a kiss to his mouth. "I thought you handled it pretty well, all things considered," she quipped. His mouth curved in amusement, just as she'd hoped.

"Yeah, I only called on the flames of hell."

Chuckling, she kissed him again. "Thank you for coming for me."

"Of course I came for you. Tanner believes I love you. Love? I don't know if you could call it that. What I feel isn't romantic. It isn't soppy or gentle. It's dark and consuming and intense – far more intense than any supposed 'love' I've sensed in another person." He skimmed his fingers down her arm and took her hand, rubbing his thumb over her palm. "Whatever the hell it is, it's strong enough to mean my soul is right there."

She gave him a watery smile. He was better with pretty words than he thought. "That's only fair, since you have mine."

Knox kissed her hard, pouring that undefinable emotion into

it, letting her feel it for herself. Levi had once said that Knox lived for her now. The reaper was right. Knox had been alive a very long time, knew exactly how it would feel to go through a lifetime without her. He couldn't go back to that numbness. His demon had no intention of doing so.

Tangling his hand in her silky hair, Knox kissed her again, indulging in a thorough tasting of his mate as he rolled her onto her back. Knox suckled her bottom lip. "This mouth is every man's fantasy. But it's mine. Only I can have it. Only I can taste it and fuck it." To punctuate that, he thrust his tongue back inside to stroke hers; dominating and exploring with an urgency that was fed by the fury still sizzling inside him. He needed to take her, claim her, and own her so completely that she'd never be free of him, just like he'd never be free of her.

Shoving his hand up her tank top, Knox possessively splayed it over her breast and squeezed. Her soft moan made his cock twitch – already he was long and full, desperate to be in her. "I want you wet." With a pinch to her nipple, he smoothed his hand down her flat stomach and into her panties, cupping her. There would be no psychic fingers tonight, just his skin and hers.

Harper curled her legs around him as he began pumping two confident fingers in and out of her, expertly stroking right over her g-spot each time. He didn't just hit the spot, he doodled circles on it, fluttered over it, swirled around it. Shit, it felt fucking amazing.

With his free hand, Knox peeled up her tank top and drank in the sight of her luscious breasts. "My marks have faded. We'll have to fix that." He latched onto a taut bud, sucking it deep into his mouth.

Moaning, Harper shrugged out of her tank top and tossed it aside. Each tug of his mouth on her nipple sent a jolt of pleasure straight to her pussy. She hissed as his teeth bit the side of her breast. There was no repentance in the dark gaze that met hers; only pure, unadulterated possessiveness. Her hiss became a sob when he withdrew his talented fingers. "The teasing has to stop." Her stomach was knotted with need – a need to have him in her, stretching her. "Fuck me."

"No. I want to savor." Knox suckled and bit his way down her body. Every part of her was imprinted into his brain; not just her taste, scent, and the feel of her skin, but every curve, every indent, every freckle, every birthmark. He danced his tongue over his demon's brand as he tore off her panties. "I'm going to taste you now. And then I'll have you. And this tight little pussy will explode all over my cock."

Fingers biting into her thighs, Knox sank his tongue inside her. The taste of her burst through him, and went straight to his painfully hard cock. Gluttonously, he licked, lapped, and sipped at her pussy; he couldn't get enough. Would never get enough. He'd always need her.

As his tongue fluttered teasingly against her inner walls, Harper pulled hard on his hair. "In me." He moved to her clit, licking and swirling … and she realized he was writing his name over her flesh. "Fuck, Knox, now." She could only get out key words at this point. Her body was wound so tight, she was shaking. "Knox!" He got to his knees and moved to straddle her chest; his sensual features alive with raw hunger.

"Get me wet, baby."

The command vibrated with enough power and dominance to make her shiver. She opened her mouth, and he surged inside. Wrapping her hair around his fists, he worked his cock in and out of her mouth, all the while looking at her like she was the most fascinating thing he'd ever laid eyes on.

Fighting the urge to stay in the heat of her mouth, Knox

stopped after only a few thrusts, and then he positioned himself between her thighs. "You ready?" At her nod, he smoothly sank into her with an agonizing slowness. She pressed her nails into his back in feminine demand, but he continued to slowly surge forward until he was finally fully sheathed.

"Fuck me hard."

Knox cocked his hips, giving her a shallow thrust. "When I'm ready." He kept his strokes sensual and wickedly slow, never moving his eyes from hers. With his cock buried in her body, he kissed her; poured everything he had and everything he was into it. She kissed him just as hard and demandingly, feeding him little moans and whimpers that made his cock pulse. He breathed her, tasted her, felt her running through his veins, and imprinted on every bone.

"Harder." She inhaled sharply as he suddenly slammed hard. "Fuck." He hooked one of her legs over his shoulder and then he was plunging in and out of her with frantic, branding strokes. The sleek muscles of his back flexed and bunched beneath her hands. Caught in his gaze, she could see his pleasure, the fury of his possessiveness, and the depth of the raw, biting need he had for her – all of it heightened and intensified her own need until she could sense her release tumbling fast toward her. "Don't ask me to wait, I can't."

"Then come," he said against her lips. He closed his mouth over hers, swallowing her scream, as her pussy rippled around his cock. Her release seemed to echo through him, making him explode with an unnatural force as he drove deep.

As she lay shuddering beneath him, Knox nuzzled her neck, inhaling her warm, honeyed scent into his lungs. "Now I feel better."

"Yeah? How's your demon doing? Calmer?"

"It's smirking. It got what it wanted." He kissed her. "You."

"Brace yourself, because I'm going to annoy you, ignore you, and surprise you for as long as we both shall live."

He smiled. "And I'm going to spoil you, fuck you, and – of course – order you around for the rest of our lives."

"You're going to *try*," she corrected.

Kissing her again, Knox chuckled. "You'll definitely keep things interesting."

"Was there ever any doubt?"

None.

CHAPTER TWENTY-TWO

"When did you tell Harper what you are?" Levi asked Knox as they stood in Jolene's large and very crowded kitchen the next morning.

"She's known since the day before her birthday," Knox replied, watching his mate laugh at something Khloë said. "As proven by the fact that she's still content to be my mate, she accepted it. In fact, she took it pretty well."

"Looking around this room," began Larkin, "I can understand why she didn't find it such a big deal. To grow up in this crazy family, you'd have to become a very accepting person."

Listening to the ongoing argument between an imp who believed he was the reincarnation of Tupac and another imp who was insisting the rapper wasn't really dead and was actually living on an island with Elvis and Michael Jackson . . . "True."

When they'd arrived at Jolene's house, it had been to find Harper's entire lair squished into the building. They had each hugged and made a big fuss of Harper, though none had been as dramatic about it as Lucian. He was sulking at the moment, angry that she was refusing to consider taking another male as her mate.

"Does she know that being your mate makes her a co-Prime?" Tanner asked Knox.

"She will soon." It wasn't often that Primes officially took a mate as it meant sharing power. Knox hadn't been in any rush to tell her that she now wielded as much power over their lair as he did, suspecting she wouldn't like it much. Being quite an individualistic person, she had no interest in ruling others. She had no aspirations for that kind of power, which was partly why she hadn't wanted to take over from Jolene as Prime of her family's lair.

"Do me a favor and tell her while I'm around," said Tanner with a grin. "Her responses are always interesting."

Levi spoke then. "If you haven't told her she's now your co-Prime, I'm guessing you also haven't told her that you want to psychically bug her, so you'll always know where she is and what she's doing."

"No, I did tell her," said Knox. "She recommended that I shove a large object up my ass. She doesn't want to be monitored 24/7."

Keenan sighed. "I can understand if she'd find it uncomfortable. But she has to know that some things – for instance, the fact that she's breathing – are more important than her privacy."

Larkin snorted. "Not to someone as private as Harper. But I'm guessing Knox will keep working at making her change her mind."

Knox would. Although he respected her wish to not be so closely watched, her safety was much more important to him. "Until she does, we ensure that she's safe." His sentinels nodded; it was a vow.

* * *

Raini took a cookie from the pile on Jolene's kitchen table before turning to Harper. "So . . . who exactly were Jeanna and Jacques?"

"Just stray demons that worked as a partnership and would do anything for the right price." Harper ate the last of her cupcake. "Even something as stupid as go after Knox Thorne."

Devon shook her head in wonder. "Stupid is an understatement. I saw what he did to Isla. It was freaky how totally calm he looked while he did it."

Khloë nodded. "He's the last person I'd ever cross. And I happen to like trouble." She turned to Harper. "I'm guessing you know the secret of what he is. I know you can't tell me what he is, and I'm not asking. I'd just like to be sure you know exactly who – what – you've mated with."

"Rest assured," was all Harper said, not prepared to reveal anything else. Hearing a husky and very sexy laugh, Harper looked to see a grinning Keenan fairly surrounded by female imps.

"He's hot as hell," commented Devon.

Khloë snorted. "Yeah, if you go for alcoholics." And Khloë had no tolerance for them. She smiled at Harper. "When are you gonna show me your wings?"

"When I learn to control them."

"I'll help. The first few times hurt like a bitch and they're super hard, but it's not so bad after that. Oh, I almost forgot to ask: When's the party?"

"Party?" echoed Harper.

"You guys declared yourselves as mates. That means you get a mating party."

Harper hadn't even thought about it until that moment.

"Ooh, she hasn't planned it yet." Khloë rubbed her hands together as she turned to Raini and Devon. "I think this is where we step in."

"Good idea," said Raini. "Our Harper's creative, but she's also too self-conscious to plan a decent event."

Devon nodded. "We can come up with something better ourselves."

"I'm right here," Harper ground out.

Devon patted her hand. "We know, sweetie. Now you just stand there and look pretty – we have this." A loud hiss escaped her as she glanced behind her. "Back off, pooch."

"Hackles down, kitten," said Tanner.

Leaving the hellhound and the hellcat to exchange barbs, Harper went to her mate and stepped right into his arms. The sentinels melted away, giving them some privacy. "I have no idea why they're all here," she told Knox.

He kissed her forehead. "They had a scare when you were taken. You're important to these people, Harper."

She looked at the male arguing with Jolene. "Maybe not to Lou."

Knox shrugged. "No one's all that important to Lou. He just came here because he's nosy and wanted all the details about what happened."

"If I *did* have OCD," Lou said to Jolene, "it would bother me that the letters aren't in alphabetical order, wouldn't it?"

"Be honest, admit that it bothers you," dared Jolene.

"What bothers me is that health professionals give fancy names to conditions or learning difficulties that will irritate the patients; like OCD not being in alphabetical order, putting an 'S' in 'lisp,' and making dyslexia a word that *no one* can spell. It's just mean."

Harper turned to Knox. "I still don't quite know how to process that guy."

"Ignore him." Knox pulled her flush against him, smiling to see that her gaze was the same warm-honey color it had been when they first met. "Ignore them all. Let me take you home."

"Will you ravish me if I do?"

"You know I don't like rhetorical questions."

She smiled, lightly scoring her nails over the brand on his nape, knowing how much he liked it. *I love you, Knox Thorne.* His eyes shone with an adoration that warmed her all over, inside and out. She knew if he could articulate what he felt, he would. She also knew it bothered him that he couldn't. *It's enough that you look at me just like that – like I'm all that matters to you.*

You are *all that matters to me.* She was everything to him. Meant more to him than he thought anything could.

Then take me home and ravish me, archdemon.

He did.